A Novel

THE GRAY FAMILY:

FORCES OF NATURE

JOHANNA DELACRUZ

DISCLAIMER

CHAPTER 1

IT'S OUR TIME

Pax

I walked to the bakery and went inside to find Shaun waiting on people. He looked different from the last time I saw him but still adorable. I strolled to the line and waited until it was my turn. After he waited on the other customers, I moved to the counter with his back to me.

"I'll be right with you," Shaun said as I stood there, waiting. He turned around and came face to face with me. "Pax," he whispered.

"Hey, Shaun," I greeted him as the corners of my lips curled into a smile. His eyes widened as I stood there. Then he diverted his eyes. "What can I get you?" He asked.

"You," I answered, smirking as Shaun looked at me with furrowed brows. I leaned on the counter and looked at him. "How about after you get off work tonight, we talk?" I asked.

Shaun looked at me with concern as I looked at him with confidence.

"Uh, I can't," he said, surprising me.

"What?" I asked.

"I got an early class and homework. Excuse me, I have work to do," Shaun said as he walked away from me.

I didn't come all this way to school to have Shaun shoot me down. Shaun would be mine. I left the bakery to see Pat waiting for me.

"Well," Pat asked.

"Shaun says he's busy with homework and an early class," I answered.

"Does he think you're stupid or something?" Pat asked.

"No, but that douche that did this to him better be glad he encountered Matthew," I huffed as Pat gave me a knowing look. It pissed me off to know someone treated someone I cared about so badly.

"Well, I guess it's time for Plan B," Pat said as I smirked. Plan B is always my favorite because plan A never works.

I finished placing items in the car's trunk for Plan B.

"It's good to know we are committing a felony while carrying on the family tradition," Kaxon remarked. He had his hands shoved in his front pockets.

"It's not a felony. It's a necessary means," Mason added.

"Cuz, it's a felony," Kaxon reminded him.

"Let's have less talking and more action. I don't have Grammy Gray's time for this bullshit. I want my guy back," I told them as I got into the car.

"Damn, someone needs to get laid. Love makes you do dumb things. Thus, I chose no love. Then I stay smart," Kaxon retorted.

"Or a loser," Pat told him, walking past him and getting into the car.

Mason shook his head as they got into the backseat. My cousins needed to get their shit together. I didn't have all night, especially when our brothers figure out what we're doing.

Our brothers and cousins hung out at the house until Payton wondered why we were quiet since he didn't hear us.

"Has anyone seen the demon twins?" Payton asked as he came downstairs.

"Aren't they upstairs?" Park asked as everyone looked at them.

"No," Payton answered.

"Better question, where the hell are Kaxon and Mason?" Markus asked as they all looked at each other, knowing what we were planning. It doesn't take a great genius to figure out the shit we do. They're slower on the uptake.

Our brothers and cousins went looking for us while we were busy committing a crime of our own.

Shaun came out of the bakery and locked up. He turned and met with a bag over his head, then dropped to the ground as Pat and Mason bound him. Kaxon pulled off the bag and shoved a sock into his mouth.

"That's so you don't scream," Kaxon said as he patted Shaun's cheek. My brother and cousin carried him to the car and shoved him into the back seat. Shaun turned to face me as I waved at him, smiling.

The others got into the car, and we drove to a secluded area. After we stopped, I got out of the car and dragged Shaun out, then untied him.

Shaun stood there, looking displeased. Okay, he looked pissed.

"Hey, I tried to talk to you, and you blew me off, so we do this the Gray way," I said.

"And you kidnap me?" He asked.

"It's effective," I replied, shrugging.

Shaun looked at me then walked over to sit down on a rock. He ran his hand through his hair in frustration.

"You wanted me to give you a chance. I'm giving you a chance," I said.

He looked at me. "And time," he added.

"That too," I said.

"Do you have any idea what it's like to look over your shoulder and wonder if you'll make someone angry? Or that someone assaults you? The hell you endure because you associate with certain people," Shaun said as I looked at him. "It's the worst feeling in the world. Then before that happened, you refused to talk to me, shutting me out."

"I was wrong, but I was angry," I reasoned.

He stood up. "That is the problem. I get to deal with anger and rejection. I got to deal with it with my family, my ex, and you. Who's saying that you won't get angry and shut me out again?"

I furrowed my brows.

"For once, I found peace, even if it's alone," Shaun told me as he walked away. My brother and cousins didn't stop him, and neither did I. Shaun was right.

Pat walked over to me as I stood there. "Pax?" Pat said, looking at me with concern.

"I want to be alone," I whispered as I turned and walked away. I wanted Shaun, and Shaun didn't want me.

I walked down the street as a car came along and stopped. The doors opened, and Pay and Park emerged as I stood there. My brothers walked over to me.

"Remember when everyone said to give Shaun time, and he would come around to me?" I asked. "I did, and he wants nothing to do with me. He prefers to stay alone than with me. I'm sure everyone was wrong about Shaun."

"Pax," Payton said as I diverted my eyes. Tears fell, but I didn't want to break. They pulled me into a hug as I buried my head into them and cried.

Matthew and Markus got out of the car and looked at each other.

"We should help the bugger out," Markus said.

"You're nuts," Matthew told him.

"Okay, we either help Pax out, or you find that cute girl you're avoiding," Markus said.

"Fine, we'll help one of the demon twins, so I can avoid that girl," Matthew groaned.

"I knew you would see things my way," Markus retorted.

While Payton and Parker took care of me, Matthew and Markus went to find the others. They walked until they found Pat, Kaxon, and Mason.

"Well, that didn't go as planned," Kaxon mentioned.

"No shit, Sherlock," Markus retorted.

"Why did you think it was a good idea to tie Shaun up after what he went through with Travis?" Matthew asked the others.

"Because Pax wanted to show Shaun that he wants him," Mason answered.

"That's not the way to do it," Matthew reasoned.

"Well, that's fine and all, but does anyone realize what happens when someone rejects my twin?" Pat asked the others.

Matthew and Markus gave each other knowing looks, as did Kaxon and Mason. Yeah, things will get messy with me. I have a temper, and it's about to blow, especially with Shaun rejecting me.

My temper will set off a chain of events bringing family members to the school to deal with it, who are our parents.

CHAPTER 2

TROUBLE'S A BREWING

Pat

Do you know how you want to help someone, and it blows up in your face? That is me with my twin. Pax and I did everything together, even getting into trouble. We dragged Kaxon and Mason along for the ride.

We got back to the house with Matthew and Markus to see Payton and Parker waiting for us along with the girls. I saw Britt and grinned.

"Will you focus instead of focusing on your woman?" Kaxon asked.

"Hey, it's been a long time," I told Kaxon.

"And your dick still won't get any action until we fix Pax's problem," Mason mentioned.

"My dick doesn't get action anyway," I retorted, rolling my eyes.

"Do you three mind not discussing Pat's dick? I prefer not to hear this shit," Parker said.

"Pat started it," Kaxon said, pointing at me.

"Well, I'm ending it," Payton told us.

"Where's Pax?" I asked.

"He's upstairs and refuses to talk to us," Payton said.

Pax might refuse to talk to our brothers and others, but he never refuses to talk to me. I went upstairs to talk to Pax and opened his door to have something thrown at my head. I ducked because I'm not a dumbass who gets hit. I stood up and looked at Pax.

Pax's anger is plausible, and he looked as if he would break any moment. I walked towards Pax as he furrowed his brows at me.

"Why doesn't Shaun want me?" Pax asked with a quivering lip.

"I don't think that's it. Shaun went through hell because of his ex. People can change you without you knowing it," I reasoned.

"How do you deal with an ache in your chest? It feels as if everything is caving in on you. Someone will explain it to me because this is bullshit!" Pax raged. His voice alerted the others who came upstairs.

"Pax, I know it hurts, but it won't stay this way," I reasoned.

"Pat," Pax's voice trailed off as he broke. I held Pax as he cried. I comforted him because he needed it.

Pax rarely broke when he cared about someone; that's what made it heartbreaking. How do you help someone when the only person who can is not here?

I let Payton and Parker take over for me, then left with Kaxon following me.

"I know what you're planning and don't," Kaxon warned me.

I turned to Kaxon. "I'll talk to Shaun, and that's it," I said.

"Talk with your words or fists?" Kaxon asked.

I looked at him with irritation.

"Pat, we aren't kids anymore. You can't force people to talk. They do or don't. Let those two figure it out," Kaxon reasoned.

"That is my twin. I can't stand around and watch Pax hurt," I told Kaxon.

"Then let Pax deal with it. Don't you have an issue of your own?" Kaxon asked.

"Yeah, but first things first," I said as I turned and walked away.

I walked around town until I found Shaun. He was coming out of the bakery, locking up. I walked up to him and touched his arm.

"Please don't touch me!" Shaun screamed while cowering.

I jerked my hand back.

"Please," Shaun begged as he started crying. I stood there, stunned. "I promise I'll be good," he whimpered.

I looked at Shaun, shocked as he shook, hiding his face.

"Shaun, I won't hurt you," I said.

I watched Shaun whimper while shaking. That's when it hit me what Payton and Parker told us about Shaun. I pulled out my phone and made a call. After speaking with the person, I hung up and stayed there.

Tonight I saw two broken people for different reasons. It wasn't right.

I heard a car pull up as Parker emerged from it with Markus. They walked over to us as I looked at Parker.

Parker looked at me, shook his head, then walked over to Shaun and talk to him. Markus stood next to me.

"I didn't know it's this bad," I mentioned to Markus.

"That's what everyone tried to tell Pax, but he thinks it's because Shaun doesn't care about him. Shaun went through hell last year because of his ex. Parker and I found Shaun drunk one night," Markus explained to me.

Parker got Shaun calmed down and walked past us. "Go home, Pat," Park ordered me. I said nothing as Parker led Shaun away from us. Markus said nothing as we walked back to the house.

When we got back, I got a lecture from hell from Payton, and things got heated. We got into a fight, with the cousins stepping in to stop us.

"What the hell is wrong with you?" Payton snapped.

"Me? I'm helping my twin, and I get a lecture from you! Newsflash, you're not Pops!" I yelled.

"Be glad because pops would beat your ass for that stunt," Payton barked.

"Payton, you're a dick and always have been," I shouted. That's all it took. Payton hauled off and hit me, startling the girls as Matthew and Markus kept Payton from killing me. Mason and Kaxon dragged me away before it got messy.

They shoved me out of the house as I fought both. Kaxon knocked me on my ass.

"Stay!" Kaxon ordered me. I sat there as Parker walked up and saw me sitting on the sidewalk, rubbing my chin.

"I don't want to know why you're on the ground," Park said.

I stood up and looked at everyone. "Since everyone feels the need to hit me, you can all suck it," I snapped as I turned and walked away.

"Patton!" Parker yelled as I flipped him off.

"Well, that went well," Kaxon mentioned as Mason and Parker looked at him. Kaxon shrugged.

School hasn't started yet, and things were already a mess. Good luck to us when it starts.

Pax

I heard yelling and came out of the bedroom. I don't know what happened, but no one looked happy. I came downstairs to hear what happened.

"You hit Pat?" I asked as everyone looked at me. "Why?"

Matthew looked at me. "Because Pat went to talk to Shaun and made things worse," he said.

"What? Why?" I asked, confused.

"Because Pat wanted to help you," Payton answered.

Parker entered the house and looked at me. "Look, I get you want Shaun, but pushing him into something he's not ready for isn't the answer," Park told me.

I looked at everyone.

"You didn't see what Shaun went through last year and found him broken. We did. Markus and I found Shaun a drunken mess after enduring a beating from his ex. Stop thinking about yourself. You need to understand not everything is about you or Patton," Park told me.

I looked at everyone as they looked at me, saying nothing.

"Don't worry, I won't get close to anyone again," I said as I went back upstairs. I hated my brothers at that moment. Shaun pursued me two years ago, then gets involved with a douche.

Since my loving brothers are tools, they need not worry about me. I can handle things on my own.

Everyone wants me to stay away from Shaun, then I'll stay away from him. I can see this year will be super fun.

Payton

"Well, school is starting off with a bang," Kaxon mentioned as I rolled my eyes at him.

"Shut the hell up, Kaxon," Parker snapped.

I made a call home to explain to pops what happened.

You got to be kidding me. Payton, you're the oldest.

"I know, but you know the devil twins," I said.

It doesn't matter. It's your brothers. I expect Parker and you to look out for the twins, not beat the hell out of them.

"I know. I let my temper get the best of me," I explained.

I don't care. Get yourself in check, Payton, or I will do it myself. If I have to come up there, none of you will like me.

Pops hung up, and I sighed.

"What did pops say?" Parker asked.

"If we don't take care of the devil twins, pops is visiting us," I answered.

Parker groaned as I shook my head. The thing about pops is he didn't play games with anyone. He hated it when we fought with each other. Yeah, brothers fight, but we took it to the extreme. Now, it was time to wrangle in the devil twins before shit went south.

CHAPTER 3

IT'S NEVER A GOOD THING WHEN A BROTHER IS MAD

Parker

We went looking for Patton while leaving Payton to deal with Paxton. We found the bugger and dragged his ass back to the house. The last thing we need is Pops visiting us. What part of chill don't my brothers get? You would think they would change coming to college. Nope, they got worst.

We sat the devil twins down on the couch and told them like it is.

"Look, I get you're hoping to jump on Shaun, but don't," I told Pax. I looked at Pat. "I understand you have some weird-ass need to help, but don't."

The twins looked at me, unamused.

"Get your shit together, or Pops is coming for a visit," I warned the twins. I shook my head and went upstairs, having enough fun for one night. Selena followed me. That is a good thing.

Pax

"We're leaving. I hope things are better tomorrow," Josie said, kissing Payton, then leaving with Britt. Our cousins left shortly afterward.

Payton went upstairs, leaving Pat and me alone.

"Well, so far, college blows," Pat mentioned.

"It only blows because everyone is too busy making orders. We should shake things up somewhat," I suggested.

"Will this get us arrested?" Pat asked.

"I hope not because it pissed off Pops when the cops brought us home a dozen times last year," I reminded Pat.

"Fun times," Pat chuckled.

I scoffed as I shook my head. If Shaun wanted nothing to do with me, then I will have my fun. The fun will come at the other's expense.

I went to bed, knowing what I planned to do tomorrow. Patton, Kaxon, and Mason were coming along for the ride, whether they like it.

Kaxon

After getting back to our rental house, I called dad.

Kax?

"Dad, we have a problem," I said.

What's going on, Kax?

"The brothers are fighting. Payton punched Pat, Shaun rejected Pax, and Mason wants to pursue some girl I don't think feels the same. I'm stuck in a precarious position with them," I explained.

Out of the four of you, you're the most sensible. I know you will keep the others out of trouble.

"But when Pax lets his temper flare, all hell breaks loose," I said.

Yeah, I heard. Lex said Payton called him and told him what's going on with the boys. Lex doesn't play games, and he doesn't play with the boys. It looks like you're in charge.

"Great, what I always wanted, to be someone else's brother's keeper," I groaned. Dad chuckled, then hung up.

That's the thing about my dad, he has a habit of irritating Grandpa, but there's never a time I can't talk to him. I made another call.

Hello?

"So, I have this problem," I said.

Who hurt you so I can hurt them?

"No one hurt me, or I will kick their ass," I answered.

Grandpa chuckled. *That is my boy.*

"But the cousins have issues, and dad put me in charge," I mentioned.

Well, frack doesn't always think when he decides.

"It's because I'm more level-headed," I reasoned.

That's because you take after me. Someone has to get the brains out of this family, considering most of everyone didn't.

"Yeah, I see that," I sighed.

Kax, you'll do the right thing. Keep the devil twins out of trouble, or mini-Nash will visit, and then major-Nash will visit. That means I visit.

I stood there, knowing when Grandpa showed up, it was never a good thing. He didn't care if he hurt your feelings.

"I'll do my best," I said as I hung up. I have a feeling tomorrow will start a spiral of events, and one guy could help.

I went to bed, hoping to get some sleep. The operative word is hope.

Pax

The next day I got up and got ready. I came downstairs to grab breakfast, ignoring Payton and Parker.

"What? Are you ignoring us now?" Payton asked.

I said nothing and went about my business. I have plans today.

"Well, it looks like we will have a peaceful morning," Parker mentioned.

I gulped my food, then left without saying a word. Pat came down and saw Payton and Parker without me.

Pat

"Where's Pax?" I asked.

"Oh, you mean the brother who is ignoring us? He left," Park answered while eating.

Pay looked at me, and I looked at Pay. Payton and I always had our issues as Parker and Pax do. While Parker and Pax fought, they never took it further. Pax could still talk to Parker. I'm the opposite. If I fought with Payton, I still didn't go to him about issues. It didn't help when Payton hit me.

Parker looked at both of us and said, "You know this tiff you have going between the both of you is stupid. We all came from the same parents, which makes us brothers."

"Stay out of it, Parker," Payton warned.

Parker got up from the table. "No, I won't stay out of it. It's bad enough to babysit one brother; we don't need unnecessary issues with you two. Suck it up and deal with it." Parker put his bowl in the sink and left.

Payton looked at me and said, "Sorry that I hit you last night. I know you worry about Pax, but sometimes you have to let people work things out for themselves."

"Do you have any idea what it's like to watch someone break?" I asked.

Payton looked at me with concern.

"I watched how people treated Pax in high school. I watched Pax struggled to admit that he's gay, then watch Shaun pursue him, then drop him. Shaun asked for Pax to wait for him. Pax did, even after hooking up with some guy from school who treated Pax like he's nothing," I confessed to Payton.

Payton looked at me, saying nothing.

"Pax had sex with some guy, and the guy treated him like the plague last year," I told Pay. From Payton's expression, I'm guessing he knew because Pax told him. "Pax found someone to fill a void, thinking it will help him move on from Shaun. Pax's in love with Shaun, but he's hurt. Rejection is a bitch."

"Look, I know we don't always get along, but you're my brother. I'm harder on you than the others because I know you can be a better person. Out of our brothers, you're more cautious and help when you feel someone needs it. Patton, I hate we butt heads. It's bad enough that Parker has issues, Pax has a temper, and Presley is a womanizer. You aren't like that," Payton explained.

"No, I get it, but it doesn't mean I won't help my brother when he needs it. Plus, I have more significant issues to deal with now," I mumbled.

"What issues?" Pay asked.

I diverted my eyes as Pay walked towards me.

"What issues, Pat?" Payton repeated himself.

"Britt's parents banned her from dating me," I answered.

"What? Why?" He questioned.

"Something about our families having a beef with each other," I answered as Pay looked at me. "Britt's a Tilson," I admitted.

Payton's expression contorted in shock.

"I don't know the full story, but it's not fair to hold a grudge for so long that we deal with it," I reasoned.

"Pat, one of the Tilson family members, tried to kill Nana and Pops. Another family member attacked Aunt Larkin. It isn't a small grudge they have with each other. It's worst," Payton told me.

I looked at Payton, stunned. I didn't know any of this, and I doubt Britt knows.

"Payton, I won't drop Britt because she has a psycho family," I declared.

Payton shook his head in disbelief.

"Why should I give up my happiness because others are assholes?" I questioned. My brows furrowed. I know my family went through a lot, but it's unfair to suffer because people can't let things go.

"The minute the family finds out, it'll piss them off. Be careful, Patton. History is hard to erase because you want happiness," Payton warned me as he walked away.

Now, I didn't know what to do. I needed advice and went to someone in particular. I made a call and explained what I needed. The person agreed to meet me and talk. I hope this works.

CHAPTER 4

BROTHER ADVICE

Pat

I sat in a diner, waiting as someone walked into it. The person saw me and joined me at the booth I sat in the diner.

"I didn't think you would get here this quick," I mentioned.

"I came to visit one of Marshall's boys," Nathan said. "What's up?"

I took a deep breath, then explained everything to Uncle Nathan. He sat there and listened until I finished. I watched him rub his chin, contemplating what I said.

"What do you think?" I asked, feeling hopeful.

"You should talk to your dad about this, Pat. I knew the Tilson family growing up and what they did. They're a nasty bunch of people. It doesn't help that you and Mason became involved with two family members," Nathan advised.

"I know, but knowing Pops, he won't be happy to hear it. Uncle Nathan, I like Britt, and I don't want to lose her because her family is assholes. Britt's nothing like her family," I reasoned.

Nathan looked at me and sighed. I didn't want to lie to my parents or anyone else. What do you do when it involves your heart?

Nathan

After I visited Pat, I left to meet up with Noah, who is also in town.

"What's up with Lex's boy?" Noah asked.

"Well, it seems Pat likes a certain family member of a family we all hate," I answered.

Noah looked at me, surprised. "No," Noah said with surprise.

I nodded.

"Dude, that's messed up," Noah mentioned.

"Well, one tried to off Maggie along with Nash and Maggie's kids while another one attacked Larkin. I would say so," I agreed.

"I would talk to Nash," Noah suggested.

"And say what? Oh, Nash, your grandkid likes a Tilson, even though they're assholes who went after your family. Yeah, that will go over swell with big brother," I retorted, rolling his eyes.

"Get Nolan to do it," Noah suggested.

"I'll do one better," I said, pulling out my phone and making a call. The person on the other end answered, and I explained Pat's dilemma. The person listened, then hung up.

"Well," Noah asked.

I smiled. When you need help, you call the one person everyone loves besides Grammy Gray. This person was the best at taking care of business.

Patty

I hung up the phone as Nate looked at me. "What did Nathan want?" He asked.

"Nathan went to see Patton and found out Patton likes Britt Tilson, who is Mike Tilson's granddaughter," I said.

Nate looked at me.

"Nathan wants me to talk to Nash and explain things," I explained.

Nate looked at me. I knew that look. As much as our families didn't get along, you can't hold someone accountable for another person's actions. I hated Brian and Trish Holloway, but I love Maggie. That will benefit me.

Nash and Maggie came home and found Nate and me at the table.

Nate looked at Nash. "Sit," Nate ordered as they sat down at the table and joined us. "Your mother has something to tell you."

Nash and Maggie looked at me as I told them what Nathan said. After I finished, Nash's reaction was less than favorable.

"No way! That family is nothing but trouble!" Nash yelled.

"Nash, not every person turns out like their family," I reasoned.

"The Tilson's tried to kill Maggie and my kids. One raped Larkin, and you want me to understand one person is good in that family! Over my dead body!" Nash yelled.

"Look, I get that you're unhappy, but I didn't hold Maggie accountable for what her dad did to me," I admitted. Maggie and Nash looked at me with confusion.

"What does my dad have to do with this, not that I care?" Maggie asked.

"Remember when I told you about a boy who I liked in school and Nate dealt with said boy," I mentioned.

"Yeah, you said the guy wasn't a guy anymore, but a girl," Maggie mentioned.

"Well, that's not true, and it was your dad," I confessed. Maggie did a double-take, and her eyes widened. Nash furrowed his brows. "Before you both jump to conclusions, it was before I dated Nate. I had an insane crush on Brian, but Brian turned out to be a toad. He made the mistake of hitting me."

Maggie looked at me, shocked as Nash sat there, speechless.

"Nate found out and handled Brian, then he called the cops. I fibbed and said Nate was with me, then offered to press charges for Brian hitting me since I was seventeen. He was an adult. I learned that sometimes a crush is nothing more than that, and it led me to Nate," I said, looking at Nate with adoration. Nate returned the same look, taking my hand in his hand.

I looked at Nash and Maggie.

"Sometimes, we move past situations and find a better person. I did that with Brian and received a daughter in return," I reasoned.

Nash sighed. "I understand, but we have to talk to Lex and Larkin. They need to know, especially Lex," Nash told me.

"Give your kids more credit, Nash; they may surprise you," Nate said.

Sometimes we visit the past to help the future. It's not always pleasant but works out for the best.

Maggie

I can't believe Pat had a thing for my loser dad. That is recent information. Then again, I liked Bryson. I'm still wrapping my brain around the fact I forgot about my husband, but remember Bryson. Why couldn't I lose my memory of Bryson and keep my memory of Nash?

We went over to Lex's house and had Larkin meet us there. I hope they take the news well.

"Mags, relax. It'll be okay," Nash reassured me.

"I hope so," I said as I sighed.

We arrived at Lex's house and went inside to find Larkin waiting with Maverick. We hugged the kids and their spouses.

"What's going on, Ma and Dad?" Lex asked us.

"You and Larkin need to sit. We have something to tell you," I answered. They sat down next to Piper and Maverick. I explained what Pat told us and waited for the fallout.

Lex and Larkin looked at each other, then at us.

"Look, we understand if you're upset," Nash said.

"But we aren't," Lex said, surprising us.

"What?" I asked.

"We moved past that," Lex said.

"Lark?" Nash said.

Larkin looked at us, then at Maverick, who nodded. She turned back to us.

"I forgave Roger a long time ago," Larkin admitted, shocking us. "I spent endless hours in therapy with Jordan. I understood forgiving Roger wasn't for his benefit, but for mine. If I resent Roger and hold a grudge, then I can't move forward and feel happy. I don't want Roger to have any power over me, even if he is dead," Larkin reasoned.

Nash and I sat in two chairs, looking at our kids.

"Anger is a useless emotion, and it's not worth it. We moved past everything that happened. Isn't it time you both did the same thing?" Lex asked us.

Nash sighed. "I watched how that family went after my family and felt helpless. I saw your mom get hurt countless times, then watch family hurt you kids. It's terrifying to watch people attack someone you love. You want to protect that person," Nash explained.

"That's the thing, Dad, no matter what, you came when we needed you. That's why it's easy for us to move past everything. We know you will protect us no matter what," Larkin told Nash.

That's when I understood more about my husband than I ever did. Nash made mistakes because it terrified him he would lose the people he loves, his family. Nash looked at me.

"What?" Nash asked me.

"You lost us and couldn't stop it. First was when I lost my memory, next was Larkin with her innocence, then Lex with his accident," I said.

Nash furrowed my brows.

"It terrified you would lose me, you pushed me away until I lost memories of you, then you realize you lost me. You thought I would pine over Bryson because I did before, and it hurt you," I said as everyone looked at me.

"I don't want Patton to suffer from rejection the way I did. The Tilsons have a way of hurting someone I care about. I hate the thought of it happening to my family," Nash reasoned.

"Who says it will happen?" Lex asked Nash.

"Dad, you have rotten apples in a bushel, but it doesn't mean all are bad. You pick through the bad ones to find one good one. Isn't that what Ma did with you? She picked through your undesirable traits to find the good ones," Larkin reasoned.

Nash looked at me. "Well, did you?" Nash asked me.

"No," I answered. Nash furrowed his brows. "My heart did. The heart wants what the heart wants," I said, smiling. Nash smiled at me.

"No offense to anyone, but I don't want to get dragged into my kid's love life. We're dealing with Pax as it is," Lex mentioned.

"What's going on with Pax?" I asked.

Lex told us about Payton's phone call. Nash and I looked at each other. Nixon spiraled out of control when Nash and Kat rejected him. We had a feeling the same thing will happen with Paxton unless we can stop it.

CHAPTER 5

TROUBLE WITH A CAPITAL T

Pax

Pat, Kaxon, and Mason met up with me in town. We walked around town until some dumbasses messed with us.

"Look what we have here, boys," one guy said, rubbing his hands together. "It seems the idiot train derailed and resulted in assholes."

Pat and I looked at each other, then back at the stupid asses in front of us.

"They look like nothing but fags to me," another guy remarked.

Pat and I looked at the tool who thought he's funny.

"Here we go with the derogatory remark about someone's sexuality. Didn't anyone tell you Nancy boys that make you an asshole?" Kaxon asked as we stood there.

"What the hell did you say, rim job?" A third guy huffed.

"Are you deaf on top of stupidity? Damn, I didn't know this campus contains that many ignorant fools," Mason mentioned.

As these tools tried to one-up us, which they failed at it, someone walked up.

"If it isn't the pee-pee brothers," Sable said, making the guys who stood in front of us laugh. "You reek so much that Shaun won't lower his standards for you," Sable told me, waving her hand in front of her nose.

"Ah, hell, here we go," Kaxon said. Pat and I laid the four guys out, then I grabbed Sable's hair. I dragged Sable while holding her hair as she screamed.

"You want to run your mouth, then I should give you a reason to run it, you cumdumpster," I barked as I dragged Sable.

Sable slapped at me, but I didn't care. She deserved it, considering the bullshit she put Parker through in high school. I got Sable to the campus and held her down as I removed her clothes.

"Whoa, Pax. Don't you think that you're taking things too far?" Kaxon asked.

"Shut the hell up, Kax. You can help or keep your trap shut," I snapped as I stripped Sable down to her underwear.

"Let go of me," Sable screamed.

"You get everything you deserve, you stupid bitch," I said, yanking Sable up and smacking her.

"Pax!" Pat yelled, trying to stop me. I released Sable, shoving my brother as she started running. I caught Sable as she kicked and screamed. I'm not finished with this bitch.

Pat and Kaxon tried to stop me as I went after Sable. Mason left to get help. I have a temper like no other.

"Get off of Sable!" Kaxon yelled as I hauled off and hit him.

"Paxton!" Pat yelled, trying to subdue me. I ended up hitting Patton as Sable screamed.

During this incident, people arrived, seeing everything happen. The situation got messy when I heard people yell and restrain me. I didn't stop until someone said something.

"Paxton," I heard someone say and looked to see Shaun standing there, furrowing his brows.

I looked at Shaun as he helped Sable.

"What the hell is wrong with you?" Shaun asked as I stood there while Parker and Payton restrain me. Shaun shook his head as he helped Sable. They walked away, and I said nothing.

Payton and Parker released me as I turned around to face them. Mason, Kaxon, and Pat gave me a disapproving look while Kaxon and Pat rubbed their jaws.

"I get that you're upset, but what was that?" Payton asked me.

"Sable deserved it for what she did to Parker," I answered.

"Pax, you hit Sable and stripped her clothes off her like an animal. That's assault," Kaxon informed me.

I looked at my family as they shook their heads. Campus security showed up, and my brothers explained what happened, but it didn't matter. I was in trouble for what I did.

Security took me to the Dean's office, who called my parents, fantastic.

Pat

We waited near the Dean's office to find out if the school is kicking Pax out for what he did to Sable.

"School hasn't started yet, and Pax's in deep shit. Pops will kill me," Payton said, pacing.

"Not if Pops doesn't find out," Parker mentioned.

"And how will we keep that from happening?" Payton asked.

We all looked at each other and made a call. We explained what was happening, and the person agreed to help. Let's hope this works.

Pax

I sat in the Dean's office, waiting for Ma and Pops to arrive. That's all I need now. Then I heard two voices as I looked at the doorway to see Aunt Larkin and Uncle Maverick enter the office. What the hell are they doing here?

"Mr. and Mrs. Gray?" The Dean asked.

"You betcha," Maverick answered as Larkin elbowed him.

I sat there, saying nothing because I'm hella confused.

"I expected you to look different," the Dean mentioned.

"Well, we're old," Lark said.

"Okay," the Dean said, confused.

"Let's cut to the chase. Pax has a temper and let it get the best of him," Lark said.

"Your son assaulted Sable Andrews," the Dean said.

"Sable Andrews assaulted our other son, Parker. She distributed child pornography," Lark informed the Dean.

The Dean looked at Lark, shocked.

"Dean, this is a misunderstanding, and Sable told Paxton that she gave him the Clap," Lark said.

I sat there, shocked.

"Wouldn't you want to hit someone who gave you a nasty STD?" Lark questioned.

"Oh, my," the Dean said, stunned. Lady, you're not the only one.

"Look, we promise Paxton will not do stupid shit again if you let him off with a warning," Lark said, shooting me a look.

"Well, if your son doesn't commit any other serious offenses, we can give him probation," the Dean offered.

"We'll take it," Maverick blurted as I groaned.

"That includes no campus parties or anything college-related for six months. If there's no further incident, I'll lift the probation. Paxton Gray must keep a distance from Sable Andrews," the Dean informed us.

"You got a deal," Lark agreed as I shook my head. She turned to me. "Let's go, you twit."

I stood up and left the office. I came out to find everyone waiting for us.

"Well," Payton asked.

"I can't attend any college functions, including parties. I can't have any contact with Sable. If I'm a good boy, they will lift my probation. I also can't misbehave," I answered.

"You got off light. Be glad your dad didn't come," Lark told me.

"Yeah, sure. I get to attend college single and with no social life. I'm living the dream," I retorted as I walked away.

I know I should be happy that the school didn't kick me out. This reinforces the fact Shaun messed with my life as he did in high school.

As I walked down the hallway, I heard someone say, "Before you storm off, we should set some ground rules."

I turned to see Maverick walking towards me. I furrowed my brows.

"You seem ungrateful that we put our neck on the line for you. We didn't want you to get a visit from your parents," Maverick told me.

"Do you want a cookie?" I asked with annoyance.

"No, you act grateful. But then again, you don't understand the concept," I heard someone say.

I turned around to see Pops standing there. Well, shit. Pops walked up to me, grabbed my shirt, dragging me away. Yep, I'm a dead man.

We got back to the house as everyone followed. Pops tossed me onto the couch.

"Stay and say nothing," Pops ordered me as the others watched. "I'm finished with you boys and your bullshit. You're adults, and now it's time to act like it. Since you disregarded my warnings, this is how it will go down. Pax, you're getting a job if you want to attend school," Pops told me.

"What?" I exclaimed, standing up. "That's not fair!"

"Life isn't fair, and your behavior is ridiculous. You are getting jobs," Pops told us. My brothers shot me a glare.

"Where will I get a job?" I questioned.

"I'm glad that you asked. You have a job waiting at the bakery. Our family knows the family that owns it. They are more than happy to give you a job," Pops said.

"But Shaun works there!" I exclaimed.

"Guess you will work together," Pops informed me.

I groaned.

"No jobs. No school," Pops said as my brothers groaned. "You'll appreciate the shit you put your ma and me through growing up."

I sat down on the couch. So much for keeping my distance from Shaun. It will suck ass. Well, Pops punished me his way. He's forcing me to work around someone he knows I have no choice but to interact with, FML.

CHAPTER 6

WELL, THIS SUCKS A**

Pax

The next day I got up and got ready. Pops stayed the night to make sure I showed up for my job. The others went to apply for jobs while I came downstairs, finding Pops waiting. He gestured me with his finger to follow him, and we went to the local bakery.

Pops also felt the need to talk to me on the way to the bakery.

"Pax, I'm not doing this to be mean. If you're busy, it will keep you out of trouble," Pops said.

"Well, it's not like I will do anything, considering I'm on probation and single," I replied, shrugging.

Pops gave me a look, and I sighed. What more is there to say? After my stunt, if I had any chance with Shaun, I blew it.

We arrived, and an older guy greeted us.

"You must be Lex and Pax," the guy said, shaking Pops's hand.

"Are you Frazier?" Pops asked.

"That would be a big fat no," the guy said.

Then another guy came out who was much older.

"Welcome to Kate and Frazier's sweet treats! Where we make all your sweet dreams come true. It's like Disneyworld in your mouth," the much older guy announced.

The other guy pointed at the much older guy. "That is my dad, Frazier. I'm Nik," the guy introduced us.

Frazier walked over to us and looked me up and down. "Didn't anyone tell you if you hit a skank, you get a classy lady to do the job?" Frazier asked as I looked at him.

"That is true. Uncle Ryan disapproves of us touching women, so we find women who can touch another woman, except me," Nik said. That answer made me confused.

"Nik's gay, so he gets his sister to do his dirty work," Frazier explained. This information surprised me.

"I want my son to stay out of trouble, not get into it," Pops informed both.

"Oh, you don't worry, we will make sure your son stays out of trouble. Plus, I like Maggie," Frazier said, smiling. "Your dad needed some work, but I'm glad he got his shit together," Frazier told Pops, who gave Frazier a look. "Don't give me that look. I'm happily married to a crazy woman who's Nik's mom. She gave me four crazy kids," Frazier explained.

This conversation is getting weirder at the moment.

"Come on, Pax. I'll show you around the bakery and get you situated," Nik told me as I followed him to the back. We left Frazier and Pops to talk.

Nik showed me where everything is and gave me an apron; then, he showed me the cash register. As I learned the cash register, a door opened, and someone said, "Sorry, I'm late. I had to take care of something."

We stopped and turned to see Shaun come in from the back. Shaun saw me as I stood there.

"No worries. It's not like you're always late," Nik said.

I stood there, saying nothing.

"Shaun, this is our new employee Pax. He will wait on customers while you help me with orders," Nik told Shaun.

"Sounds good. I'll get to work," Shaun said as he put on an apron.

Nik taught me the register and let me attempt it a few times before turning me loose on it. It didn't seem hard as I picked it up. Nik left me to get situated as Shaun brought out a tray of muffins to fill a container.

I stood there like a big dope.

"I didn't know you needed a job," Shaun mentioned, filling a container.

"Yeah, Pops thinks we all need a job to stay out of trouble," I answered.

Shaun looked at me as I sighed.

"Don't worry, I got the hint and won't bother you," I said as I shifted from foot to foot.

The door chimed as Pops and Frazier turned to see Sable entered. Fuck. I turned and walked into the back, away from crazy. Sable walked over to the counter.

"Can't a girl get some service?" Sable asked with a smirk.

This bitch is trying to get me into more trouble. I hid in the back. If anyone from the school catches me near Sable, I will get kicked out.

"It looks like someone isn't doing their job," Sable announced.

"What are you doing, Sable?" Shaun asked.

"Well, I want to order something, and your co-worker isn't doing his job," Sable sneered.

"Pax can't wait on you or be around you, and you know that," Shaun told Sable, who smirked.

"Oh, well, I will let everyone know not to come here since you get lousy service," Sable declared.

Great, now I will get fired because of Sable. I looked at Nik and removed my apron, handing it to him. Nik looked at me with concern.

"I don't want to cause problems for you and your dad. I can't be in the same place as that chick, or the school will kick me out. So, yeah, I need to find a job, and I doubt I will," I said as I walked past Nik and Shaun as Sable smirked.

I walked over to Frazier and Pops.

"I'll pack and return with you, then I'll figure out something when we get home," I said to Pops, who furrowed his brows. "Your rules." I turned and walked away.

Someone hates me enough to make my life a living hell. As I walked, Pops caught up with me, stopping me.

"Pax," Pops said as I turned and saw my tear-streaked cheeks. That's all it took, and I broke. Pops pulled me to him as I cried. I'm not one to complain about anything, but I felt like everything is falling apart.

Shaun

I look at Sable. She did that shit on purpose, and I know she set Pax up, knowing his temper. Sable stood there like the cat that ate the canary.

The bell chimed, and two girls walked into the bakery. They stopped to speak to Frazier for a few minutes, then walked over to Sable. Nik came out of the back to watch the exchange.

"Can I help you?" Sable asked the girls.

"It depends if you want to keep your tits," one girl said, cracking her knuckles.

"Excuse me," Sable said, appalled.

I said something when Nik stopped me.

"You touch me, and I will go to the school," Sable told the girls.

"Go ahead, then we will explain a few key details to the school about the shit that you're doing," one girl said.

"I will have you kicked out," Sable announced.

"How will you do that? Do you even know who you're talking to here?" The other girl asked, looking at Sable like she's stupid.

"I will go to the dean," Sable answered, acting proud.

"Good, you tell her the Shaw family says hi," one girl said as Sable looked at the girls confused. "Since you don't know who you're talking to, we will tell you. I'm Jesse Shaw, and that's Skylar Shaw. Our family owns the school."

Sable's face contorted in horror as I stood there.

"You're in our family's bakery, which means we can deny anyone service, including you. Isn't that right, Uncle Frazier?" Jesse asked as Frazier walked over to us.

"That is correct. Now, run along and don't come back. If you feel the need to leave a critical review, go ahead, but be careful. There are a lot of Joneses, Shaws, and Fraziers attending this school. I doubt your critical review will make them happy," Frazier informed Sable, smiling.

Sable slithered away like the snake she is.

"Excuse me, I have to persuade someone to take a job," Frazier said, leaving as I shook my head.

More people came into the bakery, including two guys, whom I recognized as Kaxon and Mason.

"Why is Pax bawling like a baby?" Kaxon asked.

"Because Sable showed up," I answered.

They looked at each other, then at me.

"What?" I asked.

"Don't tell me you defended that hoe?" Kaxon asked.

"Nope," I answered as I finished placing the muffins in the case.

"Then do us a favor and don't play with our cousin," Mason told me as I looked at him. "Pax doesn't deserve head games."

I looked at Kaxon and Mason as Lex walked back in with Pax. Pax walked past me as Nik handed him an apron.

"So, how can I help you?" Pax whispered.

We all looked at Pax as he avoided eye contact.

"We would like two cappuccinos and two apple muffins," the girls ordered.

Pax nodded and retrieved the order as I watched him. Pax said nothing to me as he got the girl's request. I watched as he waited on people, not saying much. That bothered me.

Pax

Pops watched me, as did others as I waited on people, waiting to see if I got out of line. There's nothing like someone putting you under the microscope while working. Once Pops felt satisfied, he left to check on my brothers.

My cousins tried to talk to me, but I didn't say much. The less that I said, the better it was. Everyone got what they wanted. I kept my mouth shut, along with my anger in check.

My brothers showed up near the end of my shift and said something to me. I kept working, restocking the cases while waiting for people. When I wasn't filling cases, I cleaned up.

"Paxton," Parker said as I moved from table to table.

"Paxton, talk to us," Payton coaxed.

"What's there to say? I'm behaving myself and working. Everyone got what they wanted. So do me a favor and leave me alone," I whispered as I worked.

"Pax," Pat said. I could hear the sadness in his voice.

I looked at Pat as Kaxon and Mason walked over to us.

"I'm sorry that I hit you and Kaxon. Now, I'm behaving and acting like a behaved child. If I'm lucky, I can graduate college with no issues. Now, excuse me, I need to finish up. I have to get ready to figure out my schedule since we're starting school," I said, walking away from everyone.

God will take mercy on me and put me out of my damn misery. Then again, I'm not that lucky.

CHAPTER 7

A NEW DAY, SAME OLD BULLSH*T

Pax

I figured out my school and work schedule, which are my basics, and okay. Nik scheduled me for the evening. I started classes, keeping to myself. My brothers and cousins tried to talk to me, but I stayed to myself. I did in high school and now, college.

Ma called, and I spoke to her. She tried to carry on a conversation, but I wasn't in the mood. She asked if I wanted to talk to Pops. I declined. My family thinks I'm a screwup anyway, especially Pops.

At the bakery, Shaun attempted a conversation. I kept it brief. He made himself clear that one night. So why make conversation when you're disinterested in dating someone?

I don't understand anyone. Everyone is on my case about the shit that I do; then, everyone wants to talk when I walk the strait and narrow. I don't want to talk. I want to get through school and move on.

"Man, this sucks," Mason said to the others.

"So much for the four of us taking on the world. One took a siesta from life," Kaxon mentioned.

"It reminds me of high school all over again," Pat sighed.

Kaxon and Mason looked at Pat.

"People jumped on Pax more than anyone, making him shut down. I miss my twin," Pat told Kaxon and Mason.

They all looked at each other. I walked across campus as I heard someone call my name. Now what?

I turned to see Parker walking towards me. I furrowed my brows.

"Hey, how's your first day?" Park asked.

"It's okay, but I got to get to work," I said.

"Are you okay?" Park asked.

"I'm fine, but I need to go," I said, walking away.

Markus walked up to Parker.

"What's up with Pax?" Markus asked.

"A lot," Park answered, sighing.

While my brothers hung with my cousins, I kept myself busy. I showed up to work and got ready for my shift.

"Hey, Pax," Shaun greeted me.

"Hi," I replied. I waited on customers.

"How was your first day?" Shaun asked, making conversation.

"Okay," I answered, not engaging as I waited on people.

Shaun got the hint as I worked. I helped close up the bakery as Shaun attempted to make conversation. He talked, I worked.

"So, I thought we could hang out," Shaun suggested.

I wiped off tables and straighten chairs.

"We could grab a bite," Shaun mentioned.

"I'm not hungry," I mumbled as I grabbed a broom and swept the floor.

"Okay, then we can study together," Shaun offered.

"There's no need. I have basic classes," I declined as I finished up.

"Pax," Shaun said.

I looked at Shaun. "You're not ready and disinterested in me. My family would rather tell me I'm a screwup than help me. Your sister enjoys making my life hell since high school. Now everyone gets their wish," I said as I walked away from Shaun.

"What do you mean Sable made your life hell since high school?" Shaun asked, following me.

"It's nothing," I mumbled as I removed my apron.

"Pax, talk to me," Shaun said.

"Nope, I'm okay, talking to no one. Now, excuse me," I said, leaving the bakery. It doesn't matter what I say; no one will believe me, anyway.

I walked back to the house as I encountered Sable. Well, this is fantastic.

"Since you enjoy beating on defenseless girls, you need a lesson," Sable said. Someone tapped me on the shoulder. The minute I turned around, someone's fist met my face.

"You want to jump my sister, tough guy. Now, enjoy the beating of your life," Ben yelled, beating the hell out of me. I couldn't even defend myself since he got me pinned.

Sable laughed as Ben beat the hell out of me as he did in high school. Ben would corner me alone, knowing he didn't stand a chance with Pat and me. He finished his beating and spat on me. Then they walked away as Sable laughed.

I groaned, getting to my feet. Well, that will hurt like a bitch in the morning. I held my side as I walked to a house, trying to stop my bloody nose. Yeah, I can't go home and explained to my brothers why I didn't fight back. They wouldn't listen, anyway.

I can't go to my cousins because they would tell my brothers. No way in hell, I will let Shaun help me. I don't need his pity.

I sat down on a bench and removed my shirt, holding it to my nose. I thought college would be fun, but it sucks. Let's see, I'm on probation, I work with someone who doesn't want me, my family scolds me, and I got the shit beat out of me. These are fun times, I tell you.

I sat there, contemplated my life as I heard some guys walk up to me.

"Look what we have here, boys," one guy said as I looked at the guys. Well, this sucks.

Britt

Josie and I were on our way to meet Payton and Patton when we saw someone lying on the ground next to a park bench. We looked at each other and walked over to see if it was a homeless person until we realized it was Paxton.

"Oh, my god," Josie said as we hurried over to Paxton and helped him.

"Paxton," I said with concern.

Paxton pushes us away. "I'm okay," he said, getting to his feet. We stared at Paxton, shocked. "I will find a place to clean up, then sneak home."

"Paxton, you need a Doctor," I said.

"No doctors or hospital. I don't want my family to know," Paxton told me as I furrowed my brows. "My life sucks, and this is another thing to add to it."

"Then let us help you," I offered.

Paxton looked at us.

"Please," I offered.

"Fine," Paxton grumbled as we helped him back to our dorm.

Pax

I sat on Britt's bed as she and Josie helped me. Selena walked into the dorm room with another girl as I sat there, a bloody mess.

"Oh, my god," Selena gasped.

"Yeah, God isn't helping me at the moment," I mentioned as Josie and Britt cleaned new up.

"What happened?" Selena asked.

"Well, Ben Andrews beat the hell out of me, and then four guys jumped me. I'm having a terrible night. If you could not tell my family, that will be awesome," I said with a look.

"Pax, your brothers, need to know," Selena said.

"Nope, they don't. So, I will let Britt and Josie finish cleaning me up, then sneak into the house. It's not the first time that this happened, and it's not the last. If you cannot say anything to anyone, that will be super," I said with sarcasm.

The girls looked at me with concern as Josie finished. I pulled on my bloody shirt and got up. I left the dorm room and went home. Now, I needed to sneak past my brothers and into my room.

I climbed a tree, making my way up to my window. I opened it and climbed inside the bedroom. I started stripping when my door opened, and someone turned on the light. I stopped and looked at my brothers.

"Pax?" Payton said, shocked.

"I had a shitty night and prefer no lecture or jokes," I said, looking at my brothers.

"Who did this?" Parker asked, walking into the bedroom.

I grabbed some clean clothes. "No one, I'm clumsy," I lied, knowing my brothers didn't buy it.

"Tell us, Pax," Pat said.

I looked at my brothers. "No, and don't ask because I still won't tell you. Don't call Pops because I need no more punishment," I told my brothers.

"Pops won't punish you," Payton mentioned.

I looked at Payton like he was on crack.

"Oh? Because to Pops, I'm a screwup. Thanks to me, he made you all get jobs. If Ma had Pat and not me, it would be better. Who wants to deal with someone who's a screwup and gay?" I said, emotionless.

"Is that what you think?" Parker asked.

"It's what I know," I answered.

"Pax, no matter what, you're wanted in this family. Yeah, we fight, but we're brothers," Payton assured me.

"We know that's bullshit. Let's be realistic. Ma and Pops help you. I get punished for something that someone else did," I said.

"What are you saying?" Parker asked.

I looked at my brothers and dropped a bombshell on them. It's going big or go home time.

"Sable set you up, and I found out. I went after Sable. She sent Ben and his cronies after me in high school. They waited until I was alone and jumped me. Every chance they got, they would jump me, including Shaun. Then they told everyone I was gay, even though I denied it because I wasn't ready to come out. That's why I didn't believe Shaun when he confessed to me. When he helped Sable, I knew it was all bullshit," I admitted.

My brothers looked at me with concern.

"Yeah, the Andrews family got me into a lot of trouble when they started it, but I got punished for defending myself. If you want to know why I didn't want to give Shaun a chance, there you go. Now, excuse me, I got to study so I don't get kicked out," I said as I finished dressing and picking up a book. I didn't want to talk about this anymore.

Now, people will leave me the hell alone.

Parker

We left Pax's bedroom, and Payton went looking for Ben Andrews while I went looking for Shaun. I never knew what happened between Pax and that family, but this isn't right.

I found Shaun at the bakery, locking up.

"Explain to me why you feel the need to mess with my brother," I said as Shaun turned around to face me. I walked up to him. "We helped you and didn't know what you and your family did to Pax. Why?"

Shaun furrowed his brows. "Because I was an asshole, but the truth is I care about Pax," Shaun said.

"Your sister set my brother up along with me, and you did nothing but help her," I said.

"Because I hid my sexuality and drinking. Do you know what it's like to hide things and deal with a family you don't like? You of all people should know this, Parker. Look, I'm not messing with Pax," Shaun said.

"Then, what are you doing?" Parker questioned.

"I'm opening myself up to Pax because I'm in love with him," Shaun admitted, surprising me. "It's taking a lot of time in therapy to understand who will and won't hurt me. I planned to take it slow with Pax, but he rushed things."

"Well, good luck, because you're back to square one with my brother," I said as I walked away from Shaun.

My brother might be many things, but he doesn't deserve someone to mess with his head. I returned home and went upstairs. I heard sniffling coming from Pax's bedroom. I turned the door handle and opened the door to see Pax wiping his eyes as he worked on homework.

I know the feeling of broken and feeling like no one cares. I felt that way after what Sable did to me. I walked in and crouched next to Pax. He looked up as tears fell. I pulled Pax into a hug as he cried. Sometimes a simple hug speaks more than words.

I heard footsteps as I turned to see Payton and Patton standing in the doorway. I nodded as they both came into the bedroom and offered comfort to our brother. It's something Pax needed from us.

CHAPTER 8

KEEPING A DISTANCE

Pax

I kept my head down and did what I had to do. My face looked terrible from what happened a few nights ago. I went to class, and people stared at me. I focused on the course.

After my classes, I went to work. Nik and Shaun stared at me. I went to the back, saying nothing, and got ready for my shift.

"Paxton? Are you okay?" Nik asked with concern.

"Yeah, I ran into a door," I lied as I got things ready.

Nik furrowed his brows as I set tables and chairs up. Frazier came out of the kitchen, and Nik gestured at me as I worked. They whispered as I made sure the bakery was ready to open.

"Uh, Paxton, if you want a day off, we'll be fine," Frazier reasoned.

I walked towards the three of them. "No need, I'm okay," I said as I went into the back. I refuse to have someone knock me down and not getting up. That is not me.

The bell chimed, and I walked over to the cashier register as people stared at me.

"Can I help you?" I asked.

The people placed their orders, and I ignored the stares. My brothers and cousins came into the bakery as I worked. They watched me as did my job, ignoring comments and stares.

Shaun tried helping me, but I refused his help. As I waited on people and my family watched me, the bell chimed as they parted ways. I was getting an order for a customer as the person approached the counter. Once I gathered everything, I turned, walking back to the bar, not noticing who was standing there.

I set the order on the counter as I looked up to see Ma standing there. I looked at her, trying not to cry. Pops walked up to the bar as I furrowed my brows. Then I saw Nana and Grandpa along with Uncle Noah as more family entered the bakery.

Ma touched my hand, making me break down and cry. Ma released my hand as she walked around the counter and held me. I gripped her as I cried. The one person I needed is here.

"Oh, Pax, I'm here," Ma said as she comforted me.

"I'm sorry, Ma. I'm trying," I cried.

"I know, baby, I know," Ma said, comforting me.

"Who called Ma?" Parker asked, looking at my brothers.

"I did," Pat answered as Park and Pay looked at him. "My twin needs the one person who we all need."

I stood there and buried my head into Ma.

Piper

When I walked into the bakery and saw Pax, it pissed me off. How did it get so bad? They hurt one of my babies, and no one stopped it. Frazier let Pax leave, and we took him home.

When we returned to the house, all hell broke loose. I let everyone have it with both barrels, including Lex.

"What do you want me to say, Piper?" Lex yelled.

"How about let me help you, Lex?" I yelled back.

"The boys are adults!" Lex yelled.

"And our kids! Don't stand there and tell me you never asked for help! I can't believe you or any of you!" I yelled at Lex and the boys.

The boys and Lex looked at me.

"I don't expect perfection, but I expect you will look out for each other. This family is about helping each other and not letting one fall, or did you forget that?" I asked Lex and the boys.

"It's been rough, Ma," Payton mentioned.

"That's bullshit, Payton, and you know it. Don't hand me that shit," I told Payton.

"Piper, we won't always be there. The boys have to learn," Lex told me.

"Does that include getting the shit beat out of you from others? And don't tell me it was a door," I told Pax, not looking at him.

Pax opened my mouth, then closed it.

"I want the names of the people that did this," I demanded.

"What do you have planned?" Lex asked me as everyone looked at him, then we heard a knock at the door. Lex looked at me. "You didn't?"

"Oh, I did," I said.

Parker answered the door and found the sisters standing there.

"Well, our crazy aunts are here," Park announced as Larkin smacked him, then hugged Parker. Lyric, Lakin, and Luna did the same, then Lyric and Luna hugged their kids.

The sisters walked over to Lex. "Always late to the party, aren't you?" Lyric asked Lex.

"That's not funny," Lex said.

"No, it's downright hilarious to think we would stand by and do nothing," Lakin retorted.

"Get your ass in gear and help us so that your wife can help your son," Larkin ordered Lex.

"What are you planning?" Lex asked.

"A big dose of karma," Luna answered, cracking her knuckles.

Lex sighed and left with his sisters while I handled my boys.

"Where's Presley?" Parker asked.

"Presley is with Grammy and Grampa," I said as the boys looked at me, surprised.

Patty

I heard a knock at the door to find a man about Lex's age standing there.

"Is Presley Gray here?" The man asked.

"Why?" I asked as Presley came out of the kitchen and turned around, going back into the kitchen. "No, Presley joined the circus with the other monkeys. Bye, now." I closed the door and turned around to see Presley stick his head out.

Nate sat on the couch, drinking his coffee. I gestured with my finger as Presley walked towards me.

"I will tell you what I told your Uncle Nolan, knock your shit off," I told Presley. Presley looked at me, shocked as Nate chuckled. "Now, I want you to write an essay on why women aren't sexual objects, and you're not a lothario," I ordered.

"Do you even know what a lothario is?" Presley asked me.

"Do you want to live to find out?" I asked. Presley's eyes widened as he ran upstairs.

I sat down as Nate chuckled.

"What is wrong with that boy?" I asked.

"Presley's a Gray and Grays are notorious for the ladies," Nate said, laughing.

"Yes, we know with all the women you dated, don't we?" I retorted as Nate rolled his eyes.

"Yeah, but I got the best one," Nate said, smiling.

I chuckled as I leaned over and kissed Nate.

"I worry about Paxton," I mentioned.

"I know, but Paxton will find his way. It will take longer, but he will find it. You should have faith, Patty. Look at me. My ma never thought I would settle down, but I did. It took that special person," Nate reasoned. I smiled as the phone rang.

I got up and answered it. I furrowed my brows as I listened to the person on the other end.

"Hold on," I said as I handed the phone to Nate.

Nate took the phone, then said, "Cayson? Whoa, slow down. What?"

Nate, she's gone.

"Who?" Nate asked.

Dominique.

Nate looked at me as I furrowed my brows.

I went into the bedroom and thought Dominique was sleeping. Nate, my wife's gone. What will I do?

"You will come home, little brother. We will take care of you," Nate said as Cayson cried.

Nate offered Cayson comfort, and I made calls. The first call was to Jonas; then, I called the kids. The problem with death is it comes without warning, and with us getting older, it was a matter of time.

Lucille once told me that death is inevitable, but it's what we do while we're here that counts. Plus, we take care of family no matter how big of a pain in the ass they are.

Nash

Ma called while we dealt with the situation at the college. She delivered terrible news about Aunt Dominique and asked if Cayson can come to live with us. I wondered about the triplets. Yeah, Ma has some colorful language.

I hung up after agreeing and let everyone know. Mags hugged me as the grandkids offered comfort. The kids returned a while later, and I told them about Aunt Dominique. They understood as I explained what was happening.

We had to get home for the arrangements, including the boys. God, I hate funerals, and I know the cousins are taking it hard.

CHAPTER 9

FAMILY REUNION

Patty

Everyone returned for Dominique's funeral. It was crazy seeing how the family grew, but it was nice to see the kids again, along with the brothers. When Cayson arrived, I hugged him, and he cried. Dominique was the one person who helped shaped Cayson into the man he is now.

Nate comforted his baby brother since Lucille wasn't here to do it. Then Jonas arrived with Karen and comforted Cayson. It was good to see the brothers together.

As the kids arrived, so did the triplets, Carson, Cody, and Caleb, along with Jace and Jaime and their wives. Then the boys came with their wives and kids.

"Damn, Nash, you got old," Jace said, hugging Nash.

"You're right behind me, buddy," Nash told Jace, chuckling.

"I see you're crazier than ever," Jaime said to Nixon.

"Someone has to shake things up in this family, considering you will go to hell as a lawyer and all," Nixon retorted. They laughed.

"Did you ever find your ark, Noah?" Cody asked.

"Yeah, and you're not on it, thank god," Noah answered.

"Well, Nathaniel, Jr., you're still old," Carson commented.

"So are you, and I can still beat your ass," Nathan replied with a look. They laughed as they hugged.

"So, Magazine, is everyone still getting a turn?" Caleb asked Maggie.

"How is your nose? Do you need another nose job?" Maggie asked with a look as Caleb smirked.

"Well, it seems you're all idiots, but old now," Nolan told the others as we watched the kids.

"And we can still beat your ass," Nixon mentioned.

I smiled as the kids all talked and laughed, catching up. It's been a while since everyone was in the same room. It sucks that it's for a funeral.

Cayson, Jonas, and Nate talked about the arrangements. The minute Nate mentioned Cayson staying with us, that caught the triplet's attention.

"Wait, hold up. Dad is staying with one of us," Carson mentioned to Nate and his brothers.

"Yeah, we lost Ma, and we don't want to lose Dad either," Cody said.

"I'm not living with one of you three. Are you insane?" Cayson asked his sons.

"But you're our dad," Caleb said.

"And I'm still your dad, but I raised you, and you're crazy. Your ma and I talked about what we would do if something happened to one of us. We decided not to live with either of you," Cayson told the triplets.

"Damn, that's harsh," Nixon mentioned as we looked at him.

"I love you, boys, but I can't live with you," Cayson told his sons.

I watched the triplet's expression change. Cayson got up and walked towards his boys.

"You have your lives now. I want to stay close to Nate because, like you, he's my brother," Cayson explained.

"It makes sense," Noah mentioned as we looked at him.

"What does bud?" Nate asked.

"As a brother, you have a powerful bond with each other. That's why we all live close to each other, as do the others. No one knows what it's like to have that brother bond except a brother. I can't imagine not having my brothers around me," Noah explained.

"Yeah, it's like a part is missing when one leaves," Nathan added.

"Our brothers are the ones that know all our secrets," Nolan said.

"And pulls our asses out of the fire," Nixon reminded us.

"We look out for each other even when we don't think we need it," Nash mentioned.

"Because brothers have a unique bond with each other that others don't understand," I said. I looked at Nate, who smiled.

I understood what it's like to have that bond because of my brother. Unless you have a brother, you don't understand it.

Pax

I sat off to the side, watching everyone interact with each other. I didn't know the cousins well or Grampa's brothers, but I understood the brother bond. My brothers and I fight, but I can count on them.

I got up and walked over to my brothers, who were talking to other family members.

"Damn, did you get the number of that truck that hit you?" Someone asked me.

I looked at the person with furrowed brows as my brothers took exception. I walked away as my brothers dealt with it. Did you ever feel low, and someone says something, then it makes you feel worse? Yeah, that sums up my life now.

I went into the kitchen and sat at a table alone. I stared out the window, thinking about what I did wrong in my life.

"Consider the source and ignore it," I heard someone say as I looked to see Cayson sit down at the table with me.

"I'm sorry about Aunt Dominique," I said, shifting in my seat.

"Yeah, I am, too, but Dom was a special person. I was a mess when I met her. I didn't have any direction and took Dom's food from her. She tackled me and took it back. Dom didn't take my shit, which is what I needed," Cayson explained.

"Well, you met someone that cared about you. I meet people that don't care, then get the shit beat out of me. I cause more problems than necessary. Ma and Pops tire of helping me," I said.

"Nah, that's not true," Cayson said.

"Isn't it?" I asked.

"Trust me; it's not. When I was younger, Jonas and I got into a fight, and our Ma didn't help matters. I got arrested, and Dad kicked me out of the house. I had a lot of issues I needed to deal with that I didn't. We worked things out, but I had to grow up," Cayson explained.

"I want happiness, and it's eluding me," I whispered.

"Because you're not allowing it. Anger is a terrible emotion, and it keeps you from feeling happy. When you let go of the anger, you find happiness. Give yourself a break," Cayson told me.

I nodded as Cayson got up and went into the other room. I sat there as Pops walked in and sat down next to me.

"We should talk," Pops said as I looked at him. "Pax, I know you don't feel that I don't care about you, but that's not true. I love you, boys, more than anything."

"Then why are you harder on me than the others?" I asked.

"Who says that I'm easy on your brothers? Each of you has a distinct personality from the other. I act according to your personality. Now, you're having a troublesome time, but it won't stay that way. I don't want to find you in a ditch somewhere or the morgue," Pops told me.

I looked at Pops and furrowed my brows.

"The worst feeling a parent can have is to receive a call that someone hurt their child. When Patton called us, it was the worst feeling. It terrified us that someone hurt you because we went through it before with you. No matter what you or your brothers do, your ma and I will always love you," Pops told me.

I needed to hear that.

"Yeah, even if you are a pain in the ass," Park mentioned as I looked to see my brothers standing there.

"Pax, no matter what, we will back you because you're our brother," Payton reminded me.

I looked at everyone and smiled. It was the first time I smiled in days.

We stayed for the funeral, and I kept to myself. I didn't know many people, except for the ones I saw often. This family is massive.

After the funeral, we went back to Nana and Grandpa's house to eat. I looked at the food as I held a plate in my hand.

"That's a lot of food," someone mentioned.

I looked to see a guy standing next to me.

"Yeah," I answered, looking at the food.

"Kain mentioned you were having a tough time," the guy said.

"Who are you?" I asked.

"Kaiden, Kain's twin," Kaiden introduced himself.

"Does this family know everything?" I asked.

"Yep, until you keep things from the family that you shouldn't like, I did," Kaiden said.

"What do you mean?" I asked.

"I didn't talk to my family while I was in an abusive relationship with my ex. It took things escalating with getting help. It took a long time afterward to allow someone to get close to me," Kaiden explained.

"How did you work past it?" I asked.

"I have a very crazy family that enjoys plotting and planning," Kaiden mentioned. He glanced at the family.

I looked at the family and sighed. My situation differs from Kaiden's. Shaun never abused me but rejected me. I know Shaun was in an abusive relationship, but he clarified he doesn't want me.

When we return to school, I'll keep my distance and focus on school and work. Sable and Shaun got what they wanted, and I suffer the consequences. The apple doesn't fall from the proverbial tree.

CHAPTER 10

SOMEONE IS GETTING KIDNAPPED

Pax

We returned to school, work, and courses. My brothers and cousins enjoyed their time at school with their significant others. I had school and work to keep me busy.

One night, my brothers and cousins went to some college party while I stayed home. If someone catches me at a party, then I'm screwed. I made some popcorn and got a pop before settling in to watch a movie.

As I hit play, I heard a knock at the door. I set the remote down on the coffee table and answered it. Shaun was standing at the door.

"Is this a bad time?" Shaun asked me.

"Shouldn't you be a party?" I asked.

"I don't go to parties or out much. Since Travis, I keep my distance from most people," Shaun said.

"Yeah, I noticed," I replied. I didn't need this right now. All I wanted to do is watch a movie alone.

"It took a lot of therapy sessions to understand that not everyone will hurt me. My therapist said if I take it slow with someone, it will help," Shaun mentioned.

"That's good, but I learned people would hurt you even when they say they won't. You know, like when you treated me like an animal because of what I did to Sable even though she had people jump me. Then again, it's okay for you needing time," I said.

"Pax," Shaun said.

"No one cares to hear the complete story, so excuse me while I go back to my movie," I said, closing the door.

People will say that I'm acting harsh, but when you get burned enough, you learn. If I keep my distance from people, I won't get burned or hurt. I went back to my movie, enjoying myself. I was better at doing things alone.

Shaun

I sighed as I stood on the other side of the door. I was ready to open up to someone, and the person rejects me. I turned as Parker looked at me, shaking his head.

"Well, that was a bust," I said as Parker gave me a look.

"So? It doesn't mean you give up," Markus told me.

"That was a stupid idea," I told both.

"My brother is stubborn, but that doesn't mean you stop," Parker told me.

"I need a miracle," I said as Parker and Markus looked at me and smiled.

"Leave that to us," Parker said as I looked at him with a cloud of suspicion. What did the two of them have planned?

Pax

After the third movie, I called it a night. I went upstairs and changed, then went to bed. I fell asleep since I haven't slept well since everything that happened.

Thirty minutes later, someone awoke me with their hand over my mouth and wearing a mask. My eyes widened as the person wrestled with me while two other people zip-tied me. Then someone put duct tape over my mouth before placing a hood over my head. What the fuck?

Someone lifted me, carrying me, although the person was rough. The next thing I knew, someone shoved me into something, and I lay there like a lump. I'm sure with the way it's going for me. Lately, this is the cherry on top.

I flopped around like a fish as I felt myself moving. I worked at getting loose; then, I felt the movement stop. I heard a door open as someone yanked me out of whatever container that held me. I'll take a guess; it's a vehicle. The person dragged me until they stopped, then lifted me.

I stood there as someone removed the hood from my head. I stood in front of Shaun, then looked to see Grandpa and my uncles standing there along with Parker and Markus.

Nixon turned me around to face him. "I will remove the tape, but you listen to what Shaun says," Nixon said as he ripped off the tape.

"Sonofabitch!" I yelled.

"I beg your pardon; your grammy is not. You have some respect. Now, listen to what twinkle toes have to say," Nixon said, smacking me upside the head. He turned me to face Shaun.

"Look, I know I hurt you, but I don't see you like an animal. Yes, it shocked me what you did, but I found out from others the bullshit that Sable did to you. I regret hurting you in high school because I hid who I was. I hurt you countless times, and for that,

I'm sorry. The worst part is that I wish that I never did because I'm in love with you. When you're lonely, you look to someone to fill that loneliness when your heart aches for someone else. I know you don't believe me, and you have every reason not to, but my heart wants you, Pax," Shaun told me.

I looked at Shaun, figuring out what I wanted to say.

"The heart wants what the heart wants," someone said as I turned to see Uncle Noah smiling.

"Take a chance," Nathan said.

"You like Shaun, he likes you, and we're one big happy family," Nixon added.

"God, you're slow. Shaun likes you, and you're stubborn," Nolan said.

We all looked at Nolan, who shrugged.

Grandpa walked towards me as I stood there.

"Pax, I know you're hurt, but don't make the same mistakes I did with your nana. I hurt her countless times because I acted stupid," Grandpa told me.

"It took you long enough," Nixon said to Grandpa. Grandpa rolled his eyes.

I turned to Shaun, who looked at me.

"It's disturbing that you enlisted my family to pull the same stunt that I pulled on you," I said.

"Yeah, that wasn't my idea. It was Parker and Markus's idea. I wanted to talk to you, and they said this would work," Shaun reasoned.

I chuckled as I shook my head.

"If you untie me, we will talk," I reasoned as Shaun smiled. Grandpa pulled out a knife and opened it; then, he cut off my zip ties. Everyone left us to talk alone.

"So," I said as I had my hands in my pockets.

"So," Shaun said.

"You're in love with me?" I asked, tilting my head.

"Yeah, and it's crazy that I spent many hours in therapy working up the nerve to tell you," Shaun said, raising a finger.

"I see," I said.

"But if you're unsure of us, I understand. If you want to go slow, we can go slow," Shaun offered.

I shifted in my spot, kicking the ground with my foot. I didn't want to get kicked in the teeth again. Rejection is a bitch.

"I don't know," I said with hesitation.

"What do you want me to do to prove that I'm serious?" Shaun asked me.

"Show me," I answered. Shaun looked at me with anxiousness. "Show me what you're serious about and not telling me what I want to hear. You told me you would wait for me and didn't. You told me to wait for you, and when I attempted with you, you pushed me away. My family didn't understand my reasons. They never had someone play with their feelings as you did with me."

"Okay, then I will show you. Whatever I have to do, I will do it," Shaun said.

"I'll believe it when I see it," I said, shrugging. I turned and walked away from Shaun.

"What the hell is wrong with this kid?" Nixon asked the others.

"Actions speak louder than words for Pax," Noah reasoned.

"What bullshit is that?" Nixon asked.

"The kind that people who get hurt want. I know I had to do the same thing," Grandpa told his brothers.

I walked over to Parker and Markus.

"Can you take me home?" I asked.

"Yeah, little brother, we can," Parker answered as I got into the car, and they took me home.

I know people don't understand why I didn't fall into Shaun's arms, but when you get burned enough with someone, you're gun shy. If Shaun wanted me, then he will prove it. If he doesn't, then I move on with my life.

I hoped Shaun does.

CHAPTER 11

ACTIONS SPEAK LOUDER THAN WORDS

Pax

I came downstairs and opened the front door as a guy stood there holding flowers.

"Are you Paxton Gray?" The guy asked me.

"Yeah," I answered, looking at the guy funny.

"These are for you," the guy said, handing me the flowers, then leaving.

"Uh, thanks," I mumbled, closing the door. I pulled a card out and read it.

Payton walked into the living room. "Who are the flowers for?" He asked me.

"Shaun sent me flowers," I said, handing the flowers to Payton and going into the kitchen.

Parker came downstairs and saw Payton holding the flowers. "Delicate flowers," Parker commented.

"Shaun sent flowers to Pax," Payton said as Parker looked at Payton.

It will take more than flowers to show me that Shaun is serious. I doubted Shaun for a good reason. Every time I open myself up, I get kicked in the teeth. Yeah, that won't happen.

The next day, I opened the door and found a giant stuff teddy bear sitting there with a note attached to its neck. I dragged the stuffed bear into the house and tripped on it, falling on top of the bear.

Parker walked past me. "I'm sure Shaun will prefer you to lie on him," Parker said.

I looked up at Parker and rolled my eyes. He went into the kitchen as I got off the teddy bear and stood there.

Patton came downstairs and saw the giant bear lying on the floor.

"Shaun?" Pat asked.

"Who else?" I answered.

Pat laughed, and I sighed.

I walked to the bakery to start my shift when a clown stopped me. What the fuck?

I tried to move around the clown, and he kept stopping me. That made me annoyed as he held up his hand, then handed me a bunch of balloons. I took the bundle, and the damn clown squirted me in the face with water, using a flower on his lapel.

I decked the clown and released the balloons. First, I hate clowns, and second, he had it coming.

Mason and Kaxon saw the clown lying on the ground out cold, then noticed the balloons floating away in the air.

"Paxton had a run-in with a clown," Kaxon mentioned.

"Shaun might want to change tactics since Pax hates clowns," Mason reasoned as Kaxon nodded.

I walked into the bakery as I saw Britt working. Good, Shaun wasn't here. I went into the back and put on an apron as I got organized.

"Here, this is for you," Britt said, handing me a box.

I looked at Britt funny and opened the box. Inside I found a cupcake and a note, then set it down and opened the letter: The Gray Brother's Bakery.

I set the note down and picked up the cupcake, taking a bite, realizing it came from our bakery. Pops make specialize cupcakes for me since I have an allergy and can't eat certain foods. That's why I eat nothing from Kate and Frazier's sweet shop.

I set the cupcake and swallowed the bite in my mouth. "When did this come?" I asked Britt.

"Yesterday. Shaun said you couldn't eat anything in the bakery because you have a gluten allergy. He called your parents and asked for a cupcake for you," Britt told me.

Aside from my family, the only person I told about my allergy is Shaun.

"I know you have reservations with Shaun, but last year was rough for him. We watched how Travis tore him down and abused him. Shaun wouldn't let anyone touch him and kept to himself," Britt explained.

"I'm afraid if I open myself up, Shaun will come up with some reason to not want to be with me. In high school, he terrorized me, and I gave him a chance. Then I find out Shaun was dating someone. Shaun offered long-distance after telling me we'll see how things go. I know he went through a lot, but so did I," I explained.

"Sometimes two broken people make a whole," Britt mentioned, walking away.

I looked at the cupcake. I wasn't so sure about anything.

After my shift at the bakery, I came home and went upstairs to my bedroom. I opened the door and stood there, shocked.

Shaun turned around and looked at me. "Uh, you weren't to come home yet," Shaun mentioned. I walked into the bedroom to see flowers, balloons, candy, and other romantic items.

Then I saw a box. I opened it up. It had movies, popcorn, pop, candy, and treats from Grandpa's bakery.

"I thought about the movie night at your house and how we enjoyed watching movies together. I hoped we could watch some movies together like that night," Shaun said.

I looked at Shaun.

"Your brothers suggested it along with the items I sent you. They said it would help. I'm not good at romance and asked for help. I even called your dad and asked him to send you a treat. Uh, I mean, um, yeah," Shaun stammered as I looked at him.

I furrowed my brows.

"You wanted me to show you, but if you don't like it, I will stop. I deserve rejection for what I did. I screwed up and lost a chance with someone I love. That's the story of my life, so I'll go," Shaun said as he started for the door.

"Wait," I said.

Shaun stopped and turned as I walked towards him. "Pax," Shaun said as I placed my hands on his face and leaned in to kiss him.

Shaun hesitated but kissed me back as I deepened the kiss. He placed his hands on my back as we continued to kiss. It was a long-awaited kiss.

After a few minutes, we broke from our kiss.

"When I said show me, the material things aren't what I meant. I meant affection," I explained as Shaun gave me a sheepish look.

"I told you I'm not good with romance, and I listened to your brothers," Shaun said.

"Who told you to send me a clown?" I questioned.

"Parker did. Why?" Shaun asked.

"Be right back," I said, leaving the room. I went to the bathroom and grabbed a bottle of powder, then went to Parker's bedroom. I opened the door, and the bottle of powder then shot it at Parker.

"What the fuck?" Parker wheezed and gasped.

"The next time you send a fucking clown, I'll cut off your dick. Now, let's go to the hospital before Ma and Pops kill me," I said as I helped Parker out of the bedroom.

We walked past Shaun as Parker gasped. Payton and Patton found out what I did, and Payton grabbed an epi-pen, shoving it into Parker's leg. Parker screamed, and we dragged his ass out to the car, taking him to the hospital.

After we arrived, they took Parker back, and I got a lecture from hell from Payton.

"What the hell is wrong with you? Parker is allergic to powders," Payton yelled.

"Well, Parker shouldn't tell Shaun to send me a clown," I replied.

"You hate clowns," Payton mentioned.

"No, shit, Sherlock," I responded with a look.

"Park is lucky you didn't rip off his nuts," Pat mentioned.

"Oh, I promised Park the next time I will rip off his nuts," I told Pat.

"We will need a cake," Pat mentioned as Payton smacked him.

As we waited, Kaxon and Mason showed up.

"Is there ever a time you guys aren't trying to off each other?" Kaxon asked.

"What fun is that if we don't attempt a homicide once in a while?" Pat asked.

Kaxon shook his head, then looked at me. "Why are you here and not at the house?"

"Because I caused this mess," I answered.

"And you left a guy alone that wants you. Nice mixed signals, tool," Kaxon mentioned.

Well, shit. I forgot Shaun is still at the house. I looked at my brothers.

"Go," Payton said as I left.

I got back to the house and found Shaun gone. I had Kaxon take me over to Shaun's place and rang his buzzer. I waited until Shaun came down and answered the door.

"Look," I said.

"No, I get it. You can't let things go when your brothers do something wrong. I busted my ass to show you. You had to take care of a mess you created," Shaun said with the same look that I saw the day I went after Sable.

"I knew it," I whispered.

"Knew what?" Shaun asked.

"That you will find a reason that you don't want me. Please stop sending me things," I mumbled as I turned and walked away.

"Pax!" Shaun yelled.

I shook my head as I realized it was a mistake taking a chance. I got into the car as Kaxon looked at me.

"Please don't lecture me and tell me I jumped to conclusions. Take me home so I can get rid of the stuff in my room. It's over," I whispered as Kaxon drove me back to my house.

When we got back, I got out of the car and went inside the house. Kaxon followed me as I grabbed trash bags and went to my room. I grabbed everything Shaun did and threw it into the containers.

"Pax," Kaxon said.

"I'm a fool, and it's over. I let my guard down and got rejected again. I almost killed my brother because of my temper. God hates me," I snapped as I bagged everything up.

My brothers came home and heard the commotion. They came upstairs to find me bagging items and mumbling to myself.

"What's going on with Pax?" Payton asked.

"I don't know. Pax isn't making any sense," Kaxon said.

"No one wants you, Paxton. You're a horrible person. You can't control your temper. Why do you deserve love?" I mumbled as I finished bagging everything.

"Pax," Payton said as I kept mumbling. "Pax!" He shouted, and I stopped. I looked at Payton as he looked at me, then I passed out.

"Pax," I heard someone say, but I was out. I heard voices, but I'm exhausted. I didn't tell my brothers I wasn't sleeping after getting attacked. I had horrible nightmares and did everything to stay awake. Tonight sent my emotional state into overload, causing me to break.

It was a call my brothers would make to my parents that would send everyone into a panic. It will take one person to help me through it.

CHAPTER 12

HELP

Pax

I woke up and looked around, noticing the hospital room. I went to raise my arm with something preventing me, then I saw it, restraints. What the hell?

"I see that you're awake. How was your nap?" Someone asked.

I looked to see Larkin sitting in a chair next to the bed.

"I don't call stuck in a hospital bed with restraints enjoying a nap," I replied.

Larkin stood up and put her hands on the rail of the hospital bed.

"Why am I here?" I questioned.

"Because you need help. You have PTSD from when those people attacked you," Larkin told me.

I looked at her.

"Pax, Markus called me and explained what happened. Have you been sleeping?" Larkin asked me.

"Sleep is so overrated," I told Larkin.

"A lack of sleep can affect you in several ways. When you don't sleep, it affects your life, especially your emotions. I know I went through it after what Roger did to me," Larkin admitted.

I didn't know what to say. With everything that happened, I felt my life spiraling out of control every day.

"How long have I been here?" I asked.

"Three days," Larkin answered.

"And my family? Did they visit me?" I questioned.

Larkin gave me a soft smile. "Yes, but I wanted to talk to you when you woke up and explain things," Larkin said.

I looked at her as a tear fell down my cheek. I looked to see Pops standing in the doorway as he walked into the room and over to the hospital bed.

"I'm sorry, Pops," I said with my voice breaking.

"Pax, it's okay, but you need help. When Payton called us, it was the worst feeling in the world to know your child's hurt. Your ma and I were going out of our minds, knowing something happened to you," Pop told me.

All I could do at that moment is cry. I finally broke and felt out of control. Pops comforted me as I cried. People don't understand how events can make your life spiral. You can't tell anyone because they won't listen. Trust me, I tried with my family, but they missed all the signs.

Ma came in to see me, and that made me cry more. Larkin took off the restraints so I could hug my ma. They put on the restrictions so I wouldn't hurt myself or others when I woke up.

After calming down, the rest of my family came into the room. I sat there, feeling drained.

"Lark, what happens now?" Pops asked Larkin.

Before Larkin answered, someone else answered for her. "Pax will stay here for a few weeks for therapy, and we will watch his sleep," someone said.

"Who are you?" Pops asked.

"Dr. Jordan Shaw, Jr., I will be Pax's Doctor," Dr. Shaw said.

"Are you related to Jordan Shaw?" Pops asked.

"Jordan is my dad, and my daughters attend school, who is Jesse and Skylar," Dr. Shaw explained. "Dad contacted me and explained about Paxton. He's busy with the foundation and asked me to help."

"Will Pax be okay?" Ma asked with concern.

"Pax will be fine, but he needs help. It sounds like the lack of sleep is affecting him. We will track Paxton's progress, and when he's better, we will release him," Dr. Shaw explained.

I felt exhausted. I laid down and fell asleep.

Over the next two weeks, I attended therapy sessions with Dr. Shaw and slept. He gave me something to calm my mind so that the nightmares became less, and talking about it helped. I didn't realize how much a situation can affect you, and I learned more about my temper. Dr. Shaw gave me coping mechanisms to help with my anger. It turns out I enjoy drawing a lot.

While I got help, my family dealt with things their way, like situations with particular girls.

Mason kept acting like things with Nora was terrific. Nora didn't feel the same way, but Mason didn't get the hint. Nora's interest lies with someone else.

"Why don't you tell Mason?" Britt asked Nora.

"Because Mason doesn't listen. He thinks we're picking up where we left off," Nora answered.

As Britt and Nora talked, Mason walked over, spun Nora around, and kissed her.

"Hey," Mason greeted Nora.

"Hey," Nora said.

"Let's go get some food," Mason said, dragging Nora away from Britt, who shook her head.

Josie walked over to Britt. "Is that Nora with Mason?" Josie asked.

"Yep," Britt said.

"I thought Nora liked Matthew," Selena mentioned.

"Well, Nora does but hasn't told Mason that she likes Matthew. Plus, Matthew keeps avoiding Nora," Britt explained.

"Doesn't your dad hate Mason?" Josie asked.

"Yep, and the Gray family, hence why a cousin is watching me, so I don't go near Pat," Britt said, sighing.

"I'm so glad I don't have these issues. When you're homeless, you don't have someone telling you what to do," Selena mentioned as the others looked at her. "Well, you know what I mean."

Josie giggled as Britt shook her head.

The girls discussed their love lives. My cousins and brothers discussed each other's love lives.

"So, what are you going to do about Britt?" Kaxon asked Patton.

"We're working on it, but stop avoiding the subject. What about you?" Pat asked.

"What about me?" Kaxon asked.

"You're the only one who isn't dating," Pat mentioned.

"Because I have standards like high standards," Kaxon said, raising his hand high.

"That's not what I mean. I saw you talking to some girl," Pat mentioned.

"Oh, that girl, well, I ran into her at the bakery after she threatened Sable. She has a little attitude," Kaxon said.

Pat arched an eyebrow.

"Don't even think about it," Kaxon said.

"Think about what?" Pat asked.

"You're plotting, and you have bigger issues to deal with your love life. Unlike everyone else, I don't need help," Kaxon informed Pat.

"If you say so," Pat said.

"I say so," Kaxon said.

Yeah, I found all this out when they released me from the hospital. I was busy getting help while everyone else was busy with their issues.

My family came to see me, and I felt better, but I changed. My anger wasn't prevalent like it was, and my confidence unpronounced. I drew when I felt anxious or upset. Yeah, I had a lot of drawings on a sketch pad.

After two weeks, the hospital released me. I had to take incomplete in my classes since I missed time, and I'm still on probation for a few more months. All I could do is work and draw. I didn't see Shaun at all, and we didn't work the same shift.

Dr. Shaw advised me not to worry about that part of my life but to focus on my emotional and mental health, so I did. I sat in my bedroom, sketching when someone knocked on my door.

I looked up to see Parker standing in the doorway. He walked into the bedroom and sat down next to me on my bed.

"I'm sorry that I tried to kill you," I apologized, surprising Parker. "Dr. Shaw explained my actions have consequences. I have to take responsibility for them. It's part of my therapy."

Parker looked at me.

"Dr. Shaw said I need to focus on my well-being and not worry about my love life," I mentioned, hinting to Parker.

"Pax, we haven't seen Shaun," Parker said.

"Oh," I whispered. I started sketching as Parker looked at the drawing and furrowed his brows. "It's for the best. I'm lucky to stay in school even though I took incomplete, and Nik held my job." I wiped a tear away as I drew.

"Give Shaun time, Pax. He's giving you space," Parker suggested.

"Yeah," I whispered as Parker got up and left the bedroom.

I stopped drawing and cried. It's my fault that Shaun is staying away. I let my temper get the best of me, and after what Shaun went through with Travis, I didn't blame him. I create my messes; now, I have to clean them up.

I returned to work, and Britt worked with me. She said nothing about Shaun, even when I attempted to ask her. Yeah, I was stubborn.

While I worked, some guy came into the bakery and flirted with me. The guy came in every time I worked and would talk to me. He told me his name is Richard. I thought nothing of it.

Britt watched as the guy flirted with me, as did my family when they came into the bakery. I didn't want Richard. I wanted Shaun.

His attention was kind since I didn't get any from other guys, but I was hesitant. I kept my distance until one night. I closed up the bakery alone. Britt left to sneak around with Pat, and I cleaned up.

I went into the back, not hearing the bell, and came out to see Richard in the bakery. What the hell is he doing here?

"We're closed," I told Richard.

"That's good because I thought we could hang out," Richard said.

"Why?" I asked, cleaning up.

"Because I like you and you like me," Richard said.

"And we're not a big happy family, and I'm not interested," I told Richard.

"Come on, Pax," Richard coaxed, moving towards me.

I looked at Richard. Is this guy on crack?

"We all know you won't do anything because your temper gets you into trouble," Richard said, pushing my buttons.

I furrowed my brows.

"So, if you fight back, then you're done, and if you don't, no one will believe you. You are a Gray," Richard said with a tone I hated.

I clenched my fists, knowing I had no recourse, and no one would believe me. Richard backed me up against the wall and put his hands on my pants.

"Now, be a good boy and enjoy yourself," Richard whispered into my ear as I stood there.

I closed my eyes, waiting for the inevitable when nothing happened. I opened my eyes to see Richard on the floor and Shaun standing there. Great, now people will accuse me of something I didn't do.

"I did nothing. I swear," I said as Shaun looked at me. I furrowed my brows, trying not to cry, but it wasn't working. I wiped my eyes. "If you don't believe me, I'm okay with that."

I moved away from Shaun as I went to the back, wiping my eyes. I picked up the phone and made a call.

"Pay, it's me," I sniffled. "Can you come to get me?"

What's wrong, Pax?

"I can't tell you, but please come get me," I said, sniffling.

Yeah, I'll be there in a few minutes.

I hung up and cried. I sat down on the floor and heard sirens. I sat there as I heard people come into the bakery, then heard Payton. I put my head in my knees and covered my head as I cried.

"Pax?" Payton said.

I looked to see Pay, Park, and Shaun standing there.

"I didn't fight back because my temper gets me into trouble. I didn't flirt. I did what Dr. Shaw told me to do. I promise I did nothing. So, why did this happen?" I asked with tear-streaked cheeks.

"Because people take advantage of a situation, knowing their intent," Payton explained.

"Payton, I'm trying," I said.

"We know, little brother, we know," Payton said, hugging me as I cried.

I learned people would do things to make you feel less than a person, knowing you're trying. All you can do is keep working harder. It's a lesson I learned the hard way, but it's one that will bring something important back into my life.

CHAPTER 13

REUNITED

Pax

I sat on the couch, stunned. My family attempted to talk to me, but I didn't understand why? Why would someone do that?

"Pax," someone said, and I looked at Shaun, sitting in front of me. "You did nothing wrong, and that asshole played on your situation."

"I didn't flirt with the guy or show interest. I did what Dr. Shaw instructed me to do. I sketch to handle my emotions. Why me?" I asked, furrowing my brows.

"Because the guy is a predator. The guy looks for people he knows that won't fight back. The guy is like Travis. They pick someone for a particular reason. It's not your fault," Shaun reminded me.

I had no recourse, and that sucked.

"It's time to get help with this situation," Parker mentioned as we looked at him. "A prominent family owns this school, and someone is talking to a family member."

Everyone looked at Kaxon.

"Why are you looking at me?" Kaxon asked.

"Because it's your turn to help family," Markus told Kaxon.

Kaxon looked at everyone and sighed. I needed a shower. I went upstairs while my family discussed the matter and took a

shower. I scrubbed myself raw, trying to wash away the night. Since nothing progressed, I still felt dirty.

After I finished, I turned off the water and dried off. I looked in the mirror to see myself as a shell. The last few months took their toll on me.

I put on some clothes and went into my bedroom to find Shaun sitting on my bed, waiting for me.

"I figured you left," I mentioned.

"No, I wanted to stay, if you don't mind," Shaun offered.

"That's fine," I said, sitting on my bed next to Shaun.

We said nothing, then Shaun reached for my hand as I recoiled but touched it. I relaxed as Shaun interlocked his fingers with mine.

"It's difficult after a terrible situation, but it gets better," Shaun assured me.

"It might," I said, not knowing what will happen.

"I can stay with you," Shaun offered.

I nodded, saying nothing. I laid down on the bed, and Shaun laid next to me. He wrapped his arms around me as I fell asleep. It was a comforting feeling.

I woke up the next day to see Shaun asleep next to me. I reached and brushed his hair away from his face. Shaun opened his eyes and looked at me.

"Sorry, I didn't mean to wake you," I said.

"No worries, it was nice waking up next to someone," Shaun mentioned, smiling.

"So, um, I thought we could try," I said, searching for words.

Shaun looked at me. I diverted my eyes.

"You know, try as a couple, but we don't have to, if you don't want to," I blurted. God, I was nervous.

Shaun said nothing.

"It's okay if you say no. I don't want to pressure you. If you say yes, cool. If not, it's okay — no pressure from me. No, sir," I rambled.

Shaun interrupted my ramble, pressing his lips to my lips. Our lips moved in sync with each other as I put my hands on Shaun. Then he pulled back.

"Sorry, you were rambling," Shaun told me.

"Yeah, I do that when I'm nervous," I mentioned.

Shaun smiled as I smiled. My door opened up, and we turned to see my brothers standing there.

"Well, it looks like you two got over your hang-up with each other," Parker mentioned.

We looked at Parker weirdly.

"Yeah, you don't forget the raincoat even if you can't produce children," Payton mentioned.

Shaun and I looked at Payton like he's crazy. My brothers laughed, closing the door behind them.

"Your family is strange," Shaun mentioned.

"You don't know the half of it," I said, sighing.

Shaun chuckled as I shook my head. Then he got out of bed. I laid there as Shaun picked up my sketchbook and flipped through it. He stopped at one sketch.

"You sketched me?" Shaun asked.

"Yeah, I figure I could look at it when I needed a reminder of my temper," I answered, playing with my fingers.

Shaun looked at me and set my sketchbook down on the desk. He walked over and sat down on the bed.

"Pax, I know you have a temper, but I know you wouldn't hurt me. It disappointed me that every time we tried, something interrupted us. It didn't stop my feelings about you. Last night, I came to talk to you," Shaun said.

"You avoided me after the night I sent Parker to the hospital," I mentioned.

"I didn't avoid you; I gave you space to fix whatever was going on with you. Plus, I didn't want to argue about us, knowing your anger," Shaun reasoned.

"Yeah, Dr. Shaw explained that I have misplaced anger. He taught me coping mechanisms," I explained.

"That's good because if we do this, I don't want your anger hindering it. I want someone who knows the difference between when to fight and when to step back. What I saw last night pissed me off. It reminded me of Travis and someone who intended to hurt you. So, I clocked the asshole," Shaun explained.

I chuckled.

"I pictured the person was Travis. That helps direct your anger," Shaun reasoned, making me laugh.

"So, do you want to try?" I asked.

"Yeah, and this time we'll take it slow," Shaun responded.

I sat up and leaned in, then kissed Shaun as he wrapped his arms around me and kissed me back. It was a new beginning for us.

Kaxon

Why the hell do I get dragged into drama? I avoid drama like the plague, my cousins not so much. I went looking for Jesse and found her at the bakery, drinking coffee. Okay, she's alone, and that's my cue.

I walked over and sat down at Jesse's table. She arched an eyebrow.

"I'm not stalking you. Girls assume shit, and I'm not an assuming person. I need help," I said.

"You got that right," Jesse retorted.

I gave Jesse a looked and rolled my eyes.

"The school put my cousin Pax on probation for beating the hell out a bitch that deserved it. I know guys shouldn't touch women, but she is far from one. Anyway, because of it, he can't defend himself, and some douche almost attacked him," I blurted.

Jesse stared at me. I didn't know if she seems confused or wants to kick my ass. I watched Jesse pull out her phone and make a call. I plead with this chick about my cousin, and she makes a social call. What the fuck?

"Hey, Grandpa. School is fine, and Skylar is crazy. Remember the kid that Dad is helping? Yeah, that is the one. Well, it seems the school feels he's trouble, and people are making trouble. Can you help the guy out so that his family will stop interrupting my time alone? Thanks, Grandpa," Jesse said, hanging up.

I looked at Jesse. "Who was that?" I asked.

"It's my grandfather, Jordan Shaw. He will speak to Uncle Ryan about the situation and get your cousin off probation. Now, is there anything else you need?" Jesse asked me.

This chick needs some fun. Jesse is a sourpuss from the word goes.

"A date?" I asked.

Jesse looked at me.

"Look, you hate people. I hate people. Let's hate people together. Plus, you're not annoying as most chicks that attend this school," I reasoned.

"You date little, don't you?" Jesse asked.

"Nope, I have standards. Plus, I don't need a gift from a hoe," I replied. I watched a smile form on her lips.

"You're different," Jesse mentioned.

"You got that right, sweetheart. My grandpa is a crazy reverend, and my dad is plain crazy. You try dealing with those two, and you're lucky you're normal," I remarked.

"My uncle is Frazier. He's an idiot. My uncle Liam detests everyone. My uncle Elijah is a momma's boy. My dad can break you in two. Explain to me about normal," Jesse said.

"You and I will get along fine," I mentioned, smirking. Jesse smirked back. "So, about that date?"

"I don't like heights and hate stupid people. Any place that doesn't have those two things is okay," Jesse told me.

"Okay, I will cook for you, and we can watch a movie on the floor in my living room. I'll lock the door and take everyone's key," I offered.

"Then you have a date. Don't fuck it up," Jesse told me.

Wait. Did I ask a chick out and accepted? Well, shit, thanks, Pax, I owe you one.

CHAPTER 14

DATE NIGHT

Shaun

I know it's a hit or miss with Pax and me, but I'm serious about us. I missed Pax a lot, even when I was with Travis. Pax and I talked for hours about everything, and I didn't feel stupid about my ideas.

Since Pax has a gluten allergy, I contacted his dad about recipes. Pax's dad sent me quite a few items. I went shopping and picked up things. I cooked dinner for Pax and figured we would watch a movie at my place. I enlisted his brothers to help me.

Parker makes sure Pax arrives, and Payton helps me with the cooking and baking. Payton met me at my apartment after I finished at the grocery store. We went up to my apartment, and I set the bags on the kitchen table.

"So, is everything set?" I asked Payton.

"Yeah, you relax. Parker will do his part. It's a good thing I'm helping you cook and not Parker. Our brother burns water," Payton mentioned.

I looked at Payton.

"Parker can't cook," Payton told me.

"Well, I called your dad, and he explained what to buy. I didn't realize how much food has gluten in it," I told Payton.

"Yeah, it was bad before our parents found out about Pax's food allergy. Most people think nothing of eating food, but Pax was sick a lot. He was miserable and lost weight," Payton explained.

"I remember when we dated in high school, Pax told me about his food allergy. I checked about gluten before getting Pax food," I told Payton, who looked at me.

"Most people couldn't care less about Pax and not bother, but you care about him," Payton mentioned.

"Because Pax is special to me. Pax didn't make fun of me when I told him I want to be a pastry chef. Travis told me it was a stupid occupation and made me a pussy," I said.

Payton furrowed his eyebrows.

"I remember when I didn't make Travis's favorite dish. He threw the plate of food at me, then told me to clean it up. Afterward, Travis assaulted me," I whispered, embarrassed about the abuse.

"Shaun, Travis is an asshole and doesn't deserve your attention. Pax might have a temper, but he would never hurt you," Payton reassured me as I nodded.

We got to work, cooking and baking, preparing dinner for this evening. God, I hope Pax enjoys it.

Pax

I worked at the bakery, waiting on customers as Britt helped me. Shaun said he has plans this evening, which bummed me out. While I was busy at the bakery, I didn't know a few people were conspiring.

Parker showed up while I was busy and gestured to Britt, who nodded. She signals at Nik, who nodded. I brought the order to the countertop and rang up the customer. After the customer left, Parker whistled using his thumb and finger.

I looked up, and Pat and Kaxon came out from the back, ushering me away from the counter.

"What are you, tools, doing?" I yelled.

"Helping you," Pat answered.

"My shift isn't over," I told Pat.

"It is now," Kaxon said. Pax and Kaxon shoved me to Parker as I stumbled forward. Parker caught me and dragged me out of the bakery. I looked at Pat and Kaxon, who waved and smiled.

"You'll get me fired," I told Parker.

"Oh, well, then you find another job," Parker said, dragging me away from the bakery.

Parker dragged me to Shaun's building. I stood there as he rang the buzzer. The door clicked, and we went inside, walking up to Shaun's apartment.

"Park, what are you doing?" I asked.

"You'll see," Park answered as we arrived at Shaun's door.

"I told Shaun that I wouldn't pressure him. He wants to take it slow and will think that I want to go fast," I said in an anxious tone.

"Will you relax?" Parker told me.

I looked at Parker with apprehension. Shaun will think that I planned this. Oh, hell, no, it's not this time. I turned and started walking away. Parker realized what I'm doing and ran after me.

"Oh, no, you don't," Parker said, dragging me back.

"You don't understand," I yelled.

"Chill the hell out, you anxious twit," Parker barked.

I looked at Parker. When he released me, I took off with Parker chasing me. He dragged me back, and I kept leaving. We did this for a good twenty minutes as Shaun's door opened.

Shaun and Payton watched us. Parker and I fought each other as we made our way back to Shaun's apartment. Then I saw Shaun and Payton. I sighed.

"The next time you plan something, you chase after the weasel," Parker told Shaun.

"I swear I had nothing to do with this," I told Shaun, who looked at me, puzzled.

I felt anxious, standing there, knowing everything will blow up in my face. Shaun stepped towards me as I stood there, furrowing my eyebrows.

"It's okay. I enlisted your brother's help. I wanted to surprise you with a date," Shaun assured me.

"Say what?" I asked, surprised.

"I planned a date for us at my apartment. I made dinner and dessert, then picked up some movies to watch. If we're taking it slow, then we can do it without pressure," Shaun explained.

"But we have a problem," I said, thinking about my food allergy. Ma and Pops made sure I have gluten-free food, and Payton helps me cook since Pops isn't here.

"What's the problem?" Shaun questioned.

"I can't eat anything that you make because of my food allergy," I answered, feeling terrible.

"That's why I called your dad, and Payton helped me cook," Shaun told me.

That surprised me.

"I know you have a gluten allergy from when we dated in high school. I know that if your dad doesn't cook, then Payton does. I even got the recipe for your favorite cupcakes," Shaun told me as he smiled.

"Well, you both have fun. We're out of here," Parker mentioned.

Parker and Payton left as I went into Shaun's apartment. Shaun closed the door, and I saw the kitchen table set up for dinner. I walked over and sat down at the table as Shaun joined me.

Shaun lifted the lid to the pan, and we dished our food onto our plates. I took a bite, and it surprised me how delicious the food is.

"How is the food?" Shaun asked me.

"It's great. It reminds me of Pops's cooking," I answered.

"Good, because I never cooked for someone other than myself," Shaun said.

"What do you mean?" I asked as I ate.

"After Travis, I didn't date, so I learned how to cook for myself. At first, I burned everything. Next, I screwed up the seasoning. I kept practicing until I learned. I got used to making food for Travis that I didn't know what I liked," Shaun explained.

I stopped eating and looked at Shaun.

"But I learned I like a lot of things and enjoy trying new recipes. I'm even taking culinary and pastry classes. One day, I'll open a restaurant of my own, even if Travis and my family thought it was a dumb idea," Shaun told me.

That bothered me that people belittled Shaun's goals and ideas.

"It's not dumb," I told Shaun.

"What?" Shaun asked, confused.

"It isn't dumb if you want to learn culinarily. People who dismiss your ideas are dumb. When you care about someone, you support their dreams. I say if you want to open a restaurant, then go for it. I will come every day to eat," I said, smiling, which made Shaun smile.

After dinner, Shaun set the cupcake in front of me. I looked at it, then picked it up, removing the wrapper. I took a bite, and it surprised me how much the cupcake tasted like Pops. It even had the cream filling, as Pops makes.

"Does the cupcake meet your standards?" Shaun asked, eating his cupcake.

"Yep," I answered, enjoying the cupcake. After that cupcake, I had two more. Shaun looked at me. "What?" I asked.

"Aren't you afraid of putting on weight?" Shaun asked me.

"Well, if I do, then I do. No one is stopping me from eating," I said while shrugging.

Shaun looked at his half-eaten cupcake.

"Shaun, you can eat," I mentioned as Shaun stared at me. "I'm not Travis," I added.

I watched Shaun relax and finish his cupcake, then eating another one. Travis is a dick for what he did to Shaun. I'm glad that Matthew took care of Travis, or it would be me. Let's hope I never see that asshole.

We finished dessert, and I sat down on the couch as Shaun put a movie into the Blu-Ray player. Shaun joined me on the couch, and we settled in to watch a video. I laid my head on Shaun's shoulder as he wrapped his arm around me.

Now, this date was perfect. There was no pressure, and it was the two of us together. You can't ask for a better date than that, although I have a feeling tomorrow will create unnecessary issues.

CHAPTER 15

WELL, SH*T

Pax

I snoozed. My phone kept buzzing. I didn't know someone was calling as I slept. A few minutes later, I woke up and saw Shaun sleeping next to me on the couch. Our bodies tangle with each other.

Shaun woke up and rubbed his face.

"Morning," Shaun said.

"Morning," I said, not realizing what I said.

We looked at each other, then my eyes widened. I jerked up as Shaun did the same. I grabbed my phone to see several missed calls from everyone. Then we heard pounding on Shaun's apartment door.

We got up and ran to the door. Shaun opened it to find my brothers standing there looking piss.

"Oh, hey, guys," I said.

"Do you mind telling us why you didn't bother to come home last night?" Payton asked with his arms crossed.

"Well, I would, but I can't because I fell asleep," I responded.

"Do you know what this is?" Parker asked, holding up his cell phone. "It's called a phone. A guy named Alexander Graham Bell invented it to use."

"Yes, and it's a lovely function," I retorted.

I watched Parker's eye twitch.

"Did you get lucky, Pax?" Kaxon asked as we looked at him. "What? It's an honest question," Kaxon told us.

"Boy, you need Jesus," Payton told Kaxon.

"Hey, I will have you know I get all the Jesus that I need, thanks to Grandpa," Kaxon retorted.

Someone moved Kaxon out of the way and separated Payton and Parker. We watched Matthew walk into the apartment and sit down in a chair, then he pulled out his phone and looked at it.

"What are you doing?" Parker asked.

"I'm looking through social media. Continue to give your brother the third degree," Matthew told Parker.

"You're a big help," Parker grumbled.

"Well, nothing happened last light, and Pax is safe. Did it dawn on anyone that Pax came here for a date? If he didn't come home, then he was here. Or did this concept escape everyone?" Matthew asked my brothers and cousin.

Payton entered the apartment. "After what happened to Pax, we worry," Payton told Matthew.

"That's if Pax was in imminent danger, which he's not. If Shaun couldn't take on Travis, I doubt he would hurt Pax. No offense, Shaun," Matthew told Shaun.

"None took," Shaun said, looking at Matthew.

"Look, I'm fine. We ate dinner, watched movies, and fell asleep on the couch. Nothing happened last night besides spending time together. We both agreed to take things slow," I said.

"You're a Gray. There's no Gray takes things slow with their significant other," Parker told me.

"Well, we do," I said, shrugging.

"Christ, you guys suck at this," Markus said, walking into the apartment.

"When did you get here?" Kaxon asked.

"Two minutes ago. I saw the search party and joined," Markus told Kaxon.

"Well, I came to keep Payton and Parker from pounding Pax into oblivion. I'm also keeping Pax from killing Parker," Kaxon told Markus.

"You know Payton can wipe the floor with you?" Markus asked, arching an eyebrow.

"That thought didn't escape me," Kaxon said, raising a finger.

"Where's Pat?" I asked.

"Pat's figuring out how to see his lady love. Someone is guarding and reporting back to Daddy about Britt's every move," Kaxon answered.

"Ah," I said.

"Can we get back to the matter at hand?" Payton asked.

"What matter? I overslept, and you both showed up here like apes. Did it ever occur to you I won't put myself in that position as I did?" I said.

My brothers looked at each other, then at me. Both said, "No."

I sighed and sat down on the couch.

"Look, we fell asleep watching movies. Yes, Pax should have called you," Shaun said as I went to protest. Shaun gave me a look, and I closed my mouth. "But it's hard to call when you don't plan to fall asleep."

Matthew watched Shaun with me and noticed that Shaun took control of the situation. My brothers were too worried about me not coming home; they didn't see our interaction.

"Now, if you don't mind, I will make sure that Pax comes home and gets ready for work," Shaun assured my brothers. My brothers agreed and left. My cousins follow my brothers, leaving Shaun and me alone.

I looked at Shaun, who sat down next to me.

"Thanks," I said.

"I get your brothers worry, and next time we'll make sure you call your family," Shaun reasoned.

I smiled.

As everyone left the building, Matthew stopped my brothers and cousins.

"What's going on, Matthew?" Payton asked.

"I don't think you have to worry about Pax," Matthew told Payton.

"Why not?" Parker questioned.

"Shaun's protective over Pax and keeps Pax grounded. Usually, Pax will argue but didn't in the apartment," Matthew explained.

My brothers looked at each other, surprised, as Matthew smiled. That's when my brothers realized what influence Shaun had on me.

Everyone left, and I put on my shoes.

"So, last night was fun," I mentioned.

"Yeah, it was," Shaun said.

I wanted to ask when we would do it again, but I figure that I shouldn't. My luck, it will be a one-time thing. Shaun put on his shoes and walked me home.

We walked in comfortable silence as I figured out how to approach the subject of another date.

"So I was thinking," I said.

"Yeah," Shaun said as we walked.

"We can go on another date," I mentioned.

"We'll see," Shaun said as we reached my door.

I turned and looked at Shaun. I waited for Shaun to say something. He leaned over and kissed my cheek.

"I'll call you," Shaun told me as I nodded. He left, and I stood there like a lump. Well, I felt like a tool.

I went into the house and went upstairs to get ready for work. As I got ready, I checked my phone. I sent Shaun a text to let him know I had fun. After I sent it, I regretted it. Then I sent another text. After ten messages, I sighed. Yep, I'm a tool.

I fell backward onto the bed. My phone dinged, and I opened my messages. It was a stupid meme from Mason. Okay, I'm sure that's not legal. Where the hell does my cousin find this shit?

Note to self, kick Mason's ass when I see him.

I got up and went to the bakery.

Shaun

I got home and grabbed a shower. Last night was amazing. I couldn't wait to spend time with Pax again. After my shower, I picked up my phone and saw ten messages. I chuckled when I read the words. Pax is so adorable.

I sent a message back and got dressed. After I finished dressing, I grabbed my keys and left. I stop by a place and picked up breakfast. I paid and left, carrying the bag with me.

I made my way to the bakery and entered to find Pax getting things ready. I walked over to him and held up the bag.

"Breakfast?" I asked. Pax looked at me and smiled.

We sat down and ate breakfast before his shift. Nik came out of the back and saw us, then smiled. As we ate, some guy burst into the bakery. We looked at the guy.

"Well, hello, nurse," the guy said as I chuckled. Pax looked at the guy with confusion. He walked over and pinched Pax's cheeks. "You are the cutest guy I ever saw, except that guy." The guy pointed at Nik, who chuckled.

"No offense, dude, but you're old and creepy," Pax remarked as I snickered.

"What? I'm offended. I'm not old or creepy," the guy exclaimed in the most colorful voice ever.

"Oh, you're creepy all right," Pax said.

"Well, I never," the guy huffed as he marched over to Nik. I roared with laughter as Pax looked at me, confused.

"What's so funny?" Pax asked me.

"That's Nik's husband, Leo," I answered, chuckling.

Pax's eyes widened in horror. "Oh, God, I didn't know," Pax whispered.

I looked at Pax with curiosity.

"Do you think Nik will fire me for insulting his husband? I can't lose my job," Pax whispered.

I looked at Pax with concern as he got up. He walked over to Nik and Leo, who's standing behind the counter.

"I'm so sorry. I didn't mean to insult you. If I knew who you were, I wouldn't say anything," Pax apologized as Nik and Leo looked at him with concern. "Dr. Shaw told me not to overreact, and when I do, to apologize. He explained it would help with my temper," Pax rambled.

I watched as Pax kept apologizing as Nik and Leo reassured Pax. Then Nik walked away.

"Did I do something wrong?" Pax asked, getting upset.

"What? No," Leo answered.

"I did. I'm so sorry," Pax said as I walked over to Pax. I put my hand on his arm. Pax looked at me. "Shaun, I didn't mean it."

"Pax, it's okay," I reassured Pax, comforting him.

A few minutes later, someone entered the bakery. The person walked over to us.

"Pax?" The guy said.

Pax looked at the guy. "Dr. Shaw?"

"Let's talk," the guy said as he led Pax to a table. They sat down and talked.

I looked at Nik. "Who's that?"

"That is my cousin, JJ. He helped Paxton. It seems the kid hasn't had it easy and needs people who care," Nik reasoned.

I nodded as I watched Dr. Shaw talk to Pax. We would find out something crucial about Pax that none of us knew. It's something that Pax inherited from a family member. A secret that individual family members kept guarded, not telling anyone.

It will take a visit from someone significant to help Pax.

CHAPTER 16

FAMILY SECRET

Pax

They say every family has their secrets, and ours did not differ from anyone else's. We hid it better. A few family members knew a particular mystery but didn't elaborate on it.

With the recent issues I had, Dr. Shaw pulled medical files on family members with his dad's help. His dad treated my family. Both scoured through data on my family's medical history. Then information caught their attention.

"That makes little sense," JJ told his dad.

"What does?" Jordan asked.

"Is it possible it can skip a generation?" JJ asked.

"It depends on genetics. Different disorders can pass to other family members without hitting the person. It's the same with the brain," Jordan explained.

"No wonder this kid acts the way he does," JJ mentioned.

"JJ, you need to contact the family immediately," Jordan advised JJ.

"How do you approach a situation without hell breaking loose?" JJ asked.

"You use the direct approach," Jordan advised.

It's a call that no one expected when Dr. Shaw contacted my parents, along with my grandparents. My grandparents contacted my uncles. He drove to Oakridge to speak to my family, informing them of his findings.

Nash

We met with Paxton's doctor. He explained to us the situation with Pax and what he uncovered. Lex didn't take it well.

"No way," Lex said, standing up and looking at everyone. "There's no way that my ma has issues like this. Right, Ma?" Lex asked, looking at Mags, who looked at me.

Lex looked at us, stunned.

"Lex, we didn't tell anyone because it's not something you discuss. With the health issues your mom had, it didn't help when you add anxiety to the mix," I explained.

"But Ma is okay," Lex mentioned.

"Yeah, but it wasn't always that way. We found out when your mom got sick. We told no one," I reasoned.

My brothers stood there, quiet, which is unusual for them. They're planning something.

Lex walked over to Mags. "Why didn't you tell us?" Lex asked her.

"Because we took care of it. For years, I worried about no one wanting or loving me. It didn't help that your father was a tool," Mags said.

"Hey!" I exclaimed.

"Well, it didn't," Mags told me. I sighed.

"Does Nana and Grampa know?" Lex asked.

"No, because we didn't tell your grandparents," Mags answered.

"Lex, it's not the end of the world. So, your mom is a nutcase. We're used to it," Nixon mentioned.

We looked at Nixon like he lost his damn mind.

"Trust us; it explained so much about Maggie because she's nuts," Nathan added.

"Are you serious?" I asked Nathan.

"It's true," Nathan said, shrugging.

"You're not helping," I told Nathan.

"Who cares? Maggie is crazy, and you're a tool," Noah told me.

"You're not helping either," I informed Noah.

"God, you all suck at this. Yes, Maggie has anxiety and created more issues than we needed. She took her happy pills. Now we're here. Can we move forward?" Nolan asked.

I shook my head.

"And people wonder why I have anxiety. Have you guys met you?" Mags asked my brothers.

"Yes, and we are delightful," Nixon retorted.

"I didn't come here to cause issues. I came to tell you that Paxton needs medication to help with his anxiety," Dr. Shaw said as we looked at him.

Lex looked at Piper. "Lex, if this helps Pax, then what is the harm? I want our boy happy and not worried all the time," Piper reasoned.

Lex looked at us and sighed. "If that's what it takes, then okay. I don't want Pax to hurt," Lex said.

"It will help. The mind is a complex area. We magnify situations, making scenarios worse than what they are. Paxton is a suitable candidate for a low dosage of anti-anxiety medication. It will help. I will track and adjust the medication," Dr. Shaw informed us.

Lex nodded as the doctor left. I hope it helps Pax with things because he's struggling.

Pax

Shaun went with me to meet Dr. Shaw. I sat in a chair as I bounced my leg. Shaun put his hand on my leg, and I calmed down. I can't help it. Sitting in this office makes me feel anxious.

Dr. Shaw placed a bottle in front of me on his desk. I picked the bottle up and looked at it.

"It's an anti-anxiety medication. It will help the mind relax and make you focus. Your mind is magnifying issues in a way that makes you create scenarios. They are ten times worse than what they are. It's common in a family that has anxiety," Dr. Shaw explained.

"Will it help me feel better?" I asked, wondering if it's the right decision.

"It will take a few weeks, but we will adjust the dosage as needed. Your body will adjust, helping you understand situations better. Plus, we will meet to discuss everything. Paxton, it will get better," Dr. Shaw assured me.

God, I hope so, because my life hasn't been easy. We left the doctor's office, and I stepped out into the bright sunlight. I stood there, wondering what happens next?

"Pax, it will be okay," Shaun assured me.

"How do you know?" I asked.

"Because I take medication for it," Shaun admitted.

I looked at Shaun with surprise.

"After Travis, I developed horrible anxiety. The doctor prescribed me medication to calm my mind. It's one reason I kept my distance from people. Abuse has a terrible effect on the mind and hinders your life. I knew if I wanted to be with you, I had to gain control of my life again," Shaun explained.

I sighed — one more uphill battle to overcome in my life.

Over the next two weeks, I took my medication, and it took time to adjust. Boy, it took time. I fought with my brothers, who wanted to knock me out several times. Yeah, it got rough.

I kept apologizing. My brothers told me to stick it. Did I mention my brothers wanted to throttle me? My cousins told me to stop apologizing. I can't help it.

I also drove Shaun nuts worrying about everything. He told me to relax. That didn't help. Did you ever tell someone to relax? That caused Shaun to tackle me several times.

Every time my temper flared, Shaun handled it. He shoved my sketchbook in my face. I smacked him with it. Yeah, I got tackled again. It drove my brothers nuts.

"How long does it take for medication to kick in for someone?" Parker asked Payton.

"My guess, a long ass time," Payton told Parker.

"I swear if it doesn't happen soon, I will beat the hell out of Pax," Pat said, walking past Payton and Parker.

"No shit," Kaxon added.

"Why are you here?" Parker asked Kaxon.

"I'm here for moral support," Kaxon answered.

"Well, go home and support from there," Parker said, pointing to the door.

"Spoilsport," Kaxon said, staying put.

While Parker and Kaxon went back and forth, Shaun dealt with me. He pushed me up against the wall and held me against it.

"Do you mind?" I asked.

"Will you quit acting like an ass?" Shaun asked.

"You like my ass," I answered with a look.

Did I forget to mention that while adjusting to the medication that I flirted with Shaun?

"Pax," Shaun said.

"Yes," I replied.

"Stop flirting," Shaun ordered.

I pouted as Shaun sighed.

"You're something else," Shaun told me.

"Is that good or bad? Oh, God, it's bad, isn't it?" I exclaimed.

"No, but the doctor needs to adjust your meds," Shaun said as I looked at Shaun. He pulled me into a hug as I buried my head into his chest.

"I want to feel normal," I mumbled.

Shaun held me as I wrapped my arms around him. "You will, but it will take time," Shaun assured me.

I sighed. Why can't my life be okay? Thanks a lot, Nana.

CHAPTER 17

BALANCE

Pax

The medication started working finally. I didn't feel anxious, and everything became more transparent. Dr. Shaw helped me realize my anxiety affected my temper. It was good to have control over my life again.

Shaun was working with me today at the bakery when Kaxon and Mason showed up.

"What are you doing here?" I asked my cousins.

"We come bearing good news and tidings," Kaxon answered. I looked at Kaxon weird. "Your probation is no more." Kaxon grinned. Mason rolled his eyes. I shook my head.

"What did you do?" I asked.

"Well, I chatted with a girl who agreed to a date," Kaxon mentioned. That shocked us. "She talked to her grandpa, who talked to her uncle, and they talked to the Dean. Her family owns most of the school," Kaxon explained.

"So, you used the girl to help yourself and me," I mentioned.

"No, I asked the girl to help. The date is a bonus since we both dislike people and have high standards. Plus, the girl is nothing like the girls here, thank God," Kaxon said.

Mason and I chuckled.

"How are you feeling, Pax?" Mason asked me.

"Better. I don't feel angry or out of control anymore," I answered.

"Yeah, we heard you drove your brothers up the wall," Mason said.

I felt someone wrapped their arm around me and turned to see Shaun next to me.

"I had help," I said, looking at Shaun, who smiled at me.

"What did you guys need?" Shaun asked Mason and Kaxon.

"Coffee and muffins," Kaxon answered.

"Two coffees and muffins are coming up," Shaun said, retrieving the order.

I talked to the guys while Shaun got the order. It felt nice to laugh again.

While we were at the bakery, Matthew avoided a particular girl.

"How long are you planning to avoid this girl?" Markus asked Matthew as they walked to class.

"I'm not avoiding it. I'm keeping my distance," Matthew responded.

As Matthew said as a particular girl walked over to him.

"Hey, Matthew," Nora greeted Matthew.

"So much for keeping your distance," Markus whispered, earning a look from Matthew.

"So, I haven't seen you since I got here," Nora mentioned.

"Yeah, my courses keep me busy," Matthew mentioned.

"Well, we can have coffee," Nora suggested.

Before Matthew answered, Mason, walked up.

"Hey, babe," Mason said, putting his arm around Nora and kissing the side of her head.

"Hey," Nora said.

"I brought breakfast," Mason said, handing Nora a coffee.

"Thanks," Nora said, taking the container.

"What are we discussing?" Mason asked, sipping his coffee.

"Coffee," Markus said and smirking.

Nora sipped her coffee as Matthew shook his head.

"We need to get to class," Matthew said, dragging Markus away, leaving Mason and Nora standing there.

Once Matthew and Markus were out of sight, Matthew stopped.

"What was that?" Markus asked as Matthew looked at him.

"That is keeping the peace," Matthew answered.

"Well, it's not like Nora is into Mason," Markus mentioned.

"No, but Mason is into Nora, and I refuse to be an issue," Matthew said.

"Why? Because of Sadie?" Markus questioned.

"Leave Sadie out of this," Matthew ordered Markus.

"Matthew, there's nothing wrong with caring about two people. Since Sadie, you have dated no one," Markus reminded Matthew.

"And it will stay that way," Matthew said, walking away.

"Mark my words, you will meet someone and won't be able to stop the inevitable," Markus yelled.

"Not in this lifetime!" Matthew yelled back.

"You're like your father," Markus sighed.

I waited on customers as Shaun filled orders.

"Halloween is coming up," Shaun mentioned.

"Yeah," I said, handing someone change and order.

"We could go to a haunted house, an apple orchard, or a carnival," Shaun suggested.

"Sounds good to me as long as it's with you," I said as Shaun smiled.

I didn't care what we did as long as I could spend time with Shaun. Holidays were never a big thing for me growing up. While my family got into the spirit, I was okay not doing anything.

After work, we went back to the house, and I went upstairs to get my sketchbook.

"Things seem good between you and Pax," Parker mentioned.

"Yeah, they are. We're going to a haunted house this weekend, then I figure an apple orchard," Shaun mentioned.

My brothers looked at Shaun like he was on crack.

"Why are you looking at me like that?" Shaun asked my brothers.

"You know Pax does nothing like that?" Pat asked Shaun.

"Pax doesn't?" Shaun asked.

"Yeah, little brother doesn't do holidays," Parker answered.

"Why not?" Shaun questioned.

"Because Pax doesn't get into holidays like most people. Even as kids, we all did stuff. Pax didn't join. It takes someone special to get that to happen," Payton mentioned.

I came downstairs, and we left, walking to Shaun's apartment.

"So, your brothers told me you don't do holidays," Shaun mentioned.

"Yeah, holidays never interested me," I replied.

"Oh," Shaun said as we walked.

I stopped, and Shaun looked at me.

"Because I had no reason to celebrate a holiday. Now I do," I explained, smiling.

Shaun walked over to me and wrapped his arms around my waist.

"I didn't have the best childhood growing up. Holidays sucked in my house, but I want to change that," Shaun mentioned.

"Then change it with me," I suggested as Shaun smiled. He leaned in and kissed me.

We broke from our kiss and placed our foreheads against each other.

"I'm glad that we found our way back to each other. I missed you a lot, Pax," Shaun whispered.

"I missed you more, Shaun," I said.

Shaun released me, and we started walking as he slid his hand into mine, interlocking our fingers. Yeah, Shaun and I have our difficulties, but what couple doesn't? It took time to get back to each other, but it was worth it.

We got back to Shaun's place, and he went into his bedroom. I sat down on the couch, opening the book to a blank page. Shaun came out a few minutes later in a towel. He removed the towel before positioning himself on the couch.

"If you don't want to do this, I understand," I mentioned, peeking over the sketchbook.

"I'm okay with it," Shaun told me as I sketched.

I drew an outline as I filled lines and added shadows. I was learning a human perspective with sketching. I finished the drawing, then turned to show Shaun.

Shaun pulled a blanket on him and wrapped it around his waist as he took the sketchbook from me.

"I know it's primitive, but I'm taking art classes," I explained.

"It's not primitive. It's good, considering you never took art classes," Shaun mentioned.

"I enjoy art; it relaxes me," I reasoned.

"Pax, if art is something you enjoy, then go for it. The only person stopping you is you," Shaun told me.

I smiled, knowing that Shaun supported my decision. He went back into the bedroom and got dressed while I sat down, flipping through my sketchbook. Shaun emerged and sat down next to me.

"Where did you learn to draw?" Shaun asked me.

"My grandpa Nash drew and showed me a few things. We visited our grandparents. He would give me a blank paper, crayons, pencils, and colored pencils. I would sit at the table for hours drawing pictures," I answered.

"It seems you both had a common interest," Shaun mentioned.

"Yeah, we're the only ones that draw. Everyone else found other interests. Grandpa wanted to stay close to Nana. They opened the bakery with Grandpa designing cakes and Nana baking. Pops loved working at the bakery along with Ma," I explained.

"We can follow suit," Shaun mentioned as I looked at him. "I can make gluten-free food, and you can design cakes."

That made me smile. I leaned over and kissed Shaun. I loved doing something together with Shaun. Most people can't handle being together with someone always, but I didn't mind it. I enjoyed seeing Shaun often. Plus, we understood each other.

I had a feeling Halloween will be a comedic of sorts with us.

CHAPTER 18

A HALLOWEEN CHAPTER OF SPOOKY TALES, WELL, SORT OF

Pax

Do you know how, when you're sleeping, you have this fantastic dream, then some dipshits think it's cute to wake you up? Yeah, that would be my brothers, who thought it was lovely to throw ice water on me.

I felt something wet and cold hit me, making me jump up in bed.

"Oops, we should have thought this through," Parker laughed, holding a bucket.

Payton and Patton stood on each side of Parker as I got out of bed and chased them, drenched. They ran down the stairs, and I took a shortcut, jumping the railing and landing on the tools.

"Ugh," Payton grunted.

"Thanks for breaking my fall, you dicks," I said, smacking each one in the head.

Parker threw me off him. "What have you been eating?" He asked, stretching.

"Food," I replied, standing up. I'm small, but I'm compact. Pat and I are the shortest ones in our family besides Ma.

Parker and I wrestled as Pat got into the mix, and Payton answered the door. Shaun came inside as Parker flipped me.

"Who's winning?" Shaun asked.

"No one," Payton answered as Parker jumped on me, then Pat jumped on Parker.

I saw Shaun and kneed Parker in the junk as I got up.

"You're so going to pay for that, you little shit," Parker gasped, grabbing his junk.

"It's disturbing how violent you all are," Shaun mentioned.

"It's effective," I said, shrugging. I grabbed Shaun's hand and dragged him upstairs.

"It's good to see Pax happy again," Pat mentioned.

"Little brother, it's always good to see Pax happy," Payton replied.

"I'm getting ice for my boys," Parker whispered, ambling to the kitchen. Payton and Patton laughed.

Once we hit my room, I closed the door and jumped on Shaun, crashing my lips into his lips. Shaun held me as he kissed me back. We broke from our kiss, and Shaun let me down.

I walked over and changed my tee-shirt and found a dry spot on my bed, freaking Parker.

"Why do you have ice in your bed?" Shaun asked, pointing to the ice cubes.

"My dipshit brothers thought it was cute to dump ice water on me," I replied.

Shaun chuckled.

I laid back, propping myself up on my arms.

"I thought in the spirit of Halloween. We could hit a haunted house, then watch scary movies," Shaun suggested.

I looked at Shaun with hesitation.

"Come on, Pax. This Halloween is the first one I can enjoy with someone I love," Shaun said as I looked at him. Shaun gave me the puppy dog look, making me cave.

"Fine, but a haunted house, then movies," I groaned.

Shaun grinned as I rolled my eyes. I hated Halloween, and my family knew why I hated it.

Later on, we went to a haunted house. I looked at the house and furrowed my brows. I felt two arms wrap behind me, making me relax.

"You two are the most sickening people I met," Kaxon mentioned.

"Way to ruin a moment, cuz," Markus mentioned.

Kaxon shrugged as I shook my head.

"Ignore them, and now we're here together," Shaun whispered.

"That's the only reason I came," I said, glancing at Shaun, who smiled.

While we stood in line, a few people thought it was a grand idea to make comments.

"Great, now we get stuck watching two fags make out," one guy remarked.

Shaun removed his arms, and we turned to look at the group of people behind us.

"What did you say?" Payton asked, walking up to the guy who commented.

"You heard me," the guy answered.

"No, I don't think we did, you homophobic Neanderthal. You should repeat yourself," Parker challenged.

Here's what people need to understand about us. When we ask you to repeat yourself, it's not a request. It's a challenge to see if you want your ass beat.

"It's bad enough everyone has to deal with queers taking over everything and invading our lives. How about they do us a favor and crawl back into the dark alley they live?" Another guy asked.

"How about you go back to the Stone Age and club your woman over the head?" Markus asked.

"The only reason you're allowed to walk around is that we have to accept you, freak," a girl spat.

"Sweetheart, I walk around on two legs that God gave me, and it has nothing to do with if you accept me or not," Markus retorted.

That set off a chain of events as everyone argued while I stood there, watching. I found it interesting these people didn't know us but felt the need to make stupid comments.

Kaxon whistled as everyone stopped and looked at him.

"Ah, hell, here we go," Matthew mumbled.

"Do you know how ridiculous you sound making homophobic slurs?" Kaxon asked, walking towards the other group of people.

Someone opened their mouth.

"Yeah, I would stop right there," Kaxon ordered.

The person shut their mouth.

"First, no one cares what you think. Yeah, you don't like gay people. Who cares? The only person who feels bothered with gay people is you. You don't like distinct races or cultures either. Why, may you ask? Because it's how Mommy and Daddy raised you. You have this mentality that you're better than everyone, but you're not. You're some dumbass who feels entitled to everything. Newsflash, you aren't. So, do everyone a favor and shut your damn mouth before you show your ignorance," Kaxon told the other group.

"Must be nice to know you're able to say whatever you want," another girl replied.

Kaxon looked at the girl. "Yes, because the first amendment entitles me to speak without consequence. You would know that if you paid attention in History and Government classes. You suck this poor sucker's dick," Kaxon retorted, pointing at some tool next to the girl.

"That doesn't give you the right to talk to us like that," another girl huffed.

"Yes, it does and also gives me the right to call you on your uneducated point of view. Be happy you can attend a fine establishment of a college to receive an education. Most people don't get that," Kaxon added.

"It's not our fault that our parents can afford things," a different girl mentioned.

"Sweetheart, your privilege is showing," Kaxon retorted as the people stood there, stunned. "Yep, I said what I said, and I'll repeat it," Kaxon remarked, walking away.

"You got to hand it to Kaxon; he's not afraid of calling people out on their bullshit," Mason mentioned.

"Yep," Patton agreed.

I stood there as Shaun looked at me with surprise.

"How come you said nothing?" Shaun asked me.

"Because I know my family has my back," I answered, turning to enter the haunted house.

We went through the haunted house and made it to the end. It wasn't flawed and fun. After we all made it through, the shit hit the fan. The other homophobic group of people took exception to the other's remarks. They thought it's swell to jump my brothers and cousins. It became a brawl.

I sat in the jail cell with a shiner as others sat with cuts, busted lips, and bruises. That's why I hate the holidays. We always land in jail for some stupid reason or get grounded.

Someone made a call, and we had to wait for the person to show up. Please let it not be Pops. The person showed up, and it wasn't Pops. We got the pleasure of Uncle Nixon's presence.

"You called your grandpa," Patton said to Kaxon.

"Yeah, because I'm his favorite," Kaxon replied while grinning.

"Who are you here for, Reverend?" The officer asked.

"That group, unfortunately," Nixon told the cop, pointing to us. "What are the charges?"

"Inciting a riot," the cop answered.

"That's it?" Nixon asked with a look.

The cop looked at Nixon. "That's a big deal," the police answered.

"Pft, that is nothing. How about you stop hanging out at the donut shop and do some actual police work?" Nixon retorted.

The cop looked at Nixon unamused. The next thing we knew, Nixon joined us.

"So much for calling gramps," Markus mumbled as Nixon sat on the bench with us.

"Now, who are we calling? If we call anyone else, I'm sure we're getting company," Kaxon mentioned.

We all looked at Kaxon, who shrugged. I got up and asked the cop to make a phone call. He hassled me about it.

"Look, I get my uncle offended you, but I'm entitled to one phone call. Everyone gets one phone call. We can stand here and argue all night about the legal system, or you can let me make a call. Those people started it with their homophobic slurs and then jumped us. We used self-defense. If you took this situation to a judge, the judge would throw it out. They would charge the people in the other cell with a hate crime," I said.

I surprise the cop with my knowledge. I'm gay, not an idiot. The officer opened the door and let me make a call. I contacted the one person I knew would help us.

Three hours later, Grampa Nate and Grandpa Nash walked into the room where the police held us.

"You called our grandpas," Parker said, surprise.

"No," I said as everyone looked at me. "I called Grammy Gray." I smiled, then stopped.

"Nixon? When will you learn to stay out of jail?" Grampa asked.

"When I'm dead," Nixon replied as Grampa rolled his eyes. Grampa looked at the cop. "Let my son and grandkids out."

"Sir, we arrested everyone for inciting a riot," the cop said.

"No, you want to make a point, and you don't have one. Legally, you don't have a leg to stand on since there were witnesses who saw everything. You didn't question anyone. Did you even read their rights to them?" Grampa asked.

"Yes," the cop claimed.

That response earned a doubtful look from Grampa.

"Well, no," the cop confessed.

"Yeah, I thought so. Now let those people go since you violated their rights," Grampa ordered.

The cop didn't have a choice and let us go. As everyone started leaving, Grandpa Nash said something.

"We want to press charges against that group for a hate crime," Grandpa told the cop, pointing to the other group.

"Why?" The cop questioned.

"Because those people went after my family, intending to hurt them because two of my grandkids are gay. Derek Crandall went after my kids. This police department did not stop it until the situation escalated. Someone ended up in the hospital. You might think we're overreacting, but we're not, and it stops now," Grandpa Nash demanded.

Another officer came to the back to find out what was happening.

"Joe? Why is everyone still here?" The office questioned.

"Rob, these gentlemen want to charge the other group with a hate crime," the officer said. He explained what happened tonight to the other officer.

The cop looked at the one who held us. "Then charge the other group with a hate crime. It's not rocket science. Michigan charges anyone with a hate crime who commits a violent act against someone. The person uses race, ethnic origin, religion, gender, or sexual orientation. Why did you hold these men and women under the pretenses of inciting a riot? The other group conducted a hate crime," the cop reasoned.

The cop looked at the other police, dumbfounded.

"Unless you have an issue with homosexuals?" The second cop questioned.

The first cop got a look on his face, which said everything to the second cop. The second cop released us with an apology. He questioned the first cop about his involvement with the situation.

I wanted to go home and forget about Halloween altogether. It took a group of hateful individuals to wreck a fun night. My family lands us in jail. That's why I hate the holidays.

CHAPTER 19

NEW SEMESTER

Pax

The new semester started, and I returned to classes. I had a lot of catches up to do because of what happened. I didn't mind. It was better than sitting around with my thumb up my ass. Yeah, work is okay, but when you can't go to any functions, it sucks ass.

On the plus side, I got to see Shaun more. If we weren't working, we studied together. Okay, that's a big fat lie. We made out a lot.

While Shaun and I couldn't keep our lips off each other, Matthew had issues of his own in the form of Nora. It seems my cousin attempted to keep Nora at arm's length. Nora tried not to stay there, while Mason is oblivious to it.

Matthew was with Payton at a coffeehouse when Nora made a beeline for Matthew.

"Hey, Matthew," Nora greeted Matthew.

"Hey, Nora," Matthew replied.

Payton stood there, watching the exchange unfold.

"So, I thought we could hang out," Nora suggested.

"I thought you have a boyfriend," Matthew responded.

Nora looked at Matthew and rolled her eyes.

"Why don't you go hang out with Mason?" Matthew suggested.

"Because I don't want to hang out with Mason," Nora replied.

Yep, Payton was still watching, trying to stifle his laughter.

"Then I say you do," Matthew said.

"Matthew," Nora said as Mason walked into the coffeehouse. He made a beeline to Nora, wrapping his arm around her waist.

"Hey, babe," Mason greeted Nora, who looked like someone took her last cupcake.

"Hey," Nora replied.

"I thought we should hang out," Mason mentioned.

"That is a great idea. You two hang out, and we will leave," Matthew said, walking away with Payton following and laughing. Yeah, my brother has no shame.

"What was that?" Mason asked Nora.

"Nothing," Nora lied. Yeah, that chick is a big fat liar. She will cause more issues than needed between my cousins.

Matthew and Payton walked to the house and talked along the way.

"Okay, what was that?" Payton asked.

"That is a complication that I don't need in my life," Matthew answered, referring to Nora.

"You like this girl, don't you?" Payton asked.

Matthew gave Payton a look.

"Matt, it's been three years since Sadie," Payton mentioned.

"Yeah, well, it feels like it was yesterday for me. Look, I got to go," Matthew said, walking away.

"You're in denial!" Payton yelled.

Matthew flipped Payton off, who laughed. I told you, my brother has no shame.

Matthew

What is with everyone? I don't need anyone in my life, and I sure in hell don't need a girl who's with my cousin. I got back to the house and got into my car. I pulled out of the driveway and drove until I made it to the cemetery, pulling up to Sadie's grave.

I got out of the car and walked to her gravesite. Looking at her headstone, I sighed. I crouched, brushing the leaves away from it. It might be three years for others, but it felt less for me. I missed Sadie. She was everything to me, and in a blink of an eye, she left.

"You know if you keep mourning the dead, you will never move on with your life," I heard someone say to me.

I turned to see my dad standing there. He walked over to me.

"When I lost your grandparents, I closed myself off from everyone and everything. I focused on taking care of my sister and cousins. I thought if I didn't open myself up, then I could hang on to them a little longer," Dad told me.

"How did you move on from losing Grandma and Grandpa?" I asked.

"I met a girl when I was younger. One day, I got a call from Major, telling me that the girl lost someone. The same girl locked herself away from everything, trying to deal with her grief. I refused to let her. Then one day, I married that girl," Dad answered.

"It was Ma," I mentioned.

"Yep, and I watched your mom go through what you went through with Sadie. I watched the guilt eat at her for living while Daniel died. Daniel had problems like Sadie. You can't keep feeling guilty because you lived when they died. If that's the case, then crawl in the hole with them," Dad reasoned.

"What?" I asked with a strange look.

"Isn't that what you want?" Dad questioned me.

"No," I huffed.

"Then stop mourning the dead. You can remember the time you had with the person, but stop feeling guilty that you're alive. Death is a part of life, but it's not the only thing. Live first," Dad told me.

I looked at my dad. I can't fault him for his words, considering he went through it. If anyone knows what it's like to lose someone, it's my dad.

We stood there for a while. One day, I'll meet that person and realize how important that person will be to me. Who knows? The person is closer than I know.

Pat

How is it that everyone has no issue with dating, but I have every problem with the girl I like? It doesn't help that someone is watching Britt's every move. It's like Romeo and Juliette, except I'm not dying. Screw that; I got way too many things planned.

Even Kaxon has luck in the women's department. Yeah, I'm still unsure about that situation. The dude won't admit he likes anyone, yet I see him around this chick named Jesse.

I came home and sat down on the couch, throwing my head back.

"What's your problem?" Parker asked me.

"My love life sucks," I answered.

"Besides that," Parker said.

I lifted my head and looked at Parker, who has Selena on his lap. Great, another reminder I have issues with love.

"Why don't you disguise yourself if you want to see Britt?" Selena suggested.

"As in what? I'm sure that Britt's bodyguard will find out," I mentioned.

"Not if you look nothing like yourself," Selena mentioned.

"Say what?" I questioned.

"Don't be you," Selena answered while shrugging.

I looked at Selena. I shook my head as I got up and went upstairs. I didn't need a disguise. I need my girl, which I don't have. Yep, love sucks.

Pax

Shaun and I stopped making out, making Shaun look at me with confusion.

"What's wrong?" Shaun asked.

I got up and started pacing as Shaun sat up in his bed.

"Pax, talk to me," Shaun said.

"Well, I've been thinking," I said as I stopped and looked at Shaun.

"Okay," Shaun said.

"About sex," I added.

"Say what?" Shaun questioned with a surprising look.

"I've been thinking about sex with you, and I didn't know how to approach it. You with what happened with your ex, and I had some random hookup," I mentioned.

Shaun looked at me, confused, and stood up.

"Wait. You had a random hookup with another guy?" Shaun inquired.

"Well, yeah," I replied, shrugging.

Shaun gave me the weirdest look, then left the bedroom as I stood there confused. Okay, what happened? I left the bedroom. I went into the living room to see Shaun standing there with his arms crossed, rubbing his chin.

"Is something wrong?" I asked.

Shaun looked at me and lowered his arm, placing his hands on his hips.

"Pax, why would you hook up with some random guy?" Shaun asked.

"It's not like I jumped into bed with someone. We were dating, and then it happened," I explained.

Shaun furrowed his brows. I knew that look; it's one I saw many times from people. It's the look of disappointment.

"So, it's okay that you were seeing someone, but I had to wait," I whispered.

Shaun said nothing.

"I'm going to go," I said as I put my shoes on and grabbed my hoodie, then left.

I went back to the house and walked in as my brothers were talking about something. I ignored the conversation. Parker stopped and looked at me.

"Pax? What's wrong?" Parker asked as Payton and Patton looked at me.

"Shaun and I talked about sex. I mentioned I hooked up with someone in high school," I mumbled, not looking at my brothers.

"You did what?" Parker asked, shocked.

I nodded.

"Why would you hook up with someone?" Parker questioned who looked at Payton and Pat, who stood there, saying nothing. "Did you know?"

"I suspected," Patton answer, shrugging.

Parker gave our brothers a look, then turned his attention to me. "Let me get this straight, Pax. You thought it would be a great idea to hook up with someone without a relationship? Do you know how stupid that is, or dangerous?" Parker scolded.

"But we were dating," I said, looking at my brothers. Parker looked pissed while Payton and Patton gave me an uneasy look.

"Wait. Was it Tristan?" Pat questioned.

"Yeah, why?" I asked.

"Pax, that guy had no intention of anything serious with you. Everyone knew he is the biggest player in school, and you fell for it," Pat told me.

I stood there, stunned. Now, I felt like shit.

"Shaun asked you to wait for him after what happened with Travis. That dicklicker put Shaun through hell. He assaulted Shaun several times," Parker told me.

I looked at my brothers, shocked. My brothers looked at me with disappointment.

"But you had sex with people," I mentioned to Payton and Parker.

"While in a relationship," Payton reminded me. "We didn't hook up with random people."

"Sable was my first time, and looked how that turned out," Parker added.

I furrowed my brows. The next thing I knew, our phones beeped. I pulled my phone and opened my messages as my eyes widened, making me drop my phone.

"Well, that's great," Payton grumbled.

"Ah, hell. Here we go," Parker added.

"This chick is getting on my last nerve," Pat huffed.

The front door opened, and our cousins walked in, pissed off.

"Can someone explain why we all got a picture of Pax and some random guy having sex?" Markus questioned.

Everyone looked at me as I stood there.

"It seems little brother hooked up with a player, and he took pictures. My guess Sable's behind this," Parker said.

"Your ex, the same one Pax beat the hell out of her?" Kaxon asked.

"The one and only," Parker answered.

Everyone looked at me as I picked up my phone. I said nothing and went up to my room. It's not like I can do anything about it, anyway. The last time I got probation. Shaun feels disappointed in me, and my brothers disapprove of my behavior. It's a matter of time before I get a lecture from hell from my parents.

I went to my room, closing and locking my door. I grabbed my sketch pad and started drawing, then my phone rang. I picked it up.

Pax?

"Hey, Pops," I answered.

What are you doing?

"I'm sketching, as Dr. Shaw told me to do," I sniffled.

Is it helping?

"I'm not sure, but Dr. Shaw told me to sketch when my anxiety kicks up," I whispered.

Do you know why I'm calling?

"Yeah, and I know I did something stupid. I know you and Ma feel disappointed in me," I sniffled, wiping my eyes.

I heard Pops sigh. *It was a mistake; we all make them.*

"Yeah, well, I'll stick to sketching, then I can erase my mistakes," I said as I hung up.

I went back to sketching, not realizing one crucial detail. When I hooked up with Tristan, I was seventeen. He was eighteen. When he took that picture, that is a bad thing. Sending naked pictures of a minor to people is the distribution of child pornography. It's illegal in Michigan.

Sable got in trouble with Parker for her bullshit. Now, she will go down for her role in the picture of me along with Tristan. It couldn't happen to a more beautiful person.

CHAPTER 20

SPIRAL

Pax

After that day, I did what any mature adult does; I avoided people. It didn't help that my classmates whispered about me or that Shaun and I weren't speaking at the moment. I kept my distance from everyone, including my brothers. It's a little hard when you share the same house.

I stopped seeing Dr. Shaw, which didn't help. Any appointments I had, I canceled. My medication ran out, and I didn't bother to refill it. All my progress got set back because of Sable's antics, and I let my anxiety take over.

Anxiety is a funny thing; your mind magnifies a situation ten times worse than it is. You create so many scenarios in your head that aren't true. You mix that with my temper, and you have more issues.

My brothers tried to talk to me, but I shut them out. I didn't need another lecture. Every time I saw Shaun, I avoided him. I even asked Nik to change my shift and take me off the counter. The less I dealt with people, the better.

I sat in the bakery's kitchen, working on a cake. I put a lot of time into decorating it, wanting it to look like Grandpa's cakes. I finished the cake and Nik saw it.

"It's terrible, isn't it?" I asked, looking at the finished product.

"Well," Nik said as I furrowed my brows.

Frazier showed up, and I grabbed the cake, tossing it into the trash can.

"What's going on?" Frazier asked.

"I ruined the cake. It's not like Grandpa's cakes, so I will make another one," I said, getting to work.

Nik and Frazier looked at each other, then at me as I worked. If Grandpa saw what I did, he would feel disappointed in me.

"Pax, take a break," Frazier suggested.

"Not until I get it right. I want to send Grandpa a picture, so he's proud of me," I said as I made another cake.

"I'll call Nash," Frazier whispered as Nik nodded.

I finished mixing the cake, placing the batter into pans, and baked it. I waited until it was cold, then sat there for hours decorating it. Every part had to be perfect since I'm a Gray, and my grandpa is a well-known baker.

I finished and furrowed my brows. It wasn't perfect, and I doubt edible.

"Pax?" I heard someone say.

I looked to see Pops and Grandpa standing in the doorway. I grabbed the cake and threw it in the trash can. I turned around and looked at them as they looked at me, confused.

"The cake is terrible, but I can do much better. I mean, no one wants a horrible-looking cake, and it will ruin our name. So, I will make another one," I said as I gathered ingredients.

Grandpa and Pops watched me as Grandpa held his hand up behind him. They watched as I went to work and attempted to make a cake. Knowing both were watching me made me nervous. I didn't want to disappoint Grandpa and have him think I suck at something he was excellent at doing.

"I'll get it this time, and it will make you proud, Grandpa," I said as I worked to put the batter in the pans, making a mess. "Shit, I'll clean that up. Sorry, I'm trying," I said as I cleaned up my mess. "Please don't feel disappointed in me."

Grandpa walked towards me as I took the pans to the oven, put them in, and then closed the oven door. I started mixing the frosting and made a mess. Nothing was working right with the cake, and I felt embarrassed.

I kept mumbling as Grandpa pulled me to him and hugged me, then I buried my face and cried.

"Pax, it's okay," Grandpa said, comforting me as I wrapped my arms around him tight. He let me cry, saying nothing. My anxiety went into overdrive, and I couldn't handle it.

After my breakdown, JJ walked into the kitchen and sat down with me along with Pops and Grandpa. JJ let me talk as the three listen to me. It was nice to open up and not feel so overwhelmed about things.

"Pax, when we're feeling threatened, we have a flight or fight reaction. Your anxiety sent you into a flight reaction, which is common. Have you been drawing?" JJ asked me.

"Yeah, it helps," I said.

"Good, keep drawing, and we need to get you back on your medication. The major problem happened recently. Now, it becomes a legal issue, which I'm obligated to report to the authorities," JJ informed me.

I looked at JJ and sighed.

"It was a stupid mistake, and everyone berated me for it when I didn't know," I told the others.

"The others shouldn't have said anything. It wasn't their place," Grandpa told me.

I looked at Grandpa, then at Pops, who didn't say much. Great, now the hammer will fall.

"I agree," Pops said as I looked at him, surprised. "It wasn't their place, and now it's time to fix it."

"You're not mad?" I asked Pops.

"No, Pax, I'm not. I'm disappointed in your brothers and cousins," Pops said as I felt relief wash over me.

"I have a suggestion," Grandpa mentioned as we looked at him.

JJ left to take care of my medication, and Grandpa and Pops helped me with a cake. They guided me on making one, and Grandpa sat down with me, teaching me how to decorate it. It reminded me of when Grandpa would sit with me when I drew. While Grandpa helped me, Pops took matters into his hands.

Lex

I went to the house to visit the boys, and to my surprise, my nephews were there. That saves me a trip. The boys were a little surprised at me. Okay, that's a lie. My visit shocked them.

"Pops, what are you doing here?" Payton asked, shocked.

"I came to find out why your brother stopped taking his meds and quit his therapies," I mentioned. Everyone gave me a guilty look. "What? Cat got your tongue?" I asked.

"Pops," Parker said. I shot Parker a look. He shut his mouth.

"Don't talk, listen. Paxton made a mistake, thinking someone gave a damn about him. That kid only wants someone to love him, and he feels alone. You could have helped Pax, but you scolded him. It's not your job to rebuke your brother and cousin. It's your job to love and help him. You all disappoint your parents and me," I told everyone.

They looked at me, feeling ashamed. I walked over to the door and opened it as my sisters- and brother-in-law walked into the house. They looked at the boys and shook their heads. I let my sisters handle their boys as I went to visit Shaun.

I rang the buzzer, and the door opened. I went up to Shaun's apartment and knocked. He opened it, surprised to see me. I went inside his apartment, and he closed the door behind me.

We talked. It was time to fix the situation because my boy needed me. Pax didn't need scolding; he required compassion. If any of my boys were in trouble, I would help them, not let them drown. That's what family does for each other because of family matters.

Pax

I finished decorating the cake and looked at it. I smiled, feeling proud of myself. I looked at Grandpa, who smiled. I hugged him.

"Pax?" I heard someone say.

We turned, and I saw my family standing there. I got up from my seat and stood there. I worried my family would scold me again. Then Shaun walked past everyone, and I lowered my head. Shaun pulled me to him and hugged me. I wrapped my arms around him and held on tight, gripping his shirt.

My brothers walked towards me and engulfed us with a hug. Pops and Grandpa watched us. My cousins talked to me, and for once, I didn't feel so overwhelmed.

"You did good," Grandpa told Lex.

"I learned from the best," Lex told Grandpa. They looked at each other and smiled.

"Sometimes, you need understanding when you're spiraling out of control," Larkin mentioned. Everyone watched us.

I didn't need coddling. I needed people to love me when I didn't love myself. As Pops said, family matters, and my family mattered to me.

CHAPTER 21

COMMUNICATION

Shaun

It was time that Pax and I communicated with each other and came to an understanding. After everything, we both went through on our own. The last thing we need is miscommunication between each other.

We sat on my couch and talked.

"Your dad came to see me," I said.

Pax looked at me with confusion.

"Lex explained to me that when you love someone, you love them no matter what. Then he told me about what happened to your mom and him in a car accident. It put a lot of things into perspective for me," I explained.

"What was that?" Pax asked me.

"That I don't want to lose you, and I don't want you to feel you can't talk to me about your feelings. Your dad also explained about you and your brothers. You think people care more about your brothers than you," I answered.

Pax opened his mouth, then closed it.

"Talk to me, Pax," I coaxed.

"It's difficult because no one ever talks to me. People talk at me or down to me," Pax said, shrugging.

"Then tell me about your feelings and fears. I want to know," I replied.

Pax stood up and started pacing as I watched him.

"When I realized I was gay, it terrified me. Then, when you called me names, it hurt my feelings. I had this insane crush on you and got crushed. When Parker brought you home, you made this effort with me. I thought cool, but then you left for college and tossed me away. Do you know what it's like not to talk about your hurt?" Pax asked, stopping.

I looked at Pax with empathy.

"My family thought I should understand your situation. Every time I attempted to show affection, you rejected me. Then, when I did something, you looked at me with disappointment. I can't win with you, Shaun," Pax admitted to me.

Pax was angry with me, and I didn't make it easy on him.

"Rejection is a bitch, and feel as if I'm the biggest bitch out there," Pax huffed.

I stood up and looked at Pax. "Then get angry with me," I said.

"What?" Pax questioned with a confused look.

"Get angry, show me how pissed you are at me," I demanded.

Pax stood there.

I pressed him as I walked towards Pax. "Show me! Yell, scream, but do something!" I barked.

"You want me to show you!" Pax yelled.

"That's what I said!" I yelled back.

"Fine!" Pax shouted. He shoved me as I stepped back, gaining my balance. "I hate you! You make me feel crazy! You broke my heart! Why? Why did you break my heart? What did I do to you?

Why can't you love me?" Pax screamed as he hit me, letting his anger out.

I let Pax unleash his anger as I stood my ground but didn't retaliate. Pax wasn't hurting me, as Travis did. He was angry, but deep down, he wouldn't harm me how Travis did.

I wrapped my arms around Pax as he stopped fighting. He buried his face into my chest and trembled as I held Paxton. It was difficult for Paxton to be honest with someone.

I rubbed Paxton's back, comforting him. He finally stopped shaking as I offered comfort.

"I'm sorry, Pax. I didn't mean to break your heart. It's the last thing I wanted to do to you. I didn't understand until your dad explained it to me," I reasoned.

Pax lifted his head and looked at me as I looked at him. His cheeks streaked with tears. I released him and moved my hands to his face. I wiped his tears with my thumbs. I leaned in and pressed my lips to his, kissing him.

I pulled back and looked at Paxton. "It took me a long time to understand the difference between control and love. People attempted to control me, but you didn't do that. You offered your heart, and I kept hurting it. I don't want to hurt you anymore. I want to be the one that loves you," I said.

Pax looked at me, unsure about what I said.

"I will prove it," I said as Pax nodded.

I pulled Paxton to me and held him. I didn't want to hurt Pax because he didn't deserve it. Now, it's time to prove it to him.

Pax

After that night, things got better between Shaun and me. He stopped with the disappointing looks, and I opened up more to him. It was a big step on both our parts. Being honest with my feelings proved difficult. I wanted to hide my disappointment with something or feelings. Shaun would push me to discuss my feelings.

My brothers watched us as we argued until I admitted my feelings, then I cried. I felt like a damn crybaby.

"Well, it's good to see Pax admitting his feelings," Parker mentioned. Payton and Patton looked at Parker, then rolled their eyes.

Other times, Shaun tackled me when I denied my displeasure. My cousins and brothers watched us.

"I see Shaun's therapies are getting Paxton to admit the truth," Markus mentioned. The others looked at Markus like he was nuts.

Yeah, I'm the guy who likes to deny his emotions. It's weird for me to admit anything. Have you met me?

Pops even called to check on me.

"Well, Pax is getting tackled by Shaun at the moment. Now Pax is crying. It's an effective therapy and works for these two," Parker told Pops as I laid on the floor while Shaun sat on me.

Parker walked over and handed me the phone. I took it from him.

"Hey, Pops," I said, sniffled.

How's it going with you and Shaun?

"It's a little rough. Shaun's sitting on me," I answered.

Yeah, I don't want to know. Pax, the more you open up, the better it is.

"I'm working on it. JJ said it's helpful," I mentioned.

Good, that means you're attending therapy. Are you taking your medication?

"Every day," I replied.

Well, I'll let you get back to whatever you're doing, and no, I don't want to know. We will see you at Christmas.

"Okay, Pops," I said, hanging up. I handed the phone back to Parker as I laid there on the floor.

Kaxon strolled into the house and stopped. "Well, we know who prefers the bottom," Kaxon remarked.

I rolled my eyes as Shaun got off me and helped me up. I walked over to Kaxon and smacked him upside the head. Shaun chuckled.

"I see Pax is feeling better," Kaxon mentioned.

"Is there a reason that you're here? Don't you have cousins to harass?" Parker asked, sitting down on the couch.

"Well, no. Markus is unholy with his boyfriend. Matthew is hiding from Mason's girl. Mason is oblivious that Nora isn't into him," Kaxon said.

"Then find a girl and leave me alone," Parker told Kaxon.

"Well, I found a girl, but not sure if she's digging me," Kaxon mentioned.

"Wait. You found a girl to like your stupid ass. Okay, this is priceless," Parker mentioned, sitting forward.

"Okay, I'm not stupid, dingleberry. For one to be stupid, one must know nothing. Second, I didn't say the girl likes me. Now, I need help with dinner," Kaxon said.

"And you came to me? Dude, I don't cook. I suck at it," Parker admitted.

"Can Payton cook for us?" Kaxon asked.

"Doubtful since Payton's busy with Josie," Parker answered.

"Well, I can't ask Patton because I don't trust him not to poison us. Paxton is busy with his love crisis. Yep, I'm screwed," Kaxon sighed.

"Settle down, Esmeralda. I will help you, but if we catch anything on fire, you're deaf, and I'm blind," Parker said.

Kaxon looked at Parker.

My brothers thought it's swell to rope us into helping him with Kaxon and Kaxon's date at our house. Payton and Shaun cooked, so no one got poisoned. Parker played maitre'd, while Pat and I played servers.

We dragged Selena and Josie into our mess by proxy since they were dating my tool brothers. You date us; you suffered with us when someone comes up with a scheme.

We set everything up, and Kaxon knocked on the door. Parker opened it and announced, "Welcome to Chez Gray. Get in here before you freeze us out." Parker yanked Kaxon and his date inside the house and slammed the door shut.

Kaxon looked at Parker.

"You're strange," the girl mentioned.

"No, this schmuck doesn't want to screw things up with you," Parker said, walking away.

Kaxon and the girl looked at each other. Pat and I came out of the kitchen.

"There's the table. Sit," Pat ordered. Yeah, we got looks for that comment.

"Excuse the demon twins," Selena said as she and Josie shoved us out of the way. "They're uncouth."

"Listen here, dumpster girl. No one asked for your commentary," I said.

"Don't be an ass," Josie told me.

"Says the girl that strung big brother along," I remarked.

That earned an ass beating from Payton and Parker, who tackled me. I hit both in their boys, dropping them. Shaun dragged me into the kitchen.

"Hey, I didn't finish yet," I yelled at Shaun.

"Don't make me spank you," Shaun said.

"I need to be bad more often," I retorted, smirking. Shaun rolled his eyes.

"Your family reminds me of my family," the girl said.

"Is that good or bad?" Kaxon asked.

"It's good," the girl said, smiling. Kaxon smiled as they sat down at the table.

We fed both as we spied on Kaxon and the girl.

"How's it going?" Payton asked.

"It seems like a match," Parker answered.

"Well, we didn't scare the girl off," Pat mentioned.

"That's Dr. Shaw's daughter," I mentioned.

Everyone looked at me.

"I saw the girl's picture in his office. Her name is Jesse, and good luck, Kaxon," I added.

Everyone looked at me, shocked.

Kaxon and Jesse finished their dinner. "Well, I will admit that this date turned out better than expected," Jesse told Kaxon.

"Good, because you're the first girl I ever went out on a date with," Kaxon admitted.

My brothers and I facepalmed ourselves.

"Well, your the first guy I ever went on a date with," Jesse mentioned.

We looked at the girl, shocked.

"I am?" Kaxon asked.

"Yeah, most guys are stupid and want one thing. I don't have the patience for stupidity. Plus, a guy needs to get through Dad," Jesse answered.

"Who's your dad?" Kaxon asked as I gestured at him. He ignored me. Big mistake, buddy. I wish you well.

"Jordan Shaw, Jr.," Jesse answered.

That's all it took as Kaxon got up and left the house, confusing Jesse and making us sigh. My cousin is a certifiable idiot. Explain to me how he shared Valedictorian with Pat and me? I still think Kaxon sucked someone's dick.

CHAPTER 22

HOUSTON, OUR COUSIN, IS A TOOL

Kaxon

I made my way home and ran into the house. I slammed the door behind me as the others looked at me, confused.

"Is there a reason that you came in here like something's chasing you?" Markus asked.

"Well, not something, but someone," I answered as my cousins gave me a weird look. "It seems I had dinner with Pax's shrink's daughter."

"Wait. Doesn't that family own the college we attend?" Markus asked me.

"That and I'm sure when her dad meets me, I'm a dead man," I reasoned.

"Then don't be you. Problem solved," Matthew suggested.

"That's a big help," I grumbled.

"I'm curious if you finished the date or ran out on it," Mason mentioned.

The others looked at me, and I looked confused.

"Yep, you're a dead man when Daddy finds out," Markus remarked.

Great, that's all I need. I will die before I graduate college, sooner than later.

Jesse

I sat there, wondering if my date would return, but I have a feeling he wouldn't.

"Excuse our tool of a cousin. He's not good with women," a guy mentioned.

"I take it that Kaxon doesn't date a lot," I said.

"Nope," everyone said.

A girl came out and sat down in Kaxon's seat. "I'm Selena. I lived with those guys," Selena said, pointing to the guys who waved. "That's my twin, Josie, who I didn't know about until my senior year in high school."

A girl waved to me.

"Kaxon is different and makes stupid decisions," Selena told me.

"That doesn't surprise me, considering most boys make stupid decisions. Take my family, who run rampant with boys. They all make stupid decisions. Idiot central called and wants the Jones, Frazier, and Shaw boys' back," I said, making Selena giggle.

"So, you're not mad?" Selena asked me.

"No," I answered with a look.

"Why the hell not?" A guy asked.

We looked at the guy.

"That's Parker, my boyfriend," Selena said.

I got up from my seat and walked over to the opening at the countertop.

"Because most people are nervous when they go on their first date. The person worries about screwing up that they'll make mistakes. You add the fact that someone will meet my dad, and that makes for a terrifying concept," I reasoned.

"Yeah, your dad can be scary," Paxton mentioned as I looked at him.

"My dad cares about my sister and me. He's your typical father. Skylar is dying to date, and I'm not," I reasoned.

"Please don't hurt Kaxon, or better yet, don't let your dad hurt him. That would be bad on so many levels," Patton mentioned.

"No worries," I said as I turned and left the house.

"Okay, that chick is odd," Payton mentioned.

"That makes the girl perfect for Kaxon since he's weird anyway," Parker added.

The strange part about this evening is that I enjoyed myself and found Kaxon's family fun. I returned to the dorms and went up to my room. I found Skylar in the room, writing.

"How was your date?" Skylar asked.

"It was fun until Kaxon left after finding out about Dad," I answered, going into the bathroom.

"Does that mean if you date, I can date?" Skylar yelled.

"Yep," I yelled back.

"Woo hoo!" Skylar whooped.

I came out of the bathroom and changed into my PJs.

"Out of curiosity, is there a guy you like?" I questioned Skylar.

"Well," Skylar said, sitting up. "There's this guy who's in my class, and he's adorable, but he has a girlfriend," Skylar mentioned.

"Skylar," I said.

"Yeah?" Skylar said.

"No," I told Skyler.

Skylar gave me a disappointed look.

"Our family doesn't mess with people in a relationship," I reminded Skylar.

"That is not true. Uncle Frazier's dad, who is Uncle Carrington, dated a married woman," Skylar mentioned.

"Yeah, and that turned out so well," I refuted.

"Well, phooey," Skylar pouted.

"Give it time. When the right person comes along, you will know it," I advised.

"What about Kaxon?" Skylar asked.

"I like Kaxon. He needs a shove, and I plan to give him one," I mentioned with a look.

Skylar giggled as I grabbed a book off my nightstand. Tomorrow is a new day.

Kaxon

The next day, I got up and went to get some coffee and a donut. I need delivery because, well, I'm lazy. I strolled to the bakery. Okay, that's a lie. I ran to the bakery because it's freaking cold outside. I hate this weather. One minute you have spring weather, the next rain, follow with snow, then we're not sure. It's Michigan, and Mother Nature forgot to take her meds.

It hasn't snowed, so I don't need my parka or boots, thank god. Although, heated boxers would be excellent since junior is hiding and hates the cold. I walked over to the counter to find Britt working.

"Shouldn't you be dodging my cousin?" I questioned.

Britt gave me an annoyed look.

"I'm saying that you're the dodgeball queen," I remarked.

"You're a pain in the ass," Britt mentioned.

"Well, this pain in the ass doesn't have someone watching them like a hawk, unlike you. That reminds me, why isn't your sister not watched like you?" I inquired.

"Because Nora loves to piss my parents off and doesn't care. It's annoying," Britt groaned.

"Or your sister's balls are bigger than yours," I suggested.

"I don't have time for your shenanigans," Britt told me.

"I beg your pardon, I do not, nor have I ever did shenanigans. My pappy would beat the hell out of me, then Ma would make him sleep in the doghouse. That sucks because we don't own a dog," I replied, smirking.

"What do you want?" Britt asked with annoyance.

"Give Kaxon a coffee and a donut. I'll take a latte and a muffin," I heard someone ordered. I turned to see Jesse. She looked at me and smiled.

"Why do you look like you want to eat me?" I questioned.

Before Jesse answered, the bell chimed, and we turned to see a man enter the bakery with black hair and ice-blue eyes. He walked towards us, and I stood there, confused.

"Since you feel concerned about my dad, I thought you both should meet," Jesse mentioned. The man looked at me, not smiling. Yep, I'm a dead man.

"I heard you skated on my daughter last night," the guy mentioned.

"I didn't skate since I wore shoes, and they don't have wheels," I corrected the guy.

"You left the date and my daughter. It's the same thing. Don't correct me unless you want your family invited to your funeral," the guy informed me.

"Dad," Jesse said.

"What? I must put idiots in their place," the guy told Jesse.

I watched those two bickers like hens.

"Hey, JJ," another guy said.

"Hey, Nik," JJ greeted the guy.

"Nik, will you tell my dad to stop?" Jesse asked Nik.

"No can do, sweetie. Your dad is cool, unlike Liam, who will spit out any guy he comes into contact with in his presence," Nik mentioned.

This family is strange.

"Fine, Dad, this is Kaxon Gray. I like him. Stop harassing your future son-in-law," Jesse said.

"Wait. What?" I asked, confused.

"What part of I like you, don't you get?" Jesse asked me.

"But you hate people," I replied.

"Well, I like you," Jesse said.

I facepalmed myself. JJ looked at me, and I sighed. I won't win this situation.

"Relax, I know your family. I'm sure if you mess up, your family will handle you," JJ told me.

"My family are a bunch of tools who land in jail. Trust me, I know," I mentioned.

"That sounds familiar," JJ mentioned.

Britt gave our orders to us and smiled as I glared at her. It's karma, pure and simple. I make comments, and it bites me in the ass. Now, I get stuck having breakfast with Jesse and her old man. I have to figure out how the hell I got engaged to a girl I went on one date, FML.

CHAPTER 23

CHRISTMAS FOLLIES

Pax

Christmas break arrived, and we all went home for Christmas. We were bringing people with us. I couldn't wait since it was my first Christmas with Shaun as an official couple. Plus, he was staying with us, which was even better.

We arrived home and dragged our bags into the house. I hit the door and tackled Ma before my brothers got a chance. Pops pulled me off of Ma.

"Pax, you have plenty of time to spend with your Ma," Pops told me as my brothers tackled Ma. Pops sighed.

"I've missed you, boys," Ma told us.

"We missed you more, Ma," Payton told Ma.

"It's official," Presley said.

"What is?" Patton asked.

"You and Pax are the shortest members in the family," Presley reminded us.

"That is not true. Ma is shorter than us," I said.

"Hey!" Ma yelled as we chuckled. "I'm not that short."

We looked at Ma.

"Okay, so I'm an inch shorter than the twins," Ma grumbled.

"Yeah, but the perfect fit for me," Pops said, wrapping his arm around Ma.

That made us smile. We give our parents hell, but no one can say that they don't love each other. It's the love everyone wants, and one I hope I get with Shaun.

I walked over to Pops. "Do you care if I go to the bakery and practice?" I asked.

Pops looked at me, as did the others. I bounced around in my spot, waiting for an answer.

"Only if we can go with you," Parker mentioned as I looked at my brothers, who gave me a look.

"Well, uh," I said.

"How about you, boys, and I go down to the bakery together? I'll call Dad to join us," Pops suggested.

"Okay," I said with hesitation. That's not what I hoped for with my request. I wanted to practice making cakes to surprise Shaun.

We went to the bakery, and Grandpa was waiting for us. I went to the kitchen and started grabbing ingredients. Everyone watched until Grandpa shoved them out of the kitchen.

"Thanks," I said to Grandpa.

"No worries. Your brothers worry about you," Grandpa mentioned.

"When my brothers watch me work makes me nervous," I replied.

Pops walked into the kitchen and guided me with making the cake, instructing me on what to do. I listened and followed the steps. I told no one, but I used to love coming to the bakery and watch Pops' work. He found enjoyment with it. Plus, I got to spend time with Grandpa.

I put the cake pans into the oven and waited.

"So, I was thinking," I said as both looked at me. "I want to major in culinary arts along with becoming a pastry chef, then work at the bakery."

I looked at Pops and Grandpa, who looked at me.

"Or not," I sighed as I played with a hand towel.

"It's a good idea," Pops mentioned.

"One day, I will retire. The family business can pass down to other generations," Grandpa added.

I looked at both of them with hope. "Are you sure?" I asked.

"Sure, why not?" Pops asked.

That made me smile. I couldn't wait to tell Shaun. The cake finished baking, and I pulled it out of the oven, setting it on a rack to cool. Shaun came into the kitchen as I admired the cakes.

"The cake smells delicious and looks great," Shaun mentioned.

"I had help," I said. "Plus, it will give me practice when I graduate and come to work here."

Shaun looked at me.

"I talked to Pops and grandpa, and they agreed," I explained.

"Then I guess we will work together," Shaun added, surprising me.

"Huh?" I asked.

"I talk to your dad the last time he visited. Besides discussing different things, we discussed job opportunities. He offered me a job when I graduate, and I accepted," Shaun told me.

I couldn't help but smile when Shaun told me that. Grandpa and Pops smiled as I looked at them. Those sneaky sneaks. I chuckled at their plotting.

Once the cakes cooled, Grandpa guided me with frosting and decorating the cake. As I worked, I heard a familiar voice.

"Anyone here?" Noah asked.

"They're in the back. Grandpa kicked us out of the kitchen," Parker answered.

"Nash didn't want you to burn down the joint again," Noah teased.

"I will never live that down," Parker grumbled.

Noah chuckled as he went into the kitchen.

"Hey, tool," Noah greeted Grandpa.

"Hey, demon spawn," Grandpa replied.

"What are the plans for Christmas?" Noah asked.

"Ma wants Christmas at our house since Jonas and Karen are coming in to see Dad and Cayson," Grandpa mentioned.

"Are the girls coming?" Noah asked.

"Yeah, the girls are staying with us. They're bringing their husbands, wife, and the kids," Grandpa mentioned.

"The boys are coming with their families. Marcy is going nuts waiting for them to get into town. I swear my wife is as nuts as she was when she gave birth," Noah sighed.

"Who had the bright idea was it to invite everyone?" We heard someone yell in the bakery.

Grandpa and Noah looked at each other and said, "Nixon."

Nixon walked into the kitchen. "Isn't there one Christmas where shit won't hit the fan?" Nixon asked.

Page 164

"Have you met our family?" Noah asked.

"Unfortunately, yes, and spent many times in jail because of you twits," Nixon retorted.

"That's Nolan," Noah reminded Nixon.

"Where is your other spawn half at, brother?" Nixon asked.

"Bitching at Marshall and Murphy because Macey is bitching at Nathan," Noah answered.

"Let me guess; we can't come because of blah, blah, blah," Nixon remarked.

"Sounds about right. Marshall's stuck working on a case, and Murphy's stuck at the hospital," Noah explained.

"Do we need a cake? Because I'm sure Nathan has blue balls," Nixon mentioned.

I got up and left the kitchen as they watched me, then I jumped on Parker. We fought as I kindly reminded him about the cake incident.

"Damn, look at Pax go," Noah said.

"Pax still miffed over the cake?" Nixon asked.

"Even I wasn't that bad when you got me a cake," Noah mentioned.

"Did you forget you yelled at my wife?" Grandpa reminded Noah.

"And Dad yelled at me. What's your point?" Noah asked.

Pops and Shaun walked past them as they yank me off of Parker. Shaun whispered something in my ear, and I looked at Shaun.

"Listen, you boys, knock it off before I knock you off," Pops ordered as we looked at him. "It's bad enough I have to deal with my crazy ass sisters at Christmas. I don't need my crazy ass sons helping."

"Excuse me. Would you like to rephrase that, you dolt?" Lyric asked as we looked to see my four aunts standing in the bakery, smiling.

"Nope, because you're nuts," Pops said as Grandpa came out of the kitchen while Noah made a call. Grandpa walked over and hugged our aunts as Pops did the same.

"Please tell me you saw your mother first," Grandpa mentioned.

"Well, duh," Larkin remarked.

"Dad, Ma was the first one we saw," Lakin said.

"And she tackled us, so we left our husbands and kids to keep her company," Luna added, smiling.

"Look what the cat dragged in," Nathan said as he and Nolan entered the bakery.

"Damn, you both were quick. I hope you're not like that in the bedroom," Nixon mentioned.

"No, big brother, that's only you," Nolan replied.

Our aunts hugged the brothers. They had a bond as we did with our uncles. I walked over to Aunt Lyric, and she hugged me.

"How are you doing?" Lyric asked.

"Better," I answered, making Lyric smile. I was closest to Noah and Lyric. Our personalities were similar, along with Grandpa. It was a surreal experience to see us, the brothers, and the quints in one room together.

Everyone left the bakery, and we went home. The excitement of seeing everyone tires me. When we got back, I crashed on the couch.

"What's wrong with Pax?" Ma asked as I slept on the couch.

"It's the medication. Too much excitement drains Pax, and the meds help relax him," Payton explained.

"How is he at school?" Ma questioned.

"Pax has his good and bad days. We deal with it as it comes. Plus, Shaun helps a lot," Parker mentioned as they watched Shaun sit with me.

"At least Pax is sleeping. That's a good thing," Pops mentioned as I started snoring.

"And he sounds like a dying bear," Presley mentioned as everyone looked at him.

"Yeah, we can't wait until you come to school next year," Payton mentioned, rolling his eyes. Presley shrugged.

I woke up in my bed the next day. What the hell? I sat up and rubbed my eyes as Pops checked on me.

"Did I sleepwalk?" I questioned.

"No, I carried you to your room. You lost weight," Pops mentioned. Shit, I forgot about the weight loss.

"Yeah, it's the anxiety. Plus, it's difficult when Payton isn't home to cook," I mentioned.

"Pax, you need to eat," Pops told me.

"Well, I need to learn to cook, or I will starve," I retorted. I got that look we all get from our parents that tells us not to be a dumbass. Yeah, I got that look now.

"Look, I will teach you so you can cook if Payton's not home. Then I want you to make sure you eat. You got me?" Pops said.

"Yeah, I got you," I answered.

I got out of bed and went downstairs. Everyone was eating as I walked into the kitchen. Ma handed me a plate, and I joined the others. I stared at my food, then pushed it away. The others stopped and looked at me, along with my parents and Shaun.

"Honey, is there something wrong with the food?" Ma asked.

"Not hungry," I mumbled as I sat there.

"Is it the medication?" Ma asked.

I shifted in my spot. My anxiety was through the roof because of everyone coming home for Christmas.

"Pax, answer your mother," Pops ordered.

I looked at my parents as I felt my heart race. Sweat formed on my forehead, and I wanted to puke.

"Paxton?" Mom asked as I got up from the table.

My brothers watched me as Shaun got up.

"Uh, I, um," I said, closing my eyes. I couldn't focus on anything or form a sentence.

Then I felt hands on my face as I opened my eyes to see Shaun looking at me. "Breathe," Shaun coaxed. I took deep breaths as I became calm. Tears fell down my cheeks. "Better?" Shaun asked.

I nodded as I sat back down. Shaun put my plate in front of me. "Pax is okay. He needed a moment," Shaun said to everyone while looking at me. I picked up my fork and started eating my breakfast.

Pops snapped his finger at my brothers and motioned for them to stop staring at me. Ma carried on without making a big deal about what happened. Anxiety is a bitch. Your mind goes into overdrive with every scenario, making it ten times worse than it is. Medication helps, along with support.

We finished breakfast, and my brothers and I met up with our cousins to have fun in the snow. When I mean snow, that includes snowball fights, sledding, and ice skating. It was a tradition with us when we got together.

It felt good to laugh and have fun. God knows I needed it.

Nathan

I swear I will hurt my boys if they don't come home for Christmas. Dealing with a pissed off Macey is not fun. Everyone's kids and grandkids are coming into town, except mine.

I had Marcy and the girls take Macey out for the day to get peace. I love my wife, but I know how she feels when the boys don't come home. The front door opened and closed as I leaned on the kitchen counter, drinking my coffee. Noah walked into the kitchen.

"Any word on the boys?" Noah asked.

"Marshall told me they're trying to come home, but work is busy. Macey's upset, and my hands tied," I answered.

"Not everyone can come home, Nathan," Noah reminded me.

"Yeah, I know, but it sucks. I miss the boys," I said, sipping my coffee.

While Noah talk to me and the girls kept Macey busy, Nash and Nixon were taking care of a special gift.

Nash

Nixon went to one gate, and I waited at another at the airport. I stood there as I saw Marshall come through the exit of the plane. He walked over to me.

"Where's your family?" I asked.

"Grace couldn't make it because her mom is sick, and the kids stayed with her," Marshall explained.

Someone tapped me on the shoulder, and I turned to see Nixon with Murphy.

"Where's your family?" I asked.

"They're home sick with the damn flu," Murphy mentioned.

I chuckled. Marshall and Murphy hugged.

"Do you think we'll surprise our parents?" Marshall asked.

"Definitely. Baby brother can quit bitching and moaning," Nixon answered as I chuckled. The boys laughed as we left the airport. Nathan and Macey didn't know it, but Ma and Dad contacted the boys to help bring them home for Christmas.

With everything that happened this year, family means everything, including generations. If I learned anything from Grammy Gray is without family, you have nothing. Our legacies begin and end with family, which is essential to us.

CHAPTER 24

CHRISTMAS SURPRISES

Maggie

We dropped Macey off and went home. Nash arrived with Marshall, who hugged me.

"Your brother will kill you when he finds out that Marshall didn't go see him and Macey first," I told Nash.

"Mags, it wouldn't be a surprise if the boys showed up. Nixon has Murphy at his house," Nash said.

I showed Marshall to a bedroom and let him get settled. Everything was fine until Nathan and Macey came over. Marshall and I came downstairs, then stopped midway. Our eyes widened as I pushed Marshall back upstairs.

"What are you doing here?" Nash asked Nathan.

"I came to see Ma and Dad, you tool," Nathan huffed.

"Are you PMSing?" Nash asked.

Nathan glared at Nash as I came downstairs. The front door opened as I saw Nixon and ran to shut it, then locked it.

"What the hell? Open up, you brainless wonder!" Nixon yelled.

"We don't want what you're preaching!" I yelled as Nathan and Macey looked at me.

Pat ushered Nathan and Macey into the kitchen as Nixon pounded on the door. Nash opened it a crack.

"Do you mind letting us in before I get blue balls?" Nixon asked.

"No," Nash answered.

"What the frick, dude?" Nixon questioned.

"Get rid of Murphy, you twit," Nash ordered as he slammed the door shut.

Kat looked through the window and noticed Nathan and Macey.

"Plan B it is," Kat told Nixon. They left until Nathan and Macey left. Noah showed up seeing Nixon, Kat, and Murphy. "I thought you were keeping your better half busy?" Nixon asked.

"I was, then I had to leave. Why?" Noah asked.

"Because Nathan and Macey are at Nash's house," Nixon said with a look.

"Well, shit," Noah replied.

"We're going to Kain's house to see Kaiden since my boys are dipshits and can't bother to say hi to their old man," Nixon remarked.

"Good luck, frick and frack," Noah chuckled.

I called Lakin and Mia to help distract Nathan and Macey. They came over with Larissa. Between Lakin and Noah, they distracted Nathan, all right. They tackled Nathan as Mia and Larissa rambled to Macey. Nate and Pat watched with amusement while Nash and I snuck Marshall out of the house.

Yep, Christmas should be fun.

Nixon

We left Nash's house and went to Kain's house. We walked in, and I looked at the boys.

"Hey, old man," Kain greeted me.

"I'll see an old man you. Where can we hide this twit?" I asked, gesturing at Murphy.

"I thought Murphy was staying at your house?" Kaiden asked.

"You, I will deal within a few minutes, but I need to hide Murphy," I told Kaiden.

"You're in deep shit, brother," Kain told Kaiden.

Kaiden rolled his eyes.

"You're both in deep shit," I said.

"Nothing new there," Murphy commented.

"Can we focus here?" Kat asked us. "We need to keep Murphy away from Nathan and Macey. Both didn't get the memo we surprised them for Christmas."

"What memo? That you all suck at this?" Kain questioned, earning looks from Kat and me, then a slap from me.

The next thing I knew, the front door opened with Nash, Maggie, and Marshall coming into the house.

"Why are you here and not at your house?" I asked Nash.

"Because we have Ma and Dad," Nash answered with a look.

"Good point," I agreed.

"Christmas is more tiring than a shift at the hospital," Murphy said, sitting down on the couch.

"No, shit. I thought police work was exhausting. It has nothing on our family," Marshall added, sitting down next to Murphy.

"You two twits have two days until we call all relax," I informed the Bobbsey twins.

Marshall and Murphy groaned as my phone rang. I answered it.

"What do you mean Nolan is there? We gave you one job to do. No, I will not calm down, old man. Yeah, yeah, I know. You're not too old to beat my ass," I said, hanging up. I looked at Nash. "Dad called and said Nolan showed up at your house."

Nash looked at me, and we ran out of Kain's house.

"Should we join them?" Maggie asked.

"Nah, let the dipshits deal with it," Kat answered. You got to love a woman like Kat, who lets me fall on my face. Remind me later to punish her.

"Can someone take me to see Lex since Nash forgot me?" Maggie asked the boys.

"Yeah, I can take you, Aunt Maggie," Kain said as they left.

Nash

Nixon and I got back to my house and walked in on Luna sitting on Nolan's head. The others stood around eating popcorn.

"Lu, can you get off me?" Nolan asked.

"Nope," Luna said. I chuckled. I love my girls.

Nolan shoved Luna off him and got up. "For a little thing, you got some weight behind you," Nolan mentioned.

"I'm a Gray," Luna shrugged.

"Uh, baby, you're a Harper now," Major reminded Luna.

"Yes, but I was born a Gray," Luna reminded Major.

Larkin came out of the kitchen, eating a sandwich. "You're almost out of food, old man," Larkin told me.

"Then you can pay the grocery bill since you don't live here," I told Larkin.

"Okay, now that we established Luna is a Gray and Harper, and Larkin eats Nash out of house and home. Where is?" Nolan asked. Noah clamped his hand over Nolan's mouth.

"Where is who?" Nathan asked.

"It's mo one. There is no who, what, where, when, or how," Nixon answered, shooting Nolan a look.

"Excuse us," Noah said, dragging Nolan out of the house.

"Well, this Christmas bites," Macey grumbled, sitting down on the couch. "All I wanted for Christmas this year is to see my boys since we couldn't visit them. While everyone gets to celebrate with their kids, I get a freaking phone call. Merry Christmas to me."

Nathan sat down next to Macey. "Honey, both boys are busy helping people. We can't fault them for not coming."

Macey looked at Nathan.

"I want to see the boys too, but next year," Nathan suggested as the front door opened.

"Is this a bad time?" Jonas asked as he and Aunt Karen came into the house.

"Hey, Jonas," Cayson said, coming downstairs.

"Nope, your timing is perfect," Dad mentioned.

Nixon and I looked at each other, acting innocent. Christmas will be fun this year.

Nathan

Christmas arrived, and we haven't heard from the boys. That didn't sit well with Macey. It's bad enough the boys couldn't come, but not a freaking phone call?

Macey sulked and refused to open gifts. Great, Christmas will be a blast. We got ready and went to Nash's house. The car ride was unpleasant. Thanks, Marshall and Murphy, for letting me deal with your mother.

We arrived and went into the house. Macey pouted as I greeted everyone. I let Macey sulk and went to get something to drink.

"Hey, that's my head," I heard Noah yell. He came into the kitchen. "Get your wife under control," Noah ordered me.

"Macey's upset," I said, sipping my drink.

"Christ, I didn't realize Mother Nature paid a visit!" Nixon yelled, walking into the kitchen.

"Enough, you shrew!" Nolan shouted.

"Nathan takes care of your wife before the family jumps her," Nash told me as I sighed. I set my glass down as I went into the living room.

I walked over to Macey, and we started arguing until Macey broke down.

"It's not fair, Nathan! I miss the boys! Why does everyone get their families, and I don't get a simple phone call!" Macey cried.

"Mace, I miss the boys too," I said, pulling Macey to me as she cried. People don't understand what it's like when you don't see your kids much. We make time, but it's complicated with the boys' jobs. I wished the boys came for Christmas.

Nash

My phone beeped, and I checked my messages, then smiled. I showed my brothers the news, and they laughed. We went into the living room, and I walked to the front door. I opened it and shushed the others. Kain and his family came inside as two people followed them.

I closed the door as Nathan had his back to us. Macey had her head buried into his chest. Marshall and Murphy crept towards their parents as we watched, smiling.

The boys stood behind Nathan, and Marshall tapped Nathan on the shoulder. Nathan glanced and said, "What, Marshall?"

Macey lifted her head as Nathan realized what he said. Nathan and Macey turned to see Marshall and Murphy standing there, smiling.

"Merry Christmas, Ma and Dad," Murphy said.

"Oh, my god!" Macey screamed as she hugged her boys, who embraced their mom back.

Macey let go of the boys, and Nathan hugged both. We stood there, grinning like fools.

"How? I thought you both got stuck at work?" Nathan asked.

"Nana and Grampa helped along with our uncles and aunts. They wanted to surprise you both for Christmas," Marshall explained.

Nathan looked at us, then walked over to us.

"I don't know how to thank you," Nathan said as he started crying.

"You did, brother," Nix said.

Nathan hugged us along with Ma and Dad. My brother isn't one to get sentimental, but I remember when he found out about Macey's pregnancy and wedding. The day the boys came, Nathan was ecstatic. That was a memorable Thanksgiving.

Nathan went to spend time with his boys, and I smiled. Mags walked over to me as I wrapped my arm around her.

"You did good, Nash," Mags said.

"Mags, if my grandparents and parents taught me anything, its family is everything," I said.

"Will you tell everyone that you orchestrated Marshall and Murphy coming home?" Mags asked me.

I looked at Mags. "Nope, it's time someone else got the gift of importance," I said. I looked at Ma and Dad, who were laughing with Jonas and Cayson.

My parents deserved recognition for everything. They put up with a lot from us and loved us when we acted unlovable. Because of our parents, I met my wife and had a family. The family was everything and more to me.

You can't ask for more than that.

CHAPTER 25

NEW YEAR

Pax

We return to school after the holidays. As much as I enjoy seeing family, it's good to get back to school. Pops taught me how to cook some food, and Payton told me he would teach me more at school. That's when he isn't sucking face with Josie.

I came out of class, and someone ran, picking me off the ground. That caused me to drop my books as the person set me down. I turned to see Shaun with a shit-eating grin on his face.

"Man, you made me drop my books," I said, picking up my books.

"It's not my fault you're small," Shaun mentioned.

I stood up with my books and shook my head.

"You're a nut," I said.

"Yeah, but it's nice to be playful," Shaun mentioned as I gave him a look. "Do you have another class?"

"Yeah, then work," I answered.

"How about after work, we hang out?" Shaun asked.

"Sounds like a plan," I replied as Shaun kissed me, then walked away. My boyfriend is a nut. I shook my head and chuckled as I went to class.

Shaun

While Pax was busy, I picked up a few things for tonight. I picked up food and dessert, then found some movies online. I ran into Markus at the store.

"It looks like someone has a romantic evening planned," Markus mentioned. He looked in my handbasket.

"Yeah, I wanted to plan a special night with Pax," I mentioned.

"Then you may want these," Markus said, tossing a box into my basket. I picked up the package. "Never forget your raincoat."

I shook my head and put the box back on the shelf. "No offense, but we're not at that point," I said.

"Suit yourself," Markus said while shrugging.

Parker found us in the store's aisle and noticed that we're standing next to the boxes.

"Dare I ask why you're standing next to raincoats?" Parker asked.

"I was cutting through aisles, picking up items for tonight," I answered.

"Uh, huh," Parker said.

"I told Shaun to make sure he had some. Did he listen to me? Nope," Markus said.

"Listen, for the last time, I'm not having sex," I announced as everyone looked at me.

"Are you sure about that?" Markus asked me.

"What? Haven't you seen two gay guys discuss safe sex?" Parker asked the other customers.

I facepalmed myself. The manager kicked us out of the store. My plans were blowing up in my face, thanks to ying and yang.

Pax

After class, I went to work. The bakery was busier since everyone returned. Britt, Nik, and I waited on the customers. When it slowed down a little, Frazier motioned me to the kitchen. I went to the back to find out what he wanted.

"Is everything okay?" I questioned, not sure of the answer I would get.

"Yeah, but a little birdie told me you wanted to learn how to bake. The same birdie said you have a gluten allergy. It's difficult to find items that taste decent without gluten," Frazier answered.

"My family learned how to cook special foods for me when the doctor diagnosed me. My grandpa tailored baked goods around my allergy so I could have a cake on my birthday. Most places serve gluten-free food, but I'm picky about what I eat," I explained.

"How would you like me to teach you how to bake? I have a best friend that is a phenomenal cook. He can teach you how to prepare dishes," Frazier suggested.

"I don't think your bestie would approve of you offering him to help me," I mentioned.

"Want to bet?" Someone asked in a husky voice.

I turned to see a man around six foot two, built with grayish-brown hair. The man was the definition of sex on legs. I stood in awe of him.

"Hey, kid. You got some drool right there," the man mentioned, pointing to the corner of my mouth.

That snapped me out of my thoughts as I wiped my mouth.

"Frazier explained your situation to me. Considering I know your family, I'm making an exception with you. Don't fuck it up," the man told me.

"I don't think I can screw this up because I'm sure you will beat the hell out of me. I can hold my own but look at you. You're massive," I exclaimed, pointing to the guy's arms.

"It helps to work out, eat right, and beat the hell out of people. When people chase you, trying to kill you, you do what you can," the guy told me.

I stood there, speechless.

"Ryan, you're scaring the little guy," Frazier said.

"Frazier, people need to know that not everyone is sweet and innocent. Plus, you're an idiot," Ryan responded.

"That might be true, but the kid doesn't need a crash lesson in life. He needs to learn how to cook, so he doesn't starve," Frazier reasoned.

"Fine, cooking first, then life lessons later," Ryan grumbled.

I can see this will be a fun time. It's not that I don't appreciate people helping me. When you meet a guy who's almost a foot taller and built like a shit brick house, it's intimidating. I left Frazier to argue with Ryan and went back to work. My shift was almost over, and I wanted to see Shaun.

Shaun

After my run-in with Parker and Markus, I found a store to buy some food. I checked the labels that said gluten-free. Once I got what I needed, I went to my apartment. I kept it simple and made a decent meal.

I finished cooking and set the table, making sure everything was ready. Then I searched for movies, which were comedies and action films. I wanted a lovely evening, and a drama movie, wasn't it. We had enough drama for a while.

My buzzer rang, and I pressed the button. I heard a knock at the door and answered it to find Pax standing there. I kissed him, and he walked into the apartment.

"You made dinner?" Pax asked.

"Yeah, I thought we could have dinner, then watch a movie. Your brother and cousin thought we would do something else," I said with a look.

"My brother and cousin are idiots," Pax replied.

I couldn't argue with that logic.

"It's because everyone else is doing unholy things doesn't mean that I am," Pax told me.

"Exactly, plus when the time's right, it will be special between us," I reasoned.

We sat down at the table, ate dinner, and talked.

"Can I ask you a question?" Pax asked.

"Yeah," I answered between bites.

"Are you scared to have sex after what happened with Travis?" Pax questioned.

It was an honest question.

"At first, I was. I couldn't stand anyone touching me, and a simple touch made my skin crawl, making me flinch. My therapist explained this was a normal reaction to enduring abuse. When you trust someone, and they destroy it, it's difficult to trust anyone again," I explained.

"So, what changed with me?" Pax inquired.

"I saw the way you reacted when you felt rejection. It wasn't rejection from only me, but from others. You wanted what I wanted, unconditional love. Everyone takes affection for granted, but we wanted it from someone. I know it makes little sense," I sighed.

"It makes perfect sense to me," Pax said.

I looked at Pax and smiled.

"No matter what happened between us, I still want to be with you. I can't explain it. It's like I can't breathe when I'm away from you. When we're together, I can breathe," Pax told me.

"It's the love that's deeper than the ocean," I mentioned.

"Yeah," Pax agreed.

I looked at Pax and realized that his love went more in-depth than the ocean. Pax feels more profound than most people. No one sees it because he keeps that part of himself hidden, but when you have time to find it, it's indescribable.

We finished dinner, then settled on the couch as I played a movie on my laptop. Pax snuggled up to me as we watched two videos. We fell asleep on the couch.

Tonight was easy. We didn't need a fantastic time to enjoy ourselves. Sometimes simple is better.

Pax

The next morning, I woke up on top of Shaun with our bodies tangled with each other. I gazed at Shaun, then realized I didn't tell my brothers where I was.

I scrambled to my feet, kneeing Shaun in the stomach. That woke Shaun up.

"Christ, Pax," Shaun winced.

I grabbed my phone and saw fifty missed calls and text messages from my family. Well, shit.

Bam! Bam! Bam!

Shaun got up and answered the door as I stood up. My brothers stood there, unamused. They walked into the apartment.

"Mind telling us why you can't pick up the damn phone and say, hey, I'm crashing at Shaun's place?" Payton asked me.

"It's a little hard to call someone when you fall asleep," I answered with a look.

Payton gave me an annoyed look.

"Pax, we got Ma and Pops on our back. They already think we're screwups," Parker mentioned.

"Like that's new?" I questioned. That earned a look from Parker.

"What if someone kidnapped you?" Pat asked.

We all looked at Pat.

"Who would kidnap Pax? If someone did, the kidnapper would return him," Parker replied.

"Look, I'm fine. I know everyone worries about me, but I'm taking my meds and seeing my shrink. I need to live a productive life," I reminded my brothers.

"Then we got a bigger issue," Payton mentioned.

"What now?" I asked.

"Shaun's family is fighting the charges against Sable with what she did to you," Payton told me.

"What?" Shaun and I both exclaimed.

"That's why Pops called. Sable is claiming you set her up," Payton answered.

"What?" We both asked again.

"Damn, is there an echo in here?" Parker questioned.

"Unbelievable," I huffed.

"Little brother, the Andrews might have an attorney, but we have family," Payton reminded me.

When my life is settling down, someone comes along and throws a monkey wrench into it. I made a stupid mistake and get to live with the consequences.

CHAPTER 26

FIGHTING BACK

Paxton

Knowing that Shaun's family is fighting the charges didn't help with my anxiety. The situation escalated. Shaun did what he could to help me, and Jaime worked at handling the legalities of it all. It would take an unsuspecting ally to help me.

I was up in my room with Shaun, tearing my room apart looking for items I couldn't find. Payton and Parker were in class as Pat stood in the doorway. I didn't know Kaxon came over to the house.

"What's up with Pax?" Kaxon asked.

"His anxiety is kicking in because of this mess with Sable," Pat answered.

"Wasn't this the same girl that threw Parker under the bus at homecoming? She broadcasted their sexcapades at homecoming one year," Kaxon questioned.

"Yeah, but both were under eighteen," Pat reminded Kaxon.

"It doesn't matter," Kaxon said.

"How so?" Pat questioned.

"Any sexual broadcast involving a minor. It's illegal and detrimental to a minor's health in Michigan. It's what the law refers to as child pornography," Kaxon explained.

"According to Pops, Jaime is working on the legalities of it. Sable destroyed the evidence, which doesn't help our situation.

They can nail Tristan on it, but Sable claims she knows nothing about it," Pat told Kaxon.

"You help Pax, and I got a plan," Kaxon said, leaving.

"Where are you going?" Pat yelled.

"To call in a favor! If I'm getting roped into marrying someone I don't know, then they can give me a wedding gift," Kaxon yelled back.

"Married? When did Kaxon get engaged?" Pat mumbled.

Kaxon

I left the house and went on a scavenger hunt. It isn't a real one, considering the person I'm looking for is at a well-known bakery. I hurried to the bakery to find Jesse sitting at a table, drinking coffee, and looking through her phone.

"How is it every time I find you, you're alone?" I asked, sitting down at a table. I looked at Britt. "Get me a coffee."

"What do I look like?" Britt asked me.

"Well, you look like you work here unless they're paying you to dodge my cousin," I mentioned.

"Come get your damn coffee at the counter," Britt huffed.

"I'm offended. You lack customer service skills," I retorted.

"Bite me, tool," Britt said.

"Someone else would prefer to bite you," I retorted. Britt clamped her mouth shut. I figure that would shut her up.

I turned to Jesse, who looked at me like I was crazy.

"It's difficult to find wonderful help nowadays. People lack customer service skills," I remarked.

Jesse chuckled.

"So, I will get to the point, since you told your dad I'm your future husband. I need a favor," I mentioned.

"How is telling my father I claim you entitle you to a favor?" Jesse asked me.

"Because I'm special," I answered.

"Oh, you're special, all right. There's a bus coming this way for you to catch," Jesse retorted.

"Cute," I said.

"Yes, we knew this, but continue," Jesse said.

"There's a situation with my cousin Pax," I said, then explained the situation to Jesse. She listened as I told her everything about Sable and Tristan. "I know your family owns this school and wondered if they could help?"

Jesse released a breath, giving me a look, then pulled out her cell phone and made a call. I don't know who Jesse spoke to, but she explained what I told her to the other person. After Jesse finished her phone call, she hung up.

"Up for a field trip?" Jesse asked me.

"You're not planning to seduce me, were you?" I questioned.

"Do you want me to seduce you?" Jesse questioned.

"I'm difficult. I have high standards," I answered.

"Then you're safe," Jesse replied, smiling.

"That's good to know since we didn't have our first kiss yet," I reminded Jesse.

"Because you're an idiot who ran out on our date. Be happy that I'm talking to you," Jesse reminded me.

"What can I say? I'm one of a kind," I mentioned. Jesse chuckled.

Britt gave me a coffee, and we left the bakery. Nothing like taking a field trip and not informing anyone because I'm sure my cousins will hurt me when I return. We got into Jesse's car, and she drove to our destination.

It took us a few hours, and we pulled up to a large house. We got out of the car, and I followed Jesse as she walked into the house. Great, not only will my cousins hurt me, but I can add breaking into a home as a criminal charge. Dad will hurt me.

A man came to the front door with grey hair and ice-blue eyes.

"Does your dad know you left school?" The guy asked Jesse.

"Dad is busy with his patients, plus he gave my guy here a hard time. I told Dad not to worry, that this guy is my future husband," Jesse said as I groaned.

The guy chuckled. "Well, my boys get to deal with girls while I dealt with their stupid asses," the guy mentioned.

"Dad is too severe about things. I enjoy riling him up," Jesse said. "Grandpa, this is Kaxon. Kaxon, this is my Grandpa Jordan," Jesse introduced us.

I shook Jordan's hand, and he waved us to follow him to the kitchen. A guy was sitting at the counter in the kitchen.

"Kaxon, this is Dean. He's a cousin and an attorney," Jesse told me.

I shook Dean's hand. I stared at him with confusion.

"Is there a problem?" Dean asked me.

"You're dark," I answered.

Dean chuckled. "I'm half-Mexican. My dad came from Mexico, and my mom was born here," Dean explained.

Jesse rolled her eyes.

"Excuse my idiot boyfriend. He's hanging out with Uncle Frazier," Jesse said. Dean chuckled, and I shrugged.

"So, Jordan explained the situation with your cousin," Dean mentioned.

"Yeah, my cousin Jaime is working to counteract the charges," I said.

"I can help with your cousin's situation," Dean offered. I looked at Dean with surprise. Let's hope this is the answer to Pax's prayers.

Jaime

I sat in my office, sifting through paperwork about Paxton and Parker. With all the motions I filed, the Andrews's attorney kept trying to suppress the evidence.

"Mr. Gray, you have a call on line two," my secretary announced.

"Thanks, Paige," I said as I answered the call. I spoke to the person for a few minutes and set up a meeting.

A few hours later, I met with the person at a coffeehouse close to the office. I sat down at a table and ordered a coffee.

"It seems you have a problem, and I have a solution," Dean told me. He pulled out a file and tossed it onto the table. I picked it up and skimmed through the information.

"What's this?" I questioned.

"That's your smoking gun," Dean answered. "I received a visit from a Kaxon Gray, and he explained to me everything that happened with your family."

I looked at Dean with surprise.

"The Andrews family doesn't understand that Michigan made child pornography illegal. Not only is it a severe offense, but any parties involved will register as a sex offender," Dean explained.

"I understand that, but Sable Andrews was a minor with Parker," I said.

"It doesn't matter. Sable was the age of consent, while Parker wasn't. From the timeline, Parker was fifteen. The age of consent in Michigan is sixteen with sexual consent. Parker Gray can't give legal consent about sexual activity if he was under the age of sixteen. It falls under the law of statutory rape," Dean explained.

I looked at Dean. We agreed to work together on the legalities of the situation and bury the Andrews family. To discuss Paxton and Parker's situation. We would need witnesses to corroborate Parker's story with Sable Andrews. I have a feeling we have our witnesses.

Parker

We got home from class, and as soon as I walked in the door, my phone rang. Pops called me and explained to me what was happening. I stood there as Payton looked at me.

"Yeah, I understand," I said as I spoke to Pops. After I hung up, I looked at Payton. My brothers and Shaun came downstairs.

"What did Pops want?" Payton asked.

"It seems our little cousin helped Pax. Remember the video Sable played at homecoming?" I asked Payton.

"Yeah, unfortunately," Payton said.

"I was fifteen when Sable took that stupid video. Sable was sixteen," I mentioned.

Payton looked at me, as did the others.

"Jaime is going after Sable for statutory rape and needs witnesses. He's calling you, including Kaxon and Shaun," I told Payton.

Payton looked at me with surprise as I looked at Shaun. Shaun furrowed his brows. If Shaun admits he knew about the video, he implements himself as an accessory. He'll do jail time along with registering as a sex offender.

"I will tell my cousin to exclude you," I told Shaun.

"Why? I'm guilty," Shaun admitted.

I looked at Shaun.

"Once again, when my life is back on track, someone wrecks it," Shaun said. He looked at Pax, who looked at Shaun with concern. "All I wanted was happiness and peace. I guess we don't get what we want."

Shaun came downstairs and left. Pax came downstairs and walked over to me.

"I know we don't always get along, but can't you do something?" Pax asked me.

I furrowed my brows.

"Come on, Park! Whatever you want me to do, I will do it. Please don't do this," Pax begged me. "Please."

I looked at Pax. As much as I wanted to take Sable down, I can't hurt my brother. Pax went through enough, and this will send him over the edge.

I pulled out my phone and called Pops, telling him about my decision. He said he would talk to Jaime. I got off the phone and made another call. I hoped the person would help us.

CHAPTER 27

FAMILY

Nash

I knocked on a door, and Jaime looked up from his desk. My brothers and I walked into the office and sat down in chairs. Jaime leaned back in his chair.

"Why do I have a feeling this isn't a social visit?" Jaime asked.

"Because it's not," Nix said.

Jaime looked at us.

"You can't call Shaun to corroborate the tape," I said.

"Why not? He was part of the situation," Jaime said.

"Because Shaun was in rehab," Nix mentioned.

"What?" Jaime said, looking at us.

"Look," Nolan said, handing Jaime a disc.

Jaime put the disc into his laptop and played it, which showed dates and times. It also showed Shaun's greatest hits.

"So, as you can see, there's no way Shaun could have known about the situation. He wasn't there," Nathan said.

Jaime gave us a look as I looked at him with my steel-grey eyes.

"You don't want your case to fall apart, do you?" Noah asked.

That earned an annoyed look from Jaime.

"Jaime, the boys agreed to corroborate Parker's story as long as it keeps Shaun out of it. Don't be an ass and ruin someone's life who doesn't deserve it," Nix remarked.

"Look, we want to nail this family, but sometimes a person needs a break. Shaun is family," I said, pulling the family card.

"You guys suck," Jaime mumbled.

"Nope, that's our wive's territory," Nolan mentioned.

Jaime sighed. "Fine, you win. I will remove Shaun from the list before I present it to the judge. Dean and I were trying to get the Andrews family to agree with a plea deal and the other family. If that happens, then the evidence is stored and never to see the light of day," Jaime said.

I looked at my brothers, who looked at me. We got up and left Jaime's office, walking down the hallway. As we walked, I stopped. My brothers looked at me.

"Nash?" Nik said as I fell to the ground. I held my arm as I had a hard time catching my breath. "Call 911!" Nixon told my brothers.

"Nix," I said as I fell to the floor, collapsing.

Maggie

I ran into the hospital and asked for Nash. A nurse-led Lex and me to the back where Nash and his brothers were. I ran over to Nash as I hugged him. He hugged me back.

"What happened?" I asked.

"The doctor thinks I had a mild heart attack," Nash said as I looked at Nash. I felt so much emotion when he said that. "Mags, they ran some tests to see if I did," Nash assured me.

I looked at Nash with worry as I held his hand, then heard yelling.

"Oh, hell, no! That's our dad!" Larkin yelled.

"Let us through before you meet lefty!" Lakin yelled.

"You heard my sister!" Luna yelled.

We turned to see the girls enter the emergency room and run to us. They engulfed Nash as Nash wrapped his arms around the girls, and Lex joined them.

The girls and Lex pulled back.

"Don't scare us like that, old man," Lyric told Nash.

Nash looked at the kids and shook his head as the doctor walked over to us.

"Mr. and Mrs. Gray," the doctor said.

We looked at the doctor.

"After running some tests, Mr. Gray didn't have a heart attack. His cholesterol is high, along with his blood pressure. Is there anything that would cause his blood pressure to elevate?" The doctor asked.

We looked at his brothers and the kids who looked around whistling.

"I have an inkling," Nash said, crossing his arms across his chest.

"Well, with your age, you're lucky. You need to start a low-cholesterol diet along with blood pressure medication. You need to follow up with your family doctor," the doctor said, writing a script and handing it along with the diet to me.

"Thanks, doctor," I said as the doctor walked away. I turned and looked at Nash.

"Mags, it's okay," Nash assured me.

"No, it's not!" I exclaimed as I turned, then faced Nash. "We went through too much to have it end. I'm not ready to let you go yet." I started crying.

Nash got off the gurney and walked towards me.

"I remember the times you talk to me through my window. When you talked to me after Bryson humiliated me at homecoming. Then our first kiss, along with our first date, then everything that happened after in college. When I broke up with you because you acted like a king-size tool. When we came back to school, feeling sick, then waking up," I said as Nash looked at me, confused.

"Wait. Did my brothers tell you these things?" Nash asked me.

"No, they didn't tell me," I replied. I sighed, then stopped. I started thinking, then it hit me. I looked at Nash, stunned.

"Mags?" Nash said.

I gave Nash a look and glared at him.

"I love you," Nash mentioned.

"You're a dead man, Nashville," I told Nash. I smacked Nash.

"Leave it to Maggie to get her memories back when our tool brother thinks he had a heart attack," Nixon remarked.

Nathan, Noah, and Nolan laughed.

Nash and I argued on our way out of the hospital. My husband is a tool, but I love him.

Pax

I sat in my room and drew in my sketchbook. I don't deserve Parker's help. I tried to kill him a dozen times. Yeah, you don't ask.

Shaun didn't deserve this. He changed his life, and now his sister will destroy it because she's a spiteful bitch. I hate her. If I could bury her in a shallow grave, I would.

Someone knocked at my door. I looked up to see Parker standing there.

"Don't worry. I won't beg you to help me. Sorry, I almost killed you a dozen times," I mumbled.

"A dozen, try like fifty," Parker corrected me.

"Eh, semantics," I said while shrugging.

"Pax," Parker said as he entered my bedroom.

I stood up and tossed my sketch pad onto the bed. "Look, I screwed up. I made mistakes. I'm not perfect, but Shaun doesn't deserve this," I told Parker.

"Pax," Parker said as Payton and Pat came to my bedroom.

"No, you don't understand. I had this insane crush on Shaun, and it took a lot of mistakes to give him a chance. Then we had problems. When everything finally calms down, we get smack in the face again. Do you know what it's like to love someone so much that you can't breathe? How, when you're together, you wish it lasts forever?" I asked.

"Are you finished?" Parker asked.

I looked at Parker.

"We know you're in love with Shaun. If you give me a chance to explain, I came to you tell you that Jaime isn't calling Shaun as a witness," Parker told me.

"Oh? Why not?" I asked.

"Well, drama queen, it seems our grandfather and uncles helped us. If you want to continue your pity party and dramatics, be my guest," Parker offered.

"Well, no," I replied.

"Good, because brother, you need to get on the stage. There's one leaving in a few minutes," Parker mentioned.

I rolled my eyes at Parker. Parker shook his head, then tackled me. We wrestled as Parker got me pinned to the floor and tapped my face. I kneed him in the boys as he fell over, coughing. My brother is a tool.

"Are you finished horsing around with Parker?" Payton asked me.

"For the moment," I answered, nodding.

"Then we should tell you that someone is downstairs to see you," Payton mentioned.

My brother didn't have to tell me twice. I ran out of my bedroom and flew down the stairs, missing a step as I face-planted onto the floor. I lifted my head as Shaun leaned over me.

"I meant to do that," I mentioned.

Shaun chuckled as he helped me up. We embraced as my brothers watched us while Parker fixed himself. Shaun placed his hands on my face and kissed me as I returned the kiss. It didn't matter what happens now; it won't change my feelings for Shaun. What can I say? I'm in love with Shaun.

CHAPTER 28

LOVE IS IN THE AIR: A VALENTINE'S DAY CHAPTER

Pax

For Valentine's Day, Shaun planned a special night for us. He told me to pack an overnight bag and let my brothers know I would be with him. Since I didn't know where we are going, I couldn't tell my brothers.

I put my bag in the backseat and got into Shaun's car. He pulled out of the driveway and drove to our destination. We drove for a while until Shaun pulled into a bed-and-breakfast. We got out of the car and went inside to check-in for the night. We walked to a room, and Shaun opened the door. He turned on the light as I looked at the bedroom.

Shaun decorated the room with roses and balloons. We went into the room and set our bags down on the floor, then left. We drove to a restaurant that served gluten-free food along with regular food.

I looked at the menu and ordered an entrée as Shaun did the same.

"So, did you like your surprise?" Shaun asked me.

"Yeah, I do," I answered, smiling.

"After dinner, I figure we could go to a gay club, and you can show off your dance moves," Shaun suggested as I smiled.

The server returned with our food. We ate and talked.

"I saw what you and your brothers did at homecoming and prom," Shaun mentioned.

"Yeah, my family loves to dance," I smirked.

Shaun chuckled as we ate. When we finished dinner, we left the restaurant and hit a club. We walked inside, and the music was playing. We made our way to the dance floor as I watched people dance.

I leaned into Shaun. "Do you think you can keep up with me?" I asked over the music.

"Show me what you got," Shaun roared.

I made my way out to the dance floor as Shaun followed me. The DJ started playing a song as I started moving. Shaun kept in step with me as people watched us. We moved front and back, then stepping side to side.

I progressed with my steps as Shaun followed, keeping step with me. Then he flipped me, and I landed on my feet. People started clapping as we danced in sync with each other. We finished with a double clap as people cheered us. Shaun pulled me to him and kissed me.

The DJ put on a slow song. Shaun and I danced together. He wrapped his arms around my waist as I wrapped my arms around his neck. We talked as we danced. That was the thing I loved about Shaun. When we were together, it's like nothing mattered at that moment.

Shaun

Pax and I kept dancing until we went back to bed-and-breakfast. Tonight was a glorious night. We didn't have to worry about anything and could spend time together.

We got back to the room, and it got heated between us. Our kiss became passionate, and we removed our clothes, making our way to the bed. Pax stopped me.

"What?" I asked, looking at Pax.

"Are you sure that you want to do this?" Pax asked me.

"I've never been more sure about anything in my life than this moment," I answered. I placed my hands on Pax's face and kissed him.

I made sure I wore protection and took my time with Pax. We made love, and it was terrific. It's nothing like it was with Travis. Travis wasn't loving but controlled me. I didn't want that with someone I love; I wanted more.

When we finished, I cuddled Pax.

"Are you okay?" I asked.

"Yeah," Pax said as I looked at him.

"I didn't want to rush things with us and wanted it special," I mentioned.

"Shaun, I wish I would have waited for you. That's my only regret," Pax admitted.

I leaned in and pressed my lips to Pax's lips. Tonight was unusual for both of us and a fantastic Valentine's Day.

Pax

The next day, I woke up feeling a little stiff, and I don't mean a sore body. I looked down to see myself sporting a tent. Great, that's what I need is morning wood.

I got out of bed and went to the bathroom. Did you ever try to take a leak, and it goes everywhere? It happens when you have morning wood. I finished up using the bathroom and went back to bed. Shaun was still sleeping.

The minute I closed my eyes, I felt something poke me. I opened my eyes to see Shaun cuddling me. Now I know what girls mean when they say getting a poke in the morning from a guy feels like a stick.

I poked Shaun in the forehead with my finger, waking him up. He looked at me with confusion while half-asleep.

"Is there a reason that you're poking me?" Shaun asked in a mumble.

"Yeah, because you're poking me," I replied, pointing at the blanket.

"Oh," Shaun said, scooting.

I shook my head and chuckled.

"Forgot about morning wood. Be right back," Shaun told me as he got out of bed and hurried to the bathroom. Damn, he's got a cute ass.

I leaned over and picked up a pair of boxer briefs, then pulled them on before getting back into bed. Shaun emerged a few minutes later and grabbed a pair of boxers, putting them on. He crawled into bed next to me.

"So, about last night," I mentioned.

"You didn't enjoy it," Shaun sighed.

"No, I did," I answered as Shaun looked at me with curiosity. "I'm afraid that it was a one-time thing. You know, get the prize, then move on with someone else," I added, letting my anxiety run amuck.

Shaun looked at me. "Pax, last night wasn't a one-time thing. I hope it wasn't a one-time thing because it meant a lot to me," Shaun said.

I looked at Shaun with surprise.

"Last night was special to me. After what I went through with Travis," Shaun reasoned.

I laid there as I thought about it. I looked at Shaun, who looked worried.

"Travis put you through hell, didn't he?" I questioned.

"Yeah, he made me feel as if I wasn't good enough for him or anyone. If I even attempted to talk to your family, I caught hell. Food was another issue," Shaun mentioned.

I furrowed my brows.

"If it wasn't making what he wanted, it was I needed to watch what I ate. No one wants a fatty," Shaun whispered.

When Shaun told me that, it pissed me off.

"It felt strange when I didn't have someone controlling me. I became accustomed to feeling free. Then you offered affection and got upset when I didn't accept," Shaun said.

I sat up. "But I'm not Travis," I reasoned.

"I know, and I had to learn the difference. Abuse is a horrible experience to endure. It alters your perception about everyone and everything," Shaun told me.

I looked at Shaun. We both had our issues, but we wanted someone to love us for who we are. The next thing Shaun said surprised me.

"I thought it was karma for what I did to you in high school," Shaun mentioned.

"What?" I asked, confused.

"Because I was an ass to you and mistreated you. I was so busy hiding who I was that I made your life rough," Shaun replied with remorse.

"Yeah, but I held my own. It's interesting to see your crush on a flagpole, hanging naked," I said, chuckling.

Shaun rolled his eyes.

"No one deserves to have someone mistreat them. No matter what happened before, you didn't deserve Travis's abuse," I reasoned.

"Yeah, Matthew helped me with the situation," Shaun mentioned.

"I heard about that. Matthew has a temper like an uncle Michael, but Payton has Pops and Grandpa's temper. Travis is lucky he didn't deal with Payton," I told Shaun.

I didn't want to discuss some tools that dated my boyfriend. Travis is lucky he didn't deal with me. The only reason I did nothing to that sleaze is because of Shaun.

We got dressed and packed our bags, then checked out of bed-and-breakfast. Shaun drove me home and dropped me off so he could get ready for class. I didn't have a course until later.

I walked into the house to find Patton lying on the couch, tossing a ball into the air.

"What are you doing?" I asked, jumping into a chair.

"Tossing a ball, contemplating life, and wondering how the hell I'm still single," Pat told me.

"Don't you have a girlfriend?" I questioned.

"Do you mean the one who avoids me because of her stupid daddy?" Pat asked, looking at me as he caught the ball.

"That would be the one. I guess Kaxon is giving Britt a hard time about her avoidance issues," I mentioned.

"When isn't Kaxon giving someone a hard time?" Pat asked me.

"Yeah, true," I agreed.

"Enough about my nonexistent love life; how did last night go with Shaun?" Pat asked me.

"It was awesome. We went to dinner, a club, and bed-and-breakfast, then we took the next step," I answered.

Pat looked at me. "So, why do you look like you want to hurl?" He questioned.

"Because I do," I answered as I bolted up the stairs with Pat behind me. I hit the toilet and tossed my cookies. I finished and cleaned up.

"I would ask if Shaun knocked you up, but that's a little hard with two guys," Pat mentioned.

I rolled my eyes as I shook my head. I rinsed my mouth out with mouthwash.

"I puke after sex," I mentioned.

"Say what?" Pat asked with a confused look.

"It happened with Tristan, then with Shaun," I answered.

"Are you saying that you're not gay?" Pat asked me.

I looked at Pat like he was the biggest idiot on earth. "No, idiot brother," I remarked.

"Are you still gay?" Pat questioned.

I looked at Pat, annoyed. "The last time I checked, I prefer tools over kitties. Yes, I'm still gay, and you're still an idiot," I grumbled.

"I'm checking," Pat said, shrugging.

"No, it is nerves. I overthink things with people. Plus, it doesn't help that after Tristan and I did the hippity-dippity, he hooked up with someone else," I mentioned.

"What are you two plotting?" Parker asked. We saw Payton and Parker standing in the doorway.

"Well, for one to plot, one must have a reason to plot, and we don't. Pax is tossing his cookies because of having sex, and I'm wondering why I suck at love," Pat reasoned.

Thanks a lot, Pat.

"Okay, first, stop over-analyzing your relationship, Pax. Second, figure out a way to see your woman, Pat," Parker told us.

"That's easier said than done," Pat huffed.

"Well, figure out what you want. Do you want to moan over a girl, or do you want the girl?" Payton questioned Pat.

Pat looked at our brothers, then at me. "Don't look at me. I have enough to deal with in my relationship," I reasoned.

That is the problem with Pat. He has no issue offering a beat down to someone but has many questions with girls. Everyone thinks Patton has high standards, but that's not true. Patton was a pansy with girls. I have a feeling he will need a lot of help with this girl.

CHAPTER 29

A WEIRD-ASS LOVE TRIANGLE

Pax

Do you know what happens when you have sex with someone you care about and love? You want to have sex a lot. If Shaun and I could find a place, it was on like Donkey Kong. Yeah, I got over my nervousness.

If we weren't unholy, others were. I chalk it up to the weather. Body heat is incredible in the wintertime. Unfortunately, I had a few cousins who were having difficulties of their own. When I say problems, I mean the weird-ass love triangle with Matthew, Mason, and Nora.

Let me explain a few key details, back in high school, which was last year, because we didn't graduate that long ago. Okay, let me go back to sophomore year because that's when this mess started.

Payton graduated, leaving Parker and Presley with us. We were sophomores; Parker was a junior, Presley was a freshman. Parker was busy dodging girls after that troll. Presley was finding more girls to hump. My baby brother has no shame. Patton was crushing on Britt, and I was crushing on Shaun, who made my life hell. We should skip the part of Shaun and me. I prefer to enjoy how our relationship now because it's way better.

Now, you had Patton, Kaxon, Mason, and me. We were forces of nature. What one didn't think of, the others did. Yeah, that earned us time in the principal's office. While Pat and I dealt with our crushes, Kaxon kept girls at arm's length. According to Kaxon, no girl could handle him. Kaxon is full of shit.

Then you had Mason, who dated Britt's sister Nora. Mason being Mason, pissed off Britt and Nora's dad every chance he got. He didn't care; he was hot for Nora. Nora dated Mason to piss her dad off. You get the point of this romance.

Aunt Luna and Uncle Major thought Mason needed a breather from Nora and us. They moved Mason out to Hicksville, USA. We don't even know where they moved, considering any place out of the city viewed as the boonies here.

Mason vowed that one day, he would return and reclaim his undying love for Nora. Mason needs his head examined because we all know Nora isn't into Mason as Mason is into Nora. How do we know? We see it. Yeah, we're not blind, and we're not oblivious, unlike Mason.

My cousin is a twit.

Matthew

I sat in a chair in the living room, reading a textbook, when someone knocked at the door. It's that chick Kaxon is dating or engaged to. I still chuckled at that thought.

The person kept knocking as Kaxon walked into the living room.

"Your chick is here," I mentioned.

Kaxon looked at me, then answered the door. "Nope, not my chick or fiancée, which still means nothing," Kaxon remarked.

I looked around the chair to find Nora standing at the door. I got up and walked over to the door.

"Mason isn't here," Kaxon mentioned.

"I didn't come to see Mason," Nora replied.

Markus came downstairs to find Nora, Kaxon, and me at the door.

"Then why are you here and not with Mason?" Kaxon asked as Markus walked over to us.

"Because I came to see if Matthew wanted to get coffee," Nora mentioned.

Markus, Kaxon, and I looked at each other.

"Does Mason know you want to have coffee with dear old cousin Matthew?" Markus question, patting my shoulder and smirking.

"No, it's not like I answer to Mason," Nora informed Markus.

That answer earned a look from Markus and Kaxon.

"I can't have coffee. I'm studying," I answered.

"Well, coffee could help," Nora suggested.

"I'm good, thanks," I said, walking away from these three. I needed no more trouble than I created.

"Hey, Nora," Mason said, coming home, earning a look from Markus and Kaxon.

"Hey," Nora said.

"I thought we were meeting later?" Mason asked, confused.

"Well, uh," Nora stammered.

"What's going on here?" Mason asked.

This time is the one time my cousins need to keep their mouths shut but don't.

"Well, it seems Nora here invited Matthew for coffee," Kaxon mentioned.

Markus facepalmed himself.

"What?" Mason asked.

"Yep, now, it's your rebuttal," Kaxon told Nora, who glared at Kaxon.

Mason looked at Nora. "What's going on, Nora?" He questioned.

Nora said nothing, smart girl.

"Are you interested in Matthew?" Mason asked.

Again, Nora said nothing.

"Answer me," Mason barked.

Nora jumped from Mason's tone, which brought me out of the kitchen.

"Answer me," Mason snapped.

"Whoa, hold on, Mason. You need not talk to Nora like that," Markus said.

"Stay out of it, Markus!" Mason snapped. He looked at Nora. "I thought it seemed off between us, but thought I was overthinking things," Mason said.

"Mason," I said.

"What?" Mason snapped.

"Nothing is happening between Nora and me. You can relax," I answered.

"Fine, then stay the hell away from my girl," Mason ordered, dragging Nora away.

Kaxon closed the door as Markus looked at him. "You had to say something, didn't you?" Markus asked.

"Look, we have one cousin who is mooning over some chick who's avoiding him. We have the chick's sister playing Mason like a fool. Does that seem right to you?" Kaxon asked Markus.

"It's not our place to decide about our cousin's love lives," Markus reminded Kaxon.

"Well, when this blows up in everyone's faces and it will, don't say I didn't tell you so," Kaxon answered.

I shook my head and went back into the kitchen.

Pax

Shaun and I hung out on the couch, joking with each other when the front door opened and closed. We looked up to see Kaxon jump into a chair.

"Don't you have a house?" I asked.

"Well, I pissed off three Harper boys in one go," Kaxon answered, holding up three fingers.

"What did you do?" I questioned, knowing Kaxon opened his mouth.

"I told Mason the truth that Nora has the hots for Matthew," Kaxon answered, shrugging.

I sat forward. "Are you insane?" I asked.

"I got engaged to a chick I went out on a date a few times," Kaxon replied.

I looked at Kaxon, unamused.

"We're not engaged, and if I have my way, not for a long time," Kaxon remarked.

I shook my head because my cousin is a tool. Pat came into the house.

"Did you out Matthew to Mason?" Pat asked Kaxon.

"No, I outed Nora to Mason, and Matthew was standing there," Kaxon corrected Pat.

"How did you find out?" I asked Pat.

"Britt told me," Pat answered.

"I see someone quit avoiding you," Kaxon mentioned.

"Nope, Britt is still keeping her distance. I went to the bakery to get a donut, and Nora called Britt," Pat said.

"So, Britt didn't tell you. You were eavesdropping on a private conversation," Kaxon mentioned.

Pat gave Kaxon an annoyed look.

"What's the point of ruining a relationship?" Shaun asked. We looked at Shaun with curiosity. "Shouldn't Nora be the one to tell Mason the truth?" He asked.

"You would think, but no. Not every person is forthcoming with their feelings," Kaxon said, looking at Shaun and me.

I rolled my eyes.

"We all know Nora likes Matthew, and Matthew likes Nora. Mason needs to move on to someone that likes him, and I know a girl that does," Kaxon mentioned.

"And who would that be, o'wise one?" I asked.

"Glad you asked, smartass," Kaxon retorted.

I'm two-seconds from beating Kaxon's ass.

"It seems Jesse's sister Skylar has a thing for our dear hicklebilly cousin," Kaxon said.

"Isn't Jesse your fiancée?" Pat asked as I snickered.

Kaxon rolled his eyes. "No, that was to rile up Pax's doctor. We are far from that stage in our newfound relationship," Kaxon replied.

"You should stay out of this," Shaun suggested to us.

"Or we plot, and it blows up in our faces. It's the Gray way," Kaxon said, smirking.

I looked at Shaun. "I'm not a fan of the Gray way," I mentioned.

"Because it involves kidnapping," Shaun reminded me. I agreed with Shaun.

Parker and Payton walked in to find us hanging out.

"What are you twits planning?" Parker asked us.

"Whoa, I'm not part of this," Shaun answered, raising his hands in defense, then getting up and going into the kitchen.

"I didn't mean you," Parker yelled.

"You three look guilty, and from the looks of it, Mason isn't here. I'm guessing it has something to do with the Hicktown USA," Payton told us.

"Well, Kaxon opened his mouth and caused issues between Matthew and Mason. Our cousins are in some weird-ass love triangle. Kaxon wants to plot to help them out, and Pat and I thought it's a stupid idea," I explained.

Payton looked at Kaxon. "If the devil twins think it's a bad idea, it's terrible. Don't do it."

"This coming from a guy who strung some chick along who had the hots for him. Did anyone tell you you suck at romance?" Kaxon asked Payton.

"Did anyone tell you that Payton has our grandfathers' and Pops' temper? It's worse than Matthew's temper," Parker reminded Kaxon.

"Payton might have his grandpa's temper, but I have my grandpa and dad's brain," Kaxon refuted.

"That doesn't mean shit. Even semi-intelligent people can do dumbass things. You opening your mouth about Nora is the dumbest thing you ever did, Kaxon," Parker remarked.

I agreed with Parker on this one. It wasn't Kaxon's place to say anything.

"Well, if Mason wants to stick with a chick that isn't into him, then that's on him," Payton mentioned.

I had a feeling the shit will hit the fan and cause someone to leave. You can call it intuition, but nothing good ever comes from a love triangle.

CHAPTER 30

CHOICES

Pax

They say in life, we have choices. Our decisions provide an outcome that doesn't always benefit us. Sometimes it causes heartache, if we like it or not.

Nora would find this out the hard way when she became honest about her feelings. It would cause a rift between cousins and one to leave. The situation would escalate at a party we had, inviting different people. We had a party to help Patton out, not realizing it was a disaster in the making.

"You want to have a party?" Payton questioned me.

"Sure, why not? We can invite the usual cast of characters and give Patton a chance to spend time with Britt," I suggested.

"A party where you will have family along with other people here. Are you insane?" Parker asked.

"No, plus this will allow me to deal with my anxiety. It doesn't have to be big," I reasoned.

"It's been a while since we had a party," Parker mentioned.

"Yeah, but we usually have family," Payton reminded Parker.

"Not if we keep it small," Parker suggested.

Payton looked at Parker and me, then agreed to us having a small party. What could go wrong?

Matthew

I didn't know what to do about my growing feelings for Nora. I tried to stay away from her because of Mason. I didn't like how he acted with her. Mason watched Nora like a hawk, letting his insecurities get the best of him. No woman should deal with a guy who acts like that, but I also didn't want my cousin's issues.

Dad was in town, and I met with him at a coffeehouse. I wanted to get his perspective on the situation. I walked into the place and found my dad sitting in a booth, drinking coffee. I joined him.

I ordered a coffee as Dad sat there, drinking his coffee.

"How is school?" Dad asked me.

"School's fine, but I have a slight problem," I answered.

Dad looked at me as I explained about Nora and Mason. He listened until I finished telling him everything.

"What do you think?" I asked as the server brought my coffee.

"Matthew, you have choices in your life that can affect you and the surrounding people. I didn't realize that you like this girl," Dad mentioned.

"I met Nora when she came to visit Britt last year. I didn't know who she was but found her intriguing. Nora made me laugh," I said.

"Has anything happened between you and Nora?" Dad asked.

"No," I replied.

Dad looked at me as I drank my coffee. "Matthew, I know it tears you apart to feel this way about someone who's with your cousin," Dad said.

I set my cup down and looked at Dad. "Nora is the first girl that made me laugh since Sadie," I admitted.

Dad looked at me with concern.

"But I know how important family is to us," I said.

Dad said nothing and rubbed his chin. I knew he was thinking about the situation.

"All I can say is if it happens, it will," Dad told me.

I looked at Dad.

"Matthew, I know you developed feelings for this girl, but if the girl is right for you, you will find your way to her," Dad said.

"Is that how you felt about Ma?" I asked.

"Yes, because your mom was special to me. We met as kids, then I lost my parents, aunt, and uncle, leaving me to raise Mia, Major, and Maverick. I didn't think I would meet someone until one day I received a phone call from Major. Your mom buried her boyfriend. On the day of his funeral, I came to help her. Eight years changes people, and it changed us. I remember how beautiful your mom was that day," Dad spoke of Ma.

I looked at Dad and knew what he meant. I also knew that he would never come between two people, no matter what.

"One day, you will meet the girl for you," Dad mentioned.

I nodded. I met the girl. After Sadie, I didn't think I would ever meet someone. Death is an unusual situation. When you lose someone you love, you develop this hole in your heart. You never think that you will find someone to fill that hole until a girl makes you laugh one day.

I had a choice. I could pursue a chance with someone and be happy or walk away. Leaving the hole remained. I had a feeling the latter would happen.

After Dad's visit, I went to see Sadie. I walked over to her grave and stood in front of it. Sadie was the first girl I ever loved. I thought we would be together forever. Then one day, it ended. I knew that if she were here, we would be together. I thought about how I would feel if someone tried to come between us.

It was at that moment; I made a decision that's best for everyone. I walked away from Sadie and made a stop and a phone call. After I finished my business, I went back to the house as Dad met me there.

I went upstairs and packed my belongings. When I finished, I came downstairs as Dad looked at me.

"Are you sure that you want to do this?" Dad asked me.

"Yeah, I'm sure. College isn't for me. I gave it a shot and realized that I prefer to work with my hands. Plus, if I leave, Mason will be happy with Nora," I reasoned.

"Matthew," Dad said.

"It doesn't matter. I can't break up two people for my selfish needs," I said.

Dad looked at me and nodded, then helped me take my bags to the car. I was going home until I saved enough money for a house. Cousin Beau had a job waiting for me at his garage, working on cars. Grampa Nate showed me cars when I was little, and it fascinated me. Grammy Pat said he was her grease monkey, and she was his Betty Crocker. I thought that was cool.

I got into the car, took one last look at the house along with campus, and left. I made a call while on the road.

Payton

We set up for the party, and I got a call from Matthew.

"What?" I asked. Matthew explained his decision, and I understood. Out of us, Matthew enjoyed working on cars. He took after Grampa Nate. "I understand. Let me know when you get settled," I said, hanging up.

My brothers looked at me.

"Matthew left school," I said.

"Is it because of Mason?" Pax asked me.

I gave Pax a knowing look.

"Why would Matthew leave?" Pat asked.

"Because sometimes it's better to take yourself out of the situation," I answered.

"Matthew never got between people. He's like Uncle Michael," Parker added.

"Well, it doesn't matter now. Matthew left, and the others will get pissed at Mason," I told my brothers.

I had a feeling we should cancel this damn party because tension will fill the room. Something told me that anger would fill tonight.

Pax

Everyone showed up except Matthew. Markus and Kaxon asked us where Matthew was, and we dodged the question. No need to start trouble before the party, even though the drama was coming.

Mason showed up with Nora and Britt.

"How did you dodge your babysitter?" Kaxon asked Britt.

Britt rolled her eyes. "Nora slipped our cousin a sleeping pill. He should wake up tomorrow morning," Britt answered while smirking. She left and made a beeline to Patton.

Okay, that's helpful to lose a babysitter. Shaun and I hung together. Jesse and another girl entered the house.

"Who are you looking for, Skylar?" Jesse asked, looking at the girl.

"No one," Skylar replied while shrugging.

"The guy has a girlfriend," Jesse reminded Skylar.

Skylar looked at her sister, annoyed. Yeah, this party is turning into drama already.

Nora

Britt went to find Patton, and I glanced to see if Matthew was here.

"Who are you looking for, Nora?" Mason asked with annoyance.

"I'm looking to see who is here," I answered.

Mason gave me a look as I rolled my eyes. Yeah, that wasn't a good thing to do with Mason. He dragged me out of the house as we passed Josie and Selena as they into the house.

"Mason," I yelled.

Mason let go of my wrist. I stood there, looking at him as I crossed my arms.

"You know, I want to give us a chance, but it doesn't seem like you feel the same," Mason said.

I looked at Mason and furrowed my brows.

"You make a choice, Nora," Mason demanded.

"What?" I asked.

"Make a choice, Matthew or me," Mason told me as I stood there. "If you want me, then you come to the party."

I lowered my hands as I looked at Mason. He looked at me with furrowed brows. I'm tired of denying my feelings. I said nothing and turned, walking away.

"Nora!" Mason yelled, but I didn't care. Mason told me to make a choice, and I chose Matthew. No one would stop me from happiness, not even my parents. I ran to the house and knocked on the door, then climbed in through a lower window. I should have asked Markus for a key.

I looked around and bumped into things as I found a light switch. After turning on a light, I went upstairs to see Matthew. I found what I assume was his room and turned on the light, finding his things gone. I stood there, speechless. Matthew left.

Pax

Shaun and I were hanging with Patton and Britt when we heard arguing. We turned to see Mason and Kaxon fighting.

"How is this my fault?" Kaxon asked.

"Because you couldn't keep your mouth shut, and now Nora chose Matthew over me," Mason answered.

"Wait. What?" Markus asked, confused.

"Yeah, Nora went to find Matthew," Mason said, then looked at everyone. He saw our expressions. "Wait. Did you all know that Nora liked Matthew?"

Pat and I looked at each other, as did Payton and Parker.

"My family knew and didn't tell me?" Mason exclaimed.

"Mas," I said.

"Are you kidding me, Pax? We helped you with Shaun, and you couldn't tell me the damn truth!" Mason snapped.

"Mason, it wasn't like that," Payton reasoned.

Mason walked towards us. "Then tell me how it is because I'm feeling like a fool. The girl I love chooses our cousin, and you all knew. I thought it was weird that Kaxon had no issue telling me the truth, but now I know why? You all suck," Mason huffed, leaving.

Payton stopped Mason.

"Let go of me," Mason said through gritted teeth. He looked at Payton as tears fell down his cheeks. Payton released Mason, and Mason left.

Markus pulled out his phone.

"Who are you calling?" Parker asked.

"Mason's parents," Markus said, walking away to call Uncle Major and Aunt Luna.

Tonight was an epic disaster of proportions. It didn't help when Markus and Kaxon found out that Matthew left after Markus got off the phone. That made them furious with Mason, and the shit hit the fan. It was time to call in reinforcements. Or someone will suffer; I mean, by that someone, I mean us.

CHAPTER 31

REINFORCEMENTS TO THE RESCUE

Kaxon

Do you know how, when something explodes, you take cover? Well, that didn't matter. My old man showed up along with cousins Maverick, Larkin, Major, Luna, and Lex. Britt went to take care of Nora while the rest of us dealt with the adults.

I let the other handle their parents while my old man and I bonded.

"How's it going?" Dad asked me at a diner.

"Considering the shit hit the fan swell," I retorted, earning a look from Dad.

"Kaxon," Dad said.

"Yeah, I know. I should watch the others, but it's difficult with their moaning over their girls and guy," I sighed.

Dad arched an eyebrow at me.

"I help the family and end up with a fiancée," I mentioned.

"Say what?" Dad asked.

"Oh, you didn't hear? Well, my cousins thought it would be cool to ask this chick for help. I did, then she told her old man we got engaged," I replied, nodding.

"I will go out on a limb and call bullshit," Dad said.

"It's a joke," I said, rolling my eyes.

Dad shook his head and chuckled. As I bonded with Dad, Jesse showed up, which is perfect timing.

"Dad, this is Jesse Shaw," I introduced my dad to Jesse. They shook hands, and Jesse joined us. I should let Jesse meet my old man since I met her dad.

Mason

I laid on my bed as I wiped my eyes. All I wanted is to reunite with Nora. All I got is a broken heart. I wanted my parents. Tears fell as I cried.

I heard a knock at the door as I turned to see Ma and Dad at the doorway.

"Mason," Ma said, holding out her arms. I got up and walked over to her. I threw my arms around Ma and hugged her as I cried. Dad rubbed my back as I buried my head into her.

"Mas," Dad said as I looked up at him. "It will be okay."

I lowered my head as my parents comforted me.

Markus

I sat on Matthew's bed and sighed. Everything is a mess now, and I wish my parents were here. I didn't think things would turn out this way, and Matthew leaving.

"Markus?" I heard someone say.

I looked up to see my parents standing there. They walked into the bedroom and sat on each side of me.

"Things are a mess," I told my parents.

"They're not a mess, but different," Ma told me.

"Who called you?" I asked.

"Payton called Lex and said you boys needed some help. Lex called us," Ma answered.

I looked at my parents. "Matthew left," I whispered.

"We know. Michael and Lyric called us," Dad said.

I looked at my parents.

"This isn't the place for Matthew, and he knew it," Dad reasoned.

"You didn't see what happened with Mason," I mentioned.

"Do you mean about the girl?" Ma asked.

I looked at Ma.

"It's more than about a girl. When Sadie died, it affected Matthew more than you all knew. The same thing happened with Lyric when Daniel died. Grief changes people, and it changed Matthew. It makes little sense now, but it will later," Ma explained.

I had my doubts while my parents hugged me.

Nora

I sat on my bed and cried as Britt comforted me. I didn't get a chance at happiness. Meeting Matthew was a chance; seeing him again was fate. Now Matthew leaves, and Mason breaks up with me.

"Nora, it will be okay," Britt assured me.

"When?" I asked while sniffling.

"One day," she answered.

I sat there as tears fell. I had my doubts and a feeling that this was the start of what was to come. Especially when Dad finds out. Britt was smart and stayed under the radar with Dad. I wasn't smart, seeing Mason and liking Matthew. It was a matter of time before the hammer dropped.

"Britt. Nora." I heard Dad say as we looked to see Dad standing there, looking pissed.

I wiped my eyes as we sat there.

Britt

"You can't be serious?" I yelled at Dad.

"I warned you both, and you didn't listen. I told you to stay away from that family!" Dad barked.

Nora stood there, saying nothing.

"Now, if I find out again that you go anywhere near that family, you're cut off," Dad told us.

"You would leave us broke?" I questioned.

"If you can survive on that meager job that you have in college," Dad threatened.

I furrowed my brows.

"It's your last warning," Dad told us, then left.

I stood there, pursing my lips. Josie and Selena came into the dorm room.

"Was that your dad?" Josie asked.

"Unfortunately," I replied with a sigh.

"He didn't look happy," Selena mentioned.

"Dad found out about Pat, then Nora's thing with Mason. He threatened to pull funding for school if he finds out that we go near the Gray family," I said with annoyance.

"No worries there. It's not like I have a reason to go near that family," Nora said as we looked at her. "Dad wins, and we lose."

Nora sounded defeated, and I hated it. My sister did things that made her happy while I bowed down to my parents. She never cared about the consequences of her actions. Now, it's like she gave up.

"Or not," I said as I thought about the situation.

The others looked at me with curiosity.

"I'm sick of our parents dictating our life because our family has some stupid beef with the Grays. It's not our fault that two family members were douches and caused this mess. We never met Bryson or Roger, but from what I heard, both were assholes," I told the girls.

"What did Bryson and Roger do? Mom and Dad never said, and I always wondered," Nora said.

"The only people who can answer that are the family that your family hates," Selena suggested.

"I don't think the guys will tell us," Josie mentioned.

"No, but I know someone who would tell us," Selena said.

We looked at Selena, who pulled out her phone and made a video call. Piper answered the phone. They exchanged pleasantries.

"Piper, we have an issue," Selena said.

"Is it the boys?" Piper asked.

"Kind of," Selena answered.

"What's wrong?" Piper asked with concern.

"Can you tell us what Bryson and Roger did that would make Britt and Nora's family hate the Grays so much?" Selena inquired.

We heard Piper sighed. That can't be good.

"Maggie had a crush on Bryson, but he retaliated, causing the brothers to retaliate. The situation escalated between both families. I dated Roger, and he sexually assaulted Larkin in high school. We didn't know until after I broke up with Roger," Piper admitted as we stood there. "Larkin had a crush on Roger."

I stood there, stunned, as did Nora. Selena and Josie looked at us with furrowed brows.

"My family caused problems because someone had a crush on them?" I questioned.

"Britt?" Piper said.

I looked at Piper.

"Do you care about my son?" Piper questioned me.

"Yes, but our dad threatened to cut off funding for school," I answered.

"Your dad was an ass in school, and he's still an ass now. If I learned anything about my friendship with the sisters, you find a way with the person you like. Don't let your parents stand in the way of your happiness," Piper advised.

"Thanks, Piper," Selena said, hanging up the phone.

I stood there and rubbed my chin, thinking about what Piper said. I needed a plan and help. If I wanted an opportunity to have happiness and finish school, this would take finesse. Then it hit me.

"Why do I have a feeling that you're plotting?" Josie asked me.

"Because I am," I answered with a smile.

Skylar

I sat at a table in the bakery, writing something, when someone sat down next to me. I looked to see Dad sitting there. He smiled, and I giggled.

"Did you come to scare Jesse's boy toy some more?" I asked.

"No, I met his father since Jesse called me. Plus, I met with a patient to check his meds. I figure you needed Dad's time," Dad mentioned.

I smiled. I love my dad, even if he is strict with his rules.

"How is everything?" Dad asked.

"School is okay. It's nothing like high school, but," I said, then stopped.

"But what?" Dad asked.

I set my pencil down and looked at Dad. "There is this boy who I like but had a girlfriend. They broke up," I replied.

That earned an annoyed look from Dad.

"You said I could date when Jesse did," I reminded Dad.

"Unfortunately," Dad grumbled.

I laughed.

"Skylar? What about friends?" Dad questioned.

I cringed when Dad asked me that. He arched an eyebrow at me.

"No one talks to me except Jesse," I whispered.

"Did you try?" Dad asked.

"I attempted, but people look at me like I'm stupid," I answered.

Dad looked at me with concern.

"I'm hoping this boy and I will be friends," I suggested, avoiding the topic. I didn't want Dad to worry about me. College wasn't like I thought it would be here. People act pompous and entitled.

"You should make friends with a girl before making friends with a guy, and that doesn't mean your sister. Give it a shot," Dad offered.

"Okay," I said, smiling.

I will make a friend if the teacher pairs someone with me on a project. That thought depressed me.

CHAPTER 32

UNEXPECTED FRIENDSHIP

Skylar

We started the new semester. I followed Dad's advice and attempted to talk to other girls who ignored me. I checked to make sure I looked decent and didn't smell. Every time I said hi, girls walked past me. I even said hi to boys, and they did the same thing.

Jesse would tell me not to worry about it and stop trying so hard. That's easy for her to say, considering people talk to her, and she hates people. I went to class and found an empty seat. I sat next to a girl who's doodling. Okay, here goes nothing.

"Hi, I'm Skylar. You don't have to say hi back, but my dad wants me to talk to people. He worries I will develop a serial killer complex. I say he worries too much. If I'm talking too much, say so, and I will zip my lips," I said, moving my hands and buttoning my lips.

The girl looked at me and smiled, then laughed.

"I got you to laugh, which means I'm not boring. Dull people suck because they don't laugh ever. Take my Uncle Frazier. He makes people laugh and enjoys it. He is the most lovable guy around here. Grandpa thinks he's an idiot," I rambled as the girl chuckled.

Making friends isn't bad, but I could be wrong.

"I'm Nora," the girl introduced herself.

Then I realized who the girl was. She dated the guy I like, fantastic.

"How long have you been attending school?" Nora asked me.

"This is my first year," I answered.

Nora looked at me with surprise.

"I don't have many friends," I added while cringing. Nora looked at me with confusion. "I don't have any friends except for my sister Jesse. It's not like anyone talks to me," I admitted.

"Have you tried?" Nora questioned.

"Well, a little," I replied.

"A friendship takes time to build. I will talk to anyone. It makes life more fun," Nora said with a smirk.

I giggled.

"Look, since I'm not dating anyone and don't intend to date for a long time, we can hang out. You know, girl power, and all the stuff that goes with it," Nora offered.

"I would like that," I agreed, smiling.

Class started, and making a friend made me happy, except now I can't pursue the guy I like because that's wrong. Guys have a code, and so do girls. You can't date someone or seek the person if they are your friend's ex. It's not a good thing.

Okay, so I keep my friendship with Nora and disregard my crush on Mason. I can do this, I hope.

We sat in class as the professor put us in pairs to help each other with the assignments. Nora and I got paired together, which made me happy. We had to work on a project together, creating a graphic novel for our last assignment. I hope Nora can draw because I suck at it.

We left class and went to get coffee.

"So, since I can't write for shit, how about if I draw?" Nora offered.

"Whew, I'm glad you offered to draw because I draw stick figures," I answered. Nora laughed.

We sat down at a table and ordered coffee and a pastry.

"So, why did you decide not to date anyone?" I asked Nora while eating my muffin.

"Because I chose another guy over my ex. My ex told me to choose, and I did, but the other guy left," Nora answered.

I looked at Nora with confusion.

"You seem confused?" Nora questioned.

"Well, I am. I dated no one," I replied.

"Like as in ever?" Nora asked me with surprise.

"No, Dad's rule was I can't date until my sister Jesse dates. She found a guy, and now I can date. He's a little overprotective," I explained.

"It sounds like it, but it's nice. My dad is a douche," Nora commented.

"How so?" I asked, sipping my coffee.

"He threatened to cut Britt and me off with money for school if we go near my ex's family. It sucks," Nora said, sighing.

"Yeah, you're right. Your dad is a douche," I remarked as Nora laughed.

"Skylar, this is the beginning of a beautiful friendship," Nora mentioned.

I smiled at that idea. I like Nora because she wasn't uptight and down to earth. We finished our food and coffee; then I went back to my dorm room. I walked in and found Jesse lying on her bed, reading.

"Why do you look happy that it makes a person want to vomit?" Jesse asked me.

I set my books down on the desk and turned to face Jesse. "Because I made a friend," I squealed.

Jesse looked at me with confusion.

"Her name is Nora, and we have a class together," I added.

"Wait. That wouldn't be the same Nora at the party of the crush you like, would it?" Jesse asked me.

I winced.

"Skylar!" Jesse exclaimed, sitting up in her bed.

"Look, Dad suggested I make friends, and Mason will not give me the time of day, so I'm safe," I reasoned.

"Your logic escapes me," Jesse remarked.

"My logic is fine," I said, putting up my hand.

Jesse got off her bed and looked at me with her hands on her hips.

"What?" I asked.

"Do not use this friendship to get close to Mason," Jesse told me.

"I would never do that, Jesse. Dad raised us better than that," I argued.

Jesse looked at me with disbelief.

"Since we got here, no one will talk to me. People ignore me and treat me like I'm stupid. Do you know how lonely it is, not to talk to people?" I questioned.

"Skylar," Jesse said, but I interrupted her.

"Don't tell me not to worry about it because you couldn't care less what people think about you," I said.

"Wow, then you have it all figured out," Jesse remarked.

I looked at Jesse and frowned.

"What you don't understand is that people don't care about the friendship. Most care about themselves and using people. I don't care what people think. They are self-absorbed idiots. They worry more about themselves than other people's feelings. Do you think the people who attend here care about anyone else? No, they don't. One day, you see that," Jesse argued.

I looked at my sister. "Not everyone agrees with you. If you weren't so quick to judge others, you would realize that people care more than you think," I refuted.

That pissed off Jesse, and she stormed out of the dorm room. I didn't care if she got mad because it's the truth. Jesse dishes it out but can't handle the truth when someone tells her.

Kaxon

I flipped through channels to find some useless entertainment. Someone interrupted my surfing with their knocking. I tossed the remote on the couch and answered the door to see Jesse standing there. She walked into the house.

"Come on in," I mentioned as I closed the door.

Jesse paced the room, then stopped and asked, "Do you think I'm judgmental?"

"If you mean, you get annoyed with people before they open their mouths and look at them as if they're stupid? Then yes, you're judgmental," I answered. I'm not sugar; I don't coat shit.

"You're a big help," Jesse said.

"What do you want me to say? Oh, no, you're not judgmental. You're sweet and sunshine," I mocked.

Jesse rolled her eyes.

"You proved my point," I said.

Jesse sighed and sat down on the couch. I joined her. "I prefer to be honest," Jesse said.

"Not everyone enjoys honesty, but then again, I have no filter," I reasoned.

"People don't have a problem with your honesty," Jesse claimed.

I laughed a lot. Jesse looked at me with confusion.

"Are you kidding? People have a problem with my honesty, but they also have an issue with Grandpa and Dad's honesty. We don't care," I said while shrugging.

"My family is notorious for not caring what people think, especially my grandpa, Dad, and Uncle Liam. My sister doesn't think that way," Jesse explained.

I rubbed my chin and thought about it. I didn't know much about Jesse's sister except what she told me.

"Your sister has a different outlook from you. It's not a bad thing, but it's who she is," I reasoned.

Jesse gave me a look, and I gave her one back. You learn about people when you come from a family like mine. When you deal with that level of crazy, most people are sane.

"Give your sister some space and hang with me. We can surf mindless entertainment," I offered, wiggling my eyebrows. Jesse laughed, and we hung out. Well, we made out. That's better entertainment than some lame-ass show.

CHAPTER 33

SPRING BREAK FOLLIES

Pax

After the party, we didn't see Britt or Nora. Selena and Josie told us that their dad visited them, threatening Britt and Nora. That guy is a tool.

We were going to Myrtle Beach for spring break without Britt and Nora. It sucked Britt couldn't come with Pat, but it's best if Nora didn't come because of Mason.

I like Nora, but family is family. Mason's nursing a broken heart, and the last thing we needed is drama. I had enough to last me a lifetime this year. I wanted to let loose and have fun with my family and Shaun.

It seems Kaxon invited his girl and her sister. Eh, more, the merrier, plus it will keep Kaxon busy. Pops called to make sure we have everything and would see us at the beach house. You didn't think our parents would let us run amuck, did you? Plus, they were bringing Presley and his girlfriend. Yeah, that shocked us, too.

We packed up the cars as Parker took roll call. My brother is an ass. We got into the vehicles and made our way to Myrtle Beach. It took over fifteen hours because of stops for bathroom breaks and food to reach Myrtle Beach.

Once we arrived, we grabbed our bags and went into the beach house as Pops and Ma met us at the door.

"What took you so long?" Pops questioned.

"Ask penny pees a lot," I answered, pointing at Parker, who rolled his eyes.

Then someone crashed into Pat and me, knocking us down on the floor. We looked to see Presley on top of us. Payton and Parker laughed as we shoved Presley off us.

"Nothing like having brother love to welcome you. I'm glad I don't have siblings," Markus said, walking past us.

"Damn, Presley, you make the twins look like dolls," Kaxon mentioned as we got up.

"It's not my fault that Pat and Pax quit growing," Presley said, shrugging.

Mason walked past everyone, not saying anything.

"Is Mason still upset?" Pops asked.

"Yeah, It's hard to know that someone chooses your cousin over you," Parker answered.

We looked at Markus.

"Why are you looking at me? I'm not into chicks," Markus mentioned as he gestured to Hayden.

"Look, let's not spoil this vacation with issues and have fun," Ma suggested.

We kissed Ma on the cheek and went to our rooms. Pat and I shared a bedroom as we did in utero. The others shared a room with someone, and no, we didn't share a room with our significant others. That was not with our parents.

After getting settled, we went out back and hung out. I sat in a chair on the deck next to Shaun as the others joined us. Mason went off on his own.

Mason

Last year, I had hope. This year my hopes faded. I kicked the sand with my barefoot as I walked along the shoreline. Ma and Dad said to give it time, but I gave it a lot of time when they moved me to Timbuktu.

High school sucked during my junior and senior year since I went to a new school. I didn't have Pat, Pax, or Kaxon. Since we moved towards the end of my sophomore year, I adjusted to new people who weren't welcoming.

I stopped and looked at the water.

"The ocean is peaceful, isn't it?" Uncle Lex asked, standing next to me.

"The only peaceful thing in my life," I mumbled.

"I know you're hurting now, but it won't stay that way," Lex mentioned.

"Won't it?" I asked, looking at Lex.

Lex looked at me. "Mason, you dated this girl when you were a sophomore for a brief time. Did you think you would rekindle a high school romance?" Lex asked me.

"You don't understand. I fell in love with Nora," I told Lex.

"Okay, did you write?" Lex asked.

"No," I answered.

"Did you call each other?" Lex questioned.

"No," I said.

"Did you communicate while you left?" Lex inquired.

"No," I replied while sighing.

Lex looked at me, and I shook my head. "Mason, when you love someone, you do everything you can to contact the person. You didn't contact Nora after you moved. I know you had feelings for her, but those feelings fade, and you move onto someone else," Lex explained.

"What about you and Aunt Piper?" I asked.

"Your aunt dated a tool. It took locking us in an empty classroom for me to admit my feelings. When I lost my memories, my heart didn't. That's the difference between you and us," Lex told me.

"I wish Nora was honest with me about her feelings. Yeah, it would upset me, but I would get over it," I reasoned.

"Nora didn't want to hurt you because she knew you wouldn't listen. You remind me of your parents a lot," Lex said, chuckling.

I looked at Lex.

"Your parents couldn't get it together because they were stubborn. It took them three times to get it right," Lex mentioned.

"Yeah, Dad said I get their stubbornness from them," I commented.

"Mason, one day, you will meet someone, and that person will show you why it didn't work with Nora," Lex assured me.

I shook my head, knowing Uncle Lex was right. The single life is best for me now. I didn't see anyone in my future.

Skylar

I explored the house and heard everyone talking. I kept my distance from Jesse, and it didn't help that my crush is here. I made my way to the kitchen and stood there.

"Did you need something?" A woman asked me.

"Oh, uh, I'm thirsty, but don't want to impose," I answered, feeling weird.

The woman walked over to the fridge and grabbed a water, then handed it to me.

"Thanks," I said.

"I'm Piper," the woman introduced herself.

"Skylar," I introduced myself.

"Why don't you hang out with the others?" Piper asked me.

"I don't know the others well, except for my sister, and I don't want to impose," I reasoned, unsure of my answer. "I'm going to the beach."

I hurried out of the kitchen and went outside. I walked past everyone and went to the water.

"What's up with your sister?" Kaxon asked Jesse.

"Skylar doesn't know anyone and doesn't have many friends. She's distancing herself from me after our argument," Jesse explained. The others listened.

I got to the water and sat down on the beach. I wish Nora were here; then I would have someone to talk to here. I fiddled with the water bottle.

"Is there a reason you're sitting alone?" Someone asked.

I looked to see the guy that Jesse is dating, standing there.

"I'm reflecting," I answered.

The guy sat down next to me. "Reflection is good if you have something to reflect on, not so much when you talk to no one," the guy mentioned.

"I don't know anyone," I said, looking at the group of people sitting around a table.

"Well, I'm Kaxon. The others are cousins and their girlfriends and boyfriend. Now you know people," Kaxon told me.

"I don't know their names," I said.

"Then let me introduce you to everyone," Kaxon said, getting up and dragging me out of my spot. Great, I will die on spring break.

Kaxon dragged me over to his family and introduced everyone; then Mason walked up.

"And that grump over there is Mason. He got dumped," Kaxon said, pointing to Mason.

"You're a tool, Kaxon," Mason huffed.

"How am I tool? You got dumped because you're oblivious to people's feelings. Ooh, I'm Mason and care about myself," Kaxon mocked, imitating Mason, and everyone laughed.

"No one cares about Mason's stupid high school romance that crashed and burned," Presley said. A girl sat next to him, staring at me. Okay, not sure what her deal is.

"That is true. We all saw it happen," Markus mentioned as the others nodded.

"See, my family is a bunch of tools. You will fit right in," Kaxon told me.

"Take a seat," Paxton offered, and I sat down in a chair.

Everyone started talking, and I joined in with them. I felt a tap on my arm and looked at Jesse. She gave me a knowing look, and I returned it. Yes, we fight, but we're still sisters.

Mason

I sat next to Patton as everyone talked and glanced at Skylar. I spoke to her a few times in class. I didn't notice how pretty her eyes were. They're ice blue, and she has raven-colored hair. The contrast is fantastic. Not to mention, she has plump lips.

"Hey," Pax whispered, getting my attention.

"What?" I whispered.

"Quit staring. Weren't you whining about Nora?" Pax asked me.

"I wasn't staring. I was admiring," I mumbled.

"Uh, huh," Pat said.

I shook my head. Okay, so I was staring. It's easy when someone looks like that. Quit it, Mason. You're staying single.

Skylar

I woke up the next day, changed, then went downstairs to eat breakfast. The food was unique and entertaining. I watched as the five brothers fought, then their dad broke it up. It was better than when my uncles come to visit us.

After breakfast, I went to the beach. I love the beach because it's peaceful, and I love it when the water hits my feet. I jumped around in the water, kicking it with my feet. It reminded me of when Mom and Dad took us on vacation.

"Having fun?" Someone asked me.

I stopped and saw Mason standing there.

"Well, yeah," I answered, giving Mason a cheeky smile.

Mason walked towards me as I figured out what to say.

"I loved it when my parents brought me here. The entire family would come, and we had a blast," Mason mentioned.

"You have a big family, don't you?" I asked.

"Yep, and I have no siblings," Mason answered.

"I have a big family, too. Besides my sister, I have aunts, uncles, and a bunch of cousins along with my parents," I mentioned.

We stood there in comfortable silence. I didn't know what to say to Mason. I couldn't break the girlfriend code.

"How come I don't see you around at school?" Mason asked, breaking the silence.

"We don't have classes together this semester. Plus, I stay in a dorm with my sister," I answered while nodding.

"Huh," Mason said.

"Well, it was nice chatting with you. I'll go now," I said, walking away.

I have time to speak to my crush and can't pursue it because I'm friends with his ex. Plus, I doubt Mason sees me like that.

Mason

Damn it, I was hoping to speak longer with Skylar. I need to figure out a better way to talk to her.

"Damn, you move fast," Pax said. I turned to see Pax, Pat, and Kaxon.

"What are you babbling about, Pax?" I questioned.

"That you moved on from your broken heart to chatting it up with someone new," Kaxon answered. "You, sir, are dumb."

I shot Kaxon a look.

"No, Kaxon is right. You are the dumbest one out of the four of us. Do you know Skylar is friends with your ex?" Pat mentioned.

"Say what?" I asked with confusion.

"Nora, you know the chick you're hung up on and who dumped your stupid ass. That's Skylar's new best friend," Pax answered.

I furrowed my brows.

"How do we know this? Because my girl, who's Skylar's sister, told us. Now, we all know how this will work. You will pursue Skylar. She'll reject you. Unlike most people, she doesn't believe in breaking the code," Kaxon informed me.

I looked at my cousin with annoyance.

"If you can persuade sweet Skylar to ruin a friendship," Pat said, smirking.

I walked past the guys. "You guys are dicks," I mumbled, walking away.

"This situation will blow up in Mason's face," Kaxon said.

"Yep," Pat and Pax agreed.

Welcome to spring break with the Gray family. Let the games begin.

CHAPTER 34

SPRING BREAK FOLLIES, PART TWO

Pax

The day started okay, then escalated. Someone thought it would be cute to prank another person. That someone is Markus, who started a prank war between us boys. Never get in the middle of a prank war with us.

The girls stayed out of it. I give them credit for using their brains. It wasn't bad until someone nailed Pops with a bucket of paint over the door.

"That's it! Clean this mess up and get the hell out of the house!" Pops ordered us. Yep, thanks Kaxon, you twit.

Presley

We got the paint cleaned up, and I went to change. I found Eliza in my bedroom, waiting for me.

"Why aren't you with the girls?" I asked, changing my clothes.

"I wanted to hang out with you," Eliza told me.

I knew that tone. I looked at Eliza as she got up from the bed. "You don't think Skylar is pretty, do you?"

"Eliza, I have no interest in any girl except you. We talked about this," I reassured Eliza, holding her hands.

"I know, but you dated a lot of girls," Eliza mentioned.

"True, but Grays are loyal to their girls," I reasoned.

Eliza gave me a small smile. I knew Eliza felt insecure because of my reputation, but I had no interest in any girl but her. It took me a long time to persuade her I liked her.

"Look, go talk to Selena and Josie. They're Parker and Payton's girls, and Selena lived with us for a year. You will like them," I assured Eliza.

"Okay," Eliza said. I kissed her, and she left the bedroom.

I shook my head and chuckled as I finished getting dressed.

Mason

After I cleaned up, I went looking for Skylar. I found her with the girls. Shit, well, that won't work. I stayed by the patio door and waited.

"What are you doing?" Markus asked, startling me.

I looked at Markus. "Nothing. Can't a guy stand here?" I questioned.

"Oh, you mean, acting like a stalker," Markus said.

I rolled my eyes. "I'm not a stalker. I'm curious," I replied.

"What are you two doing?" Parker asked, walking up to us.

"Oh, our cuz here is stalking Skylar after whining about Nora," Markus answered, pointing at me.

"I'm not stalking," I groaned.

"Then why are you in here and not out there?" Parker questioned.

"Because I didn't want to interrupt," I answered.

"What are you guys doing?" Payton asked.

"Oh, stalker here is eyeing a particular girl with dark hair and blue eyes," Markus answered, pointing to me.

I glared at Markus.

"What about Nora?" Payton asked.

"Nora dumped Mason, so that's a moot point," Parker replied.

"Yeah, but Nora and Skylar are now besties," Kaxon said, walking over to us.

"Damn, you're screwed," Markus told me.

I felt my eye twitch.

"Yeah, you can't break the code," Parker said.

"What code?" I asked.

"The girl codes. You break that, then people will refer to you as a code breaker, making you a pariah," Kaxon explained.

"Nora dumped me," I reminded my cousins.

"Because Nora chose Matthew, who left, leaving her single," Markus reminded me.

I raked my hands over my face, groaning.

"Then why not make sure it's okay with Nora if you ask Skylar out?" Presley asked, standing there.

"When did you get here?" Parker asked.

"I got here before you, and I know more about chicks than you," Presley answered.

"That's true," Markus agreed.

I shook my head. Us standing here is getting me nowhere.

"Look, your best bet is to talk to this girl, then talk to Nora. Don't jump into something before getting the all-clear. That way, you don't look like the biggest tool to walk the face of the earth," Presley advised.

I furrowed my brows and walked away. I wanted to talk to Skylar without the surrounding people because I didn't need their input on my love life.

Skylar

Most of the day was fun. We all played a game of beach volleyball. We split up into two teams, with Kaxon's family on one side and their significant other except me. I was the only one not with anyone here.

Lex refereed the game to keep it fair while Piper made sure we stay hydrated. The game started well until the competition kicked between the sides. It reminded me of the football games my family plays on Thanksgiving.

The Gray family laughed and cheered every time they scored a point, making us get irritated. Jesse called a timeout.

"Hurry, sweetheart! We don't have all day!" Parker yelled.

Jesse walked over to me after flipping off Parker.

"That's my girl," Kaxon announced, earning a look from his family.

"Remember what Dad taught us," Jesse reminded me. I nodded and smile.

"Are we playing or doing our nails?" Markus yelled.

"Oh, we're playing, and we will make you eat sand!" Jesse yelled.

Lex blew the whistle, and Payton served. Jesse and I went into action, setting up the ball, hitting it over the net, and regaining control of the game. After that, we went to town and wiped the floor with them.

"Damn," Payton mumbled. Jesse and I high-five each other and did the same with the others.

Lex looked at Piper. "It looks like the boys met their match," Lex said, making Piper laugh.

"All right, time for food, and a break!" Piper announced as the others ran to the house.

I walked as Mason caught up with me. "Good game. Where did you learn to play like that?" He asked me.

"Our dad taught us since we have a lot of boys in the family. My family taught us how to fight, too. Cousin Lena can knock a guy out with a single punch," I mentioned, surprising Mason.

"Can you do the same thing?" Mason asked me.

"Yep, but I don't look for trouble. I prefer fun," I said shrugging.

"I take it your family is big?" Mason questioned.

"Well, you have Uncle Ryan and Aunt Alex Jones, who have Liz, Matt, and RJ, who have kids of their own. You have Uncle Frazier and Aunt Marissa, who have Junior, Austin, Mack, and Nik. Austin, Mack, and Nik are triplets and called the hellions. They have kids. Then you have my grandparents, who have Uncle Elijah, Dad, and Uncle Liam. People know Dad and Uncle Liam as the double troubles, and they have kids. So, yeah, I have a big family," I explained.

Mason chuckled, and I giggled.

"My ma is a quint who's crazy. She's sisters with Markus's ma, and my dad is brothers with his dad. Lex is my mom's brother, and Kaxon's dad is my mom's cousin," Mason told me.

"That is crazy but cool. My dad is a twin," I mentioned.

"It's nice to have cousins around your age when you don't have siblings. It's like having brothers. Pat, Pax, and Kaxon are like brothers to me," Mason reasoned.

"I enjoy having a big family. I can't imagine not having one. Plus, my family looks out for each other. It's a delightful feeling to have with people," I said.

Mason stopped me.

"Look, I know we don't know each other, but I would like the chance to get to know you better," Mason suggested.

"We have one problem," I said.

"What's that?" Mason asked.

"I'm friends with your ex, and I don't want to ruin my friendship. If you don't mind being friends, then I'm good with it," I replied.

"Friends are good," Mason agreed.

I smiled as we talked more. I like Mason, but Nora is my friend, and I refused to hurt her.

Pax

I grabbed a plate of food and went outside, then stopped. Pat bumped into me.

"Is there a reason that you became a statue?" Pat asked me.

"Look," I said, nodding to Mason.

Pat looked and noticed Mason and Skylar.

"Why do I have a feeling Mason will drag us into his mess?" Pat asked.

"Because he will," I answered.

Pat groaned as we went to sit at the table. The others joined us. I have a feeling next year will explode on us, especially when Presley arrives at school. I ate and noticed his girlfriend is a little clingy. Change that; the girl is way clingy.

Presley sat down next to me to eat, and I tapped him on the arm.

"What?" Presley asked, annoyed.

"What's up with your girl? She's glued to you like crazy glue," I mentioned.

"Eliza is a little insecure but sweet girl. It took me forever to persuade her to date me," Presley said.

"Bro, there is a difference between insecurity and crazy. You got crazy next to you," I whispered.

Presley furrowed his brows.

"I'm saying," I whispered.

"Well, quit saying it because I like this girl and plan on keeping her a long time," Presley huffed.

I looked at Pat, who mouthed what the fuck, and shook my head. Anyone who knows our brother Presley knows he doesn't do clingy or insecure. People call him a man whore, but he's not. Girls would get obsessed with him, and he would drop them. While the rest of us deals with our issues, Presley is a different ballgame. It was a matter of time before he set this girl free.

We spent the rest of spring break doing things. We went jet skiing, swimming, playing volleyball, having bonfires, and hanging out. Shaun and I spent some quality time together and talked about next year. He agreed to move back in with us and give up his apartment, which was good for me. I missed not having him around the house. Plus, I don't have to worry about my twit brothers hunting me down. My brothers and I got some time with Ma, too.

Lex

I cleaned up the kitchen and looked out the window to see Piper with the boys. I couldn't help but smile. I knew she missed the boys while they were at college. My wife is an amazing woman in every sense.

I finished up and left the house, walking over to my family. The boys went to see what the others were doing, leaving Piper and me alone.

"It's nice to see the boys together," Piper mentioned.

"It's been a rough few years for the boys, but it's calming down," I said.

Piper gave me a look, and I sighed.

"Yeah, I know, it's hopeful dreaming," I said, sighing.

Piper laughed, then wrapped her arms around my neck. "Lex, no matter what, the boys will survive," Piper assured me.

"The boys might survive, but not sure about us surviving them," I retorted.

Piper laughed and kissed me. I pulled her into a hug as the boys watched.

"One day, I hope I have a love like that," Pat mentioned.

"Little brother, one day you will," Payton reassured Pat.

"Ma and Pops went through a lot together. If they can make it, so can we," Parker added.

"With love and guidance," Pax mentioned.

"No," Presley said as the boys looked at him. He looked at his brothers. "With family, because family matters," Presley reasoned.

None of us knew how true that statement would be through the next year when Presley arrived at school. Next year would cause chaos and end with a tragedy. It would be something that none of us saw coming, and it will take the family to show why our legacy is extraordinary.

It will test us in every aspect, showing our resilience and love for each other.

CHAPTER 35

FINALS AND GOING HOME

Pax

After spring break, the rest of the year flew by. Now it was time for finals. Nik gave us time off to study; then, we worked a few days before going home. Now I know why coffee is essential to college life.

Once I completed my last final, I went home and crashed. Sleep is fantastic when you spend nights studying. Everyone else did the same thing. While we were snoozing, Matthew was busy with his life.

Matthew

I finished working on a car, and Beau walked over to me.

"All set?" Beau asked.

"Yeah, the timing belt needed replacing along with other belts," I answered, wiping my hands on a rag.

"Here," Beau said, handing my paycheck to me. I folded it, sliding it into my back pocket of my work pants.

It was my last car for the night; then I went home to have dinner. I pulled into the driveway and got out, going inside the house. Ma had dinner ready, and I went to get cleaned up.

After washing up, I came down and grabbed a plate of food, sitting down at the table.

"How was work?" Dad asked while eating.

"Okay," I answered while eating.

Ma sat down at the table while we ate.

"I found a house for you," Dad mentioned.

"I don't have enough money saved for a house yet," I replied.

"Well, your mom and I discussed it. We will loan you the money for the house, then you can pay us back," Dad suggested.

I looked at my parents, who looked at me with soft smiles.

"It's doable," I said.

"It's a fixer-upper, but I can help you with it, and I called some family for help," Dad mentioned.

I thought about it. I didn't mind rehabbing a house. Plus, it would keep me busy.

"That works. When can we look at it?" I asked.

"Tomorrow, if you like," Dad replied.

"Works for me," I added as I finished my dinner.

After dinner, I went up to my room and read. I flipped through pages of a book, then set it down. I grabbed my phone and opened my text messages to the last message I got from Nora. I read through all the messages, rereading each one. I missed her and crazy antics.

It didn't matter because Mason and she are happy now. I talked to Payton and Markus a few times. Markus mentioned Nora, but I changed the subject. I refuse to interfere with another relationship.

Presley is graduating next week, and we were all going. Great, I needed to see Nora with Mason. I closed out my messages and set my phone down, picking up my book and reading. The new house would keep my mind and hands busy along with work. One day, I will find peace.

Pax

We finished out our last week, then packed. Payton wrangled us because Parker is always late. Once we got the cars loaded, we picked up Shaun, who is returning with us. Parker picked up Josie and Selena.

Freshman year is over, and now it's summer break. I sat in the backseat with Shaun.

"How was your first year?" Shaun asked.

"It had its trials, but it worked out better than I expected. I dealt with more than I expected but fought back with the help of people who love me," I answered.

Shaun smiled, sliding his hand into my hand and interlocking our fingers.

"Little brother, you went through hell, but you survived," Payton mentioned as I smiled.

"Yeah, I did," I agreed.

We drove home and arrived three hours later. After getting out of the cars, we dragged our stuff into the house. Ma hugged us along with Pops. It was good to be home.

I took my bags to my room and collapsed on my bed. I heard chuckling and turned to see my brothers and Shaun at my doorway.

"You never know how much you miss your bed until you leave it. I am never leaving my bed again," I said.

"Yes, you are! It's taking years to get you, boys, out of the house!" Pops yelled.

"Thanks for the support, Pops!" I yelled back.

"Any time, Paxton!" Pops yelled.

I shook my head and rolled my eyes. It's good to be home.

Presley's graduation arrived, and we all attended. Nana and Grandpa were having a party for Presley. Our cousins came in for the party, which was massive. The party also came with some issues in the form of Aunt Lyric and Aunt Luna.

It seems Aunt Luna took exception to the situation with Mason and threw digs at Aunt Lyric. We all know how this turns out.

"It's so nice that Matthew could attend a party. Will Lex's boys deal with the same issues with their girlfriends?" Luna mentioned to Lyric at the food table.

"It's doubtful. Lex's boys have girlfriends that love them," Lyric retorted while smirking.

"Oh, that's right, because no one dares to hurt Lex's boys, but my boy," Luna remarked.

"What do you mean by that?" Larkin questioned.

Ah hell, here we go.

"She means heaven forbid anyone takes responsibility for their actions," Lakin answered.

"This coming from someone who's never around here. You have room to talk," Larkin told Lakin.

"Considering your boy is notorious for screwing over Payton, I would say so," Luna claimed.

"Markus is gay," Larkin snapped.

"Only to keep Payton from beating his ass," Lakin accused.

"This situation isn't about Payton and Markus. It's about the fact that Mason is oblivious to a girl not liking him. He reminds me of his mother," Lyric remarked.

"Yeah, because I didn't use sympathy to get a guy," Luna argued.

"That's a low blow, Luna," Larkin said.

"It's the truth," Luna replied.

That was it. Lyric went after Luna with Lakin and Larkin joining them, crashing into the food table and cake.

"Ah hell, here we go," Nixon grumbled.

Now, if anyone ever met my crazy aunts, they know that they're bat shit crazy. Lyric pushed Luna's head into the cake as Larkin shoved food at Lakin, and Lakin hit Lyric. Lyric elbowed Larkin while Pops got dragged into the mess, trying to separate them.

"Damn, look at them go," Parker mentioned.

Grandpa and the uncles had to separate Pops and his sisters covered in food.

"Aren't you going to help?" Markus asked Maverick.

"Son, we learned a long time ago that you never get in the middle of their brawl," Maverick said.

Matthew shook his head and left.

"Matthew!" Micheal yelled.

Matthew waved his dad off.

Now, it gets interesting from here.

"Well, I see some things never change," Grampa Nate said as we stood there. "You're adults acting like children. Ma would enjoy the chaos because, well, she's Ma. But I saw what happens when situations get instigated. You need to stay out of your children's personal lives and let them figure it out. They're not children."

"But Grampa," Luna said.

"But nothing, Luna. While you are fighting, we have one unhappy family member who went through hell. The same hell his mother went through when she was younger. Does that seem fair to you? It doesn't seem to me," Grampa said.

"Nate is right. Yes, when your children hurt, it breaks your heart. You give them life and raise them. When they struggle, you struggle. You never stop loving your children, even when they're acting unlovable," Nana said. She looked at Grandpa and our uncles.

The next thing that surprised us came from someone significant.

"I came from a home with parents that didn't love me. They tossed me away like trash. I had two people take me and give me love. It took a lot of love to help me understand they wanted me. When you have people make you feel unwanted with their actions, you believe it with everyone. It took people to understand I didn't need those people in my life, and they were next door to me. I love you girls, but you can't keep acting like children. We're stronger, united, then divided," Nana said.

Luna walked towards Nana. "I hate seeing my boy hurt," she said.

"Honey, we all hate seeing our children hurt, but without the hurt, you can't experience the joys. Your dad hurt me countless times," Nana mentioned.

"Hey!" Grandpa exclaimed.

Nana gave Grandpa a look and shook her head. She looked at Luna. "But he gave me a lot more joy than hurt, and he gave me all you. I say the good outweighs the bad," Nana said, smiling.

Luna nodded as Larkin took a piece of cake off Lyric and popped it in her mouth.

"Do you mind?" Lyric asked.

"Nope, because I refused to let the wonderful cake go to waste," Larkin answered, eating cake.

"Can the spouses of the twits we call the quints to go hose them off?" Nixon asked my uncles and aunts, who helped my aunts and Pops.

It's never a dull moment with our family.

"Eliza, I told you I have no interest in another girl," Presley said as we turned to see him and Eliza arguing.

"Are you sure?" Eliza questioned.

"Positive," Presley answered.

"Okay, what is that?" Parker asked.

"That's issues," Payton answered.

"That chick is way too insecure," Kaxon mentioned.

Pat and I looked at each other. We both knew it's a matter of time before Presley became tired of Eliza's insecurities. It escalates to the point of no return, causing an unexpected incident. As they say, expect the unexpected with us because it's coming. We didn't know it yet, but the end of the sophomore year would prove disastrous.

CHAPTER 36

NEW YEAR, A NEW CAST OF CHARACTERS

Pat

We got back to school, and it was a long-ass drive. It wouldn't be terrible, but it's nauseating when everyone is making goo-goo eyes at each other. I didn't hear from Britt, and I'm wondering if she's still interested in me.

Ma and Pops returned with us to help get us settled, and I rode with them. Better with my parents, than listening to the others speak sweet nothings. Can I gag now?

We got to the rental house, and Shaun is staying with us along with Presley's insecure chick, fantastic.

"Okay, everyone, go get settled, then we will discuss things," Pops told us.

I took my bags to my room and set them down. I unpacked and made sure everything was in its place. While Parker is a slob, I'm not. Payton, Pax, and Presley keep their bedrooms semi-neat. I like my stuff organized.

I walked out of my bedroom to hear Presley and his girl. Pax came out of his bedroom with Shaun.

"What are those two arguing about now?" Pax asked me.

"Beats the hell out of me, but I'm not dealing with this all year," I replied.

"Christ, isn't there one day that we don't have to listen to those two argue?" Parker mentioned.

Payton walked over to Presley's bedroom and handled little brother.

"Listen, I get you two have issues, but we aren't listening to you both argue all school years. You have other people who live here and don't want to listen to you," Payton told Presley and Eliza.

"Come on, Pay," Presley said.

"No, Pres, deal with it," Payton ordered as he left the bedroom.

Presley looked at Eliza, who furrowed her brows. "See what you started."

"What? I can't have concerns?" Eliza asked.

"Concerns, yes. Insecurities, no," Presley answered.

Eliza looked at Presley with concern.

"I love you, but you can't keep worrying if I'm looking around on you," Presley said.

Eliza nodded as Presley hugged her and kissed the top of her head. Let's hope Eliza chills out, or issues will happen. We went downstairs as Pops talked to us. We went over a few things, and my mind drifted to Britt.

We didn't know what transpired over the summer between Britt and her dad. Only Nora knew.

Sam

I stepped off the bus and made my way to the admission's office. I picked up my schedule and then hit the bookstore. Thanks to scholarships, I could attend school.

Thanks to some computer skills, I secured a dorm room. I made my way to the dorm and found my room. I looked around to find another bed in it. I picked a bed and set my stuff down.

I started unpacking as the door opened and heard two voices.

"That must be your roommate, Hayden," a guy said.

"I guess so. Hey, I'm Hayden," the guy introduced himself.

I turned around and said, "Sam."

"I'm Markus," the other guy introduced himself.

"Hey," I said.

"Are you new?" Markus asked me.

"Yeah, I transferred schools," I answered.

They looked at me.

"Later, dudes," I said, leaving the dorm room.

I left the dorm and went to get my books. After collecting the textbooks I needed, I took them to the front and handed the voucher to the cashier. I waited as the cashier took care of me and heard voices behind me.

"I'm sure you will see Britt again," a guy said.

"Well, I didn't hear from Britt since the party," the other guy said.

The cashier gave me a receipt, and I grabbed my books. I turned to see two guys who looked at me while standing there. I looked at the one guy as he looked at me.

"You got a problem?" The guy asked me.

"Nope," I said as I winked at the guy and left.

The guy did a double-take. "Did that dude wink at me?" He asked.

"Looks like it," the other guy said, snickering.

"Great, not only did I have girl issues, but I have some guy flirting with me. Why can't they flirt with you, Pax?" The guy asked.

"The guy finds you cute," the other guy teased.

I left the bookstore and went to the bakery. I walked in to see a guy working. I made my way to the counter and set my books down. The guy looked at me, confused.

"Did you need help?" The guy asked.

"Yeah, I need a job," I answered.

"I don't know if Nik is hiring," the guy mentioned.

"Can you check?" I asked.

"Yeah, hang on," the guy said. He went into the back and returned with another guy.

"Shaun said that you're looking for a job," the guy mentioned.

I nodded.

"Well, I haven't heard from Britt, which leaves a position open. If you want the job, it's yours," the guy said, rubbing his chin.

"Cool," I responded.

The bell chimed, and someone came into the bakery. The girl walked over to the counter.

"Hey, Nora," Shaun said.

"Hey, Shaun. Hey, Nik. Hey, some guy I don't know," the girl said to me.

"Where's your sister?" Nik asked.

"Britt and my dad got into a tremendous fight, and Britt left," Nora told the others.

"Did she call you?" Shaun asked.

"Nope. She packed and told me she's over my dad controlling her. I don't care what my parents think," Nora told Nik and Shaun.

I grabbed my books and left. I didn't want to hear about someone's family drama. I wanted to know more about the passionate guy I saw in the library. I returned to the dorm room to find it empty and removed my baseball cap. I ran my hand through my short hair.

This year will be a change, but worth it. Now to insert me into a specific family and see what happens.

Pat

Pax and I returned to the house, and Parker looked at me. "Why do you look like you found out Santa's not real?" Parker asked.

I looked at Parker unamused.

"Pat had a guy wink at him in the bookstore," Pax said, sitting down on the couch.

"No, shit. Did the guy blow you a kiss?" Parker questioned.

I glared at Parker while Pax chuckled.

"I'm not freaking gay!" I exclaimed.

"First sign of denial," Parker mentioned.

"Fanfuckingtastic," I huffed, sitting down on the couch and crossing my arms. First, I don't hear from Britt, and now, I have some dude eyeing me. It's bullshit.

"Batting for the same team isn't terrible, especially when the guy is," Pax said. Parker and I stopped him.

"Whoa, we need not know about your kinky shit," Parker remarked.

"No shit," I added.

Markus and Hayden came into the house.

"You lost?" Parker asked.

"No, we went to get our schedules and met Hayden's new roommate," Markus answered.

"What happened to the last roommate?" Parker asked.

"Beats me, but the kid that is rooming with me seems weird," Hayden mentioned.

"Weird like eccentric weird?" Parker asked.

"No, weird as in serial killer weird," Markus replied.

We looked at Markus. It's a what the fuck moment.

Nora

I went to get a coffee, and Skylar met me.

"How was your summer?" Skylar asked me.

"Stupid," I answered, drinking my coffee. "Britt and my dad got into a fight, and she left. It's because my dad has some weird-ass grudge against Patton's family."

"That sounds like my family. They had some history with another family where the other family tried to kill my family," Skylar said.

I looked at Skylar, speechless. I had no words.

"So, I wanted to ask you a question, and if you say no, I will understand," Skylar mentioned.

I looked at Skylar, drinking my coffee.

"I went on spring break with my sister and her boyfriend. Mason was there," Skylar said as I set my drink down. "We talked, but I know that he's your ex. I will understand if you don't want me to talk to Mason. Your friendship is more important than a guy."

I looked at Skylar as she fidgeted in her seat.

"Skylar?" I said.

"Yeah," Skylar replied.

"It's okay if you talk to Mason," I told Skylar.

"Are you sure?" Skylar sounded surprised.

"Yeah, the truth is I liked Mason in high school, but feelings change. He's a sweet guy when you get past the jerky part," I mentioned.

Skylar giggled as I laughed. I didn't hate Mason. I followed my heart, and it belonged to someone else. I wondered what Matthew is doing?

Skylar and I talked. We talked about different things and laughed. It was nice having a friend to hang out with now. Sometimes friendship wins over a guy, and I would rather keep Skylar as a friend than lose her because of Mason.

This year would be crazy to epic proportions, throwing everyone into a situation it didn't prepare us.

CHAPTER 37

THE NEW GUY IS WEIRD

Pat

I went to get a breakfast sandwich and a latte at the bakery. I walked into the place and over to the counter as I saw the guy who winked at me working. Great, that is my luck.

"Yo, can I help you?" The guy asked.

I looked at the guy's name tag. "Sam?" I said.

"The last time I checked," Sam said.

"Aren't you the guy that winked at me at the bookstore?" I questioned.

"Are you seeing things?" Sam asked me, arching an eyebrow.

I distorted my face, looking at Sam.

"Why do you look like you had a bad chicken?" Sam asked me.

"I'm trying to figure you out," I replied.

"I thought I smelled something burning," Sam remarked.

I narrowed my eyes and pursed my lips. Sam took his finger and poked me in the forehead.

"Didn't anyone tell you you can get wrinkles that way?" Sam asked me.

I slapped his hand away from my face.

"Didn't anyone tell you I will beat your ass?" I replied.

"Feisty. I like it," Sam flirted.

I stepped back from the counter. I'm not sure if coming here to get breakfast was a good thing. This dude is weird.

I stood there as Sam made things, then wrapped something in the paper, and placed the counter items.

"Your latte and breakfast sandwich," Sam said.

Wait. What?

"How did you?" I asked, confused.

"Know? A good worker learns their customers," Sam said, then kissed the air at me.

I tossed my money on the counter, grabbed my stuff, and got the hell out of there. I bumped into Kaxon, who was with Mason.

"Why do you look like you caught Pax and Shaun doing unholy things to each other?" Kaxon asked me.

"The new guy Sam in there is weird. He got my order for me and kissed the air at me," I said.

Kaxon and Mason looked at each other.

"I didn't give the guy my order," I added.

They did a double-take. I shook my head in disbelief as I went home. I didn't need this shit. I got back, and Parker opened his mouth. I shot him a glare and went up to my bedroom.

Sam

I smirked as two guys entered the bakery.

"Are you, Sam?" A guy asked me.

"Yeah, who are you?" I questioned.

"Kaxon," the guy said.

"Yeah, I don't care," I replied.

Kaxon looked at me.

"Are you always this rude to customers?" Another guy asked.

"Are you always oblivious?" I questioned.

The guy looked at me with confusion.

"Did you want to order or stand there, holding your dicks?" I questioned.

Their eyes widened as I looked at the guys with boredom. The two guys turned and left the bakery. I rolled my eyes.

The bell chimed as a girl walked into the bakery. She walked up to the counter. "What are you doing?" The girl asked me.

"Uh, you know, acting casual," I answered.

The girl giggled as I laughed.

"How's it going?" The girl asked me.

"Much better than expected. You know what people say?" I mentioned.

"What's that?" The girl asked me.

"Expect the unexpected," I answered with a smirk.

The girl smiled, and so did I.

Pat

I finished breakfast and cleaned my room. Now that everything was neat, I came downstairs and opened the door to see Kaxon and Mason standing there.

"Didn't I see you?" I asked.

Kaxon pushes me into the house. He and Mason came in and closed the door.

"What's up with that guy, Sam?" Kaxon asked me.

"Beats me. The dude is weird as hell," I answered.

"Weird doesn't explain shit. Where's Pax?" Mason asked.

"How the hell should I know? It's not like I have twin radar," I said.

The front door opened. Pax and Shaun walked into the house. Kaxon and Mason turned and grabbed Pax, dragging him out of the house. I shook my head and followed, closing the door behind me.

Pax did a flip and dislocated his arms, getting out of Kaxon and Mason's grip. Then he dropped both as they hit the pavement with their knees.

"Dare I ask why frick and frack shoved me?" Pax asked me.

"Reinforcements," I responded.

"Ah," Pax said.

Kaxon and Mason got to their feet and gasped, holding their boys.

"Christ, Pax, what is with you and our nuts?" Kaxon gasped.

"I told you to keep your hands off me. Why does everyone think that because we are smaller, it gives them liberties with us?" Pax asked me.

I shrugged.

"We need you to check out that guy, Sam," Mason said, wincing.

"Why?" Pax asked.

"Because you can tell us what his deal is with Pat and why he's a dick," Kaxon said, standing up.

Pax shook his head and turned as he started walking. We walked with him and went to the bakery. I react with my fist, but Pax is quick. People don't see him coming until they're on the ground.

We went into the bakery, and Pax saw Sam. He walked over to the counter as Sam stood there. Kaxon, Mason, and I stood there, watching.

Sam looked at Pax with disinterest.

"I heard you're giving my cousins and brother shit," Pax said to Sam.

"Let me guess; you're their reinforcements. You're a little small, aren't you?" Sam asked, pissing off Pax.

Pax jumped over the counter as Sam swapped and landed on the other side of it, facing Pax.

"What is this ninja shit?" Pax asked.

"A little slow like your height," Sam retorted.

Kaxon, Mason, and I looked at each other.

"You don't scare me like those yutzes who had to get their bodyguard. Which seven dwarfs are you? Let me guess; you're dopey," Sam told Pax.

Pax jumped over the counter as Sam stepped aside. Pax cornered Sam and pulled his fist back as someone nailed him in the nuts. We watched Pax drop to his knees as Sam push him over, then walked past Pax. "Pussy," Sam said.

We stood there, shocked. Sam walked past us and winked at me.

"What the fuck was that?" Mason asked.

"That was someone taking Pax down," Kaxon said, pointing to Pax, who laid on the floor, squeaking.

"Good luck, Pat," Mason said as they looked at me, then looked at Pax.

I sighed. Great, that's what I need. I have some dude flirting with me while taking down my damn brother. Kaxon and Mason are of no help.

I will have to avoid the bakery when Sam is working. I hope I don't see him on campus. So, why am I so curious about him?

Sam

How does someone get close to a person without interference from others? I need an ally, and I know the person for the job, my roomie.

I scoured the campus looking for Hayden and found him getting food, perfect. I walked into the diner and tapped him on the shoulder. He looked at me.

"Yo, Hayden, my man," I said.

Hayden looked at me. Okay, new tactic.

"I need your help," I mentioned, acting aloof.

"With what?" Hayden asked.

"Patton Gray," I answered, pushing out my lips.

"Why, Patton?" Hayden asked me.

"Because I like him," I mentioned.

Hayden looked at me.

"Come on, bro. Help a roomie out," I said, slugging Hayden in the arm.

Hayden arched an eyebrow at me as I lowered my hands.

"Okay, how about I tell you the real reason I need your help, but not here?" I suggested.

Hayden gave me a skeptical look.

Hayden

"Are you kidding me?" I asked as I paced our dorm room. "How do I keep something like this from Markus?" I questioned.

"You say nothing, duh," Sam said, rolling his eyes.

I stopped and looked at Sam.

"Look, I need help with the others accepting me, then I will tell everyone the truth. You and one other person know the truth," Sam reasoned.

"If this blows up in our face, your deaf, and I'm blind," I said.

"It won't blow up in our face, I promise," Sam said.

"Okay, but first you need some work. No one will believe you," I said, gesturing at Sam.

I know I will regret this, but I hope it works. Sam and I got to work. I don't know what Sam is thinking, but I knew why he's doing this.

CHAPTER 38

PARTNERS

Pat

Classes started, and I found my seat in English. Usually, Pax and I have a class together, but he was behind because of what happened last year. I sat there as someone sat down next to me. I looked to see Sam, fantastic.

I got up and found a different seat far away from Sam. It didn't work because he moved to a position next to mine.

"Will keep following me if I change seats?" I questioned.

Sam looked at me. "Yep," he said.

I groaned. I didn't need this shit. I went to get up, but the professor came in and started class.

"Welcome class, this is creative writing. This semester you will write a piece on personal experience. You will create a story and include details from your life," the professor explained.

"Why can't we write a piece of fiction?" Another student asked.

"Good questioned. Anyone can write fiction, using proper grammar and structure. When the person writes this way, the person leaves out an important element. It is a human emotion. A reader needs to connect with a story. They must connect with the characters," the professor answered.

"What about writing what we know?" A guy asked.

"What do you know?" The professor asked.

Everyone looked at the professor.

"Do you know about relationships?" The professor asked.

"Yeah," the guy answered.

"Okay, but do you understand the different relationships? What kind of relationship? Is it family or romantic? Do you understand the other people involved, or do you assume?" The professor questioned.

Everyone looked at each other.

"That's the difference between writing what you know and understanding it. You," the professor said, pointing to me.

"Me?" I asked, pointing to myself.

"Well, you are the one I chose. Do you have a family?" The professor asked.

"Yeah," I answered.

"Pick a family member and tell us about that person," the professor instructed.

"My brother, Paxton. Pax is my twin, who's younger than me by two minutes," I said.

"Okay, tell us about Paxton," the professor said.

"Paxton worries about people and approval because he has anxiety. He has a tender heart that he hides because he doesn't want to disappoint people. What people don't see is that Pax's funny and honest. He enjoys sketching because of our grandpa Nash. Pax will fight back when pushed and let no one hurt me," I explained.

"Why is that? Why won't Paxton let anyone hurt you?" The professor asked.

"Because he's my brother, and we have this bond. We help each other and take care of each other. I can't imagine my life without Pax or my other brothers," I answered.

"What this student said about his brother, did it make you connect with his brother?" The professor asked.

The class thought about it.

"Do any of you have siblings? Raise your hands," the professor instructed.

Most of the class raised their hands, including Sam.

"Okay, so you understand what it's like to have that bond with your sibling. This student explained it," the professor mentioned.

The class nodded.

"Congratulations, you connected to this young man's experience," the professor said, smiling.

Damn, I didn't think of it that way.

"Now, I will pair you with another student, and the topic you must write about is relationships. Explore different relationships and pick one, creating a story. Show your readers what the characters are doing. Create human emotions and connecting people to your characters. Make the story fun, including key elements such. Use love, heartache, humor, anger, and any other emotion. Breathe life into your piece because it will count for fifty percent of your grade," the professor told us.

It made me curious to know who my partner is with this assignment. I listen to what the teacher said. He made sense. I never looked at writing this way. Everyone considers writing art. People convey their emotions in art in different ways. Pax uses sketching to channel his feelings, but I use writing.

At the end of the class, the professor assigned partners to us.

"Your partner is the person to your left. Why, may you ask? We read left to right, so it makes sense who your partner is with the assignment," the professor announced.

I looked to my left at Sam.

"So, I guess we're partners," Sam mentioned.

"I guess so," I sighed.

"Did you want to hit the library or get something to eat?" Sam asked.

"Or we could each work on the assignment," I suggested.

"Yeah, I don't think so, buddy. No offense, but I need not flunk a class because you have issues," Sam said, standing up and walking away.

Wait. What? I got up and ran after Sam. I caught him in the hallway.

"I don't have issues," I told Sam, stopping him.

"Oh? Then why ask to do the assignment on our own?" Sam questioned me.

"You dick punched my brother," I replied.

"Because your brother threatened to beat my ass. Didn't you ever hear of self-defense?" Sam asked me.

"Pax didn't touch you," I reminded Sam.

"Not yet, but I refuse to give him a chance. Now, if you're done acting like a tool, I would like to work on the assignment," Sam told me.

"I'm not a tool," I refuted.

"If it acts like a tool and looks like a tool, then it's a good chance it's a tool," Sam retorted.

I looked at Sam, annoyed.

"Are you afraid that I'm smarter than you?" Sam questioned me.

I scoffed. "Newsflash, buddy, I was valedictorian of my class."

"Yeah, along with two other people," Sam remarked, rolling his eyes, then walking away.

"What?" I asked as Sam kept walking.

Sam

Patton caught up with me and argued with me. It didn't matter because if this assignment allowed me to get close to him, I would use it.

I stopped and looked at Patton. "Is that all you do?" I asked.

"Do what?" Patton asked me.

"Argue over stupid shit. Do you need to prove your point?" I questioned.

"Well, you don't seem to understand me," Patton replied.

"I understand you," I said, stepping close to Patton. Our faces were mere inches apart. "You're so busy talking that you don't listen to other people. If you listen more, you will see what you're missing."

Patton furrowed his brows as I looked into his steel-grey eyes. I needed Patton to see me. Then he would understand.

"That is the problem. You won't see what's in front of you because you don't want to see it," I said as I walked to the bakery.

It seems I need a new tactic if my plan works. Plan A and B aren't working. Now it's time for plan C, and if that's a bust, then

I moved to another plan. For someone so brilliant, he sure is dense.

Mason

I came out of class and saw Skylar. I ran and caught up with her.

"Hey," I said.

"Hey, Mason," Skylar greeted me.

"So, I thought we could grab a bite to eat," I suggested.

Kaxon and Jesse walked up to us.

"What's going on?" Kaxon asked.

"Mason suggested getting a bite to eat," Skylar said.

"I could go for food," Kaxon mentioned.

"Food is good," Jesse added.

Skylar looked at me and smiled. "Let's get some food," she said.

I smiled as the four of us walked to a diner. We went inside and found a booth. I sat next to Kaxon as Skylar sat next to Jesse. A server walked over and started flirting with us.

"Would you like to keep your tits?" Jesse asked the server. She looked at Jesse, shocked. "Then, you take our orders and stop eyeing my guy."

The server scampered off as Skylar giggled.

"Savage, I like it," Kaxon mentioned.

"What's so funny?" I asked Skylar.

"Because we're Shaws and don't approve of people flirting with the people in our lives," Skylar answered.

"Does that include me?" I asked as Kaxon and Jesse watched us.

"It's possible," Skylar mentioned.

I looked into Skylar's ice-blue eyes with my steel-grey eyes. She differed from Nora in every way. How come I never noticed her? Skylar has so many exceptional qualities to her, and it had nothing to do with her looks. I like that she's bubbly.

Another server came to take our order as we sat there and talked. I never laughed as much as I did with Skylar. I have to remember to keep it friendly with Skylar because she didn't want to ruin her friendship with Nora.

Kaxon leaned over and whispered, "You okay?"

"Yeah," I whispered, lying. Kaxon looked at me. Sometimes we don't get what we want. I learned that with Nora.

Eliza

I sat on a bench, waiting for Presley. I fiddled with my thumbs. Everyone knew his reputation at school, but I thought it made me special when he pursued me. I had a boyfriend who treated me like dirt. Presley made me feel unique.

Someone sat down next to me. I looked to see Selena.

"I know we don't know each other well, but we should," Selena suggested.

"I know people don't like me because they think I'm clingy. It's that I had a boyfriend treat me horribly. I'm scared that Presley will find someone else," I explained, furrowing my brows.

"I know you worry, but Presley doesn't want anyone else. The key to relationships is having interests of your own. You don't make the guy your world," Selena reasoned.

"You sound like you know what you're saying," I said.

"I lived with the brothers for two years. They're crazy, but when they meet someone, that person is it for them. The worst thing you do is to let jealousy take over your relationship. Give Presley a reason to keep pursuing you," Selena suggested.

"I'm not sure how to do that," I said, feeling confused.

"I can help you," Selena offered, smiling.

I nodded. I didn't want to lose Presley. I love him, but I didn't want my heart to get broken either. I hope Selena's suggestion works.

CHAPTER 39

WORKING TOGETHER

Pat

I relented and invited Sam over so we can work on the assignment together. We sat down on the couch, and Sam took out his notebook.

"Okay, so, what should our paper be?" I asked.

"I have an idea," Sam said.

I looked at Sam.

"How about we write about how a parent interferes with their child's relationship?" Sam asked.

I arched an eyebrow.

"Think about it. The story will have all the elements along with human emotion. It's the criteria of the assignment," Sam reasoned.

"Do you understand this topic?" I questioned.

"Yep," Sam answered.

"Okay, smartass, give it your best shot," I remarked. I'm curious to see what Sam writes.

I sat there as Sam started writing and waited. It took a few minutes, but Sam finished, then read to me what he wrote.

Jason strolled through the school hallways with a reputation that proceeded him. He didn't care what people thought about him and kept most people at arm's length. It's not that Jason didn't want to get close. He felt people would see the tenderness that existed if he opened his heart.

The only person Jason allowed seeing that hidden feature was his friend Clare. Clare wasn't like most people. Her personality was unique and enticing. She had an infectious laugh that made you chuckle. Her lips curled into a mischievous manner when she was deep in thought. Jason knew Clare was planning something humorous. That's why they were friends.

But like most friendships, their relationship developed further with affection. It was something they understood with each other that others didn't know about them. Both shared inside jokes, making them connect more than most people.

This closeness didn't sit well with Clare's parents, who forbade them to see each other. Clare's father raged at the thought of a relationship developing. He made Clare chose Jason over her family.

"You don't understand," Clare wailed.

"No! You don't understand. We will never welcome Jason here. You make a choice, your family or Jason," Clare's father growled.

Claire furrowed her brows as tears escaped her eyes, falling down her cheeks. How do you choose the love of your family over someone that holds your heart? An ache filled her chest as she stood there, clenching her shirt.

It was a decision Clare would make that will tear her life apart. A decision she didn't want to make but had no choice.

Sam finished reading what he wrote, and I furrowed my brows.

"So, yeah, I thought we could go with that angle," Sam said, clearing his throat.

"You sound like you went through it," I mentioned.

"Something like that," Sam mumbled.

"Did you love the girl?" I questioned.

Sam looked at me and gulped. I looked at him with curiosity.

"Uh, nope," Sam answered.

"Was it a guy?" I asked.

Sam shifted in his seat while I waited for an answer.

"You know, this topic is a terrible idea," Sam said, gathering his stuff.

What? Sam grabbed his stuff and got up, hurrying to the door. I went after him. He opened the door, and I closed it.

"Let go," Sam mumbled.

"Not until you tell me why you changed gears on me?" I questioned.

"It's a stupid idea. Now let go," Sam ordered through gritted teeth.

"It's not stupid. What's wrong with you?" I questioned as I spun Sam around to face me. Wait, he's crying. What the fudge?

I narrowed my eyes and furrowed my brows as I looked at Sam. Then he did something unexpected. He crashed his lips into mine. I stood there, shocked, as he gripped my shirt and deepened the kiss. I closed my eyes. Our lips moved in sync as we kissed, then Sam broke from our kiss.

"Sorry," Sam said as he bolted out of the house.

I stood there, speechless, with my mouth agape. That wasn't any kiss, and those weren't any lips.

"Why do you look like someone destroyed your room?" Parker asked, walking up.

"Uh, um," I stammered. "I got to go," I blurted, turning and running upstairs. No way was I gay, and no way will I tell anyone about that kiss. The worst part is, I liked it.

Sam

Shit, I shouldn't have kissed Patton. I ran back to the dorm and upstairs until I reached my dorm room. I ran in and closed the door, leaning with my back against it.

"Why do you look like you saw a ghost?" Hayden asked, looking up from his books.

"I kissed Patton," I blurted as I paced the room.

Hayden sat up. "You did what?" He questioned, confused.

"I kissed Patton," I announced.

"I heard you the first time. Why?" Hayden asked.

"He kept pushing me and wouldn't let me leave his house. So, I kissed him," I declared as I stopped and threw my hands up in the air.

"Who? Patton?" Hayden asked.

"No, it's the tooth fairy. Pay attention," I demanded.

Hayden got up from his bed and walked over to me.

"Okay, so you screwed up," Hayden mentioned.

"Yes, I know I screwed up. How do I fix this?" I questioned.

"Well, you could kiss Patton again," Hayden suggested.

I smacked Hayden and waved my hand. "Ow," I said, holding my hand.

"I play football. What did you expect? The Pillsbury Doughboy?" Hayden asked me.

"No, but I didn't expect you to break my hand. Why do you need muscles, anyway?" I questioned, holding my hand.

"It helps when you have a two hundred and a fifty-pound guy coming at you," Hayden answered with a look.

"How do I fix this?" I asked.

Hayden blew air past his lips and rubbed his chin. "Plan D," Hayden said.

"What?" I asked.

"Plan C is a bust. You failed at the friendship situation. Now Plan D. Tell Patton you're insane," Hayden suggested.

I pursed my lips and looked at him unamused. Hayden is no help.

"I got it," Hayden said with a look. Oh God, now what?

The next day, I went to class and sat next to Patton. I diverted my eyes and hid my face.

"Hey," Patton said.

"Hey," I mumbled.

"So, about yesterday," Patton mentioned.

"Forget about it. It was a moment of insanity," I said, waving Patton off.

"What?" Patton asked.

I opened my mouth, but the professor walked into the classroom. The gods have answered my prayers.

"Okay, class today, we will conduct a lesson showing chemistry between two characters. We need volunteers," the professor said.

I sunk in my chair.

"You and you," the professor said, pointing at Patton and me.

"Uh, I got a cold," I lied, hacking.

"Nice fake cough, but save it," the professor told me.

Great, not even my cough can save my stupid ass. I got up and made my way down to the front of the class along with Patton.

"Now, in every story, there is a romance between two characters. These people need chemistry. To find the chemistry, it starts with a look. Turn and face each other," the professor instructed.

We turned as I looked at the floor. The professor walked over and moved my head, so I faced Patton. My heart rate increased as I gulped.

"Now, look into each other's eyes. You want to feel the emotion, and their eyes are the window to the soul. Look at the body language," the professor mentioned as he spoke to the class.

I felt my forehead bead with drops of sweat as my hands became clammy. My body temperature rose as Patton looked into my eyes.

"Now, to further show, I want you to place one hand on his cheek and the other hand on his waist," the professor instructed.

Patton did as instructed as my breathing hitched while the teacher spoke. I stared into his steel-grey eyes, and he leaned in, pressing his lips to mine. Patton deepened the kiss as he pulled me close to his body. I raised my hands and placed them on his chest as I let the kiss take over me.

"Now, that's what I call chemistry," the professor said as we broke from our kiss and let go of each other. "Thank you, now you can have a seat."

You didn't have to tell me twice. I ran back up to my seat as Patton strolled to his. I sat down and sunk in my chair as my face heated. Yep, I'm blushing.

I glanced at Patton, who smirked. I will kill Hayden for Plan D. It looks like Plan E is because I'm heading, and my plan will fall apart.

After class, I darted out of the classroom and ran back to my dorm room. The less I saw of Patton, the better. Then I remembered I had to work. Well, FML, because I'm sure he will show up, not to mention I will deal with Paxton and hitting him in the nuts. Why me?

CHAPTER 40

THE CHASE IS ON

Sam

I walked into the bakery for my shift to see Paxton standing behind the counter. He looked up from the register at me, shit. The bell chimed on the door. I turned to see Patton enter, double shit.

Both looked at me as I stood there. Paxton glared at me, and Patton smiled. Okay, I need to get out of here with little hassle, which is easier said than done with customers in the bakery.

I started making my way to a different exit when Paxton stepped in front of me. "Going somewhere?" He asked.

"Yeah, and you're in my way," I replied.

"My boys and I have an issue we need to correct," Paxton threatened.

"Well, I'm sure your boys understand you don't threaten someone," I reasoned.

I faced off with Paxton as I felt someone behind me. I glanced to see Patton looking at me and smiling. Patton leaned in and whispered, "So, about that, kiss?"

Now here is where the situation spirals out of control. Imagine someone, that's me, trying to avoid others, that's Paxton and Patton. One wants to hurt me while the other wants to kiss me. I will let you figure out which one wants to do what.

"Hey, isn't that Britt who worked here?" I asked.

"Where?" Paxton and Patton asked as I maneuvered away from them.

The twins realized I duped them and went after me.

"You go left, and I'll go right," Paxton told Pat, who nodded.

The twins chased me, and I moved around the tables as customers watched. Shaun, Nik, and Frazier came out to see the commotion in the bakery.

"Why are Pax and his brother chasing Sam?" Nik asked.

"Beats me," Shaun answered.

"Popcorn, anyone?" Frazier asked, holding out a bag of popcorn. Shaun and Nik shrugged as they grabbed a handful.

"Come here, you little rat. I will rip off your legs and beat you with them," Paxton growled.

"Now, that's not nice," I said, crawling under the table. "Didn't your parents teach you manners?"

"No, my parents taught me to beat someone's ass," Paxton answered.

I crawled out on the other side and looked at Paxton and Patton.

"Well, that's a damn shame. Here, have some dessert. You're not you when your sugar is low," I said. I picked up a piece of pie from a customer and throwing it at Paxton, except I missed.

My eyes widened as Paxton looked at Patton and laughed. Patton has pie on his face.

"That reminds me of the great pie prank in high school," Frazier said, smiling. Shaun and Nik looked at Frazier.

Patton wiped off his face. The people sitting at the table got up and moved out of the way.

"Since we're playing with our food, our parents taught us to share," Patton said. He picked up a piece of cake and threw it at me. I ducked, and it went flying, hitting someone else.

"What the hell?" We heard someone exclaimed. I turned to see Kaxon with a cake on him. He removed the cake as Mason chuckled.

I looked at Patton. "Didn't anyone say you throw like a girl?" I asked.

That earned a glare as the twins grabbed donuts and whipped them at me. Did you ever get hit with a jelly donut? Those hurt like a bitch. I grabbed cookies and chucked them like Chinese stars. I smacked the twins in the face, along with their dipshit cousins.

"This is better than daytime television," Frazier mentioned.

I ran, moving around tables as the twins chased me. Kaxon grabbed a piece of pie and smashed it into Mason's face, getting it into Mason's mouth because he kept laughing. Paxton slipped on jelly and falling as I ran from Patton.

Then I heard a yell. Oh, no, I thought as I climbed onto a table and hopped to another one.

"Samuel!" The girl screeched as everyone stopped and watched her march over to me. I hopped to another table to get away from the banshee. "You can't avoid me forever!"

"Want to bet?" I yelled as I stood on a table, covered with jelly.

"You can't dump me, then think that's okay!" The girl huffed, stomping her feet.

"Natalie! I don't like you! Go away!" I ordered as Natalie lunged for my feet. I danced around on top of the table.

"When did Frazier get table dancers?" A guy asked another guy.

"You never know with that idiot," the other guy answered.

The two guys walked over to Frazier, Nik, and Shaun, then watched me as I avoided the screeching banshee. I grabbed a muffin and shoved it into Natalie's mouth.

"Here, you need this, you skinny ass bitch," I said.

That made Natalie bolt from the bakery, wailing as I got down from the table. The bakery was a mess as people left, and our food fight covered the rest of us in food except Nik and company.

Pat

Okay, I'm hella confused. Was that chick Sam's ex? Did I kiss a guy? I went to ask Sam, but he left the bakery. I swear I thought that was someone else.

"Go home and get cleaned up, Pax," Nik told Pax, who nodded.

We left and went back to the house to take showers. I stripped off my clothes and climbed into the shower, washing every nook and cranny. I got pastries in areas I didn't need. I still didn't know what Sam's deal was, but I intended to find out.

I finished showering, then got out, dried off, and put some clean clothes on. I left the bathroom with my dirty clothes and went downstairs, tossing them into the washer. Pax followed suit, throwing his dirty clothes into the machine.

"What is with this guy? Between getting nailed in the junk, we all end up in a food fight," Pax mentioned.

I started the washer and leaned on it.

"There's more to Sam than meets the eye," I reasoned.

"Whatever it is, the dude has issues. Who was that screaming banshee?" Pax asked me.

"I don't know. I didn't recognize the girl," I answered.

"It's time to do recon on Sam," Pax suggested.

I nodded. Something told me we would find out more than we bargained for with Sam.

Sam

I stripped down and climbed into the shower. I washed up, then put on some clean clothes. I can't believe Natalie goes to school here. I didn't need this shit now. That's all I need is Natalie opening her big ass mouth.

She drove me nuts in high school, and now she's driving me insane here. I thought Sable was horrible. Sable has nothing on Natalie. If I can keep Natalie at bay, I'm golden. I will need help.

Unknown

I hit my alarm on my phone and sat up in bed. After standing up, I stretched and went to take a leak. I brushed my teeth while checking my messages. I groaned at most of them. Some texts made me laugh, especially from Nora.

I spit and got a shower, then dressed. Checking my flight times, I made sure I didn't miss my flight. It would take a few days and fight changes when I got back to Michigan. It had been a while since I was home. Not home with my douche parents, but the home state. The best thing I ever did was leave home.

No one knew where I went except Nora. I didn't tell anyone else. When I return, I will go to school up north, which gave me time to get situated. My classes got picked out, financial aid set up, and a dorm room waiting for me with a guy named Hayden.

I hope Hayden's not a dick because I have enough family members that are one. I made a call, and the person answered.

"Yeah, it's me. I'm on my way. I will see you in a few days," I said, hanging up.

I zipped up my bag and picked it up, carrying it out. I know my family has issues with people, but I don't. There comes a time to let shit go and move on with your life. That's why I left home. My dad couldn't let shit go. All because he blames people for my grandparent's death. It's not like the family killed his parents, but he resented them. Grudges are a terrible thing to hold on to all your life.

I took a cab to the airport and waited. I would soon be home, and certain people had a lot of explaining to do when I get there.

CHAPTER 41

EXPLODING PLANS

Sam

It's been a few days since the bakery fiasco. I figured out a different avenue with Patton. I didn't know someone is coming to school because a particular girl didn't tell me. It didn't help that I got stuck working with Paxton.

I waited on customers as Paxton hassled me. I didn't need this shit. I grabbed an order as Paxton stood in my way.

"Get out of my way, dingleberry," I ordered.

"Why? Does it involve my nuts?" Paxton asked.

"You deserved that," I replied.

"No guy deserves slammed in the nuts, you half-wit," Paxton retorted.

"If you weren't a freak of nature, your nuts would stay intact," I said, smirking.

"Give me one good reason not to toss you over this counter," Paxton warned.

"Hey," someone whispered, getting my attention.

"Hold that thought or better yet, don't," I told Paxton as I went to the counter. "What?" I asked the person.

"We have a slight problem," Nora told me.

A few minutes later, my eyes widened as someone walked into the bakery, carrying a bag.

I leaned in and whispered, "What's he doing here?"

"Going to college?" Nora asked as I facepalmed myself. I glanced to see Paxton glaring at me. I had to get out of here and switch spots.

I turned around and strolled over to Paxton. "Paxton, buddy, amigo, pal," I said.

Paxton looked annoyed.

"I have to leave," I said.

"Why?" Paxton asked with an annoyed look.

"I have a family emergency. So, bye," I said, hurrying through the kitchen area and out the back foot. I looked in each direction and took off running to the dorm.

Nora

I turned and walked over to the guy. He looked at me.

"Hey," I greeted the guy, smiling.

"Hey," the guy said. "Where's Britt?" The guy asked.

"Oh, you know, here and there," I answered.

The guy looked at me. I glanced to see Paxton walking towards us. Well, shit. I turned the guy around and pushed him towards the door.

"Nora!" The guy yelled.

"No time to chitchat," I said as I shoved the guy to the door.

"Wait a minute," Pax yelled, stopping us. "I thought you had a family emergency," Pax mentioned to the guy.

"What a family emergency?" The guy asked.

"The one you had a few minutes ago, and why are you wearing different clothes?" Pax questioned, gesturing at the guy's attire.

"I don't know what you mean, but I got here," the guy said.

"What?" Pax asked.

"That is enough, chitchat. Let's go," I said, pushing the guy out of the bakery, leaving Pax confused.

The guy stopped and looked at me. "Nora, what is going on?" He asked.

"Who says anything is going on?" I asked.

The guy looked at me as I dragged him away from the bakery.

Pat

I worked on an assignment when Pax came home. He looked confused.

"Did you realize that you're straight?" I asked.

"No, I'm still gay. Thanks for asking," Pax answered.

"So, what's with the confusion?" I questioned.

Pax walked over and sat down on the arm of this chair. "What do you know about Sam?" Pax asked me.

"Not much, except we have the same creative writing course. Why?" I questioned.

"Because Sam left the bakery, claiming he had a family emergency, then the next thing I know, he's with Nora," Pax claims.

I looked at Pax, confused, as he gave me a curious look back.

"Now, I'm confused," I said.

"Something is afoot, Watson," Pax claims.

"Okay, Sherlock," I replied, arching an eyebrow.

"Don't you find it's odd that we haven't heard or seen Britt, but Nora is happy?" Pax asked.

I sat back and rubbed my chin.

"If one of us disappeared, the Calvary would look for us," Pax mentioned.

"Only because Pops would need bail money," I added.

"That's true, but I'm sure Pops micro-chipped us like a dog so he could track us," Pax said.

"Okay, let's say Sam isn't who he claims to be, then who the hell is the guy that looks like Sam?" I asked.

"Good question, which means we will investigate and unmask the villain," Pax announced.

I got up from the couch. "You aren't Shaggy, and I'm sure in the hell, not Scooby," I said, going into the kitchen. Leave it to my twin to conduct recon on a guy we don't know.

Sam

I made my way to the dorm room, packed my stuff, and got the hell out of dodge. I needed to find a place to sleep and figure out my next move. I will kill Nora when I see her.

I left the dorm room and made my way to Shaun's apartment building. I could crash with him until I found a new place. I used the key he gave me for emergencies and went to the apartment. I opened the door and looked around the vacant place.

There was some furniture, but not much, and Shaun's belongings were gone. Great, he moved out. I set my bag down and went to the kitchen, opening the fridge. This fridge has nothing on Old Mother Hubbard.

I will stay here for a few days, then see about changing rooms. I didn't have much money, so renting an apartment was out of the question. I sat there, contemplating my next move when I heard a key in the lock. I grabbed my bag and went to the bedroom, exiting out of the window and down the fire escape.

I walked until I came to a door and knocked. The door opened.

"Sam?" Nik asked, confused.

"Hey, Nik. I'm wondering if I could stay a few nights until I find a dorm room," I mentioned.

"That will be difficult," Nik mentioned.

"Why's that?" I asked.

"Because all dorms have students living in them. You won't get a dorm room. What about the one you have?" Nik asked me.

"My roommate is an ass and kicked me out," I lied.

"Sam, I would let you stay here, but," Nik said.

"But you don't know me. It's cool. Thanks, anyway," I said as I left. So much for plan A through Z. I went to the diner and sat down in a booth. I dug through my pockets to find some cash.

"What can I get you?" The server asked.

"A turkey sandwich and Coke," I ordered.

"One turkey sandwich and Coke coming up," the server said, walking away.

I stared out of the window and furrowed my brows. Since it wasn't cold yet, I could sleep on a park bench. It's better than nothing. I can't crash with Nora since she's in an all-girls' dorm.

I pulled out my phone and made a call.

"Yeah, it's me. Remember when you said if I needed help, I could come to you? Yeah, I need help. I'm at a 24-hour diner. Okay, see you soon," I said, hanging up.

I sunk in my seat. Everything was going well until he came back. Why?

Unknown

I found my dorm room and set my bag on a bed. This day has been weird. Nora was acting weird, and I have Paxton Gray asking me questions. Where the hell is Britt?

As I unpacked, the door opened and closed.

"There you are," a guy said.

"Here I am," I replied, looking at the guy.

"I figured out our next move with Patton," the guy said.

"Patton Gray?" I questioned.

"Yeah, who else do you know who's named Patton Gray?" The guy asked.

I stared at the guy with confusion. He saw my bag. "Why are you packing?" He asked.

"I'm not packing. I'm unpacking," I answered.

"It's no time for shenanigans. Come on," the guy said, grabbing my arm and dragging me away.

I'm guessing this guy is Hayden, and Britt is up to something. I know I won't like it.

CHAPTER 42

THE TRUTH WILL SET YOU FREE

Nixon

I drove to the college and pulled up to the diner. I got out of the car and made my way into the restaurant, finding the person I came to see. I looked at the person as they looked at me.

"Hey, Britt," I said.

"Hey, Rev," Britt replied.

"Want to fill me in on what happened?" I asked and ordered a coffee.

"Well, the plan was working until my brother showed up," Britt mumbled.

"The same brother that no one knows about here," I mentioned.

Britt nodded. "It's because of my dad. He hates you guys a lot, and I don't know why?" Britt said.

"I can fill in the blanks," I replied.

Britt looked at me.

"When we were in college, on New Year's Eve, Mike and Sarah Tilson died in a car accident. Sarah was my brother's ex. We didn't find out later that they had a child who was your father," I explained.

Britt looked at me, stunned.

"There was bad blood between the families. At the funeral, we figured things were cool until a lawsuit got filed," I said.

"My dad kept saying the Grays killed his parents. It got so bad that my brother left when I was a freshman in high school," Britt said.

"That's why the boys don't remember Samuel. Plus, they dealt with the Andrews family," I reasoned.

"I didn't want this to happen, but I love Pat. We can't help that the heart wants what the heart wants," Britt said.

I smiled. Sometimes we help to lead the heart. No matter what differences our family has, no child should suffer for it.

"Get your bag, and we'll clear this up," I said as Britt grabbed her bag. I followed her out of the diner, and we got into the car. I drove us to the house to fix this mess. When don't I fix messes?

Pat

I sat on the couch as Pax was plotting. I didn't have time for my brother's plotting. Parker and Payton walked in as Pax filled them in on his plans.

"You want us to do what?" Parker asked.

"We spy on Sam and uncover what he's hiding," Pax answered.

"Okay, Nancy Drew. How do you expect us to do that?" Payton asked.

"Kidnapping is effective," Pax suggested.

"Yeah, when people are acting like twits. You want us to kidnap some guy to find out his secret. Did Ma drop you on your head as a baby?" Parker questioned.

That's all it took as Pax and Parker fought. I kept working on my homework.

The door opened, and Hayden came in with Markus and Sam. What the hell? I stood up as Pax smacked Parker.

"Can someone tell me what's going on and why my roommate dragged me over here?" Sam asked.

"I'm curious myself," Markus mentioned.

"Because it's time for the truth," Hayden said.

"What truth?" Payton asked.

"That Sam isn't Sam," Hayden said.

"I knew it!" Pax yelled. We all looked at Pax. "Well, I did," Pax said, shrugging.

"If Sam isn't Sam, then who is he?" Parker asked.

"Britt," Hayden answered.

We did a double-take.

"Show them," Hayden said, pushing Sam to me.

"What do you mean?" Sam asked.

"Prove that you're Britt. Kiss Patton like you did," Hayden said.

"What?" My brothers yelled.

I frowned.

"Okay, first, I'm not kissing a guy. Second, I'm not Britt," Sam exclaimed.

"Sure, you are. Now kiss," Hayden said.

"No," Sam yelled.

Hayden and Sam argued. I stood there, confused until Hayden pants Sam as Presley came into the house.

"Whoa, what did you guys do here at college?" Presley exclaimed, shielding his face.

"Yeah, that's a dude," Markus said to Hayden, who's eyes widened.

I facepalmed myself.

"I guess I was wrong," Pax said, checking out Sam.

Shaun walked into the house and caught Pax checking out Sam, then shot Pax a look. Pax looked around, whistling.

"Can I pull my pants up?" Sam asked, hanging all out.

"Please do. No one wants to see that shit," Nixon said as we all looked to see Nixon with Sam.

They came into the house as Sam pulled up his pants.

"I'm so confused," Payton said, sitting down.

"You're not the only one," Parker agreed.

"Let me clear this up," Nixon said. He removed Sam's hat and pushed Sam towards me.

I looked at Sam as he looked at me, then I saw it.

"Britt?" I asked.

"Hey, Pat," Britt said, smiling. I reached and pulled her into a kiss, deepening it. She kissed me back.

"Okay, suck face later. We have an issue we need to clear up," Nixon said.

Britt and I broke from our kiss.

"Okay, if that's Britt, who's that?" Parker asked, pointing at the guy.

"That's my brother, Samuel, aka Sam," Britt said.

We looked at each other, surprised.

"I need a drink," Parker said, sitting down.

"No, you need to get to a meeting," Nixon told Parker. Parker rolled his eyes.

We all sat around as Britt explained what happened.

"After my dad visited Nora and me at school, it got worse at home. I packed a bag and left. When I had enough distance, I cut my hair and borrowed Sam's clothes. Our dad wouldn't look for a boy. Nixon found me in his church, sleeping. He let me stay with him until school started. We planned with only Nora knowing the situation," Britt explained.

"Okay, that explains that part. How come we didn't know about your brother?" I asked.

"Because I left during my sophomore year. I'm tired of dealing with my parents," Sam said.

"I don't understand why your dad hates us so much," I mentioned.

"I can explain that," Nixon said. He explained about Britt and Sam's grandparents and our family's history. Damn, that was a lot of history.

"So, let me get this straight, no offense to anyone who's gay in this room," Parker said. He looked at Markus, Hayden, Shaun, and Pax. "Britt and Sam's dad blames our family because a drunk driver killed his parents when he was a baby. Even though the driver went to jail and our Grampa went with the police to tell the Tilson's. That's messed up."

"No, that's bullshit," Payton said as we looked at him. "You can't use a situation that involved no one as a reason to control your kids. Why do parents feel the need to control their kids?"

"Because parents don't want their kids to make the same mistakes that they did," Nixon said. "Look, I'm not good with mushy crap. That is my brothers' department. When you make mistakes, you pray your kids don't do the same thing. You hope they do better than you did with your life."

"Our parents aren't like that," Pax reminded Nixon.

"Have you met your parents? Your aunts were busy dressing your dad up like a girl or dragging him into a mess. I'm sure your grandpa was more concerned about your aunts than your dad," Nixon informed us.

"That's disturbing that my ma dressed your dad up in a dress," Markus mentioned to us.

"Eh, we did the same thing to Nolan when he was little," Nixon mentioned.

"The bigger question is why you went to great lengths to conceal your identity," Pax said.

I sat there and thought the same thing.

"Our dad gave me an ultimatum. I can quit seeing Pat and stay in school or say goodbye to my future. I chose Pat," Britt said, surprising me.

"You're willing to give up your future for our brother?" Presley questioned.

"The heart wants what the heart wants, and my heart wants Pat. He's my best friend," Britt admitted, stunning me.

My family and Britt's brother looked at me. Britt and I started as friends, and over time, my feelings grew for her. When she didn't show for our date, it sucked. I didn't think she liked me until we got a second chance.

I looked at Britt. "I'm relieved that it turned out a girl kissed me and not a guy," I said as the others laughed. Britt giggled.

"So, what now? With Britt and Nora's brother here, that blows your plan," Payton mentioned.

That's a good point. I furrowed my brows.

"Who says Britt can't keep pretending?" Pax asked us.

"Elaborate, little brother," Parker ordered.

"Britt is using the name Sam. We alter it so that both can attend, and Britt can pretend to be someone else. We have a cousin that is dating someone influential at the school," Pax mentioned.

My brothers and I looked at each other, smiled, then looked at Nixon.

"Oh, no, you allow me to call my favorite grandchild," Nixon grumbled.

"You have one grandchild," Parker mentioned.

"That's why Kaxon is my favorite," Nixon retorted as he called Kaxon.

CHAPTER 43

THE SH*T HITS THE FAN

Pat

Uncle Nixon called Kaxon, who brought Jesse and Skylar along with Mason. Britt called Nora. You can see where this is heading.

"Grandpa? What are you doing here? Wait. Why do I see double?" Kaxon asked, pointing at Britt and Sam.

"Because that's Britt and her brother Sam," Nixon answered.

"Say what?" Kaxon asked, surprised.

"Pay attention, or you won't be my favorite grandchild," Nixon remarked.

"I'm your only grandchild," Kaxon reminded Nixon.

"Semantics," Nixon said, shrugging.

Nora walked over and hugged Sam and Britt, then sat down next to Sam.

"Now it seems we have a slight issue. Britt disguised herself as Sam, and Sam is attending school. We need to keep Britt hidden, and she needs help with financial aid," Nixon explained.

Kaxon rolled his eyes, earning a look from Nixon.

"So, you thought you would use me to get to Jesse?" Kaxon questioned.

"You make it sound devious," Nixon said.

"Well, it is and not cool, old man," Kaxon remarked.

"I'll show you, old man," Nixon huffed.

"That still doesn't explain this whole situation. Why are there two Sams sitting on the couch?" Kaxon mentioned.

"Allow me to explain. Now pay attention," Nixon told the others as he explained the whole situation.

"So, Nora knew about all this? Why doesn't that surprise me?" Mason questioned with a tone we knew too well.

Nora looked at Mason and furrowed her brows.

"Mason, this isn't the time," Pax said.

"Why? Because Nora isn't honest about things?" Mason asked with sarcasm.

"Mason," Kaxon said.

"No, I'm sick of people defending someone who lies all the time," Mason told Kaxon. He looked at Nora. "Isn't there a time that you don't lie?"

"Dude, what the hell is your problem?" Pax asked Mason as I sat on the couch with the others.

"It's the fact that Nora knew and didn't bother to tell anyone. Nora knows a lot of things she isn't forthcoming with Pax," Mason snapped.

"That's enough," Nixon ordered Mason, who shut his mouth.

"Excuse me," Nora said, getting up and leaving.

"I'll go after her," Britt offered.

"No, let me," Sam said, leaving as we looked at Mason.

Nora

I left the house and walked back to my dorm room as tears fell down my cheeks. I wiped my cheeks. I didn't hear Sam yelling as I kept walking until he caught up with me.

"Nora," Sam said, stopping me.

I turned to Sam. "Everything's screwed up, and Dad is making things worse. You don't know how it felt when Britt left this summer, leaving me alone," I said as Sam furrowed his brows.

I looked at Sam. "I had to listen to Dad berate me for my poor life choices with the people I hang out in my life. I had no one to protect me while I dealt with Dad's tirade. He wouldn't let me leave and told me if he found out I went near the Gray family, he would cut me off," I told Sam. The others found us.

"Nora, I didn't know," Sam reasoned.

I furrowed my brows.

"When I left, it's I go, or I would do something that I didn't want to happen. I knew Britt would take care of you," Sam explained.

"But no one took care of me when Britt left. I don't have anyone, Sam. I broke someone's heart for another, and the person left. I'm so alone," I said as I started crying.

Sam pulled me to him and hugged me. I buried my head into my brother. I missed my big brother.

Kaxon looked at Mason. "Congratulations, you broke, Nora," Kaxon said as Mason looked at him.

I cried as Sam held me. All I wanted was what anyone wants to love someone and have them love back, but the one that has my heart isn't here.

Skylar

I stood there and watched everyone. I knew Mason is hurting, but I know what it's like to like someone who doesn't notice you. Jesse looked at me.

"What?" Jesse asked.

"We're lucky," I said.

"Why?" Jesse asked me.

"Because we have people who love us. All Sam, Britt, and Nora want are what everyone wants," I replied.

"What's that?" Jesse questioned.

I looked at Jesse. "Unconditional love from people who should love them, and a future. We can't let them suffer because of past grievances. If that were the case, our family wouldn't love Uncle Frazier," I mentioned.

Jesse smiled as she pulled out her phone and made a call. You can't hurt others because of something that happened in the past. They had nothing to do with it. It wasn't right.

Jesse walked over and handed her phone to Kaxon's grandpa.

"Who's this?" The guy asked.

"Someone that will help," Jesse answered.

"Hello," Nixon answered.

Hey, buddy.

"Frazier," Nixon mumbled.

Jesse explained the situation. We can help you out, that's if you want my help.

"Will I regret this?" Nixon questioned.

Frazier chuckled. *Sometimes we need people who understand better than most people. I'm one of those people. I know we don't see eye to eye on things, but I know what it feels like to have family hate you and other family loves you. Tell those kids not to worry. I will handle it.*

Uncle Frazier hung up as Nixon handed the phone back to Jesse. Jesse looked at me as I looked at her and smiled.

Nixon took everyone back to the house except for Mason. He stood there, looking defeated. I walked over to him as he looked at me.

"What you did back at the house was wrong," I said.

"I let my anger get the best of me," Mason reasoned.

"I understand. I know how it feels to like someone, and the person never notices you," I said, looking at Mason, who furrowed his brows. "You told Nora to choose, and she did. You can't hold a grudge against someone for their choices you force them to make, not if you want a future with me."

I turned and walked away, leaving Mason surprised. A person can hurt for a while, but they need to let it go at some point. Nora was my friend, and I refuse to ruin a friendship over a useless grudge.

Pat

After this fiasco, I sat next to Britt. I kept looking at her.

"What?" Britt asked.

"You cut your hair," I mentioned.

"Do you hate it?" Britt questioned.

"No, I like it," I replied, smiling.

Britt smiled at me as I slid my hand into her hand and interlocked our fingers. I looked into Britt's eyes as she looked at me.

"I always saw you, even when I didn't see with my eyes," I said.

"How?" Britt asked.

"My heart did," I answered.

I leaned over and pressed my lips to her lips. I gave Britt a sweet kiss, then pulled back and pulled her to me. I wrapped my arms around her. No one will ever keep us apart again, not even her dad.

Sam

I walked Nora back to her dorm. Once I got her situated, I went to my dorm room. I love my sisters and regretted leaving them with my parents. I knew if I stayed, it would get worse.

I went up to my dorm room and saw Hayden.

"Hey, I want to apologize for pantsing you earlier," Hayden apologized.

"That's now what I expected when I returned to show the world my goods," I mentioned.

"So, when you left, where did you stay?" Hayden asked me.

"I stayed with an aunt, figuring my life out. I dated this girl, but she was horrible," I said.

"Natalie?" Hayden asked.

"Yeah, did you meet Natalie?" I asked.

"No, but Britt filled me in about your ex," Hayden chuckled.

"I don't want a high maintenance girl. That is not me. I want someone who is unique and enjoys life," I explained.

"You're lucky. When I admitted I was gay, my parents threw me out. My sister, Leslie, worked to support us," Hayden mentioned.

"Your parents sound like my parents, real winners," I mentioned.

"It doesn't matter. I'm better without my parents, plus my sister is awesome. She worked so I could finish school and moved with me here," Hayden explained.

"That's cool that your sister did that," I agreed.

"So is Nora, okay?" Hayden asked.

"Who's Matthew?" I asked.

Hayden looked at me, surprised. There was a reason that I needed to come home. I didn't remember Mason Harper well. It surprised me that Nora dated Mason since they didn't match well. There's a reason that my sister likes this Matthew, and someone will tell me the truth.

CHAPTER 44

THE GRAY FAMILY MEETS THE FEARSOME THREE FROM SAINTWOOD

Pat

I woke up the next day on the couch with Britt sleeping on me. We must have fallen asleep on the couch last night. I looked down, noticing her short, messy hair. Britt's haircut was different but cute. I never dated a girl with short hair before, but I like it.

Britt stirred as I laid there and lifted her head to look at me.

"Morning," Britt yawned.

"Morning," I said.

Britt propped herself up on my chest. "Do you think Jesse and Skylar's uncle will help me?" Britt questioned.

"God, I hope so. Although, pretending that you're a guy will take getting used to with you," I mentioned.

Britt giggled.

"Good morning, sleepyheads. You didn't disgrace our couch during the night with your sinful behavior, did you?" Parker asked, leaning on the back of the couch.

"Doubtful, considering that's Presley's area," I answered.

Parker chuckled as Presley came downstairs. "Have you guys seen Eliza?" Presley asked.

"Isn't the cling wrap with you?" Parker asked.

"No, she didn't come home last night," Presley said, shaking his head.

Parker and I looked at each other. Then the front door opened, and Eliza walked into the house.

Presley walked over to Eliza. "Where have you been?" He asked.

"I hung out with Selena and Josie, watching movies. We fell asleep," Eliza answered.

"Next time, call," Presley said, walking away.

Eliza stood there, confused, as did Parker, Britt, and I.

"I should have called. Presley is right to feel upset," Eliza said, excusing Presley's behavior.

Britt and I sat up on the couch.

"Don't tell me you're cowering to baby brother," Parker mentioned.

"It's respect," Eliza said, making an excuse.

"Since when?" Parker questioned.

I got up off the couch. Payton and Paxton came downstairs.

"What's going on here?" Payton asked.

"Oh, baby brother thinks he will act like an ass to his girl and expect her to take it," Parker said as Pax walked over to me.

"Oh? That's a damn shame," Payton said, going into the kitchen. He dragged Presley out of the kitchen and into the living room.

"What the hell, Pay?" Presley yelled as Payton gripped Presley's arm.

"You don't treat your girl with disrespect, ever," Payton ordered.

My brothers and I looked at each other. Presley yanked his arm away. "I would never do that," Presley said.

"Oh? So, you didn't make your girl feel insecure?" Payton questioned.

Presley's expression changed.

"You're better than that, Presley," Payton told Presley.

"Eliza, why don't we go upstairs," Britt suggested as Eliza nodded. The girls went upstairs as we stood there. Shaun passed them on the way down, and Britt shook her head. He turned and went back upstairs. It was a brother's moment.

"I didn't mean to make Eliza feel insecure, but I know guys will chase her," Presley admitted.

"Real smooth, ex-lax," Pax said.

Presley glared at Pax.

"Don't glare at Pax. You're acting like a certified tool with your girl. It's no wonder she worries about you. Get it together, Presley," Parker snapped.

I watched as my brothers laid into Presley and thought about them. They weren't innocent and acted like tools themselves.

"Look at the pot calling the kettle black. Hey, pot," I said to my brothers. They all stopped and looked at me. "You want to berate Presley for doing stupid shit when you all did the same thing," I reminded my brothers. "The difference with me is I want my girl, and her douche father kept her from me."

My brothers looked at me, furrowing their brows.

"Britt and I started as friends. She stood me up on a date because she was afraid that I would treat her like other girls. I got lucky when I got a second chance. I didn't even get the first chance," I reasoned.

I shrugged and went upstairs. I walked to a bedroom, hearing Britt and Eliza talking with Shaun. They were discussing us. The conversation wasn't malicious but honest.

"Did you have issues with the brothers?" Eliza asked.

"Oh, yeah," Britt and Shaun said.

"But it worked out, didn't it?" Eliza asked.

"Not without issues, but all couples have issues. I dated a guy that abused me. It took a long time for Pax and me to get back on an even footing," Shaun admitted.

"It's the same with Pat and me. I stood him up on our first date. His reputation scared me, but I found this guy who would do anything for me. Even if that meant disobeying his family," Britt confessed.

Pax came upstairs, and I grabbed him, shoving him away.

"What the hell?" Pax asked me.

I shushed Pax.

"Don't shush me, you tool," Pax huffed as I pushed him downstairs. "Do you mind? The only person I want to maltreat me is Shaun."

"Ew, gross. No one wants to hear about your kinky fetish," Parker groaned.

"You're jealous because you aren't me," Pax told Park.

"Thank god for that," Presley mumbled.

Someone knocked on the door, and Payton answered it.

"Who are you?" Payton asked.

"Who I am is not important, but who are you? Well, I'm significant, but that's unimportant," the guy said.

"Frazier, you idiot, will you get on with it," another guy said, walking up with a different guy.

The three guys walked into the house as Payton closed the door. We stood there and looked at the three guys. One was massive, and the other had ice-blue eyes.

"I'm Frazier. That's Ryan and Jordan, my besties," Frazier grinned.

Ryan and Jordan rolled their eyes. "Yeah, you don't remind us," Ryan said.

"Here," Frazier said, handing me a manilla envelope. I opened it and read it.

"What's this?" I asked as my brothers looked at the information.

"We pulled a few strings with the help of Ace and his crew to help your girl and her family," Ryan explained in a husky voice.

"Frazier told me that my granddaughter called him, and I talked to Jesse and Skylar. They explained the situation to me. Why they called this idiot and not me is beyond me," Jordan said, thumbing at Frazier.

Frazier gave Jordan a look and shook his head. "What bestie two means is that everyone loves Frazier," Frazier said, grinning.

I chuckled.

"This is a record with name changes and school information," Parker said.

"Sometimes, people need to disappear to find peace," Frazier mentioned.

"Or have friends in high places," Ryan mentioned.

"Does that mean we're friends?" I asked.

"No," Ryan answered. Well, okay, I thought.

"Let's say we're doing you a favor," Jordan mentioned.

I didn't question it but went with the situation. Something told me not to ask questions. While we dealt with these guys, Kaxon dealt with others.

Kaxon

Jesse and I were hanging out at the bakery, minding our business, when two guys entered the bakery. They walked over to our table and took a seat with us.

"Can we help you?" I asked.

"It depends," the guy said.

"On what?" I asked, looking at the guys.

"If you plan to hurt our niece. Pay attention," the other guy remarked.

"Kaxon meets Uncle Elijah and Uncle Liam," Jesse said.

The guys waved at me and smiled. Liam looks like Jesse's dad, and Elijah looked like an older version.

"We were in town to visit family and thought it swells to meet the idiot who's dating our niece. See, we're overprotective of our family. If you hurt her, I hurt you," Liam warned, smiling.

Liam's smile terrified me. Elijah grinned, then we heard, "What are you both doing?"

I looked to see Jesse's dad walk in and sit down next to Liam. Well, damn. You couldn't tell them apart.

"Will you all stop scaring my boyfriend? Kaxon is cool," Jesse mentioned.

"We'll be the judge of that," Elijah said, cracking his knuckles.

It's a good thing that my grandpa is a minister because I need prayers with this family. I didn't realize Jesse came with bodyguards.

"Where's your sister?" JJ asked Jesse.

"With Mason," Jesse mentioned.

"Mason? Who's Mason?" Elijah asked.

"Mason is my cousin who likes Skylar," I answered, throwing Mason under the bus.

"Then we'll meet Mason and offer advice," Liam said as the three got up and left. Good luck, Mason, I thought as I chuckled.

Mason

Skylar and I were sitting on a bench, talking when someone grabbed me and dragged me away. I didn't recognize the guys as Skylar chased us down.

The next thing I knew, I was up on a flagpole, hanging there. The three guys laughed.

"Will you get Mason down?" Skylar asked.

"Oh, honey, I would, but this is so much fun. Now I know why Drew enjoyed doing this," the guy in the middle chuckled.

"Dad," Skylar said, giving her dad a look.

"Okay, fine," her dad said, rolling his eyes.

They let go of the rope, and I hit the ground with a thud. I laid on the ground, groaning. Skylar checked on me.

"Are you okay?" Skylar asked.

"I broke something," I cringed.

"What?" She asked, checking me out.

"My dignity," I groaned.

Skylar shook her head as her dad helped me up. Until he took my hand, making me scream.

"Shit," her dad mumbled as I grabbed my arm. I dropped to my knees in pain. "The guy broke his arm."

"Dad will kill us," Elijah grumbled.

"What else is new?" Liam asked.

They helped me up, and I held my arm as they took me to the hospital. When we got there, the staff took me back and helped me with it. Skylar and her dad went in the back with me as her uncle made a call. I don't know who they called, but I heard the f-bomb dropped often.

The doctor checked my arm and took x-rays. The doctor confirmed I broke my arm. They gave me something for pain and put a soft cast on it. I was beyond loopy. It took three hours until the hospital released me.

Payton and Parker showed up as Parker called my parents. I looked at Payton and raked my hand over his face. "Such a good cousin," I slurred, then patted his face.

"Come on, dopey, let's get you home," Payton said, helping me. I took two steps and face planted on the floor.

Parker came to the back where we were and looked at me on the floor. "Damn, what did they give Mason?" Parker asked.

"Beats me," Payton said as I held up a thumb.

"I'm okay. The floor is my best friend and comfy," I mumbled.

"Aunt Luna and Uncle Major are on their way," Parker told Payton as I laid on the floor.

"Mommy and Daddy are coming. Woo hoo!" I cheered.

"Let's get happy, Harry, home," Payton said as they picked me up. Payton and Parker dragged me out of the back and through the emergency room.

"Remember the Alamo!" I yelled as people looked at me.

"No one remembers the Alamo. I doubt you will remember this conversation tomorrow," Parker retorted.

"But I love the Alamo," I said, sniffling.

"You never went to the Alamo," Payton mentioned.

"But I love it," I exclaimed, then passed out. Tomorrow will bring pain. Good thing that I have pain killers to help me.

CHAPTER 45

WELL, THIS SUCKS

Mason

I woke up the next day in pain. I looked down at my arm in a splint and wrap, then remembered what happened. After groaning, I got out of bed and made my way downstairs to find my parents waiting for me. Why are my parents here?

"Are you okay, Mason?" Ma asked, getting up from a chair and checking me out.

"Besides a broken arm, I'm peachy," I answered.

"Don't be an ass, Mason," Dad warned me. "Your mom and I worry about you."

"Sorry," I mumbled.

"What happened?" Ma asked.

"Skylar's dad and uncles hung me on a flagpole, then dropped me," I answered.

"They did what?" Ma exclaimed.

"Yeah," I answered.

That's all it took as Ma stormed out of the house with Dad going after her. I will let them figure it out; I need something for my arm.

Skylar

I told Grandpa what Dad and my uncles did to Mason. Grandpa wasn't happy, and I thought he would kill Dad, Uncle Elijah, and Uncle Liam. It serves them right for hurting Mason.

I stood there in the bakery as Grandpa yelled at them. The next thing I knew, a woman and man came into the bakery and storming over to us.

"Which one of you is Skylar's dad?" The woman questioned through gritted teeth.

We pointed at Dad, who rolled his eyes.

"Explain to me where the hell you get off hurting my boy," the woman snapped as the man held her back. "Major?" The woman said.

"Yes, baby," Major answered.

"I will give you two seconds to let go before I rip off your balls," the woman said.

Major let go and stepped back. Smart move there, buddy.

The woman got into Dad's face as we watched.

"How dare you go after my boy?" The woman questioned.

Uncle Liam stepped towards the woman.

"I wouldn't do that if I were you," someone warned. We turned to see three women standing there.

"Who are you?" Liam asked.

The women walked towards us.

"Luna's sisters and we won't hesitate to make you a female," a woman mentioned, cracking her knuckles.

"I'd like to see you try," Liam said.

I'm not sure what happened, but that's the first time I saw women take on Liam and win.

"Okay, that's new," Elijah said as Grandpa smacked upside the back of the head, then helped Liam up.

"I apologize for my idiot sons. I didn't know about their stupidity until Elijah called me," Grandpa explained.

"My boy has a broken arm," Luna reminded Grandpa.

"I'm aware, and the boys will pay for his medical bills," Grandpa reasoned.

The woman looked at me. "I'm not sure who you are. If you had something to down with Mason getting hurt, then you stay away from him," Luna told me.

That left me speechless. I looked at the women, the guy, and my family. Thanks to my dad and uncles. I got blamed for their actions and looked at Grandpa, who furrowed his brows.

"I thought college would be fun, but I'm finding out that it isn't. I don't have time to know my crush. Dad, Elijah, and Liam resorted to their antics. I get blamed," I said, walking away as Dad went after me.

Grandpa shook his head and looked at Luna and her sisters. "Parenthood is difficult. We worry about our children. Sometimes their happiness is more significant than our happiness. Don't let the actions of my boys hinder the chance my granddaughter has with your son," Grandpa said.

"I watched someone hurt our son, and I worry about him," Luna explained. "I don't want Mason dealing with that again or someone's family going after him."

"Trust me, I understand, but Skylar isn't like that. My granddaughters care about people, and Skylar has a tender heart. We worry about her out of the girls," Grandpa explained.

"Okay, but no more hurting our son," Luna said.

Dad caught up with me. "Skylar!" Dad yelled as he stopped me.

I looked at Dad.

"I'm sorry," Dad apologized.

"You can't keep hurting any guys I like or have a chance with," I said.

"I know, but honey, it's difficult for me to know that you're growing up. The day you and your sister were born was the happiest day of my life. I wanted to keep you small forever because I knew one day a guy would take you both from me," Dad explained.

I took Dad's hands in my hands and looked at him. "You will be the first guy who loves me. No guy will take that from you because no one can take the place of my dad," I explained.

Dad looked into my ice-blue eyes with his brown eyes and smiled; then he pulled me into a hug.

Grandpa looked at Luna. "You don't want your son hurt, and JJ doesn't want his girls hurt. A father's love is like no other," Grandpa reasoned.

"Yeah, I know," Luna sighed.

Mason

I took some ibuprofen for the pain, putting an ice pack on my arm. I sat down on the couch, releasing a sigh. I didn't think college would be like this when I got here. First, Nora dumps me, then Skylar's family hurts me.

I'm thinking that God is laughing at me. Kaxon came into the house and sat down next to me.

"Your ma and aunts are at the bakery causing trouble," Kaxon mentioned.

"What else is new? The way my luck is going, I will be lucky to survive college as a single guy," I replied, looking at Kaxon. "Out of the four of us, you and the twins never had issues with girls as I do."

Kaxon laughed a lot. "Are you serious?" He asked me.

"Yeah, why?" I asked.

"Let's see, Pax is gay, Pat got stood up, and I refuse to date girls in high school because of the way they acted. Who wants to date a girl that worries about what other people think about her? Most girls are insecure people who fret over the dumbest things. It's not a bad thing, but not my thing," Kaxon said.

"Yeah, but the one girl I liked dumped me for Matthew," I reasoned.

"Are you still hung up on Nora? Dude, let it go. There's more to life than pining for some chick that wouldn't work out anyway," Kaxon said.

"What do you mean?" I questioned.

"You dated Nora for a short time, then your parents moved. You can't base feelings on someone that you dated for a short time. Did you bother to talk to Nora or make out with her?" Kaxon questioned.

I thought about it.

"No, you didn't. You confuse lust with love. You can lust after someone, but you can't base a relationship on that. Take your parents, for example. Your ma and Dad had difficulties, but it took time to reach the love stage," Kaxon said.

"How do you know about Ma and Dad?" I asked.

"I read Aunt Luna's book," Kaxon answered.

Someone knocked on the front door, and Kaxon answered it. He waved to the person who walked over and sat down in front of me. Oh, great, Skylar's dad is here.

"I want to apologize to my brothers and my actions. We forget people aren't like us," Skylar's dad explained.

I held up my arm. "You broke my arm," I said with an annoyed look.

"I'm aware, and we will pay for the medical bills. It's difficult to know that your child likes someone. There's a possibility that the guy will capture their heart," Skylar's dad said.

I looked at her dad.

"I worry about my daughters. I was present when their mother gave birth to them. I held them in my arms and promised to love them until my last breath. That doesn't mean a lot to people, but it means a lot to me. I don't want my daughters hurt," Skylar's dad reasoned.

"I like Skylar. She doesn't let me act like an ass," I reasoned, shrugging.

Her dad smiled.

"I'm getting to know Skylar. If anything progresses, cool, but I want to know her better before that happens. I don't want to make the same mistake that I did in the past," I explained.

"I prefer that," her dad agreed.

I get that parents worry. God knows that my parents always worry about me. It's not wrong, but sometimes you have to let us grow up and make mistakes. It's how we learn.

Nora

I went to the bakery and heard people discussing Skylar and Mason. It made me realize that they have people who care about them. I have busy siblings. I pulled out my phone and sent a message.

Hey. I hope everything is okay. I'm all right, well, not really, but that's not your concern. I hope you find happiness. I miss our talks. I won't bore you with nonsense. Take care.

I put my phone back into my pocket and ordered a coffee.

"Nora," I heard someone say.

I closed my eyes and cringed. I turned around and saw Dad standing there. He grabbed my arm and dragged me out of the bakery as I fought, alerting people in the bakery.

"Let go!" I screamed. Dad yanked me as I felt pain sear through my arm. I screamed. "You're hurting me!" I screamed as people came out of the bakery.

"I warned you and your sister, but you don't listen. I know you know where your sister is," Dad snapped as I cried from the pain.

"Let the girl go!" Someone barked as I cried.

"Stay out of this! It's a family matter!" Dad barked as I cried.

Someone tapped Dad on the shoulder. Dad turned as a fist hit him, making him release me and fall to the ground. I held my arm, falling to my knees, screaming.

"Elijah and Liam take the girl to the hospital. I will deal with this piece of shit," the guy said as I bawled.

"Come on, sweetie," Elijah said, helping me.

"Christ Elijah, we'll never get help with your slow ass," Liam said, picking me up and carrying me. I held my arm as I sniffled. My phone beeped as I buried my head into Liam. He brought me to the hospital and got me help.

The doctors gave me something for the pain and reset my shoulder. Dad dislocated my shoulder after he yanked my arm. The doctor gave me a sling and some medication to help with the pain.

I sat on a hospital bed in the ER and wiped my face with my free hand.

"Nora?" Sam said, walking towards me.

I looked at Sam as tears fell down my cheeks. "God is laughing at me," I sniffled.

Britt showed up and walked over to me.

"Why do you say that?" Sam asked me.

"Because no one cares about me," I answered as I cried.

Sam and Britt furrowed their brows as I sat there. Today was the final straw for me. When I felt better, I would look for a job and focus on school. My dream as a graphic artist is over, and I had to find something to support myself.

I didn't bother to check my phone. What's the point? I doubt Matthew would text me back. Mason hates me, and Skylar is busy with Mason. Britt is busy hiding while Sam is figuring out his life. One day, things will work out for me, but it's doubtful how things were looking.

CHAPTER 46

WHEN LIFE HANDS YOU LEMONS, DON'T USE TEQUILA

Nora

Sam and Britt helped me back to my dorm room. I sat on my bed, wondering what I did wrong in my life?

"Nora, it will be okay," Britt assured me.

I looked at Britt. "Will it? Do you know why Dad dislocated my shoulder? He wanted me to tell him where you are, and I refused. While you and Sam left to escape Dad, I got stuck with him," I told Britt and Sam.

My brother and sister looked at me with concern. Honesty sucks because the minute you tell the truth, people resent you. When you protect people, you suffer the consequences. I reached into my pocket and looked at my phone. I had a message waiting for me.

I opened it up, and it was from Skylar.

Are you okay? Dad told me what happened. Please let me know. Btw: Grandpa knocked out your dad, lol.

That made me smile. I sent a text back.

I'm in pain, but okay. Your uncles are sweet and tell your grandpa, thank you. You're a good friend, Skylar.

All I wanted to do is sleep and forget about what happened. I laid down, and the tears fell as Britt laid with me. Sam stayed with us.

Matthew

I checked my phone and found a message waiting for me. I opened it to see it was from Nora and read it. I closed out my message and got ready to finish working on a car when my phone rang. I answered it.

Hey, we got a problem.

"What's the problem?" I asked Markus.

Markus told me what went down at school between Nora and her dad. I hung up the phone.

"Hey, Beau!" I yelled.

"Yeah?" Beau asked.

"I need to take care of a personal matter. I promise to come back and finish the car," I said.

Beau looked at me and nodded. I got into my car, pulled out of the parking lot. I pulled up to a house and got out of the car, walking to the front door. After knocking, a guy answered with a busted nose.

"Are you Nora and Britt Tilson's old man?" I questioned.

"Yeah, who are you?" The guy answered.

That's all I needed confirmation as I grabbed him and dragged him out of the house, then beat the hell out of the guy. After I finished, I looked at the guy.

"You ever lay another hand on either of those girls, I'll kill you. Stay the hell away from Nora," I demanded as the guy laid on the ground, groaning.

I watched the guy get to his feet. "Thanks for the threat. I will use that when I press charges," the guy said as cops pulled up.

"Yeah, I will make sure they know what you and your family did to my family," I warned. The police arrested me and read my rights to me. They led me to the back of the squad car and put me into the back seat.

I sat there as they closed the door as the guy smirked. After the police took me to the police station, they booked me and put me into a jail cell. I sat there and waited for my parents to show up. I didn't care what happened to me. I didn't want Nora to suffer at the hands of that man.

Nash

Michael called me and explained what happened. I told Dad, Ma, Mags, and Uncle Cayson about it. Then I made a call. I'm sick of that family and their beef with us. Mike's kid is taking it too far.

I left the house and picked up Nix, then paid a visit to Mike Tilson's kid. Plus, we had to pick up Matthew's car. We pulled into the driveway and got out of the vehicle.

"So, what if Mike's kid disagrees? It's not like we can beat the hell out of him," Nix mentioned.

"No, but it's time for the truth. That family's lies keep causing trouble for us, and it stops," I said.

"Not like the truth always works with this family," Nix retorted.

I rolled my eyes as we knocked on the front door. A woman answered it.

"Hi, my name is Nash Gray, and this is my brother, Nixon Gray. Is your husband home?" I asked.

"No, the paramedics took him to the hospital. I'm on my way there now," the woman said, grabbing her purse and closing the door.

"Can we speak to you for a few minutes? We promise not to keep you long," I assured the woman.

"Speak for yourself," Nix said.

I gave Nix a look. He shrugged.

"Look, your husband doesn't know the truth about my family, and we got blamed for something we didn't do," I explained.

The woman looked at me.

"His father, Mike, was my best friend when we were younger. Our friendship ended because he cheated with my ex-girlfriend and married her. His brother tormented my wife and tried to kill our kids. His nephew attacked my daughter. I know you won't believe me, but it's the truth. The car accident that killed his parents, a drunk driver caused it. Our dad went to tell the Tilsons the news. I know he's your husband, but he's misdirecting his anger," I explained.

The woman furrowed her brows.

"Mickey," the woman said.

"As in the mouse?" Nix asked, arching an eyebrow.

I looked at Nix.

"No, as in his dad's name. Mickey is a nickname," his wife said.

"Well, the mouse would sound better," Nix remarked.

"Hey, Ma and Dad named you after a disgraced president," I reminded Nix.

Nixon glared at me.

"My husband's grandparents raised him. His family made it seem like your family caused problems for them, but I didn't believe it. Then he controlled the kids. Our oldest son, Sam, left home because of it," his wife said.

"So, why stay with a man like that?" Nixon asked.

"I thought if I stay, then I could protect the girls, but Mickey got worse, causing Britt to leave. My husband didn't get a chance at a loving life. His family filled it with hate and anger. I thought if I love him enough, he would see life better," his wife explained.

"Lady, no offense, but your husband won't change. When you have kids, you love them even when they're acting like little jerks," Nixon informed the woman.

My brother has no filter.

"If you want to stay with a man like that and lose your kids, be my guest, but don't say we didn't warn you," Nixon added.

"Nix," I said.

"Hey, I'm not sugar, I don't coat shit," Nixon remarked.

I shook my head and rolled my eyes.

"I don't want to lose my kids, and that's why I contacted an attorney. Mickey doesn't know yet, and I'm serving him with papers. Sometimes it takes a harsh reality to wake a person up. I should have done this a long time ago," his wife told us. "Excuse me; I have to go to the hospital and play the dutiful wife."

Mickey's wife walked past us as we stood there.

"You know, Nash, we were jerky kids to Ma and Dad, but they always loved us," Nixon mentioned.

"Even when we weren't lovable ourselves," I added.

"Frick and Frack might drive me nuts, but I can't imagine making them hate me. Mickey will lose everything thanks to his family," Nixon said.

My brother wasn't wrong. You can't change Tilson's mind about people. I knew growing up. They never take responsibility for their actions. They place the blame on others for their shortcomings. It's a sad state of affairs, but not every family has a family like ours. We were one of a kind.

We went back to the house.

"How did it go?" Ma asked, coming out of the kitchen, drying her hands.

"Mickey Mouse's wife is divorcing him, and he's in the hospital," Nixon said as Ma shook her head.

"I don't think it matters," I said.

"Why do you say that?" Ma questioned.

"Because no family will turn out like ours," I answered.

"That's because no family has a legacy like ours," Dad said, sitting on the couch. We walked over and sat down in chairs.

"What do you mean?" I asked.

"Nashville, all families have **legacies**. When our Ma and Dad met, I doubt they expected to produce a legacy like ours. If I left it up to Ma, she would have killed me if I didn't get together with your mother. That woman was batshit crazy," Dad said, making us laugh.

"Yeah, but we carried on Ma's **legacy**," Cayson mentioned.

"All families endure a legacy as generations expand to future generations. It's our goal that people remember past family members with love and laughter," Dad reasoned.

"I'll admit the old man is right," Nixon said.

"I'll old man you," Dad warned Nixon.

I chuckled. My phone rang, and Jamie said he would take care of the situation with Matthew. That surprised me, considering Jaime told me to get bent.

"What did Jaime want?" Nixon asked.

"Jaime said he would help Matthew. His offer surprises me, considering he refused," I replied.

"That's because big brother called the red-headed stepchild," Cayson said. He thumbed at Dad.

"Only because I got Patty involved with the conversation. Jonas loves helping Peppermint Patty," Dad said, chuckling.

"You wait until I see your brother," Ma told Dad and Cayson, giving them both a look.

Nixon and I laughed as we watched Ma, Dad, and Cayson bicker. I can imagine what they were like growing up with each other.

They say we come from a legacy of people before us who started it all. It started with my grandparents and carried on through generations. Generations of families who fought, loved, and laughed but had a family bond like no other. I couldn't wait to see the future generations, but someone would suffer in a way we didn't expect.

CHAPTER 47

CHANGES

Pat

After what Britt, Sam, and Nora's dad did to Nora, Britt stopped hiding her actual identity from people. Jesse and Skylar's family help the three of them live a life without fear. I can't say that I didn't see this coming. Their dad was crazy in every aspect.

Britt and I went to class and sat next to each other. We were partners. The professor came in and started class.

"Today, I want to try an exercise with everyone. Look around the room at your classmates," the professor instructed.

We looked at everyone in the classroom.

"Now, you all see different genders, skin colors, ethnic backgrounds, and so forth. We all come in different shapes and sizes, making us unique. It's the same with characters. Our characters drive a story and add depth to it. Most people make the mistake of writing a character that looks unrealistic. You come down to the front," the professor said, pointing at me.

I got up from my seat and made my way down to the teacher. I stood in front of the class.

"How tall are you?" The professor asked.

"Five foot six," I answered.

"Weight?" He asked.

"One hundred and sixty-five pounds," I replied.

"Okay, so you're not a tall, muscular guy with a billion tattoos," the professor mentioned. The class laughed.

"I have a few tattoos, but not a lot," I mentioned.

"Do you have a girlfriend?" The professor asked.

"Yep," I answered.

"Was it love at first sight? Did you look at her and say, I love this girl? She is my genuine love," the professor questioned.

"No, we started as friends, then she stood me up on our first date," I replied.

Britt giggled.

"See, love happens at different times. Most people write a story with these key elements, which are cliche. That scenario doesn't happen in actual life. Couple's fight, makeup, fight some more, tease each other, and let emotions fly. Emotions aren't logical, and people respond," the professor explained, then let me go back to my seat.

I sat down next to Britt.

"I want you to write a description of your partner, explaining details about them. Pick interesting concepts and let your imagination soar. Do not write that my partner is tall, beefy, dark-skinned, who's part of the thug life," the professor joked. We laughed.

"Show us things about your partner. Here is an example. Brad hit the gym all the time. He focused on different aspects of his body to provide the sculpted look that he hopes to achieve. Sweat glistens over his body, revealing the cuts in his toned arms and torso. Brad hoped one day, he would make the cover of a fitness magazine. He hoped to reveal the extra hours he spent grunting on the machines," the professor explained.

Why do I imagine some dude named Brad at a gym? I looked at Britt, who's drooling. I rolled my eyes.

I started writing and described Britt. It wasn't difficult, considering I noticed different details about her. I used most of the hour drafting a paper; then, I gave the piece of paper to the professor at the end of class. We left class and walked down the hallway.

"This class differs from what I expected," Britt mentioned.

"I like it. Most teachers want you to spew verbatim back to them, but this teacher makes you think," I said.

"I take it you didn't like high school," Britt said.

"High school was okay, but it didn't challenge me as college does. I hate teachers that don't challenge you. It's like they expect you to follow along with their ideas. It's all bullshit, if you ask me," I replied.

"No one asked you," Kaxon said, walking up to us with Jesse.

"Don't you have someone to terrorize?" I questioned.

"Not at the moment," Kaxon answered. He looked at Britt. "Nice to see you looking like you and not some dude we want to donkey punch."

"Yeah, sorry about the bakery incidents," Britt said.

"That is okay. Mason learned the hard way about Jesse's family," Kaxon mentioned with a look.

"Yeah, we heard Mason had a rough moment. Did he get his cast?" I asked.

"Yeah, and whined like a baby when they put it on him. You would think that's the simple part, but no. Mason hit the guy who applied the cast," Kaxon told us.

"Mason's always been a big baby. Pax broke his leg when we were little, and Mason cried. You thought he broke his leg," I said.

"Well, Mason broke Pax's leg and cried because Major punished him," Kaxon reminded me.

"What did you guys do?" Britt asked us.

"We were playing who can jump from the house to the garage. Pax hesitated, and Mason pushed him off the roof. It didn't end well," Kaxon mentioned.

Britt's eyes widened.

"Yeah, but Pax got even and broke Mason's nose. That was a fun summer," I added.

"Wow, you guys were crazy," Britt mentioned.

"Crazy is as crazy does. Grammy Gray electrocuted Grampa Nate," Kaxon mentioned.

I facepalmed myself.

"The crazy train derailed and landed in crazy town. The next stop is the Gray family," Jesse chuckled.

You got to love our family. It's our circus, and we are the monkeys.

Mason

I came out of class and saw Nora with a sling and struggling with her books. I could walk away but helped her. I walked over to Nora as she dropped her books and helped her with them.

"Thanks," Nora said.

"What happened to your arm?" I asked.

"Oh, this? It's courtesy of my dad's visit," Nora answered.

I furrowed my brows.

"It's fine. Nothing new there with my dad," Nora said. "Thanks for the help." I watched Nora walk away as I stood there.

Nora

Well, that was fantastic. It's a good thing I get my sling off in a few days. I walked to meet Skylar at the bakery. My stomach growled, and I needed to take some medicine.

I walked in, and Skylar waved at me. I walked over and set my books down on the table, then took a seat.

"How is your shoulder?" Skylar asked.

"It's healing but hurts," I replied.

"Your dad is an idiot," Skylar told me.

"My dad is an asshole. That's why I'm getting an education and learning to support myself," I informed Skylar.

"Oh?" Skylar asked.

"Yeah, I thought hotel management would work, and then I could save up for a place of my own. I need nothing fancy, but a home," I replied.

"That's cool," Skylar agreed.

Pax brought over a muffin for me, and I struggled to get money out of my pocket with my one hand.

"Don't worry about it," Pax told me.

"I can't accept this without paying," I mentioned.

"Someone already paid for it," Pax told me as he pointed at Eliza. She waved, and we looked at her. We sat there as Eliza made her way over to us.

"I didn't want to intrude," Eliza said.

"Do you want to join us?" Skylar asked.

"If you don't mind," Eliza mentioned.

"Not at all," Skylar said as Eliza joined us.

"You're dating Presley Gray, aren't you?" I asked.

"Yeah, Presley said I should make friends, and Selena and Josie are helping me," Eliza told us.

"Friends are good to have. I didn't have many," Skylar mentioned.

"Are you sure?" Eliza asked.

"Yeah, it's difficult when you come from a family like mine, but then I met Nora," Skylar said, grinning.

I laughed. We sat and talked. Eliza wasn't evil; she needed a friend. I required several since my love life sucks.

Pat

Britt and I went to get food and saw Presley chatting with some girl. My brother is a twit. I walked over to him, tapped him on the shoulder. He turned, and I hit him.

"Patton!" Britt yelled as Presley grabbed his nose.

"Do you mind explaining why you're chatting it up with some hoe?" I asked Presley. I looked at the girl. "Bye, hoe." I waved her off.

"We were only talking," Presley said, muffled.

"Dude, you're lucky it's me and not Pay," I reminded Presley.

Britt gave Presley a napkin for his nose. I want to shove my brother's head into the water and drown his stupid ass.

"Look, you're not my keeper," Presley snapped.

"No, but someone needs to put a chastity belt on your stupid ass," I remarked.

"Screw you, Pat," Presley huffed.

"Nah, I have standards," I retorted. Presley left, and I shook my head. My brother is a tool and worse than Payton. That's not saying much since Payton is a king tool.

Britt looked at me, and I shrugged. The thing about Presley is he's dating a girl and treating her like shit. Once you get past the clingy personality, Eliza isn't evil. My brother was in for a rude awakening with Eliza.

We didn't know it yet, but the end of this year would shock us and affect the family we didn't think possible. If you feel our family dealt with issues before, you have seen nothing yet.

CHAPTER 48

HOMECOMING WEEKEND

Pat

This weekend was a homecoming, which meant a football game and a dance. We all went to the game to see if our school's team wins. Yeah, our football team lost because they suck. They need a new coach and captain since Hayden can do so much on the field. The football team reminds me of the Lions, a bunch of losers. We're diehard Lion's fans, but we know our team sucks ass. We can say it, but no one else can.

We went back to the house after sitting outside, watching the game to warm up. Not only did we lose, but we froze our asses off. We got back to the house. Britt and I got under a blanket, with Pax joining us. Our brothers laughed at us.

"A little cold?" Parker asked.

"Man, the weather up here sucks worse than Pax does," I answered through chattering teeth.

"Hey, I suck pretty well. Ask Shaun," Pax retorted through chattering teeth.

"Yeah, we didn't need to know that. Thanks for sharing, little brother," Payton said, walking past us.

"Sharing is caring, big brother," Pax remarked.

Kaxon, Jesse, Mason, and Skylar came into the house as we sat there, warming ourselves.

"Where's Markus?" Parker asked.

"Consoling Hayden, if you know what I mean," Kaxon said with a look.

"Yeah, unfortunately," Parker mumbled.

Mason grabbed a pen and shoved it into his cast, itching his arm.

"It will thrill me when I get this stupid cast off," Mason grumbled, scratching.

We laughed.

Presley walked in with Eliza, arguing about something.

"I wasn't flirting," Eliza said, defending herself.

"Then what do you call it?" Presley asked.

"The guy asked me for the time," Eliza answered.

"More like making time. Eliza, you're my girl. Don't forget that," Presley reminded Eliza.

"Yo, tool, stop acting like a dick," Pax said.

Presley looked at Pax. "Stay out of this. It's none of your concern," Presley told Pax.

"It becomes our concern when you act like an ass," Parker said with a look.

"You have your significant others; I have mine. You deal with your girlfriend or boyfriend; I'll deal with mine. I don't tell you how to treat them, don't tell me how to treat mine," Presley told Parker.

"Then stop acting like a jackass, because that's what you are now," Parker remarked.

Presley glared at Parker, then went upstairs. I looked at Pax. "When did our brother become an asshole?"

"When he got taller than us," Pax replied.

Payton came out of the kitchen.

"Pay, you better handle Presley before the twins do," Parker warned Payton.

"What did the tool do this time?" Payton asked, eating a sandwich.

"He accused Eliza of flirting with some dick," I answered.

"Here, hold my sandwich," Payton said, handing his sandwich to Parker. We watched Payton go upstairs, then heard items break and crash. Presley yelled, and so did Payton. The rest of us stay put because we weren't stupid. Payton has a temper, and Presley is learning the hard way how bad Payton's anger is.

My baby brother is a tool.

The next day was the dance. While the girls shopped, Pax and I hung out at the house, watching TV. Did you think we would spend hours getting ready for a dance? We take ten minutes to get ready—the perks of being a guy.

Presley came downstairs with a black eye courtesy of Payton. He sat down in a chair.

"Payton warned you about your attitude," Pax told Presley.

"Yeah, I know," Presley said.

"Why are you dating a girl if you don't want her?" I asked.

"I care about Eliza," Presley answered.

"Yeah, but you act like a tool with her. Dude, you got to stop making her insecure," I warned.

"I never had a relationship with someone. I dated but nothing long-term," Presley reasoned.

"Well, it isn't treating the person like shit. One day, Eliza will get sick of your shit if you don't knock it off," Pax told Presley.

I agreed with Pax. People will take so much shit before they end things. The problem is Eliza cares more about Presley than he did about her. It will take one incident to put everything into perspective.

Sam

I stopped at a diner to get something to eat. I walked in and took a seat at the counter as a server walked over to me.

"What can I get you?" The server asked.

I looked at the name tag that read Leslie. She must be Hayden's sister.

"I'll take a BLT, fries, and a Coke with some company. If you don't mind?" I mentioned.

"Well, the diner isn't busy at the moment. Let me get your order, and we can talk," Leslie offered.

I sat there. I didn't expect Hayden's sister to look young. I didn't know much about his sister except what he told me. Ten minutes later, she returned with my order and stood behind the counter.

"I never saw you around here. Did you start school?" Leslie asked.

"Yeah, I came home a few weeks ago from abroad. I stayed with my aunt for a few years," I replied.

"How do you like school?" Leslie asked me.

"It's a lot different from high school. The education systems differ between the states and Europe."

"My brother Hayden attends school," Leslie mentioned, leaning on the counter.

"Yeah, he's my roommate at the dorm. When I got here, I found out my sister was pretending to be me," I said between bites.

Leslie snickered. "Yeah, Hayden said he had a crazy roommate," she told me, laughing.

"That wasn't the worst part. Hayden pants me in front of a bunch of people. I let it all hang out because of him," I mentioned.

Leslie laughed more. "Sounds like my brother," she giggled.

"He told me you took care of him when your parents kicked him out of the house after he admitted that he's gay," I said.

Leslie stopped laughing. "Our parents don't understand the fact my brother is gay. It took a lot for Hayden to tell them. Since I'm older, I got jobs and a place for us so he could finish school. I love my brother, and he didn't deserve my parents' reaction," Leslie explained.

"Tell me about it. My dad holds a grudge against another family for a situation they didn't do. Our mom stayed with him, even though she's better off without him. She reasons everyone needs love," I said.

"Your mom hopes that if she loves your dad, it will help him move on. It's difficult when you get one side of a story and not the full version. People take sides and make decisions that aren't correct," Leslie reasoned.

"It doesn't interest me to maintain a family history full of spite. My family is hateful people, and I prefer happiness. You can't feel happy if you carry around anger. It doesn't work," I reasoned.

Leslie smiled at me. My sisters and I didn't deserve to carry a burden with the last name Tilson. The things my aunt told me blew my mind about what my uncle and cousin did.

They say generations carry a legacy. I didn't want my heritage to be the same as my family. I wanted it better. I didn't want my sisters to suffer, and that's what my dad did to them after I left. I wish I would have stayed to protect them, especially Nora.

I finished my lunch, paid, tipping Leslie well since she deserved it. Then I left the diner and went to see Nora. I wanted to know more about Matthew.

Nora

I worked on homework since I wasn't attending the dance. Who would I dance with, myself? Yeah, I felt like a loser already. I didn't need to make it more clear.

Someone knocked at the door, and I got up to answer it to find Sam standing there.

"Who's Matthew?" Sam asked.

"What? No, hi, how are you?" I asked, arching an eyebrow.

"Hi, how are you? Now, who's Matthew?" Sam questioned.

I rolled my eyes as I went back to my bed. Sam entered my dorm room and closed the door behind him. He sat down on my bed with me.

"Matthew is Mason's cousin," I answered.

Sam looked at me, confused.

"I met Matthew when I visited Britt my senior year. We hit it off. When I came to school last year, Mason thought we could pick up from when we dated in high school," I explained.

"So, the guy you dated thought you could pick up from high school, and you like his cousin," Sam said.

"In a nutshell," I added.

"Did you tell Mason that you had no interest?" Sam asked.

"Did you ever talk to someone who refuses to listen and cares about their opinion?" I asked with a look.

Sam chuckled.

"Mason is oblivious to things," I mentioned.

"It's better to be straightforward than beating around the bush with someone. What about Matthew?" Sam asked.

"Matthew left, and I haven't heard from him," I answered.

Sam looked at me as I diverted my eyes. I didn't want to discuss Matthew.

"You're in love with Matthew," Sam said.

My head snapped in Sam's direction.

"What?" I asked.

"You're in love with Matthew. I can see it in your face. You can deny it all you want, but you wear your emotions on your sleeve, Nora. You always have," Sam responded.

I furrowed my brows.

"There's nothing wrong with how you feel. You can't help who you fall in love with," Sam reasoned.

"Yeah, well, Matthew left, and I'm on my own. I applied for a job and studying hotel management," I said, changing the subject.

"What about your dream of becoming a graphic novelist?" Sam questioned.

"It's a dream, and I need to support myself," I responded.

Sam gave me a look.

"It's okay. Sometimes we forgo our dreams and act like an adult. I have to learn independence and not rely on a guy. Plus, when you love someone, it's a little hard to move on from the person," I reasoned.

Sam gave me an emphatic look, then hugged me. I needed a hug because I was drowning in my emotions and heartbreak. I will be that woman with cats and plants, which reminds me I need to buy a plant. That will give me experience with caring for a plant. I will get a cat later.

CHAPTER 49

HOMECOMING SHENANIGANS

Pat

Homecoming arrived, and since Britt is staying with us, I didn't have far to go to pick her up. She is sharing a room with Eliza. We figure it was better than Eliza sharing a room with our dipshit brother. It's sad when you side with a girl over your brother.

I knocked on the door, and Britt answered it. She dressed in a navy blue, form-fitting, knee-length, lacy dress. With Britt's dark hair, the dress suited her. She looked stunning.

"What do you think? Does the dress suit me?" Britt asked, posing.

I chuckled. "That dress suits you in every way. You look gorgeous," I complimented Britt.

Britt grinned as Eliza came to the door. She was wearing a baby blue, knee-length dress that flared from the waist. Presley walked over and looked at Eliza.

"You ready?" Presley asked.

I looked at my brother, weird.

"Yeah," Eliza said as Presley walked away.

"Presley said nothing about your dress," Britt mentioned.

"It's okay," Eliza said, shrugging. She walked past us as we watched her go downstairs.

Pax and Shaun came out of another bedroom and walked over to us.

"Isn't my date hot in his suit?" Pax asked us.

"You both look dashing," Britt complimented.

"It's a suit, and you're dudes. I don't think dudes are hot, including my brother," I remarked.

Britt giggled as Pax rolled his eyes.

"Where's Payton and Parker?" Pax asked.

"They went to pick up Josie and Selena. Presley is acting like a tool," I answered.

"What else is new? I hate to say it, but Eliza deserves better. What am I saying? I don't hate to say it. It needs saying," Pax told me.

"Yeah, well, someone will show Presley the errors of his way," I mentioned.

Pax and I looked at each other. Britt and Shaun looked at us. Homecoming was about to get a lot more interesting since we roped some schmuck into helping us.

When your cousin dates someone from a big family, they have a spare cousin lying around. They help you out with a slight issue. Jesse made a call, and her cousin was more than happy to oblige. I thought our family was crazy; we don't compare to her family.

We left for the dance and arrived to set the stage. Now pay attention to this dance because the tables will flip on, baby brother. Payton and Parker didn't know what we planned with Kaxon and Mason, nor did Markus. We didn't tell them.

The dance was in full swing as I led Britt on the dance floor. We danced as the night started. We should get in a few dances before all hell breaks loose.

While we danced, Presley left Eliza alone. That's mistake number one. Mistake number two is that it gave us an opening to put our plan in motion. People have insecurities no matter what they say; even the most secure people have issues. My brothers, cousins, and I will exploit Presley's vulnerabilities and teach him a lesson.

"Would you like to dance?" A guy asked Eliza.

Eliza looked at the guy with confusion.

"Sorry, my name is Evan Jones," the guy introduced himself.

"Eliza," Eliza said, shaking his hand.

"Now that we know each other's names, would you like to dance?" Evan asked.

"I don't think my boyfriend would like it," Eliza replied.

"Who's your boyfriend?" Evan asked.

Eliza looked around and saw Presley with some girl, talking.

"That guy," Eliza said, sighing.

"If I were your guy, I wouldn't leave a beautiful girl like you alone," Evan mentioned.

Eliza looked at Evan as he smiled. She smiled in return.

"I would love to dance," Eliza said, taking Evan's hand.

Evan led Eliza out onto the dance floor and started dancing. They talked. Now, here is some background information. Evan has a girl, and no, he isn't cheating. He's helping us with our situation. His girl is at the dance talking to Jesse and Skylar, along with Kaxon and Mason. Mason isn't dating Skylar, but they're working their way to it.

While Evan made Eliza feel special, Presley noticed the closeness between them. Yeah, the shit is about to hit the fan on so many levels. Pax danced over to me with Shaun and got my attention. We watched as Presley marched over to Eliza, yanked her from Evan, and acted like an ass.

"What the hell, Eliza?" Presley snapped.

"Presley," Eliza said.

"You're my girl. Why the hell are you dancing with this jerk?" Presley yelled.

"Whoa, you hang on there. Your girl? You didn't think Eliza was your girl when you spent more time with another girl," Evan informed Presley.

"Who the hell are you?" Presley asked.

This exchange caught the attention of the others as we all stopped to watch the shit hit the fan.

"Evan Jones and who I am isn't important. You acting like an ass to 'your girl' is," Evan answered.

Presley frowned.

"Let me guess, in high school, you had girls galore, then picked a girl who you don't deserve," Evan said.

"You know nothing about me," Presley snapped.

"Oh, I know more about you than you realize. You're the guy that flirts with girls, making them feel special, then ignores them. You use your charm to your advantage, chipping at their self-esteem and self-worth. If you keep a girl under your thumb, when you get bored and you will, you move onto someone new.

Guess what, sunshine? That doesn't make you significant. That makes you an asshole," Evan countered.

Presley stood there, furrowing his brows. It took him a minute to realize we weren't coming to his defense.

"Eliza is better off without you than with you. No girl deserves your treatment with them. If you want to date, then be honest and stop stringing a sweet girl along like a toy," Evan told Presley.

Presley looked at us as we shook our heads. I know it was a shitty thing to do, but our brother needs a dose of reality. What happened next surprised us.

"Presley?" Eliza said.

Presley looked at Eliza.

"It's over," Eliza said, then turned and walked away.

Well, damn, didn't see that coming — nothing like getting dumped in front of everyone at homecoming. People went back to dancing as Evan walked over to his girl while our baby brother stood there, shocked.

Selena

I whispered something to Parker and left the dance. I found Eliza leaning with her back against a car and walked over, standing next to her.

"Why am I feeling like a jerk?" Eliza asked.

"You shouldn't," I reasoned.

"Did you see Presley's face?" Eliza asked.

"Sometimes, it helps to put things into perspective. Presley needs to know what he's missing, and he can't do that when you cave to him. If he cares about you, then he will realize what he's lost," I explained.

"What if Presley doesn't?" I asked.

"He will. It helps when you learn the family history and get sound advice," I answered with a smile.

Parker came out to make sure we were okay.

"So, now what?" Eliza asked.

"Now, you go about your business and let us handle baby brother," Parker advised. "Uncle Nixon told me it took Nana dumping Grandpa to make him see what he did. I'm not sure how that guy fits into this. I have a feeling the devil twins, along with the devil cousins, had a hand in it," Parker said.

"Why didn't you all work together?" I questioned.

"Have you met my family?" Parker asked me.

"Unfortunately," I replied.

"Look, we sit back and wait. I know my brother. He got Uncle Nolan and Grandpa's genes. Those two combinations are never good," Parker advised.

No argument there, considering what happened in high school. Parker's still miffed at Presley for ruing our Valentine's date. We took Eliza back to the house.

Presley

I left the dance and went to a diner. I didn't want to go home and deal with my brothers, especially after getting humiliated in front of everyone. I sat down in a booth and removed my tie as a server brought me coffee.

"Rough night?" The server asked.

"Something like that," I mumbled.

The server walked away as I sat there. I stayed there for a while; then someone sat down in the booth across from me. I looked to see Uncle Nolan sitting across from me.

"I heard you had an exciting evening," Nolan said.

"If you mean getting humiliated and dump, then sure," I replied.

"Did you expect anything less with your attitude?" Nolan asked.

I looked at Nolan. "Says the guy that had no issue with girls," I said with sarcasm.

Nolan ordered a coffee.

"Except I got my shit together and didn't get your grandpa's genes," Nolan retorted.

I frowned.

"If you want sympathy, you won't get it from me. You were an ass to that girl, and you deserve to get dumped," Nolan said.

"Uh, thanks," I mentioned.

"My brother was an ass to Maggie and deserved to get dumped. It took her breaking up with him to get his shit together," Nolan told me.

"Eliza hates me," I mumbled.

"Then make her un-hate you," Nolan advised.

"How do I do that?" I asked.

"Do you like this girl, Presley?" Nolan asked.

"Yeah, Eliza is sweet, funny, kind, caring, smart, and beautiful," I answered without missing a beat.

"Then why make her feel insecure? When you have all those qualities in a girl, you cherish them. With your aunt, I knew I found someone significant in my life. She had every quality I wanted, and I fell in love with those traits. Plus, I grew up to appreciate her. Presley, relationships are difficult but rewarding. If you want this girl, then fight for her," Nolan advised.

"What if Eliza doesn't want me back?" I asked.

"Then accept it. You created this mess. Now you get to clean it up," Nolan said, smirking.

I sat there, thinking. My brothers won't help me, and I'm on my own. How the hell do I win someone back when I was an ass to the person?

Nolan left the diner and got into his car. He pulled out his phone and made a call.

"Yeah, Presley took the bait. No, I didn't screw it up. I'm not Nash. Thanks for the vote of confidence, Nix," Nolan said, rolling his eyes.

Nolan started the car and left. I sat there and figured out what my next move is with Eliza. It paves the road with good intentions. Unless the path results in devastating consequences. A situation that would shock us all at the end of the year. It will alter someone's life and show why the Gray legacy is significant.

CHAPTER 50

NOTHING LIKE CONSPIRING TO KEEP FAMILY TOGETHER

Pat

After homecoming, we had to keep Eliza from running back to Presley. Do you have any idea how difficult it is to keep someone like Eliza from giving into Presley? It's difficult.

Every time Eliza would cave, we worked to keep that from happening.

"Why can't I talk to Presley? He looks so sad," Eliza commented as we stood in the school's quarter.

"That defeats the purpose of you dumping Presley. You make him a bigger schmuck than he is acting," Kaxon answered.

"But I love Presley," Eliza said, defending Presley.

"Do you love how Presley is treating you?" Pax questioned.

"Well, no," Eliza answered.

"Then don't cave and deal with an ass like Mason here," Kaxon remarked, thumbing at Mason, who gave Kaxon an annoyed look.

"Kaxon isn't wrong. You are an ass," I told Mason.

"Can we leave me out of this?" Mason asked.

"Stop acting like an ass to Nora," Kaxon told Mason while shrugging.

"Look, we know our brother," I said, gesturing between Pax and I. "Presley never dealt with girls telling him no. When you think you're king shit, you end up as shit. Plus, Presley has a habit of making terrible decisions. Ask Parker," I reasoned.

Eliza looked at me with confusion.

"Damn. You're slow. Don't cave to Presley and make him work for you. It's not that complicated," Pax remarked.

We all looked at Pax.

"I tire of tiptoeing around people," Pax said.

I shook my head. Pax isn't the most patient person. Case in point, Pax and Shaun - need I say more?

"Schmuck, three o'clock," Kaxon announced, pointing at Presley.

We whisk Eliza away before Presley talked to her. I know we're shits for doing it, but Presley needed to learn.

Presley

I saw Eliza with my brothers and cousins and started walking towards them when they left. What the hell? Now, my family is helping my ex?

All I want to do is talk to Eliza. I sighed and went to class. After class, I stopped and got a coffee. I saw Eliza and approached her when Selena and Josie stopped me.

"You don't want to do that," Selena advised.

"Why not?" I asked with irritation.

"Because the girl broke up with you. Do you want to make the situation worse?" Josie asked.

"No," I mumbled.

"Then let us help you," Selena said as she and Josie shoved me out of the coffee shop.

Pat

We lowered our menus and watched Selena and Josie push Presley out of the coffee shop. We smiled at each other as Eliza got her coffee and walked over to our table.

"Now what?" Eliza asked.

"Next phase of the plan," I answered as the others nodded.

Eliza furrowed her brows.

Parker and Markus found some random guy.

"You come with us," Parker said, escorting the guy away with Markus, making the guy confused.

When Parker and Markus were alone with the guy, Markus handed the guy a fifty-dollar bill. The guy held up the money in his hand and looked at Parker and Markus.

"What's this?" The guy asked.

"What does it look like?" Parker asked.

"A fifty-dollar bill," the guy replied.

"Well, we know your parents didn't waste money sending you to college," Markus remarked.

The guy looked at Markus.

"That is the payment to pay attention to this girl and make my tool brother jealous," Parker said. He handed the picture of Eliza to the guy.

"Yeah, because this plan worked so well the last time," Markus told Parker.

"It would have gone better if Matthew did it and not you," Parker reminded Markus.

"Matthew has problems of his own," Markus refutes.

"Let me get this straight," the guy said, earning a look from Parker and Markus. "You want me to make your brother jealous?" The guy pointed to Parker. "Hoping that he comes to his senses."

"In a nutshell," Parker replied.

"Is your brother dumb or something?" The guy asked.

"Do you want your ass beat?" Parker questioned.

"No," the guy answered with a sigh.

"Then stick to the plan and stop asking questions," Parker ordered.

The guy shoved the money into his pocket and shrugged. Parker and Markus explained to the guy what to do. There's not a chance this guy could screw this up, but then again, there's every chance.

Britt and I sat on the couch, hanging out when someone knocked on the front door.

"I'll get it," Pax yelled, running down the stairs and opening the door. "Who are you?" Pax asked, feigning ignorance.

"I'm Robert. I'm here to pick up Eliza for a date," the guy said.

Presley came out of the kitchen and stood there, confused.

"I didn't know Eliza had a date," Pax said, feigning shock. "Did you know Pat?" Pax asked me.

"Nope," I said, feigning ignorance.

Pax put his hand to his mouth, acting shocked.

"What date?" Presley questioned.

"I guess Eliza has suitors," I answered, shrugging.

We watched as Eliza came downstairs in a skirt and top, greeting Robert. The dress was Britt's idea.

We watched Presley as he watched Eliza and Robert.

"Ready?" Robert asked.

"Sure am," Eliza answered.

"Wait. You can't go out like that," Presley said.

"Why not?" Eliza questioned.

"Your skirt is too short," Presley replied.

"Sorry, your opinion doesn't matter," Eliza said, shrugging. We watched Eliza leave with Robert.

"Interesting that you think you have a say with someone who dumped you," Pax reminded Presley.

We watched Presley's expression turned to defeat.

"You want someone to care about your opinion. You should care about the other person's opinion," Britt mentioned.

"Yeah," Presley mumbled, going upstairs.

Eliza

I got into Robert's car, and he pulled out of the driveway. We drove and realized that he passed Selena and Josie's dorm.

"Wait. You missed our stop," I mentioned.

"Oh? Did I? I didn't notice," Robert lied.

"Yeah, It's back that way," I said.

"I thought we could have some fun," Robert said with a look that I didn't like.

I pulled out my phone.

"Who are you calling?" Robert questioned.

"Oh, it's my mom. She worries about me," I lied as I made a call.

"Hey, Mom. Yeah, it's me. I'm okay. I'm on a date with Robert, and we're driving down 28th street. Where are we going?" I asked. I looked at Robert. "Where are you taking me?" I asked.

"To someplace private to have a good time," Robert said.

"Oh, my date is taking me to a secluded place. Don't worry; I enjoy nature and a bonfire. Yes, I remember what you said. I promise I remember," I said, hanging up.

I sat in my seat and played with my bracelet. Robert pulled into a secluded area and parked, then locked the doors. I looked at Robert as he looked at me, then he attempted to attack me. I kicked and smacked him, pissing him off, then I nailed him in the balls as someone jiggled the door handle.

Robert grabbed his boys as the person motioned at me, and I shielded my head. The person smashed the car window and reached for me. I grabbed the person's arms as they pulled me out.

I looked up at Presley, who held me.

"I did what you told me," I assured Presley.

"Good girl," Presley said, pulling me to him as I wrapped my arms around him.

I glanced to see Presley's brothers get Robert's car opened and drag Robert out of the car, then beat the hell out of him.

"Piece of shit, sonofabitch," Payton yelled, delivering a swift kick to Robert.

"Presley, take Eliza home," Parker instructed Presley as he took me home.

"Presley, I did what you told me to do," I promised.

"I know," Presley said, comforting me.

Pat

Payton finished unleashing his anger on Robert, then turned to us.

"What were you thinking?" Payton asked.

"That Presley shouldn't treat his girl poorly," Pax answered.

Payton grabbed Pax and smacked him.

"Who's next?" Payton asked Parker and me as Pax rubbed his face.

We stood there, not smiling.

"I told you to stay out of it and look what happened. A girl almost got attacked because someone thought it was a grand idea to plan this," Payton said. He looked at Parker.

"It's not like I thought this asshole would rape someone," Parker snapped.

"No, because that's a smart thing to know," Payton remarked.

"It's not like you agreed with what Presley did to Eliza," I stated.

Payton walked over to me and grabbed my shirt, yanking me to him.

"I would never do what everyone did. I warned Presley, and I'm warning you. Stay out of it," Payton ordered, shoving me away.

Payton stormed off as we stood there.

Presley

I took Eliza home, and she sat in the car, sniffling. I glanced at her as she looked out the car window. We got home. I walked

Eliza inside the house as Britt came downstairs with Selena and Josie.

"Eliza, what happened?" Selena asked, noticing Eliza's disheveled clothes.

"Robert took me to a secluded spot and tried to rape me," Eliza sniffled.

The girls looked at Eliza as I stood there.

"I called Presley and used our signal that he taught me. Then I fought Robert, using what Presley taught me. I didn't know if Presley would show up, but he did. That means he cares about me, doesn't he?" Eliza asked as tears fell down her cheeks.

Eliza looked at me as I looked at her.

"I'm sorry that I broke up with you. Everyone thought it would teach you a lesson," Eliza admitted.

"A lesson about what?" I questioned Eliza.

"That you would treat me better. If I didn't listen, this wouldn't happen. I'm sorry, Presley," Eliza said, walking away and going upstairs.

My brothers came into the house.

"Presley," Payton said.

I felt nothing but anger. I clenched my fists and looked at Payton.

"What?" I snapped.

"How's Eliza?" Payton asked.

"Why do you care? Why do any of you care? To you, I'm a tool, schmuck, ass, and any other name you can think of with me," I snapped.

"That's not true," Payton said.

"Isn't it? You hit me because you thought I was maltreating Eliza," I reminded Payton, who furrowed his brows.

"You all thought I was making time with other girls because that's what you expect. You didn't bother to ask me anything," I told everyone.

"Then fill us in because your actions speak louder than words," Parker said.

"Okay, I met Eliza senior year and worked my ass off to get her to agree to date me. I knew she hesitated because of my reputation, but I never gave her reason to doubt me. When everyone saw me talking to other girls, I asked questions to help Eliza," I explained.

"Do you expect us to believe that?" Pax questioned.

I walked over to Pax. "Do you know what it's like to worry about someone and people hurting the person? Did you know Eliza had a boyfriend that hurt her?" I questioned.

Everyone looked at me, shocked.

"What about homecoming?" Pat asked me.

"A girl made a comment about Eliza, and I confronted her," I answered.

"You can't blame us for thinking the wrong thing, considering how you were acting," Selena told me.

"Because Eliza told me things you and others said to her, making her doubt me. Why would I hurt someone I love?" I questioned.

Everyone was speechless. My family doubted me and my intentions. They never asked, and my girl broke up with me. I walked to the steps and stopped.

"Stop helping. You're making things worse," I mumbled, then went upstairs.

I went into my room and closed my door. I sat on my bed. I didn't realize my family thought so low of me. Yeah, I will admit I get jealous, but I would never hurt Eliza. I saw what Randy did to her in high school. I told no one because Eliza made me promise not to say anything.

Thanks to my family, I lost someone who I love. All I can hope for is that I can fix my friendship with Eliza since we were friends before dating.

CHAPTER 51

FIXING A MESS

Pat

We have to fix a mess that we created. Presley wasn't talking to any of us after what happened. We also filled in Markus, Kaxon, and Mason on what happened and the truth.

"Damn," Mason said as we sat there at the bakery.

"It's not like we knew everything. Look at how Presley acted," Kaxon reasoned.

"Yeah, but it didn't give us the right to interfere," I said.

We sat there and sighed. Yep, we're tools.

Presley

I saw Eliza in the hallway at school and strolled over to her.

"Hey," I greeted Eliza.

"Hey," Eliza said.

"Are you okay?" I asked.

Eliza nodded.

"Did you want to have coffee with me?" I asked.

Eliza looked at me and furrowed her brows.

"You don't have to if you don't want," I mentioned.

"I guess coffee is okay," Eliza said as we went to a coffee shop.

We ordered two coffees, and I paid for it. Eliza refused me to buy her coffee, but I reassured her it was okay. She relented, and we found a table.

"So," Eliza said.

"I'm sorry about what happened," I mentioned, sipping my coffee.

Eliza looked at me.

"I thought if I kept people from making comments, it would help," I explained.

"So, you weren't looking for another girl?" Eliza questioned.

"No," I admitted.

I watched Eliza's expression change.

"I wanted you to hang out with the girls, so you had friends, and people didn't harass you when I wasn't around you. I knew you distrusted people after Randy," I reasoned.

Eliza looked at me.

"I thought you tired of helping me and looked around for someone with confidence," Eliza said.

"Why would you say that?" I asked.

"Because who wants to keep reassuring someone all the time? It's not like I'm pretty or thin. I know people talk about me. You told me to block it out, but it's difficult when you hear people say you're clingy," Eliza answered.

"But you're none of that, and I don't care what people say. You're more than that to me," I reasoned.

Eliza looked at me.

"I know I made mistakes with you. I'm worried that you would walk away from me because I wasn't good enough for you," I admitted.

Eliza looked at me in awe.

"When you carry the last name Gray, it's a lot to live up to with people. If I dated a lot, it would make me stand out from my brothers, but all it did was show me how lonely it is. When we started talking, I could be myself around you. You didn't care if I was imperfect. You cared about me," I confessed.

I looked at Eliza. All I wanted was my girl back. I missed holding her hand and laughing.

"I won't push you. All I want is your friendship. If you meet someone, I hope the guy makes you happy," I said.

Thanks to my family, I lost the one good thing in my life all because they didn't talk to me. Now I hoped to salvage my friendship with Eliza.

Pat

We sat around the living room, figuring out how to fix this mess. We heard a knock on the door as Payton got up to answer it. We all got up and walked to the door to see Grandpa and our uncles stand there. They came inside the house.

"When we created this plan, you left out a few details," Nixon said with a look.

"Didn't anyone tell you to leave the matchmaking to the pros?" Nathan asked.

"If we can get this tool together with your nana, we can do anything," Noah mentioned. He pointed at Grandpa, who shot Noah a look.

"Sometimes the Gray way works best," Nolan smirked.

"And sometimes family matters," Grandpa added.

My brothers and I looked at each other. What did they have planned?

Presley

I came home to find Grandpa and my uncles here.

"Is everything okay? Is Grampa Nate okay?" I asked with concern.

"Your Grampa is fine, but it seems we have a slight issue," Grandpa said.

I looked at Grandpa and my uncles with confusion.

"It seems a little birdy told us the entire situation about you and your girl. We came to help," Nixon said.

I know it's not my family, considering they created this mess.

"That's why we will help you get your girl back," Nathan mentioned.

"Yep," Noah agreed.

"Don't screw it up," Nolan reminded me.

I have my reservations about this plan because someone gets kidnapped.

Eliza

I came home and went to my bedroom. I started working on homework when someone knocked on the door. I looked up to see Markus standing there.

"Do you want to see a movie?" He asked me.

I looked at Markus.

"Don't you have a boyfriend?" I questioned.

"Eh, I'm mad at Hayden. I saw him flirting with another guy. I thought I would switch teams," Markus mentioned, shrugging.

I didn't know what to say to that.

"Our nephew is an idiot," Nixon whispered.

"We blame Nash," Nathan whispered, earning a look from Nash.

"Damn, you all suck at this," Nolan whispered.

I stood up as Nolan appeared in the doorway.

"Go out with Markus and cheer his stupid ass up," Nolan mentioned.

Markus rolled his eyes.

"Why?" I asked with confusion.

"Because Markus feels upset. It's not that complicated, sweetheart," Nolan said, pulling out his wallet. He pulled money from it and shoved it at Markus. "Here, movie and concessions are on me. Now go."

I left the bedroom and followed Markus down the stairs. I thought someone watched us and glanced as I saw Nolan smiling and waving. Okay, Presley has a strange family.

Presley

"Okay, Markus and Eliza left," Nolan said as I stuck my head out of my bedroom along with Grandpa and my uncles.

We left my bedroom as we followed Markus and Eliza to the movie theater. I let my jealousy get the best of me when I saw Markus close to Eliza and started charging towards them. Nathan and Noah grabbed me as Markus and Eliza turned. They dragged me behind a poster board.

Grandpa, Nixon, and Nolan darted out of sight as they turned back around to get concessions.

"Chill, you tool," Nathan ordered.

"Why are the devil twins easier to deal with than this one?" Noah asked.

"Because Presley got most of Nash's idiot genes," Nathan answered.

"That explains so much," Noah said.

We peered around the poster board, watching Markus and Eliza walked into a movie theater. We made our way to the theater until security caught us. Grandpa walked over to the admissions booth and bought six tickets. He gave the tickets to the employee and went to the theater until Nolan went to get refreshments.

Nixon walked over to Nolan. "What are you doing?" Nixon asked.

"Getting popcorn," Nolan answered.

"Ooh, I want nachos," Nathan said, joining them.

"As you need any more nachos," Nixon remarked.

"I'll take a pretzel," Noah ordered.

"Are you kidding me?" Grandpa asked my uncles.

"Give me some junior mints and cookies," Nixon ordered.

"Are you tools finished?" Grandpa asked.

"Yeah, you buy the drinks," Noah answered.

"Give me six pops," Grandpa ordered.

I went into the theater and found a seat a few rows back. Grandpa and my uncles walked into the theater, arguing as I sunk in my place and hid my face. Eliza saw them as Markus look up and shook his head.

"What are you looking at, sweetheart? Turn around and face the screen," Nixon ordered Eliza.

"What are you doing?" Eliza asked.

"Going to the dark side because we got cookies," Nathan answered.

Eliza looked at them with confusion.

"We came to see a movie, do you mind?" Noah asked.

"Nothing to see here. Focus on the screen," Nolan said as they sat down in a seat next to me. I hid my face as Eliza turned around to face the screen.

If we survive this plan, it will shock me.

The movie started playing. Halfway through the film, Markus and I got up, switching seats.

"Did you find the bathroom?" Eliza asked.

"Yeah, it's not that difficult next to the entrance," I whispered as Eliza looked and did a double-take. I held up a bag. "Popcorn?"

Eliza smiled and took a handful of popcorn. We settled into our seats and finished the movie. After the video ended, we got up and started leaving the theater. I gave Grandpa and my uncles a signal.

"Phase one finished, now onto phase two," Nixon said as they got up and followed us.

We left the theater, and Eliza looked around outside.

"Is something wrong?" I asked.

"Markus brought me to the movies, but I can't find him," Eliza answered, looking at me.

"I can give you a ride home since I'm headed there," I offered.

"Are you sure?" Eliza asked.

"Yeah, it makes sense," I answered.

Eliza agreed, and we got into the car. I drove back to the house as I saw red and blue lights behind me. I pulled over as I sat there. I looked at Eliza.

"Give me a minute," I said.

Someone knocked on the window, and I unrolled it as the person shined a light into my eyes. I held up my hand, shielding my eyes.

"Step out of the car, sir," the person said.

"Is something wrong, officer?" I asked.

"Step out of the car," the person ordered.

I got out of the car, and the person shoved me up against it as they frisked me. Eliza got out of the car and made her way over to us.

"What's happening?" Eliza asked.

"Ma'am, we need you to sit back in the car while we handle this suspect," the guy said.

"Suspect? What suspect?" Eliza questioned, raising her voice.

"We suspect this person of illegal activities," another guy said. "Isn't that right, dirtbag?"

"What activities? Presley, what do the police officers mean?" Eliza asked me.

"It's nothing but a misunderstanding," I grunted.

"Oh, you don't let this lothario fool you. We know this perp is doing shady shit," the officer who held me said, holding me against the car.

"What?" Eliza asked, confused.

"Should we tell this young lady or you?" The second officer asked.

"No, I will tell Eliza," I answered, sighing.

The cop let me go, and I turned to Eliza. She looked at me with concern.

"I have a confession, and it will get me ten to twenty, or longer," I said.

Eliza's eyes widened. I took her hands in my hands.

"I'm in love with you, and I hoped you would give me a second chance," I said with sincerity.

"What?" Eliza asked, stunned.

Someone tapped Eliza on the shoulder. She looked to see Grandpa, my uncles, and Markus standing there.

"Presley is asking for a second chance," Nolan answered with a smile.

Eliza looked at me. The officers removed their disguises, revealing Major and Maverick.

"Who are they?" Eliza asked.

"That's Uncle Major and Uncle Maverick, Mason and Markus's dads," I answered, surprising Eliza.

I looked at Eliza.

"I like this plan a lot better than your brothers and cousins," Eliza said, smiling.

I leaned down and kissed Eliza as she kissed me back.

"And our work's done here," Nixon mentioned, smirking.

Sometimes you need the experts to help you over the amateurs. No one will match Grandpa and my uncles in matchmaking and not screw it up completely.

CHAPTER 52

LOST AT THE APPLE ORCHARD

Pat

After the situation with Presley and Eliza, our grandpa and uncles talked to us. They told us to stay out of Presley's relationship. In their words, "They're too old for this shit." Pops never gets involved with our love lives, only us when we screw up.

Since it's autumn in Michigan, we have a trip to the apple orchard, which has a fall festival. What is with our state having carnivals in the fall? I prefer amusement parks when it's warm.

The group of us went to an Apple orchard and got out of the cars. That's when everyone split off from each other. We usually meet up after climbing trees. There are signs everywhere that say no climbing the trees. We never listen.

Britt and I went into the building and looked around at the items for sale. Let's see; you have apple pie, apple cider, cookies, donuts, apples, apple butter, and more apples. I picked up apples, looked at them, then set them back in their bins.

"What is your brother doing?" Britt asked.

I turned to see Pax plastered against the glass of the area the people are making donuts.

"Pax loves donuts. Pops had to peel him off of the glass," I answered, making Britt laughed.

I shook my head as I looked around inside the building. Kaxon found me near the cider.

"Dude, the place has a corn maze," Kaxon mentioned.

"You hate corn mazes," I reminded Kaxon, raising an eyebrow.

"It's different now that I have a girl. If I get lost, we can make out," Kaxon said, grinning.

"You have no shame," I replied.

"No shame," Kaxon agree, moving his hand in front of him.

"Who's all going to the maze?" I questioned, picking up a jar of apple butter.

"Mason, Skylar, Pax, Shaun, and Jesse," Kaxon answered.

I put the jar back on the shelf. "You remember Pax hates mazes," I mentioned.

"We all hate corn mazes because our parents used to take us to a spot and leave us there to find our way out. So not cool to do to four-year-olds," Kaxon said.

"I thought Nixon would hurt your dad for that stunt," I chuckled.

"Well, Grandpa did and then bought me donuts, hopping me up on sugar," Kaxon grinned.

"Donuts, which you can't eat because it makes your blood sugar loopy," I reminded Kaxon.

"I can have donuts, but not a lot," Kaxon told me, shrugging.

"Between you and Pax, you make mealtime so much fun," I mentioned.

Kaxon rolled his eyes while shaking his head. Paxton has a gluten allergy, and Kaxon is a diabetic. We don't make a big deal about it since our parents taught them how to handle their situations. Mason is a picky eater, and I prefer not to eat junk. Birthdays and holidays are fun at our houses.

Kaxon looked at his watch. "Before we do anything, I need to test my blood and eat before my old man has my balls in a vice grip," Kaxon said. He left the building.

Pax walked over to me after Shaun pulled him off the glass. "Where's Kaxon going?" Pax asked.

"To test his blood and eat," I answered. "I see Shaun peeled you off of the glass."

"Yeah, which sucks because I want donuts," Pax said.

"I'm sure the place has gluten-free since most places offer it. People having an allergy or Celiac's disease," I reasoned.

Pax gave me a knowing look and pivot, walking to the counter. Yep, my brother is a goner with donuts if they're gluten-free. I will never see him again. Britt looked at different apples when Kaxon returned, and someone threw an apple at him.

We looked as Jesse smirked. I roared with laughter as Britt giggled. Pax walked over, eating a donut.

"What's funny?" Pax asked, eating his donut.

"Jesse smacked Kaxon with an apple. I see the cider mill has gluten-free donuts," I mentioned.

"Yes, and the donuts are delicious," Pax comment, shoving the donut into his mouth.

"Hey, losers! We're going to the corn maze," Parker announced, sticking his head in the doorway.

I rolled my eyes as Kaxon chased Jesse out of the cider mill. Pax ate another donut, leaving the cider mill. If it wasn't for Pax's allergy, I'm sure he would be five hundred pounds with all the donuts he eats. Did you ever see that chick on Charlie and the Chocolate Factory that turned into a blueberry? It's the same concept.

We made our way to the corn maze and entered it. Everything is fine. Britt and I walked through the maze until she veered off into another opening.

"What do you think?" I asked, looking to see Britt gone. I looked around the maze and went hunting. How the hell do you lose someone in a corn maze? Dumb luck, I guess.

I searched for different paths, coming to a dead end. I turned and went in another direction as I ran, turning my head and slamming into Kaxon. We went tumbling onto the ground as Parker and Markus roared with laughter.

"Get off of me," I said, shoving Kaxon off of me.

"No offense, but I prefer someone with boobs," Kaxon replied as we got to our feet and chased after Parker and Markus.

During our chase, we crashed into Pax, causing the three of us to fall to the ground. Mason stepped over us, waking in a different direction. We got up and split up as I went searching for Britt. I saw a girl and ran over to her.

I grabbed the girl's arm. "There you are," I said. The girl looked at me, confused, as the guy with her swung at me. I ducked, and he hit the girl. "Oops, my bad," I said, standing up.

The girl held her face as the guy chased after me. I ran, darting into another opening. I glanced to see the guy chasing me, then crashed into Mason. The guy reached us as Mason grabbed his leg and tripped him. We got up and ran.

The guy got to his feet and chased us as we slid into other people, knocking them down. That pissed off the people we crashed into in the corn maze. We got to our feet as the guys took a swung at us. Mason and I ducked, and the guys hit the guy chasing us.

Mason and I looked at each other as the guy who got hit charged the others. The next thing I know, a brawl broke out in the corn maze. Pax and Kaxon found us and lent us a hand. A girl jumped on Pax's back, and he tossed her into corn stalks.

Another girl went after me, smacking me. I shoved the girl back, making her fall on her ass.

"Stay doggy," I ordered.

"A little help here," Kaxon yelled as he had a girl on his back, smacking his head.

Pax and I helped pull the girl off Kaxon as another girl hit Mason with her purse. Mason clocked the girl as we stopped and looked at him.

"Hey, if a girl wants to hit a guy, then she gets what she deserves," Mason reasoned.

Yeah, we're Grays and don't discriminate. If you hit us, prepare for us to defend ourselves. I guess their dates didn't see it our way and chased after us.

"We need to get the hell of this damn maze," Pax yelled.

"No shit," I yelled as we ran.

This is the reason the four of us hate corn mazes. We get lost and have people chasing us. We made it to the exit. Our brothers and cousins were waiting for us, along with Shaun and the girls. They saw the group chasing us and helped us out a bit. After a few minutes, the group was lying on the ground, and we walked away from that stupid corn maze.

The next time Kaxon mentions a corn maze, I will strip his clothes off and shove him in one naked. We walked back to the cars, and Shaun opened the car door, grabbing some bags. He tossed a packet to each of us, including Pax. Payton walked past Kaxon and grabbed his bag.

"Oh, come on!" Kaxon yelled.

"No, your old man will have my ass if your sugar lands you in the hospital," Payton told Kaxon.

"Here, have a pickle," Markus said, handing Kaxon a pickle.

Kaxon took the pickle and tossed it away. Yeah, pickles aren't one of Kaxon's favorite foods. Parker bought a sandwich and handed it to Kaxon.

We're asses, but we take care of the family.

"Ah, man, this bag has cinnamon sugar donuts," Mason whined, looking into his bag.

I looked in my bag and switched with Mason. I prefer cinnamon sugar donuts over the plain. I handed a donut to Britt, and she took it, taking a bite out of it.

"Well, we got apples to make a pie," Payton mentioned.

"Look at you, Betty Crocker," Markus commented to Payton, who rolled his eyes.

We laughed. We finished our treats, then Pax, Kaxon, Mason, and I chased each other as the others watched us, smiling.

"It reminds me of when they were younger," Payton mentioned.

"Yeah, those four are still a pain in the ass," Parker remarked as Payton chuckled.

Separate, we were okay, but together the four of us were forces of nature. People say that your first friends are your siblings and cousins. It's true because family is everything, and family matters.

CHAPTER 53

A FORCES OF NATURE ON HALLOWEEN

Pat

Pax and I are alike because we're twins, but we differ in tastes. Pax hates holidays, and I love them. Kaxon likes holidays to see how many treats he can get, even though he can't have them. Mason prefers Halloween over any holiday.

Jesse suggested we check out this old, abandoned asylum on the outskirts of town. I'm down for it, but Pax opted out. He hung with Shaun and watch It's The Great Pumpkin, Charlie Brown, wuss.

Kaxon, Jesse, Mason, Skylar, Britt, and I explored the old nuthouse. Since my family is crazy, it made sense to check out where they originated from in the past. I'm sure Grammy Gray lived in one at some point, considering everyone mentioned she was bat shit crazy.

We got into the car, and Jesse drove to the abandoned asylum. She pulled up to the building, and we got out of the vehicle.

"Okay, there's nothing creepy about this," Kaxon mentioned. He looked at the dilapidated building.

"It's cool," Mason said, staring at it.

"You would since you find the stupidest shit cool," Kaxon remarked.

I chuckled.

"Well, no time like the present," Jesse said to us.

"Shouldn't you say that when you're making out with me, not smacking my hands away?" Kaxon questioned.

"Listen, you horny toad, no girl enjoys a guy groping them all the time," Jesse countered.

"I wouldn't mind if a guy groped me," Skylar mentioned.

We all looked at Skylar strangely.

"If someone were to grope me, I wouldn't object," Skylar reiterates, looking at Mason. Mason was busy checking out the asylum.

Kaxon walked over to Skylar. "Yeah, you're barking up the wrong tree. That dude is oblivious with chicks," Kaxon informed Skylar.

Skylar looked at Britt and me. We nodded. Jesse grabbed Kaxon's arm and dragged him to the asylum.

"Tell my parents I'm sorry for anything I ever did. I didn't mean to put the spicy sauce in Dad's underwear and blame Pat," Kaxon yelled.

I did a double-take. "Wait. Pops beat my ass for that stunt," I exclaimed, running after Kaxon.

Kaxon got loose from Jesse and took off towards the insane asylum, entering the building. Kaxon stopped, and I crashed into him, making us fall to the ground.

"Ugh," Kaxon grumbled, and we got up. Kaxon dusted himself off and wiped his hands on me. I smacked him. Neither of us likes to get dirty and prefer neatness over messy surroundings. Yeah, we're an oxymoron.

The others entered and looked around the place.

"This is cool," Mason commented.

Kaxon and I looked at Mason and rolled our eyes.

"Why don't we split up and meet back here?" Jesse suggested.

"Are you crazy? What if someone attacks us?" Kaxon asked.

"Like who? Oh, hey, Mr. Ghost, would you attack my idiot boyfriend," Jesse retorted with a look.

"No need for an attitude, but that's nothing new," Kaxon remarked.

Jesse rolled her eyes and dragged Kaxon away from us. Mason and Skylar went in a different direction, exploring the building. Britt and I walked down the main hallway, looking into rooms, finding items left behind from the staff.

"It seems sad," Britt mentioned.

"What does?" I asked as we walked.

"A long time ago, people lived here, knowing this place as their home. Can you imagine your family putting you in place like this?" Britt asked me.

"I don't think my family would allow it. Remember, years ago, the doctors didn't have the advancement in science that they have now," I reasoned.

Britt looked at me as we walked and found a stairway. We walked up the stairs until we reached another floor.

"Doesn't it worry you it's a possibility?" Britt questioned me.

I looked at Britt. "No, because I know my family. We have our issues, but we would never abandon each other. The people who lived here didn't have a choice. Their families didn't know how to care for them and used this as a last resort," I explained.

We went into a room and looked at the empty room, which held a bed frame along with toys. I picked up a doll and looked at it. Britt picked up a dirty teddy bear. Knowing that people lived here, including children, left you with a feeling of sadness.

"Hey! What are you both doing here?" Someone yelled.

We turned to see a security guard shining a flashlight at us. We dropped the stuff, and I grabbed Britt's hand as we started running. The security guard chased us while yelling.

We ran through the hallways as someone stepped into our view, making us come to a screeching halt.

"You're on your own," the security guard yelled, running in a different direction.

We stood there as the person stood there wearing a Michael Myers mask and coveralls. The person raised their hand, holding a butcher knife. Our eyes widened as we spun and ran. The person walked behind us as we ran.

We reached the end of the hallway as someone stepped out into view dressed as Leatherface and a chainsaw. What the fuck? The person started the chainsaw and started running towards us as we took off running.

We found another stairway and ran down the stairs, reaching the bottom step. We ran down the hallway as someone stepped in front of us dressed as Jason Voorhees with a machete. Britt screamed as the person started walking towards us; we turned and ran.

We met up with Kaxon and Mason without Jesse and Skylar.

"What the hell is going on in here?" Kaxon yelled.

"Beats the hell out of me!" I yelled back.

"Hey, kids, do you want a balloon?" We heard someone say in a creepy voice. We turned to see Pennywise standing there, holding a red balloon.

"Oh, hell, no," Mason screamed.

The four of us stood there with our backs to each other. Pennywise, Leatherface, Michael Myers, and Jason Voorhees walked towards us.

"I'm too young to die a virgin!" Kaxon yelled.

We looked at Kaxon weird.

"Well, dying a virgin will suck ass," Kaxon told us.

"Worry about your lack of sexual experiences later," Mason snapped.

"I told you not to act so damn picky," I shouted.

The horror characters swung at us as we screamed, covering our heads, then we heard laughing. We lowered our arms and opened our eyes as the four of them roared. What the hell?

"Damn, I miss scaring the shit out of people," Michael Myers said, removing his mask.

"That was awesome," Jason chuckled, lifting his hockey mask.

Leatherface and Pennywise removed their masks, revealing two other guys who confused me. I didn't recognize them. We heard laughter as Jesse and Skylar came into view, clapping.

"What the hell?" Kaxon asked, confused. He wasn't the only one.

"Kaxon, Mason, Pat, and Britt, let me introduce you to my family. Mason and Kaxon meet my Uncle Liam, dressed as Michael Myers. Uncle Elijah dressed as Jason Voorhees. Cousin

Austin is Leatherface. Cousin RJ is Pennywise," Jesse introduced us to her uncles and cousins. They bowed as we heard clapping.

We turned to see our family and Jesse and Skylar's family standing there, clapping and cheering. I saw my brothers, including Pax, laughing.

"You guys suck," I grumbled, grabbing Britt's hand as we all walked towards everyone. The group of us went to another room, everyone decorated with Halloween decorations. Music started playing as people talked. Tables had food on them, along with beverages. I spoke to some people as Parker walked over to the DJ and made a request.

The DJ nodded and put on Michael Jackson's Thriller. Parker waved to us. We walked over and started dancing to the music. We recreated the moves while the video played behind us.

Payton, Parker, Markus, Pax, Kaxon, Mason, Presley, and I danced to the song as people watched. We slid across the dance floor, keeping step with each other. After the song finished, we paused as people clapped and whistled.

We smiled and hugged each other, giving each other high fives. The DJ put on Halloween music as we all danced, enjoying the night with each other.

After the party, we went home. I walked into the house and sat down on the couch. My brothers and the others found a spot and sat down.

"Man, see the look on your face," Parker laughed.

"That was a dirty trick," I said as my brothers laughed. I shook my head and rolled my eyes.

"Does your family do this a lot?" Britt asked Jesse and Skylar.

"Every Halloween. Uncle Liam and Dad started hosting haunted houses to have fun. They raised money for Grandpa's foundation, helping sexual assault victims," Jesse explained.

We looked at Jesse with surprise.

"Nana experienced sexual assault as a teen, along with some family members. My family felt every person who experienced sexual assault deserves help. The foundation provides counseling, support, and understanding, which every victim requires," Jesse explained.

We sat there, thinking about what Jesse said. With Shaun experiencing sexual assault, we knew how close this hit home for us.

I looked at Markus, who sat there along with Shaun.

"People sexually assaulted both of my parents," Markus said as we looked at him.

We looked at Markus, stunned. Markus got up and left the room. Payton went after him. He found Markus leaning against the countertop, rubbing his forehead.

"Markus," Payton said.

"I don't understand how someone can do that to another person. What kind of animal does that?" Markus asked Payton as his voice cracked.

"An animal," Payton said as Markus cried.

We watched as Payton comforted Markus.

"Markus," Payton said, pulling back. Markus looked at Payton with tear-streaked cheeks. "No matter what, it doesn't change how your parents feel about you. Uncle Maverick and Aunt Larkin didn't let this defeat them; don't let it defeat you."

Markus nodded as Payton hugged him.

"Love you, cuz," Payton said as Markus nodded.

My brother might be a lot of things. With family, he feels the same with us as our grandparents and parents do about our family. We fight and give each other a hard time, but there isn't anything that Payton wouldn't do for any of us. Family matters to Payton, along with the rest of us.

CHAPTER 54

CRAZY IS AS CRAZY DOES

Pat

Britt and I walked into class and sat down in our seats as our students came into class. The professor walked in and started writing on the magic erase board.

"Social diversity," the professor announced, turning to face the class. "What is social diversity, and how does it factor into a story? Glad that you asked."

We laughed.

"Social diversity is a classification of different ethnic and racial backgrounds. You are of a distinct race and have a different ethnic background. The definition of race is different physical characteristics that a person inherits. Observable traits of skin color, cranial features, or type of hair," the professor explained.

"You two students, please stand," the professor said as two classmates stood up. "As you can see, both people have distinct features. Will you please stand?" The professor asked, pointing to another classmate. "These two people have similar visual features. You three can sit, thank you."

The classmates sat down in their seats.

"Some writers stick to what they're familiar with when writing characters. It's what we refer to as our comfort zone. As a creative writer, branch out and write about distinct characters. It makes your writing diverse, but it enriches your story. No one says you should make particular races one way. That's a stigma which we will drop," the professor explained.

"But most media displays certain races a particular way," one classmate mentioned.

"That's true, but who do you believe, the media or what you see with your eyes? How many of you assume that people of Asian descent are rich?" The professor asked.

Most of the class raised their hands.

"Okay, how many assumed that people of color come from poverty?" The professor asked.

A third of the class raised their hands.

"What if I told you that my mother is a person of color, and my father is Asian, but we came from the states?" The professor asked, surprising us. "My father and mother are both teachers, and I have a sister who owns a shop. It's a myth life destines you to particular occupations or geographical location. Your assignment is to create a character. You'll destroy the perception of a race or ethnic background. You have all the class hour to work on it."

I started writing, creating a character, and describing the person. I spent most of the class on the paper, and at the end, of the course, we handed in our assignments.

"Mr. Gray," the professor said, making me stop.

I walked over to the professor.

"I read some of your assignments," the professor mentioned.

I looked at the teacher.

"What I find unique about your writing is that it shows us a human aspect to it," the professor said.

"Is that bad?" I asked, unsure about my writing.

"No, it's good. It shows you care about people and makes people enjoy the characters. Most writers fret over details, forgetting one important detail," the professor mentioned.

"What's that?" I asked.

"Why should a reader care about this person? What makes them human? As a writer, it's our job to make our reader fall in love with a character. It's not their description," the professor answered.

"What's a better way to make people fall in love with a character? Write about people who you love," I reasoned.

The professor smiled as I left the classroom. While my family is crazy and does crazy shit, we don't look at people other than the person's content of character. If someone's an asshole, it doesn't matter their race, ethnic background, or any characteristic. They're an asshole.

"What did Mr. Chin want?" Britt asked.

"He wanted to know how I captured the essence of my characters," I replied.

"And?" Britt questioned.

"I write about people who I love. What better way to immortalize someone than creating a character who everyone loves? That gives me an idea," I mentioned as Britt looked at me with curiosity.

I made a call and asked someone for a favor. I explained my reason, and the person thought it was a great idea. I got off the phone, and we went to our next class. I couldn't wait to work on our last paper.

Britt and I were working on math when we heard a knock at the door. I set my books down and got up to answer the door.

"Hey, Grammy," I said, hugging Grammy Pat.

"Hey, Patton. Where are your brothers?" Grammy asked, walking into the house.

"Payton and Parker have class, Pax is working, and Presley is at the library with Eliza," I answered.

Grammy walked over to a chair, carrying a bag. She sat down and rifled through the bag, pulling out some books. She handed the books to me as I took them. I opened the books up and skimmed the pages.

"What is that?" Britt asked, looking at the books with me.

"These are Lucille's journals," Grammy answered. "We didn't know that Lucille kept a written history of her life, including the family. We went through her personal effects after she passed away."

"This book talks about Grandpa Grayson. This one talks about you and Grampa," I mentioned, flipping through the books.

"Oh, my god," Britt exclaimed, laughing.

"What?" I asked.

Britt handed me the book, and I read it, then laughed. She wrote about when she electrocuted Grampa. We read through the journals and laughed.

"Did Grampa pet Uncle Jonas?" I asked Grammy.

"Yep, and then your grandpa smacked your Grammy Gray when she told him to stop," Grammy answered.

We laughed.

"The thing about Lucille is she was one in a million. People assumed she was crazy, but she wasn't. Lucille enjoyed life, and that drove everyone else crazy," Grammy explained.

I got to a part and read it.

Today Nathaniel is marrying Patty. I never thought that boy would settle down, but I knew Patty would make it happen. Nathaniel needs someone like Patty to take care of him. Heaven knows if I left it up to Nathaniel, he would marry some damn floozy.

My boys aren't the brightest bulb in the pack, but this decision is smart. I knew Patty would keep Nathaniel in the strait and narrow. The girl is intelligent and has her head on straight. They remind me of Gray and me. Let's hope Nathaniel doesn't make the same mistake that Gray did with that hussy and cost him, Patty. Gray was damn lucky when I showed up, or the boys wouldn't be here.

Men are infallible people and act like tools. It's our job as women to show our men the error of their ways. I did it with Gray, and Patty will do it with Nathaniel, plus I got a daughter finally. That damn Gray.

I looked at Grammy Pat, who smiled.

"How did Grammy know you and Grampa belonged together?" I asked.

"Because Lucille saw our friendship. There was a time when your Grampa and I weren't friends. It was a misunderstanding between us before we cleared up. I learned love comes with friendship, and Nate is my best friend," Grammy explained.

Payton and Parker came into the house and hugged Grammy. Grammy had me call the others so she could see them before she went home. The others showed up and hugged Grammy. Who doesn't love Grammy Pat?

We visited with Grammy for a while, then her phone rang. She answered it.

"Whoa, calm down, Jonas. What happened?" Grammy asked as she listened. "Oh, my," Grammy said, stunned. "It will be okay, I promise."

Grammy hung up as we looked at her. She made a call, and someone answered.

Patty? Is everything okay?

"Jonas called me. They rushed Karen to the hospital," Grammy said.

How's Karen?

"Karen passed away, and Jonas feels devastated," Grammy answered.

I will give my brother a call. When are you coming home, Betty Crocker?

"I'm leaving in an hour, and I'm bringing company," Grammy said as we looked at each other. Grammy got off the phone and looked at us. "I want you boys to pack and get Paxton. We have to return home."

We didn't argue as Payton and Parker went to get Paxton while the rest of us went to pack a bag. I didn't know my Grampa's brothers well since they lived in different states. As a family, when one hurt, the others pulled together.

As I packed a bag, I thought about what Grammy Gray wrote. The one thing I understood is she enjoyed life and saw it with a realistic view. Grammy Gray lived the same way that she loved. She did it without fear. If you can live like that, then you know life. I couldn't wait to write my paper with Britt.

CHAPTER 55

GOING HOME

Pat

We returned home with Grammy. I'm not a big fan of funerals, but I understand why you have one. Funerals give people a chance to find closure. It doesn't make the person feel better but lets them say goodbye.

We got home and hugged Ma. Pops was at Grandpa and Nana's house, helping them get ready for the family to stay with our grandparents. I hope I never attend a funeral for a long time, but it will dash that hope.

Patty

I walked into the house to find Nate and Cayson on the couch, talking. I walked over and kissed Nate. He kissed me back, then whispered in my ear, "Don't you leave me, Betty Crocker."

I pulled back and smiled. "Grease, Monkey, I plan to stick around for a long time," I whispered, then winked.

"Jonas is planning with Jace and Jamie to bring Karen home," Cayson informed me.

"Those boys must be so heartbroken," I said, sitting down on the coffee table.

"It's the same way when we lost Ma," Cayson said.

"Okay, the rooms are ready," Nash mentioned, coming downstairs with Maggie and Lex.

"What did your brothers say?" I asked Nash.

"Jonas and Jace, along with Jace's family, are staying here with the girls and husbands. Jaime and his family are staying with Nixon and along with Frick and Frack. The triplets are staying with Nathan and Noah. Nolan is taking in stragglers," Nash answered.

"Nashville, those stragglers who you're calling is family," I told Nash.

"Ma, this family has more strays than we can count," Nash said.

I rolled my eyes: my son, the comedian. I swear Nixon is rubbing off on Nash. A few minutes later, Nixon came in with Kat.

"Don't you have a home?" Nash asked Nixon.

"Why, yes, I do, and it's a lovely home," Nixon answered.

I swear my boys are something else.

"When are the strays coming into town?" Nixon asked.

Nash chuckled as I shook my head while Nate and Cayson chuckled.

"You got to love family," Cayson remarked.

"That's debatable," Nate said.

I looked at Nixon and Nash. "I want you both to pick up your Uncle Jonas," I said.

"Why us?" Nixon questioned.

"Because I said so, and Nixon Richard, you don't argue with me. I'm not in the mood for your shenanigans," I answered with a look. Nixon groaned.

Nash chuckled. "Ma called you by your first and middle name," Nash snickered.

"That goes for you too, Nashville Nathaniel," I told Nash. Nash rolled his eyes as Nixon laughed. Nash and Nixon left to check on the grandkids.

"Those boys never changed," Nate sighed.

"Neither did you and your brothers," I reminded Nate.

"That is true. We're still the lovable people we have always been," Cayson said.

"That's debatable," I replied as Cayson rolled his eyes.

It would be a long few days with everyone returning for the funeral. I know most of the family didn't like Karen, but Jonas loved her. People need to remember that every relationship is different. What happens between a couple is their business.

Maggie and Kat helped me make Nate and Cayson a meal, then they watched a show about cars on TV. I smiled, knowing Nate will always be my grease monkey. I'm glad that Beau opened a mechanic shop, and Matthew went to work with him. I had to keep Nate from sneaking off to work on cars with the boys.

I went into my bedroom and opened a closet door, then reached, pulling a photo album down. After closing the door, I sat on the bed and flipped through the pages. Maggie and Kat walked into the room.

"What are you looking at, Pat?" Maggie asked me.

"Photos of the family," I said, looking up at the girls.

They joined me as we looked through the photo album.

"That picture was when I was four years old and told everyone that Nate was my boyfriend," I said. I pointed to a picture of Nate and me. "This photo is Nate working on a model car. Lucille said he would spend hours working on them. I broke one when I was younger, and Nate got so angry."

"It sounds like you and Nate went through a lot," Maggie mentioned, looking at pictures with Kat.

"We did, but it helps when you grow up together as I did with Nate and his brothers," I reasoned.

"Wasn't it weird having so many boys around you?" Kat asked me.

"Well, I had my mom, Lucille, and Liz, to help me. I knew that if I needed anything, I could go to them or my dad, brother, or Nate and his brothers. People don't understand when you grow up with people; you become family. That's what happened with the Grays and me," I explained.

We flipped through photographs, and I explained who was in the picture and what happened. We laughed as I reminisced with Maggie and Kat. It was incredible to remember everything that happened over the years.

"Oh, my god, look at Nixon on a bearskin rug," Kat squealed, and we laughed.

"Look at Nathan and Noah in the tub," Maggie exclaimed, laughing.

"Here is a picture of Nash with flour all over him. He wanted to help me bake cookies," I said as we laughed.

"I remember this," Maggie said, pointing to a picture of the kids eating ice cream together in the kitchen. "Nash said I was a princess because Nate told him that princesses wear dresses."

I smiled, remembering that moment. I knew then that Nash liked Maggie. We looked at photographs; then people started arriving in town. It will be a long few days for Jonas and his boys to say goodbye to Karen.

Nash

Nixon and I went to pick up Uncle Jonas at the airport. We made our way to the area that Jonas was in and stood there. Uncle Jonas came walking off the plane and hugged us.

"We're sorry to hear about Aunt Karen," I said.

"Yeah," Jonas said as we walked to another section of the airport.

We stood with the funeral director as the employees delivered the casket to Uncle Jonas. I never thought that watching this would be difficult.

"Mr. Gray, we'll take your wife to the funeral home and prepare for visitation. You have our deepest sympathies," the funeral director offered to Uncle Jonas.

Jonas nodded. The funeral director and another man took the casket. Uncle Jonas stood there, watching them take Aunt Karen.

"Nixon, I'm wondering if you would conduct the services for us?" Jonas asked Nix.

"It will be my honor, Uncle Jonas," Nix said without hesitation.

Uncle Jonas looked at us. "Thank you," he said as we nodded.

We walked with Jonas out to the car. Aunt Karen had her moments, but our uncle loved her. I drove us back to my house. We came inside to find the girls there, along with others. Dad and Uncle Cayson met us at the front door.

"Nate," Jonas said, his voice cracking.

"I know, little brother," Dad said, pulling Jonas into a hug. Cayson hugged Jonas next; then Ma looked at Jonas as he cried. She didn't hesitate to hug and comfort him.

Mags got my attention as I turned to see Jace and Jamie standing there. We turned as they came into the house with their families. My brothers and I, along with the triplets, hugged Jace and Jaime.

"Nixon, my mom's gone," Jaime cried as Nixon hugged him.

"I know, Jaime," Nix comforted Jaime.

"How are you doing, honey?" Ma asked Jace.

"You know," Jace said, his voice cracking as he cried. Ma hugged Jace and Jaime. They held onto Ma and cried.

Sometimes you need your mom, and Jace and Jamie needed their mom. Ma was the next best thing for them. After comforting Jonas and his family, Nixon took Jaime and his family to his house. Jace and his family stayed with Nathan, while Jonas stayed at my home.

It would be a long few days with the visitation and funeral. Mags and I left Ma and Dad with his brothers. They needed this time together.

Patty

I brought Jonas some tea.

"I don't understand. Everything was okay. Then Karen complained of chest pains. We went to the hospital, and the doctor said it was heartburn. He gave her medication and sent her home. Why didn't they keep my wife?" Jonas questioned.

"Because that doctor was a quack," Cayson said.

"Cayson," Nate said with a look.

"Nate, that hospital sent Karen home, assuming it's something simple," Cayson argued.

Nate and Cayson started arguing as Jonas sat there. I sat down in front of Jonas. I reached and held Jonas's hands.

"Remember when you rescued me from Brian Holloway in the grocery store?" I asked.

Nate and Cayson quit arguing. Jonas looked at me.

"You risked humiliation, so I didn't deal with it because that's the guy you are, Jonas," I reasoned. "You do the right thing, even when people questioned it. When Karen got pregnant, you could have walked away from her, but you didn't. Do you know why?" I asked.

Jonas looked at me with red eyes.

"Because you loved Karen as Nate loves me, and Cayson loved Dominique. Lucille wanted you boys happy and knew it would take someone unique to do that," I reasoned.

"Karen and I planned to move back home to be closer to the family," Jonas mentioned.

"Then why not move in with us?" I suggested.

"I can't do that to Nash and Maggie," Jonas answered.

"Sure, you can," Nash said, walking in with Maggie.

Jonas looked at Nash and Maggie.

"Nate and Pat took me in when my parents dumped me. You were always nice to me, even when you broke my nose," Maggie said.

Jonas chuckled.

"Jonas, when your mom passed away, she told me she wanted me to take care of you, boys. She left, knowing you were in excellent hands," I reminded Nate, Jonas, and Cayson.

Sometimes we need the one person who loves us like family. I married Nate and his family since Jonas and Cayson were like brothers to me, growing up and became my brothers. They made it more comfortable with my brother out of state. Liz and Danny couldn't make it to the funeral because of Danny's health. I missed my big brother, but I had two brothers to help me.

"I will discuss it with the boys. I don't want them left out of a decision like this one," Jonas reasoned.

"Let's take it one step at a time, little brother," Nate told Jonas.

Nate needed his brothers around him. It seems like old times with having the three of them here. I miss those times. Lucille would be proud of her boys.

CHAPTER 56

A FUNERAL

Maggie

Do you know how most funerals have a somber tone to them? People grieve and mourn for the departed, except Nixon didn't get the memo. He went a different route with Karen's funeral.

"Nixon, please do me a favor and don't act like you," Nate warned Nixon as we stood there.

"You offend me with your lack of confidence in performing a funeral," Nixon told Nate.

"I don't give a shit if I offend the Pope. Do not screw this up," Nate told Nixon.

"Nate! We're in a funeral home. I don't think people would appreciate you swearing," Pat cautioned Nate.

"Patty, I'm in my nineties. I don't give a shit what people think," Nate retorted.

Pat sighed as I wondered how this funeral would go. If your ninety-something father has to warn you not to act like yourself, that's bad.

"Look, Uncle Jonas asked me to perform the funeral. I will give Aunt Karen the same courtesy she gave our family," Nixon offered.

"That's the problem, you won't," Nate argued.

Nate and Nixon argued while we watched. Cayson walked over to us.

"What are you both arguing about now?" Cayson asked Nate and Nixon.

"Dad doesn't have faith in my ministerial duties," Nixon grumbled.

"No one has faith in your ministerial duties, but the funeral won't bore people," Cayson reasoned.

"You're not helping," Nate told Cayson.

"Nate, Karen was a wet blanket. She sucked the fun out of everything," Cayson said, making a sucking noise.

"It doesn't matter. Did we forget Jonas lost his wife, or the boys lost their mother?" Nate asked.

"No, that thought didn't escape me since Jonas cries all the time. No wonder Ma had to trick him into doing things like taking Patty to Homecoming," Cayson confessed.

Pat's eyes widened. Nate looked at Cayson with confusion.

"Oh, that secret should have died with Ma," Cayson mentioned.

Nate looked at Pat. "Did you know about that?" Nate questioned.

"How would I know your mom did some shady stuff like this? Your mom always did shady stuff," Pat told Nate.

Cayson made a hasty retreat and went to find Jonas. Nate followed Cayson as Pat followed Nate. I learn about situations like these. Everyone spills the tea, resulting in chaos.

"The funeral should excite," Nathan mentioned.

"If Nixon is performing it, believe it," Noah added.

"I need popcorn," Nolan said, walking away.

"Dad will hurt you if you screw this up," Nash told Nixon.

"Dad can't do shit except for shuffle towards me. He's slowing down in his old age. Grammy had her cane," Nixon reminded Nash.

Nash and Nixon went back and forth on this, and the funeral director walked over to us.

"Reverend Gray, the family would like to start," the funeral director instructed.

"It's showtime," Nixon announced, rubbing his hands together. He walked away from us.

"Why do I have a feeling Nixon will screw this up?" Nash asked me.

"Because it's Nixon," I answered.

Nash shook his head, and we found a seat. Nixon walked over to the podium and stood in front of it. Jonas and his sons wept for Karen. The rest of us covered our faces. We knew what was coming.

"Dearly departed. We gather today to send Aunt Karen off in style," Nixon said, making everyone look at him except us.

"Christ, here we go," Nate grumbled as Pat sighed.

"Now, if you didn't know Aunt Karen, you were lucky," Nixon told everyone.

"What the hell?" Jaime asked with confusion.

Jace shook his head, and Jonas sat there perplexed.

"The rest of us weren't so fortunate," Nixon said.

I hid my smile as Nash rolled his eyes.

"What can I say about Aunt Karen, which no one said? Well, not much, because she stayed away from the family except for our trip to Hawaii. Do you know she smacked Maggie in the snout with fruit?" Nixon asked everyone.

My eyes widened as Nash put his hand on his face. Nathan, Noah, and Nolan started snickering.

"I know we come to a funeral to mourn, but we came to support Uncle Jonas, Jace, and Jamie. We tolerated Aunt Karen," Nixon said.

Nathan, Noah, and Nolan got up and left the room. When they vanished from the main hall, we heard a lot of laughter.

"This funeral is better than Dad's funeral," Cayson chuckled. Nate smacked Cayson while Jonas has a horrified look on his face. Jace and Jaime didn't look thrilled. Yep, Nixon did a bang-up job, and he didn't finish yet.

"I'm sorry, Uncle Jonas. I can't in my right mind stand here and speak pleasantries about a person who made it their goal to dislike our family. Most people can; I'm not most people. So, I will say, Lord, let's hope Grammy is kind to Aunt Karen. Oh, who am I kidding? Good luck, Aunt Karen," Nixon said, leaving the podium.

Nash and I heard laughter, and we turned to see our kids laughing along with their cousins. Jonas stood up as we looked at him.

"I know my wife didn't try with people. I get it, but she was my wife, even if she was a pain in the ass," Jonas said.

"Dad!" The boys exclaimed.

"Boys, I loved your mom, but that's the truth. You can love someone and not like them much. It happens with all couples.

All I can say is I will miss Karen and love her for the rest of my life," Jonas finished, then left the room.

This funeral is the strangest funeral I ever went to in my life. People got up, and I walked over to the casket. I looked at Karen lying there, looking peaceful.

"Mags?" Nash said.

"When Grayson died, we mourned. When Lucille died, we mourned. We did the same thing with Dominique. Why can't we do that for Karen?" I questioned as people stopped and looked at me.

I turned and faced everyone.

"Most people detest funerals because it's the last goodbye. You have a funeral for closure. Even if you didn't care for the person in life, you allow the people who did to mourn them. This funeral isn't for everyone else. It's for Karen's family," I said. I glanced back at Karen, then left the room.

I made my way downstairs and got a cup of coffee.

"Maggie," someone said.

I turned to see Jonas standing there.

"Thank you," Jonas said.

"I understand what couples deal with while they're together. Nash and I had our difficulties, but I know what it's like to love someone deeper than the ocean," I reasoned with a smile.

Jonas walked over to me and hugged me. I hugged him back. I didn't know Jonas well, but I knew he was a good guy that deserved respect. We went upstairs to find Nate arguing with Nixon.

"Did you want me to lie?" Nixon asked.

"No, but for the love of God, you don't act like an ass," Nate snapped. Damn, you go, Nate.

"Well, if I lie, that wouldn't be right. Thou will not lie," Nixon countered.

"Thou will have my foot up in your ass," Nate remarked.

Nathan, Noah, and Nolan saw the exchange between Nixon and Nate. They turned to leave when Nate snapped his fingers.

"My monkeys stay put," Nate ordered the boys. He turned to Pat. "This is our circus, and those are our monkeys."

Pat sighed.

After the funeral, we went back to the house. Jace and Jaime had words with Nixon, causing Nash and the brothers to intervene. Jonas smacked Cayson, and Nate smacked Jonas for smacking Cayson. Pat had to separate those three.

"How does a funeral turn into a fight?" Kat asked me.

"It's the Grays. When doesn't everything turn into a fight?" I replied.

Macey whistled, using her two fingers, getting everyone's attention.

"My God, you people need to relax," Macey said.

"You stay out of this," Jaime snapped.

"Don't talk to my wife that way," Nathan demanded.

"Then tell your wife to keep her trap shut," Jaime barked.

Jaime's wife intervened, and I sighed.

"I didn't think funerals brought out the worst in people, but they do for this family," Marcy mentioned.

"Welcome to the family where anything can and will happen," I said as Marcy giggled.

Sometimes a family legacy creates a remarkable thing. The Gray family creates chaos. Welcome to the family.

CHAPTER 57

AWAY FROM THE CHAOS

Pat

We returned to school, and it thrilled me. When you go to a funeral of someone you don't know, you get stuck talking to cousins you never met. Yeah, we have a massive family.

I came in and went up to my bedroom, setting my bag down, then unpacked my stuff. Pax tossed his bag into his room, along with Payton and Presley, who left to see their girls. Parker added to his mound of mess.

Pax walked into my bedroom.

"Why do we always get stuck around a family that we don't know?" Pax asked me.

"Beats the hell out of me. The entertainment was fun," I commented.

Pax laughed.

"I know if I ever get married or die, Uncle Nixon Can perform both ceremonies," I mentioned.

"The best part of the funeral," Pax smirked.

We heard the front door and footsteps, followed by someone dropping their books. I turned, and Britt charged me, tackling me to the ground.

"On that note, I'm leaving to see tall and sexy," Pax said, stepping over us and leaving the bedroom.

Britt crashed her lips into my lips and kissed me. I wrapped my arms around her and kissed her back. After a few minutes, we broke from our kiss.

"I see someone missed me," I mentioned.

"With every bullet," Britt retorted, smirking.

I chuckled, then got up from the floor and helped Britt up.

"How was the funeral?" Britt asked.

"Different, considering Uncle Nixon performed the funeral, and the family argued," I replied.

Britt looked at me. "Isn't a funeral sorrowful?" Britt questioned.

"You would think, but not in my family," I answered.

Britt giggled as I chuckled. She walked over and picked up her books, then set them on the desk.

"I read your grandma's journals," Britt mentioned.

"Oh?" I asked.

"I laughed a lot, but your Grammy made sense," Britt told me.

"How so? Everyone said she was bat shit crazy," I mentioned.

"But she wasn't," Britt said, grabbing a book and opening it. "Listen to this," Britt mentioned, opening to a page.

Gray is a dumbass. We fought, and he went to the bar, getting drunk. I caught him with some floozy who thought she would take my man. I smacked him and told him like it was with us.

Why marry someone if you mess around with them? Drinking is an excuse for a weak person. Gray is weak. He allows the wrong people to lead him around by the nose. Now, he will learn and choose if he wants this marriage or not. I refuse to let someone hurt me because they are selfish and think about their manhood.

You can love a person and not like them much. It doesn't mean that it's wrong; it means you see their faults and imperfections, accepting that's who they are. I learned about Gray. One day, I hope he learns my love runs more profound than the ocean, or he will have a long, hard road ahead of him.

Britt finished reading as I looked at her. She flipped through a page and started reading another part.

Nathaniel comes home late every night. I know he's seeing some hussy. My boy has his head up his ass. I don't want a daughter-in-law who I can't stand. Since Gray couldn't give me a little girl, our boys are my last resort.

Now Patty is my pick for Nathaniel. She is smart, kind, funny, and a cute little thing. I love it when Patty comes over to visit me, even if the boys give her a hard time. It's nice to spend time with another female, considering my house is overrun with idiot males.

You have Gray, who lets his temper get the best of him. Nathaniel has questionable tastes in women. Jonas, who has his face in a book. Then Cayson, who finds trouble every chance he gets. What is wrong with my family? I'm the ringleader of a flipping circus.

I chuckled.

"Your grandma understood her family and said it like it was with them. She accepted their faults, even though she didn't like them," Britt explained.

"The funny thing is, people loved my Grammy Gray. I didn't meet her because she passed away years ago," I said.

"I can see why. I read a lot of her journal and loved it," Britt mentioned.

I walked over and picked up a book, then opened it. I started reading it.

I don't know what I did to Nate. He changed to me. I went to see Lucille, and he told me to go hang out with someone my age. I thought we were friends; I guess not.

It doesn't matter, because this year I will talk to Brian Holloway. I can't wait for my senior year to start. Liz thinks I'm crazy, and Brian isn't all that, but I beg to differ. Brian is fantastic and so cute.

I know if I say hi, Brian will talk to me. I even think about how it will be with us. Would Brian spend time with me? Does he like action movies or have any hobbies? All I have to do is open my mouth and say hi. Senior year will be the best year ever.

"Who's Brian Holloway?" Britt asked me.

"That is Nana's dad. She doesn't talk about him," I answered with confusion.

I flipped through the pages and found a distinct part of Grammy Pat's journal.

I can't believe I didn't listen to Liz about Brian Holloway. I had to lie to Nate and Cayson when I came home with a bloody nose after Brian hit me. I don't think they believed me. I didn't care. I didn't want Nate and Cayson to laugh at me, knowing my crush hit me.

I lied to my mom when I came into the house. She asked what happened? I told her I ran into a door because I'm a klutz. The lie wasn't a stretch, considering I am a klutz.

So far, senior year sucks. Thanks to Jonas, helping me in the store, I didn't humiliate myself in front of Brian and Trisha. Now, I get punched by Brian after school.

When does a crush, crush you? When the person hurts you, that is when.

I furrowed my brows.

"Damn, that's horrible," Britt mentioned.

I flipped through the pages and started reading another section.

It's official; I'm an idiot. I made a complete fool out of myself last night. I went to a party and got drunk, then called Nate and told him off. He hates me, and I don't blame him. Whatever friendship I had with Nate is over.

Plus, I'm stuck with a stupid hangover. I lied to my mom, and I don't think she believed me, but she didn't punish me. Thank god for that because I'm getting punished enough.

So far, I have liked the wrong person and made someone hate me. The worst part is I still like Nate; I figure he didn't feel the same about me because of the age difference. Well, I have school and work to keep me occupied and dealing with a guy at work that won't leave me alone.

I will never meet someone, and if I do, they will be the wrong person because that's my luck.

"Your nana had a tough time with guys, didn't she?" Britt asked me.

"It looks like it," I answered.

I flipped through some pages and started reading.

Today is my eighteenth birthday, and I get a small party with my family and friends. Mom invited the Grays. I doubt Nate will come.

After my drunken excursion, Nate hates me. I don't blame him. I gave myself liquid courage, and it bit me on the butt. I am never drinking again. I can't believe I did that. Liz is lucky that we are still friends.

Now to deal with school, which sucks on your birthday.

I flipped the page.

Okay, so Mom had a party for me. Lucille, Jonas, and Cayson came to the party. It disappointed me that Nate didn't come to my party. I didn't blame him.

I went into the kitchen to get some pop and felt someone behind me. I turned to see Nate standing there. That made me nervous. Nate acted seductively and told me he would kiss me and say that he's kidding. That pissed me off, so I took the cake and shoved it in Nate's face. We argued, and he kissed me! Like lips and tongue and...

"Yeah, I didn't need to read that," I said, gagging. Britt giggled.

I skipped the mushy part.

Nate asked me on a date, and I caught my brother and Liz sucking face. That is so gross. I didn't want to see that on my birthday, no less gag. This birthday will forever be my favorite birthday. Not only did I get my first kiss, but it came from someone special to me.

I'm happy that I saw Brian's true nature because it opened my eyes to someone who I knew my entire life. Nate started like a brother to me. It grew into friendship, following with someone who always cared about me. I didn't realize it, but Lucille saw the potential of us. I will thank her later.

"That's so cool how your Grampa and Grammy became a couple. You don't hear many stories with people starting one way. Then they finish a different way," Britt mentioned.

I looked at Britt. "We did," I reminded her.

Britt smiled. "We did, didn't we?" She asked.

I leaned over and kissed Britt. We started as friends, and our friendship evolved into more. I'm happy that it did because Britt is my best friend. She understood me in a way few people did.

We sat on the bed and read through Grammy Pat's journal. That gave me an idea of our last paper for class. We had the information, and now it's time to use it. What better way than the source themselves?

CHAPTER 58

THE LAST PAPER

Pat

Britt and I scanned the journals and created a story as our last paper. It took us three days to write, edit, and polish it. We argued during the process. Never write a paper with your girlfriend.

The last day of the class arrived, and we went to class, sitting down in our seats. After the students sat down, the professor walked into the classroom.

"Morning, everyone. Today is the day you turn in your last paper. I changed the assignment," the professor announced. It earned a collective gasped from the classroom.

"What? That's not fair!" Students yelled.

As the class yelled about the teacher changing the assignment, he stood there, watching us. People stopped and sat in their seats, grumbling.

"Most of you will give a generic story with the same theme writers use. It's not wrong, but it's not what I want from you. What I want is someone to come up here and tell us a story. You," the professor said, choosing me. "Come, tell us a story. Let's see if you understood the course."

I got up and made my way down to the front of the classroom. I stood in front of the class.

"You have our attention," the professor said, sitting down in his seat.

I looked at everyone as I took a deep breath.

It was a dark and dreary night. I'm kidding. It's night, but it wasn't gloomy, and it's dark. It's night, duh. People are way too severe and treat life like it's this horrible thing.

Bad things happen. We get it. Let's move along, will we?

That is one reason I refuse to watch the news. It's too dark and miserable, always reporting the bad and never the good, pft.

In case you're wondering, my name is Lucille Adams. I'm eighteen and enjoying life to the fullest. My parents worry I need to settle down and fear that they are boring. I'm eighteen, not eighty.

I graduated from high school and skipped college. It wasn't for me. I'm done with school. So, I got a job. Hey, I can still have fun and act responsibly. I need money to pay for said fun; logic 101.

I went to work at a store stocking shelves, and it wasn't bad. I got to meet new people and make fun of said people. It's all good.

Well, that was before Grayson Gray came along, downer.

Everyone looked at me with surprise. The teacher sat forward. I continued telling my story, weaving information from Grammy Gray's journal. I changed my voice from high pitched to deep as I talked, taking on the roles of Grammy Gray and Grandpa Grayson. The class laughed as did the professor.

I finished my story and looked at the professor. I didn't what they thought or if they liked or hated it. Then the professor started clapping, as did the class. I guess they loved it.

"Now, that's a story," the professor announced.

I went back to my seat.

"It's interesting that you chose this story to tell. Explain your reason," the professor said to me.

"Lucille and Grayson are my great-great-grandparents. Grammy Gray kept journals of her life with Grandpa Gray. She included my other grandparents and family. People thought she was crazy," I explained.

"Was your Grammy crazy?" The teacher asked.

"No, Grammy saw situations like they are and enjoyed life," I answered.

"What did you learn from this assignment?" The professor questioned.

"That life isn't terrible. It has those moments where you think it is, but someday you look back on it and laugh. Laughter is key; it keeps us young," I replied.

The professor smiled. "Exactly," he said. "That story showed us who Lucille Adams was to people. It gave us a reason to connect to the character and fall in love with her. The character can be any person sitting in this room. It doesn't matter what the person looks like, who they are, or where they come from in life. What matters is how they tell us their story. Now, everyone will tell us their story. Mr. Gray, you and your partner get an A."

Britt and I looked at each other, shocked. I recited our paper. Other students got up and told us their stories as the professor questioned them. I found it interesting the different perspectives that people have with their stories. It made a person wonder.

Nora

I finished up my last class and came out, bumping into someone. We dropped our books, and the person helped me pick up my books. I looked to see a guy standing up with me.

"Sorry about that," the guy apologized.

"No worries," I said.

"My name is Clyde," the guy introduced himself.

"Nora," I said.

"It's nice to meet you," Clyde said, smiling.

"Same," I said, smiling back.

Clyde walked with me, and we talked. He seemed nice, but so did Ted Bundy, and we all know how that turned out.

Britt

Pat and I came out of class and saw Nora talking to Clyde Baker. I shook my head.

"What's wrong?" Pat asked me.

"Nora is talking to Clyde Baker," I answered.

Pat looked to see Nora chatting with Clyde.

"Do you know Clyde?" Pat asked.

"I had a class with Clyde, and he's the type that turns on the charm, if you catch my drift," I replied.

"The guy is different," Pat suggested.

I looked at Pat. I didn't want to say anything to Nora because I could be wrong. The last thing I want is for my sister to get hurt.

"Watch what happens, and if you suspect anything, then say something," Pat suggested.

"You're right," I sighed.

Pax jumped on Pat; then, they played fought with each other. I shook my head and chuckled.

"I'm heading to the bakery. Do you want to come?" Pax asked us.

"Yeah, I could go for food," Pat said as I nodded.

Oh, Nora, you don't get your heart broke.

Nora

Clyde and I exchanged numbers. He walked away, and I stood there looking at my phone. It's not like I have many options, and I haven't heard from Matthew. What's the worse that can happen? We go out and have fun.

I turned and came face-to-face with Skylar and Mason.

"Hey, Nora," Skylar greeted me.

"Hey, Sky. Are you done with classes?" I asked.

"I have one more than I'm ready for winter break," Skylar replied.

Mason said nothing to me. Talk about awkward.

"Was that Clyde Baker?" Skylar asked.

"Yeah, we bumped into each other and exchanged numbers," I mentioned as Mason stood there.

"Are you planning on a date with Clyde?" Skylar inquired.

I cringed. I didn't want to discuss this in front of Mason.

"Not sure," I answered. "Look, I have to go. Let's hang out," I told Skylar, leaving.

Skylar looked at Mason.

"What?" Mason asked.

"Could you be any more awkward?" Skylar asked.

Mason looked at Skylar unamused.

"Look, Nora and I are friends. Deal with it," Skylar told Mason, walking away from him. Mason went after Skylar.

I didn't want to stand there, discussing a potential love interest in front of my ex. It has nothing to do with Matthew, but Mason is my ex. I went back to my dorm room, set my stuff down, then changed for work at a hotel. I got a job as a housekeeper. I figure I would work my way up in the hotel and take management classes.

I arrived to work and started my shift. It's honest work, and the pay is decent. Whatever I have leftover from paying for school, I would save for an apartment or house. One day, I would have a home with plants and cats. Even if I dated, I doubt it will go anywhere.

Clyde is the first guy that took an interest in me in a long time. Then again, if I date, I will end up alone. I pushed my cleaning cart down the hallway to a door. I knocked, then used my key card to open the door.

"Housekeeping," I yelled as I heard the shower running.

"Can you take out the trash and clean up a bit?" A voice yelled from the shower.

"Sure," I yelled as I cleaned. I made the bed and emptied the trash, then left as the shower turned off. That's the part of the job I don't like.

Matthew

I washed up as I heard someone yell housekeeping. I yelled for the person to clean up and empty the trash. I turned off the shower and got out, wrapping a towel around my waist. I'm meeting Payton in an hour.

I came out of the bathroom as the door closed and noticed the room cleaned with the trash emptied. I grabbed a water and went into the bedroom, dressing in clothes.

I finished as someone knocked on the door. I answered to see Payton standing there.

"That was quick," I mentioned.

"I like to be quick," Payton smirked.

"Don't let Josie know that," I retorted.

Payton rolled his eyes.

"Hurry, before Markus gets suspicious," Payton ordered.

We left to meet with Markus and the others to celebrate Markus's birthday. Markus didn't know it, but I came to surprise him.

Payton and I walked down the hallway.

"You know, since you're here, you could visit a certain brunette," Payton mentioned.

I gave Payton a look.

"I'm saying," Payton added.

"Look, I came to see Markus for his birthday, then I have to get home," I told Payton.

"I'm sure Beau won't mind if you take a few days off," Payton told me.

"Beau doesn't mind, but I'm working on a house," I said.

Payton shook his head. I didn't want to show up at Nora's door and get her hopes up. A lot can change over the next few years with people. I doubt Nora will wait, and I don't expect her to.

Who knows what will happen?

CHAPTER 59

MISSED CHANCES

Markus

My cousins helped celebrate my birthday, and I got a surprise in the form of Matthew. He showed up at the house with Payton. I gave Matthew the biggest hug.

"Man, what are you doing here?" I asked Matthew, looking at him.

"Payton called me and said you were pouting since I left. He said it would make you feel better if I came for your birthday. Here I am," Matthew said, smirking.

I shook my head and chuckled.

"I'm glad Payton has a big ass mouth because it's not the same without you," I told Matthew.

"You do what's best for you. College isn't for me," Matthew replied, shrugging.

"Whatever the case is, I'm glad you're here," I said, hugging Matthew again.

Matthew and I grew up together because our moms lived near each other. Besides Payton, I was closest to Matthew. The other cousins said hi to Matthew; then, we celebrated my birthday.

Later on, I cornered Matthew about Nora.

"So, did you see Nora?" I asked.

Matthew gave me a look.

"Why are you looking at me like that?" I questioned.

"Because I didn't come to see Nora. I came to see you," Matthew told me.

I looked at Matthew and arched an eyebrow. "So you'll raise cats and plants," I mentioned.

Matthew rolled his eyes as I shrugged.

"No, tool, I don't like cats, and I'm not a botanist," Matthew retorted.

"Well, you need a hobby since you refuse to see a certain brunette," I retorted.

"I have a hobby; I work on cars and a house. One pays, and the other gives me a roof over my head," Matthew countered.

"Yeah, that is a fun life. You work and don't date. I can see it now; you're that old man who sits on his front porch and yells at kids to get off your lawn. Hey, get off my lawn, you brats!" I mocked, waving my hand in the air. "Would you like a cane now or later?"

"Cute," Matthew answered.

I chuckled.

Pat

It surprised me that Matthew came to Markus's birthday party. I didn't expect him to show up here.

"It's a good thing Nora is working tonight," Britt mentioned.

"Even if Nora wasn't working, I doubt she would come to a birthday party with Mason here," I replied.

"How is it that Mason can forgive Matthew, but not Nora? Nothing happened between Nora and Matthew," Britt mentioned to me.

Page 442

"Because it's more difficult to disown family than walk away from a girl or guy," I reasoned.

"I don't know about that. I disowned my dad," Britt told me.

"That's because your dad is a dick and interfered with us," I reminded Britt.

"Good point," Britt said.

I kissed Britt, and Pax interrupted our kiss.

"Don't you have a guy to keep you busy?" I questioned Pax.

Pax gave me a look.

"Yes, and Shaun's socializing with people. I'm not clingy," Pax told me.

"Want to bet?" I asked with a look.

"It differs when you share utero," Pax countered.

"I don't see the difference," I replied, shrugging.

"Yeah, you wouldn't. You're slower on the uptake," Pax told me.

"How are your nuts since Britt donkey punched you?" I questioned. Pax glared at me, and Britt hid behind me.

"Don't think I forgot about your cross-dressing girlfriend hitting me in the nuts," Pax grumbled.

"In my defense, you threatened to hit me," Britt said from behind me.

"Sweetheart, Grays don't discriminate. You nail us in the nuts, expect retaliation," Pax told Britt.

"There will be no retaliation and no more nut crushing happening," I warned Pax and Britt.

I spent most of the party playing referee between my twin and my girl.

Mason

I walked over to Markus and Matthew.

"Matthew, can I talk to you?" I asked.

Matthew looked at me along with Markus.

"Yeah," Matthew said, setting his drink down on the table.

We went into the kitchen to talk.

"What's going on, Markus?" Payton asked Markus.

"Matthew and Mason are talking," Markus answered, earning a look from Payton.

Matthew leaned his back against the counter as I stood there.

"Look, I know everything is tense between our families, but I don't want tension between us," I said.

"That's why I left," Matthew told me.

"What?" I asked.

"I thought I could handle school after Sadie, then met Nora. I didn't know she was your girl until later. I left, so you didn't get hurt. Plus, Sadie didn't like the fact I met someone. I promised forever with Sadie," Matthew answered.

I furrowed my brows.

"Mason, we're family. It's not right to hurt family, and I won't do it. I hope you're happy with Nora," Matthew said.

I didn't know what to say. Matthew left the kitchen as I stood there, dumbfounded.

Matthew

I don't know why everyone insists I see Nora? Mason and Nora are a couple, and everyone needs to stay out of it. Sadie was right. I will never meet someone better than her. So why did I hate Sadie?

I stayed for a while, then went back to my hotel room. I relaxed, reading a book, then went to bed.

"Why so glum, chum?" Nora asked grinning.

I looked at Nora and chuckled.

"Who says I'm glum?" I asked with a devilish smile.

"I know you well enough to know when you're thinking about Sadie," Nora reminded me.

I looked at Nora and sighed.

"Matthew, it's okay. She was your first love, but I'm your last," Nora reminded me as she wrapped her arms around my neck.

I looked at Nora and smiled as I felt something tug on my pant leg. I released Nora and lifted Elias.

"This little guy wants ice cream," I said, looking at Elias. He put his hands on my face and smiled, showing two teeth.

"Matthew, Elias needs dinner," Nora reminded me.

"Okay, dinner, then ice cream," I said, and we pouted.

"Okay, fine, ice cream after dinner," Nora sighed.

I smiled as Nora giggled. I love my wife and family.

I woke up startled. What the hell was that? I reached and turned on the lamp next to the bed as I looked around at the hotel room. I can't stay here. I'm dreaming about things that aren't real. I got up and dressed, shoving my clothes and stuff into a bag. After I packed up my stuff, I left the hotel room to check out. I didn't realize I forgot something in my haste.

Nora

I had an early shift at the hotel since I didn't have classes. I got dressed and went to work. After clocking in, I grabbed my housekeeping cart and made my rounds.

I used my keycard to open a hotel room. It wasn't bad, thank god. I cleaned the room, including the bathroom, then changed the sheets on the bed. As I was preparing the place for the next person, I found something on the floor. Picking up the item, I noticed a chain with a cross on it. A guest must have forgotten it.

I put the chain in my pocket and finished my job. When we find something left behind in the hotel room, we report the item to the front desk. I forgot about the necklace while working my shift.

I finished and went back to my dorm room. After I returned, I changed, and something fell out of my pocket. I picked up the item and held the necklace in my hand. Shit, I have to turn this into the front desk, but knowing the employees won't return it to the owner.

I looked at the necklace. The cross was simple and not flashy. I know most people wear crosses as an accessory, but this cross is simple. I shrugged and put it in a box on top of my dresser. One day I can return it to its owner.

Matthew

I got home and unpacked, then realized I forgot my necklace. Shit, I never take that off. I can forget about contacting the hotel, considering someone will snag it.

I heard a knock at my door and came downstairs to answer it. Dad walked in, and I closed the door.

Page 446

"How was the party?" Dad asked.

"Fine," I answered.

"What's wrong?" Dad questioned, noticing my frustration.

"I lost the cross Uncle Nixon gave me after Sadie's funeral," I answered. I ran my hand through my hair in frustration.

Dad looked at me. Uncle Nixon performed Sadie's funeral, then gave me the cross to help me. He said that becoming a minister helped him through tough times.

"Did you contact the hotel?" Dad asked.

"Why bother? Someone snagged the necklace," I answered.

"I'll see if Nixon can get you another one," Dad offered as I sighed.

"That is not the point. Uncle Nixon gave me the necklace after Sadie's funeral. It was the one thing I had left of her," I told Dad.

"Matthew, I know you miss Sadie, but if you forgot that necklace, there's a reason. It's time to let Sadie go," Dad said.

"I can't," I replied.

"Why not?" Dad asked me.

"Because if I do, then that means I have no one!" I exclaimed.

Dad looked at me with empathy.

"If I have the necklace, then I held on hope that I wasn't alone. Sadie is still with me," I explained.

"But when do you realize that while you're holding onto the past, you miss the future? Matthew, you can love and miss someone, but don't let it rule your life. You need to move on and feel happiness," Dad reasoned.

"No, what I need is that damn necklace," I retorted.

"You are your mother's child, stubborn," Dad remarked.

I shook my head. Between losing the necklace and that dream, I didn't know what to think. I figure if I worked on cars and the house, that would keep my mind off both. Something told me I didn't realize that dream was a glimpse of what was coming in my life.

CHAPTER 60

CRAZIER SEMESTER

Nora

The new semester started, and Clyde pursued me. I had my reservations, but it's not like anyone is knocking on my door to ask me for a date. While everyone was finding love and romance, I'm working and attending school. Woo-hoo for me!

Skylar and I hung out without Mason. It seems they're getting close, which is okay, but I can't stand the awkwardness between Mason and me.

"Clyde asked you out?" Skylar asked, surprised.

"Yeah, but I'm not sure if I should accept," I answered, sitting on my bed.

"Why not?" Skylar questioned, standing in front of me.

"What if I go out and it's a disaster? Or we go out, and Clyde turns into a toad?" I questioned with a look.

"Or you can go out and find happiness, then get married and have babies," Skylar mentioned. She wiggled her eyebrows.

I chuckled.

"You're a nut," I commented.

"Yeah, but sometimes you feel like a nut, and sometimes you don't," Skylar remarked, grinning.

I laughed. Skylar walked over and sat down next to me on the bed. I hugged her. Skylar became my best friend.

"What about you and Mason?" I asked.

"Well, we're going slow, I mean a snail's pace," Skylar remarked.

I looked at Skylar and shook my head.

"You need to take the bull by the horns and show Mason. The dude is oblivious," I mentioned.

"I noticed," Skylar added as we giggled.

I have a feeling Skylar and Mason would work things out. I wasn't so sure about myself. My phone dinged, and I opened a message to Clyde. I sighed, and Skylar took my phone, responding to the text.

"Here, you have a date," Skylar said, holding up my phone to me.

"Thanks a lot," I grumbled, taking my phone back.

Thanks to Skylar, now I have a date with Clyde Baker. Who knows, Clyde could be sweet? Then again, I have a better chance of monkeys flying out of my butt.

Britt

I came out of class and saw Clyde. I know Pat said I should stay out of it, but this is my sister. I walked over to Clyde as he stared at his phone, grinning.

"Hi," I said.

Clyde glanced up at me.

"I'm Nora's sister. If you hurt my baby sister, I will hurt you," I warned.

"Uh, okay, I don't know what to do with that information," Clyde mentioned.

"I don't care what you do with it. I care about how you treat my sister," I replied.

"I like Nora. If you have an issue with that, that's your problem," Clyde said, walking past me.

I picked up a stone and threw it at Clyde, hitting him in the back. He stopped and turned, shooting me a glare. I smiled and waved as Clyde stormed off.

"Didn't anyone tell you not to throw stones?" Pat asked in my ear.

"Yeah, but I'm not one to listen to people," I answered, turning my head.

Pat looked at me as I shrugged. We went to our next class.

Kaxon

Most people take the next step in their relationship. They have sex with their significant other. I'm not most people, and neither is Jesse. When I say most, I mean sex scared the shit out of me.

Jesse and I made out a lot, but I put the brakes on with her when it progressed. It's not that I don't want to. It's that I don't know what I'm doing. Since I never had a girlfriend, I don't have experience.

Like most guys my age, I researched sex the best way I knew. I watched porn. Do you know how much porn exists on the internet? A lot of it does.

I watched different videos and turned my head. How the hell do the people do the positions they do? Mason walked into my bedroom and heard the moaning.

"Are you watching porn?" Mason asked me.

"Yes, because I need research," I answered, watching some guy in an ice cream parlor with a chick.

Mason sat down next to me and looked.

"That gives a whole new meaning to soft serve," Mason mentioned.

"More like enjoying your dessert in different ways," I said as we turned our heads.

Markus found us sitting on my bed, watching porn. He walked over and looked.

"Well, I didn't know people could bend like that," Markus mentioned.

"The woman must be flexible," I said as we watched.

Then our eyes widened as a customer entered and stood there, looking at the ice cream.

"What the hell?" Markus asked.

We stared at the customer, and our jaws dropped.

"Someone has some explaining to do," I mentioned.

While the chick was moaning, the customer spoke and ordered ice cream.

"Can I get tutti-frutti ice cream?" The customer asked as the chick nodded while a guy was ramming her from behind.

I hit stop and looked at Markus and Mason.

"Can someone explain to me how the hell Pat ended up in a porno?" I asked.

"Good question," Markus said.

I closed out the browser and closed my laptop. After setting the computer down on the bed, we busted our asses to find Pat.

We left the house and hit a patch of ice on the sidewalk, sliding and falling—damn Michigan weather. You never know when there's ice.

We got to our feet and made our way to the other house. It started snowing, covering the ice. We kept hitting patches and sliding as we fell. I moved to the grass to keep from falling as we ran over to the brothers' house.

When we got there, we ran inside. Payton and Parker looked at us. Pax came out of the kitchen with Presley, eating a sandwich, as Pat came downstairs with Britt.

"Is there a reason you three barged into our house?" Parker asked.

"Is there a reason Pat was in a porno?" I asked.

Pat stopped as Britt looked at Pat. Pax and Presley choked on their sandwiches as Payton and Parker looked confused.

"Why are you watching porn?" Pat questioned.

"Research and don't change the subject," I told Pat.

"How the hell does one end up in porn?" Markus asked.

"Wait. I thought you never had sex," Parker said.

"I haven't," Pat said, confused.

"So, you took part in a porno for the hell of it?" Payton asked Pat.

"What porno? I never filmed a porn film," Pat replied.

"We saw you," Mason accused Pat.

Pat came downstairs. "Well, you saw someone, and it wasn't me. Why the hell would I be in a movie like that?" He questioned.

"That's our question," Markus mentioned.

Pat looked at us, unamused.

"I'm calling Pops," Presley announced.

"You do that, and I will beat your ass," Pat warned.

"You beat Presley's ass, and I'll beat yours," Payton told me.

"Look, I never was in porn or have been on set with one. I don't even watch that shit!" Pat exclaimed.

We started arguing as Pax attempted to sneak away until Payton caught him.

"Freeze!" Payton yelled, snapping his fingers. We turned to look at Pax as he turned to face us.

"Oh, this is good," Parker mentioned.

"How the hell did you end up in a porn film?" Payton question as Shaun walked into the house.

"What? Who was in a porn film?" Shaun asked.

"Pax," Britt answered.

Pat shot Britt a look, and she shrugged.

Shaun looked at Pax.

"Okay, yes, I was in a porn film. This guy asked me if I wanted to make some money. All I had to do was go into this ice cream parlor and as for tutti-frutti ice cream. So I did," Pax said.

"Dude, Pops will kill you when he finds out," Parker said.

"Why? It's not like I had my wanger out, and I don't even like tutti-frutti ice cream," Pax said.

"That's not the point," Payton said.

"I earned five hundred dollars," Pax mentioned, shrugging.

We did a double-take.

"When the hell did this happen?" Shaun questioned.

"Our senior year in high school. I was out driving around with Pat and Kaxon. They went to some stores, and I wandered around town. Some guy asked me if I could help him out," Pax explained.

"I remembered that day. You disappeared on us," I said. "We came out of the store and looked for you. You came walking over to us with sherbet."

"After the scene, I tossed the tutti-frutti and asked for a sherbet," Pax told me.

"I'm still wondering how you got into a porno," Shaun mentioned, scratching his head.

"Dumb luck, I guess," Pax said, shrugging.

"How about we get back to why Kaxon is watching porn?" Parker questioned.

"Bye," I said, leaving the house. That's what I get for questioning someone else, and then I get challenged. Yeah, I don't think so.

Pat

I swear my family is something else. I have no interest in porn or magazines. Shaun and Pax discuss his side work. I didn't want to know anything about it. Payton, Parker, and Presley went to find their girls. Markus and Mason left after Kaxon left.

Britt and I sat on the couch alone.

"So, you never watched porn?" Britt asked me.

"No," I answered.

Britt looked at me with surprise.

"When sex happens, I don't want some expectation that doesn't happen. I didn't want to hook up with random girls, and it meant nothing," I explained.

"And the make-out sessions?" Britt questioned.

"That's different," I replied.

"How so?" Britt asked me.

"Sex is more intimate between two people. You create a connection with the other person. I didn't want to have sex with someone I didn't love. Plus, you get one first time," I reasoned.

"You know sex will be awkward as hell the first time?" Britt asked.

"Psh, yeah," I said.

Britt giggled as I put my hands on her face and kissed her. I figure when sex happens; it happens. Why rush something?

CHAPTER 61

NOT ALL IS AS IT SEEMS

Pat

Do you know when you love someone, you're willing to do anything for them? Yeah, boundaries need set with the emphasis on the word anything because this will bite me in the ass.

Nora went on a date with Clyde, and he made a move on her. That is not cool, dude. It's a date, not a hookup. Nora told Britt, and Clyde didn't want to take no for an answer when he asked Nora on another date. Britt came up with an idea to help her sister out, enlisting my help. Why do I get dragged into these situations?

"No way!" I exclaimed.

"It's perfect," Britt reasoned as Pax and Presley looked at me.

"For you, but not for me," I replied.

"Look, you're calmer than Pax," Britt reasoned.

"It doesn't matter because I'm not dressing as a chick," Pax informed Britt.

"Plus, we know Pax's temper," Presley reasoned.

"I got better," Pax countered.

We looked at Pax.

"Well, I'm working on it. Dr. Shaw said my therapies are helping," Pax added, grinning.

I shook my head. "Why can't Presley do it?" I questioned.

"Do I look like I can pass for a chick?" Presley asked with a look.

"Pat, if you go out with Clyde, then you can put him in his place," Britt mentioned.

I looked at the three of them and shook my head. I know I will regret this decision.

"Fine, but no pictures, and if anyone asks, you're blind," I said, pointing to Britt. "You're mute." I looked at Presley. "And you're deaf," I mentioned to Pax.

"Huh? What was that? Sorry, I'm deaf!" Pax yelled.

"Cute," I mumbled.

"Well, you said I'm deaf. I should practice" Pax retorted.

I stepped towards Pax and hit him in the stomach with my fist, knocking the wind out of him. He dropped to his knees, holding his stomach.

"Damn," Presley commented.

Pax is my twin, but it doesn't mean I won't beat the hell out of him. Did people forget that he's my brother and the gloves come off with your siblings? Considering we had WrestleMania growing up in our house, it's the norm with us.

"Pat didn't hit you in the nuts. That's a plus," Presley mentioned.

Pax shot Presley a glare. I shook my head. Here we go, back at it again with the unexpected.

Britt

I showed Pat how to shave his legs and armpits. We used an electric razor first, then a lot of shaving cream. Pat nicked himself a lot.

"How the hell do you girls do this?" Pat questioned me, nicking himself with the disposable razor.

"We shave all the time and learn to shave when we grow hair. No guy wants to date an ape," I reasoned.

"If I were a chick, I would go natural," Pat told me.

"Then you would never get a date," I remarked.

"This is some bullshit here," Pat huffed.

"Make sure you shave anywhere you show skin. No guy likes a hairy chick," I informed Pat.

Pat glared, and I shrugged. Pat finished shaving, then took a shower. I waited in his bedroom with Pax and Presley. Pat showered, then got out, and came into his bedroom with a towel wrapped around his torso. Damn, my boyfriend is hot.

Pat walked over to the bed and saw the items laid out. He looked at us.

"Look at it this way, brother; Ma will get the daughter she never had," Presley mentioned.

"Yeah, an ugly daughter," Pax remarked.

"Don't listen to Tweedledum and dumber," Britt said, giving my brothers a look. They shrugged. "After we finished with you, you won't look like you," I reasoned.

"Who's this we?" Pat asked with a look.

I smiled, and Pat didn't smile.

Pat

A woman helped me get dressed. When I say a woman, I meant a drag queen. He, she, they, I'm not sure what to call the person.

"Call me Lulu, sweetie," Lulu said.

I arched an eyebrow.

"My stage name is Lucious Lulu, and I'm the best queen around town," Lulu told me with confidence. "When I get done with you, no one will recognize you, Patricia."

My eyes widened as my brothers facepalmed themselves.

"What?" Lulu asked with confusion.

"That is our Grammy's name. I doubt Grampa would love knowing we're using it for this reason," Pax answered.

"Is your Grammy a queen?" Lulu asked.

"Well, if you mean is Grammy, a female, then yeah," Presley answered.

"Sunshine, powerful women are queens, drag, or not. Now let Lulu work her magic," Lulu said as I sighed.

I dressed in layers to hide my manhood. Then Lulu gave me a chest, using makeup. She placed a cap over my hair and did my makeup, then fitted me for a wig. Next is a prosthetic chest and clothes.

"Lady and gentlemen, I present Patricia," Lulu announced. I opened the bathroom door and entered the room.

Britt, Pax, and Presley looked at me in shock.

"What?" I asked with a look.

"Damn, dude, you look hot," Pax commented.

"And not like a dude," Presley added.

"I'm done with my work here. I will see you at the bakery," Lulu told Britt, then left.

I looked at my brothers and Britt, unconvinced. No one would accept that I'm a female.

"Let's put it to the test," Presley suggests.

I looked at Presley and arched an eyebrow.

Britt

We came downstairs to find Payton and Parker in the living room. Pat turned and started going back upstairs when we stopped him and pushed him down the stairs. He fought us, and we shook our heads, pointing downstairs.

Pat glared at us as we went downstairs. Payton and Parker looked up at us. They saw us with Patricia and looked at each other.

"Who's this?" Parker asked us.

"Meet Patricia. Say hi, Patricia," Presley instructed Pat, elbowing him.

Pat glared at Presley as Pax looked at the ceiling.

"Hi," Pat said in his voice. Presley slapped him on the back. "Hi," Pat said, making his voice higher.

Payton and Parker looked confused.

"Mosquito," Presley mentioned.

Before Payton and Parker said anything, we hurried Pat past them and out the door. The last thing we need is to blow our plan.

We went to the bakery as Pat shivered.

"How the hell do girls dress like this? I'm freaking cold," Pat said through chattering teeth.

"Why do you think we wear pants in the wintertime? We're no dummies," I answered. That earned a look from Pat.

We got to the bakery and found Clyde at a table alone.

"Perfect, Clyde's alone. We'll go behind the counter while you turn on the charm," I said, patting Pat's back. The three of us went behind the counter and watched the show.

Pat

I took a deep breath and made my way to Clyde's table. He sat there, drinking coffee, and stared at his phone. I cleared my throat, and he looked at me, surprised.

"Hi," I said, imitating a female voice.

"Hey," Clyde said, smiling.

"Do you care if I join you?" I asked flirting.

"No, you be my guest," Clyde said, gesturing to a seat.

I sat down and crossed my legs, sitting like how Britt showed me. I put my hands on the tabletop and smiled in a flirtatious manner.

"Are you new?" Clyde asked me.

"Oh, yes, I transferred this semester. See, I'm new and looking for a vigorous man to show me around campus," I answered.

Presley took Britt's hand and showed me what to do. After this situation, I'm beating Presley's ass. I glared as Clyde looked at me. Pax gestured to me. I looked at Clyde, and he turned his head. I grabbed his hand. Clyde turned back to me as the others ducked behind the front counter.

I giggled. "You have muscular hands," I flirted, stroking Clyde's hand, gag.

"Yeah, it comes in handy with a girl," Clyde said. He leaned forward. "Girls love how I touched them."

"Is that so? How about you show me how you enjoy touching girls? I heard you went out with Nora Tilson," I mentioned with a smirk.

Clyde licked his lips. "Yeah, Nora couldn't handle me. No wonder she can't get a guy, that frigid bitch," Clyde said.

Britt started charging Clyde when Pax and Presley dragged her back to the bakery counter. Clyde turned as Pax pushed Britt down to the floor. I glared at Pax. Pax and Presley waved to me.

Clyde turned to face me as I smiled. Pax dropped, and I figure Britt donkey punched him in the nuts. Good, he deserves it. Presley got dragged into the fight, trying to break it up.

"So, how about we go somewhere more private?" Clyde asked.

"I thought you would never ask," I replied as we got up. We started for the door, and I stopped. Clyde looked at me. "You go ahead. I will meet you."

Clyde shrugged and left. I walked over to a shelf, picked up some muffins, and threw them at the others, getting their attention. I gestured to them as I turned and left. They followed as I caught up with Clyde.

We walked until he grabbed my hand and pulled me behind a building. He got me pinned against a wall and started feeling me up. I looked at Clyde, getting pissed. Then he found a surprise.

Clyde looked at me as I looked at him. "Is that what I think it is?" Clyde asked me.

"I guess you should have bought me dinner first, you tool," I said.

Clyde's eyes widened.

"Surprise, asshole," I said as I hauled off and clocked him. Clyde leaned down, grabbing his nose. He stood up as I hit him again. Then I beat the shit out of him. If a guy will act like an asshole and treat a girl like shit, he deserves to get his ass beat.

The others found us as I delivered a swift kick to Clyde's nuts, dropping him to his knees. Clyde groaned.

"The next time I find out you put your hands on a girl when they tell you no, you won't be breathing. Stay the hell away from Nora Tilson," I told Clyde.

"Damn!" Presley and Pax exclaimed.

"That's hot," Britt said.

We looked at Britt as she grinned. I have a screwy girlfriend. I walked past them and started running home.

"That's the fastest I ever saw Pat move. It sure wasn't with a girl," Pax mentioned.

Presley and Britt shook their heads as they chased after me. It's freaking cold, and I'm done dressing like a chick. I will never argue when Britt wears pants in the wintertime. She can dress like an Eskimo for all I care.

CHAPTER 62

IT'S ALL FUN AND GAMES UNTIL SOMEONE GETS A BUTT CRAMP

Pat

I got back to the house and ran past Payton and Parker, leaving them confused. I went upstairs and ran to the bathroom, then started removing everything so I could pee. I did the shake, then turned on the shower. I made the mistake of not waiting for the water temperature.

I danced around the shower in my haste, trying to avoid the water until I adjusted it. Then I scrubbed all the makeup off of my body. I didn't realize how much makeup drag queens use. I give them a lot of credit, considering I couldn't do it. I'll stick to looking like a guy. It's way easier to handle.

After I finished washing my body, face, and hair, I got out of the shower and dried off. I pulled on a tee-shirt, briefs, and sweats. That's much better than a skirt, although my legs and armpits feel weird without hair.

I came out of the bathroom to find Britt sitting on my bed.

"Feel better?" Britt asked me.

"So much better," I groaned.

Britt laughed. I walked over to the bed and sat down next to her.

"How the hell do you girls do it? I did everything girls do for half a day, and it drove me nuts," I said.

"You get used to it after a while. It becomes second nature," Britt explained.

"I'll stay a guy," I mentioned.

Britt giggled, and I leaned over to kiss her. She kissed me back. I pulled back, looked at Britt as she looked at me, then crashed my lips into her lips. Our kiss intensified as we made the work of our clothes.

Before I dipped the stick in the jar, I grabbed a raincoat. I didn't need to explain to my parents that they will have grandkids. I placed on the protection and thought I hit the right hole.

"Exit only," Britt grunted.

I didn't. I hit the wrong hole. I tried again and made contact, which is more challenging than I thought. I grunted, pushing myself inside Britt as she tugged my hair.

"It's a little tight," I mumbled.

"You're a little big," Britt said through gritted teeth.

"Stop pulling my hair," I grunted.

"Stop moving," Britt ordered.

I stopped moving. Britt wiggled as I laid on top of her, waiting to move. Little man ached, stuck in a tiny hole.

"Okay, move," Britt whispered.

"You sure?" I asked.

Britt nodded, and I pushed more into her as we figured out what to do with our hands and legs. Then I hit something sturdy. What the hell?

"Pat!" Britt huffed.

"What? Something's blocking, little man," I told Britt.

"Do it," Britt ordered.

Who am I to deny an order? I pulled back and pushed into Britt harder. She screamed as I stopped. I didn't know what I'm doing, and it's not like you know these things when you have sex. I should have watched porn. Kaxon is smart.

"Keep going," Britt demanded.

"Decide, woman. Stop, go, stop, go," I huffed, thrusting in Britt.

I felt the tightness leave, and it felt like a glove around my manhood. That felt much better as I picked up the pace. I got so into the moment that my butt cramped.

"Mother of God!" I screamed, pulling out of Britt and hurrying from my bed.

Britt propped herself up as I moved like someone who got sunburnt, and a person slapped their ass. My bedroom door flew open as Britt covered herself, including her head. I grimaced as I worked out the cramp, naked. My brothers stared at me.

"Do you mind? Can't a guy deal with an ass cramp in peace?" I yelled, moving around with my pecker flapping in the wind.

My brothers noticed the raincoat on my manhood and laughed. I didn't need this shit. I got the cramp to go away and shut the door on my dipshit brothers, then locked it. Note to self, close the damn door the next time.

I stood there as Britt lowered the covers from her head. She pulled her lips inward.

"Do not laugh," I ordered.

Do you know when you tell someone not to laugh, it makes them laugh? Yeah, that happened as Britt burst out laughing. I groaned. So much for my first time to feel amazing. It was awkward as hell.

I sat on the bed after I removed the raincoat and put on a pair of boxer briefs. Britt tried to touch me, and I looked at her. She recoiled her hand.

I sat there and shook my head. Britt moved and sat next to me, covered with the blankets.

"It's not that bad," Britt mentioned.

I looked at Britt. "It was terrible," I replied.

We sat there.

"I'm sure everyone's first time is awkward," Britt said.

"Sure, because that's how it goes," I responded, feeling defeated.

When you have your first time, you expect it to be excellent; then reality kicks you in the nuts. I should ask Pax since people hit him in the nuts.

"Pat, I doubt anyone's first time was awesome or amazing. No guy is born knowing how to have sex, and no girl enjoys it because it is freaking hurts," Britt reasoned.

I looked at Britt as she looked at me. Well, shit, I didn't think about that. I turned to Britt.

"It sucked for you, didn't it?" I asked.

"Because I never had sex, and it's painful at first. People assume it's pleasurable, but it's not," Britt answered.

"I feel like an ass," I sighed.

"Don't, because it's the first time. It doesn't mean we can't try again," Britt reasoned with a look.

Well, the second time is the charm until I noticed blood. I got up from the bed.

"What?" Britt asked.

"That's a lot of blood," I answered, pointing at the sheets.

Britt looked down and screamed. My brothers rushed to my room. I forgot I locked the door. I stood there, shocked as they pounded on the door, then Payton kicked in the door. My brothers saw the blood and facepalmed themselves.

I looked at my brothers with furrowed brows. "I broke Britt," I said, then looked at Britt. She looked at me with worry.

My brothers calmed us down, and Parker called Selena to help Britt. I paced as Pax changed my sheets. Yeah, I hate messes, and I'm about to lose my shit.

"Okay, so you didn't break Britt," Parker told me.

I stopped and looked at Parker.

"You broke Britt's hymen," Parker added.

Payton rolled his eyes as I looked at Parker.

"What big brother means is that when that happens, there's blood," Presley said.

"But that's not normal," I reasoned.

"It is when you have sex for the first time. We know Britt stayed faithful," Presley reasoned.

Parker smacked Presley.

"I don't understand. Why?" I asked.

"Because it happens with every girl," Payton answered.

"What?" I asked with confusion.

"Don't look at me. I never had sex with a girl," Pax said, walking past me with the dirty sheets.

"Pat, every girl bleeds their first time. It's because you tore the piece of skin inside them. Every girl differs from sex. Some don't have a problem, and some have pain," Payton explained.

"Okay, but was it awkward for you guys the first time?" I questioned.

"Hell yeah, it was. It's like pushing a bratwurst through a keyhole," Parker answered.

Ew, gross. That's a visual I will never get rid of with bratwurst and doubt I will ever eat one after that analogy.

"Unless the girl is willing and able," Presley smirked.

We looked at Presley as Pax walked past and smacked him upside the head.

"Look, every guy has a unique experience with sex. You're nervous as hell, and it's uncomfortable. You don't know what you're doing the first time," Payton mentioned.

"Speak for yourself," Presley said.

"Will you shut up, peanut gallery? Not everyone is quick to dip their hot dog in someone's bun," Parker told Presley.

"Can we stop talking about food? I don't want to eat bratwurst or hot dogs now," I said.

Parker shrugged.

"Now, I'm hungry," Pax said, leaving the room. I rolled my eyes.

Selena and Britt emerged from the bathroom.

"Britt is okay, and we are leaving," Selena announced.

"Says who?" Parker asked.

"Says the woman that won't give you her cupcake if we stay," Selena answered with a look.

Page 470

"On that note, we're leaving," Parker said. Parker and Selena left the bedroom, and Payton followed them.

Now I don't want cupcakes. I shook my head and looked at Britt.

"So, about those Tigers," Britt said, making me chuckle.

I got over my issue as I groaned, then rolled onto my back as Britt and I caught our breaths.

"That was way better than the first time," Britt giggled.

I chuckled. "Much better, although I will never eat another bratwurst, hot dog, or cupcake. Parker ruined it for me," I mentioned, making Britt laughed.

I pulled Britt to me, and we snuggled. After the initial time, sex gets better. I could do without the running commentary from my brothers or help. I have to remember never to mention this to anyone, ever.

CHAPTER 63

CHRISTMAS WITH THE FAMILY

Pat

For Christmas, we brought Sam, Britt, and Nora Tilson, along with Shaun. Since our house is full, Sam, Britt, and Nora stayed with Nana and Grandpa. I didn't know how that would go with my grandparents, considering their history with Britt's family. I guess we will find out.

I took Britt and her siblings to my grandparent's house, introducing them to everyone.

"It's nice to meet you," Grammy said. Britt and her siblings shook hands with everyone. "Nash will show you to your rooms."

Grandpa showed the others to their bedrooms as I watched.

"Pat, they'll be fine," Nana assured me.

"I know you have a history with their family," I reminded Nana.

"Yes, with their family, not them," Nana reasoned.

"Patton, we knew the Tilsons for years. I went to school with their great-grandfather," Grampa mentioned.

"I don't want Britt and her siblings to suffer because of their family," I mentioned.

"They won't. We aren't that bad," Jonas reminded me, looking at Cayson.

"Why are you looking at me like that?" Cayson asked.

"No one is looking at anyone," Grampa answered with a look.

"I will go," I said, leaving.

Britt

Pat's grandpa showed us to three bedrooms. Nora and I walked in and set our bags down. I looked around the bedroom.

"This bedroom is Larkin's old room," Nash told me. "My parents have Lyric's old room, Jonas uses Lakin's bedroom, and Cayson has Luna's bedroom. Sam will stay in Lex's bedroom."

We looked at Nash. He looked at us with his steel-grey eyes.

"Thank you for allowing us to stay here. We were staying at school until Pat and his brothers persuaded us to come with them," I said to Nash.

Nash looked at us. Nora turned to me.

"We should find another place to stay," Nora whispered to me.

I looked at Nora with empathy. I knew Nora's look. It was the same one she got when Dad terrified her. I felt something gripping my arm and looked at Nora's hands. She did that a lot when we were younger when Dad got upset. Nash noticed Nora's actions and left the room.

"See, we can't stay here," Nora told me.

"Nora," I said.

"Britt, they don't want us here. Our last name proves it. I hate our family," Nora huffed.

I looked at Nora. I didn't want her to feel miserable at Christmas.

"Let me talk to Sam, and we will find other arrangements," I offered.

Nora nodded. I turned to see Pat's Nana standing in the doorway. She came into the bedroom.

"Nash said you seem upset. Is everything okay?" Pat's Nana asked.

"We appreciate you letting us stay here, but we can't accept," I answered.

"Oh?" Maggie asked.

"I know our family wasn't the nicest to your family. We don't want to make you uncomfortable," I reasoned.

"I see," Maggie said.

We picked up our bags.

"Drop the bags," Maggie ordered. We dropped our bags. "I had a habit of running away from home, well, the Grays' home. I thought no one wanted me, but that's not the case. See, Pat had an issue with my parents when she was younger. She didn't hold it against me because my parents are assholes."

We looked at Maggie with surprise.

"So, consider this a repeat of my youth," Maggie offered.

"What happened to your parents?" I questioned.

"Rotting in jail somewhere," Maggie answered, shocking us. She turned and left the bedroom.

"This family is crazy," Nora whispered.

"Yeah, but I'm in love with one, and you're one love with another who is oblivious," I remarked. Nora sighed.

"I'm not in love with Matthew," Nora denied.

I looked at Nora.

"What?" Nora asked.

"You're such a liar," I answered.

"It doesn't matter because Matthew left and won't return my calls or text messages," Nora reasoned.

I looked at my sister. One day, I have a feeling that her excuses wouldn't work, and she would face her feelings. I let the matter rest.

Sam

I put my bag down and looked around the bedroom. It has pictures of family adorning the walls. I picked up a picture frame of a family who looked happy. Why couldn't my family have happiness?

Someone knocked at the doorframe, and I looked to see a guy standing there. I set the frame down on the desk.

"Did you find everything, okay?" The guy asked me.

"Yeah," I answered.

The guy looked at me with steel-grey eyes.

"Look, I know our families have issues, but I promise that my sisters and I won't cause problems. It's not like we had a great upbringing," I mentioned.

"Yeah, I knew your grandfather," the guy said.

I looked at the guy.

"Mike and I were best friends growing up. After I started dating my wife, I found out he cheated with my ex, who he married. Your uncle Bryson hurt my wife and attempted to harm my family. Your cousin Roger hurt my daughter. So, I know the issues well," the guy said.

I felt terrible.

"But we don't hold you and your sisters responsible for your family's actions. If that were the case, I wouldn't have my wife and family," the guy mentioned. He gave me a smile, which made me feel better.

"I'm Nash Gray," the guy introduced himself, holding out his hand.

I shook Nash's hand. "Sam," I said.

Nash nodded and left the bedroom. Sometimes forgiveness is key to healing past issues. It's what helps us move forward in life.

Nora

Britt went to see Pat while Sam talked to Nash and Maggie. I sent a text message.

Merry Christmas, Matthew.

I doubt Matthew will answer it and sighed. My phone beeped. I opened the message, and my eyes widened.

Merry Christmas, Nora - Matthew

My lips curled into a smile as I stared at my phone. Then my phone beeped again.

Tell Mason I said hi - Matthew.

My brows furrowed, and my lips turned downward. Well, everyone is wrong, and I hate Christmas. Looking at that message, I deleted my messages from Matthew and his number from my phone. I grabbed my bag and snuck past everyone as I heard laughter.

"Merry Christmas, Sam, and Britt," I whispered, then left. I walked to a bus stop and waited. A bus pulled up, and I got on it.

I found my seat and sat down. I figure I would call someone to pick me up.

The bus dropped me off, and I made a call. The person answered.

"Can you pick me up? I'm at the corner of Oakland and Hayes. Thanks," I said, hanging up the phone. I stood in the cold, shivering as a car pulled up. I opened the door and got in, then closed the door. I looked at Skylar.

"Do you want to talk about it?" Skylar asked.

"No," I answered. Skylar smiled and pulled away from the curb. I sent Britt and Sam a message, letting them know that I'm spending Christmas with Skylar.

I put my phone away as tears escaped my eyes. I wiped the tears away as I stared out the window. God is punishing me for breaking Mason's heart. Karma is a bitch.

Pat

Britt and I were hanging out when she got a message. Her brows furrowed as I looked at her.

"What's wrong?" I asked.

"Nora is spending Christmas with Skylar," Britt answered.

We looked at each other, and Britt sighed. I have a feeling this had something to do with Matthew.

Markus

I visited Matthew at his new house that he's fixing up when his phone went off. He texted someone and sets his phone down on the table.

"Was that your Ma?" I asked.

"No, it was Nora. She wished me a Merry Christmas, and I wished her one," Matthew said.

"Oh? Anything else?" I questioned, acting nosy.

"Yeah, I told Nora to say hi to Mason," Matthew added.

"What? Why?" I asked.

"Because Nora is with Mason. What part doesn't anyone understand with that?" Matthew asked me.

"Because Mason and Nora aren't together," I told Matthew.

"What?" Matthew asked me, confused.

"Christ, you're oblivious. Mason told Nora to make a choice. She freaking chose you!" I exclaimed.

Matthew sat there, stunned. I got up from the table.

"You're so consumed with doing the right thing. You missed an opportunity with someone who cared about you. I love you, cuz, but you're a twit," I said, leaving.

Matthew had an opportunity and blew it. Christmas will be fun this year at Grandpa and Nana's house.

CHAPTER 64

CHRISTMAS WITH THE FAMILY, PART TWO

Pat

Christmas is a time of happiness and joy unless a cousin screws it up and sends my girl's sister packing. Markus informed us he told Matthew about Nora and Mason. That leads to dysfunction at its best.

Matthew went to our grandparents to talk to Nora but found her gone.

"She left," Sam said as Matthew stood in the bedroom that Britt is staying in.

Matthew turned and looked at Sam. "What?" Matthew asked.

"My sister left. You must be Matthew," Sam mentioned.

Matthew looked at Sam. Grandpa and Nana watched. Sam walked towards Matthew.

"Nora told me about you. I'm surprised that someone could capture my sister's heart how you did," Sam told Matthew.

"Nora's special," Matthew said.

"Yeah, she is, and she didn't deserve to get her heart broke. I watched my dad treat Nora and Britt terribly. I made the mistake of leaving, but I refuse to make the same mistake again," Sam told Matthew.

"I thought if I left, it would help Mason and Nora," Matthew reasoned.

"Did you leave to help them or run away from a situation?" Sam questioned.

Matthew looked at Sam.

"If you care about my sister, then make her happy, but give her time," Sam reasoned.

"I thought we would have world war three happening?" Grandpa whispered to Nana.

Nana shrugged.

"I don't know you, and I'm not my family, but I love my sisters. I want my sisters happy," Sam explained.

Matthew nodded as he turned and left. He came downstairs as we watched him.

"Matthew," Payton said, grabbing Matthew's arm.

"I should have listened to everyone," Matthew said as he pulled his arm away and left.

I looked at Britt, and she looked at me. Would Matthew and Nora ever connect? We didn't know.

"Look, it's Christmas time, and there's plenty of time to deal with a love crisis later," Grammy told everyone.

"Grammy, what about Matthew?" Markus asked.

Grammy walked over to Markus. "If I learned anything from Lucille, sometimes you need to help people along. You and Mason are to make that happen," Grammy told Markus and Mason.

"Why us?" Mason questioned.

"Because you acted like a king-size tool. You remind me of your parents," Grammy told Mason. She looked at Markus. "You are closest to Matthew. Now, chop, chop," Grammy ordered, clapping her hands.

Markus and Mason left to hunt Matthew down.

Grammy looked at us. "You boys help your cousins and retrieve the runaway," Grammy ordered.

We groaned.

"How the hell do we find this chick?" Pax asked.

"Nora's with Skylar," Kaxon answered, walking past us.

"Thank you, peanut gallery," Parker remarked.

Kaxon flipped off Parker as Kain smacked Kaxon upside the head.

"No way will Nora come," I informed my brothers.

"Then use the Gray way," Nixon mentioned.

"Sure, and let's add kidnapping to the list of charges we will get," Presley mentioned.

"Get the girl. Damn, are you slow?" Nolan asked.

"I can't get arrested, or I won't be a paramedic," Presley replied.

"Don't worry. Brody is a cop. He will make sure your charges disappear. Poof, all gone," Nolan said.

"Let's go so I can spend Christmas with my girl," Payton huffed.

"Aw, is someone not getting any lovin'?" Parker asked.

Payton rolled his eyes as we left to retrieve Nora. Okay, here's the problem with this scenario. We fucked it up. Nora and Matthew refused to come back to the house. We attempted the Gray way but got met with resistance from Skylar's family. They threatened to beat our ass. Have you met Skylar's dad and uncles?

We all returned without Matthew or Nora. Grammy rolled her eyes and shook her head. I prefer not to sit in jail on Christmas. I look at this way, let Matthew and Nora figure it out.

The next day I felt more weight on me than needed. I opened my eyes and glanced to see my brothers on top of my back.

"Didn't you hear of someone sleeping?" I questioned.

"Didn't you hear that it's Christmas break, and we do all things Christmas related?" Parker questioned with a look.

I looked at my brothers and smiled. I got up and ate breakfast, then got ready. Our Christmas break comprised everything holiday-related. We used it since we're all dating someone. Pax even got into the spirit. He hates holidays. My twin and I differed in so many ways. How people confused us is beyond me?

Britt and I went Christmas shopping, picking up gifts for everyone.

"You surprise me," Britt mentioned.

"Why's that?" I asked.

"Most guys hate shopping and doing anything holiday-related," Britt answered.

"I'm not most guys. I love holidays and enjoy giving people gifts. Our family feels it's important to give someone a special item. It's better than spending money on things that no one will remember," I reasoned.

"Yeah, I remember growing up, Mom would make the holidays special, and Dad would make them miserable. Nora would decorate her room in construction paper and find things to give to us as gifts," Britt informed me.

"Nora has a kind heart, doesn't she?" I asked.

"Yeah, that's why Nora didn't tell Mason the truth. She didn't want to hurt him because she liked Matthew," Britt explained.

"Isn't a harsh truth better than a pretty lie?" I questioned.

"It depends on which version of the truth you want? Your truth or theirs. Not everyone's version of the truth is the same," Britt reasoned.

I stopped and turned to Britt. "I have a truth," I said.

"What's that?" Britt asked with curiosity.

"I love you," I replied.

Britt smiled. "I love you, too," she responded as I kissed her.

We finished our Christmas shopping and went back to my house. We wrapped gifts while my brothers bought a tree. Yeah, that is stupidity on my parent's part. Who the hell sends my brothers to buy a tree?

Pax

Who in the right mind sends us to buy a damn tree? Oh, that's right, my parents do. They thought we could use brother bonding time. Have our parents met us? When don't we bond with each other? Considering one of us has some issues, we bond all the time.

"Hurry, Pax, before I freeze my balls off," Parker yelled.

I caught up with my brothers. "I don't even like the holidays or shopping for a tree," I mentioned.

"I don't like people, but I still deal with them. What's your point?" Parker asked.

"How do you become a nurse if you don't like people? That's an oxymoron," Presley replied.

"Because most people don't talk when they're sick," Parker remarked.

"I'm still fascinated that you and Eliza will be paramedics," I mentioned to Presley.

"We saw which career we like in high school. Plus, we did great in science," Presley said.

"Don't you have to be an EMT before becoming a paramedic?" Payton asked Presley, checking out trees.

"We did. Eliza and I took a training course over the summer and became EMTs. We spent part of the school year working towards our certification. At the end of this year, we'll become certified paramedics. We're still taking classes for different levels of certification," Presley explained.

"Damn, that's impressive," Parker remarked.

"It's easier to marry someone who understands your career. It's better than someone who doesn't," Presley reasoned.

"Well, while you both are saving the world, I'm feeding it, and Payton is advising it," I mentioned.

"What's your better half doing with his life?" Parker asked me as Payton dragged a tree over to a guy.

"Teaching," I answered.

Parker arched an eyebrow.

"Patton wants to be a teacher. Who better than him?" I asked.

"That makes sense. Patton has the patience to help people learn," Presley mentioned.

"Better Pat than me," I reasoned.

My twin and I were nothing alike in personality. I react where Patton doesn't. We both have a temper, but my temper flares, and Pat is a slow burn. We have different interests in movies, music, people. I prefer guys; he prefers chicks.

Payton paid for the tree, and we helped him load it on top of the car. Well, Parker and Presley helped since I'm shorter. It sucks being five foot six and one hundred and fifty pounds. I'm the smallest boy in the family, and Pat is the same height but fifteen pounds heavier than me. That's why I'm quicker to react than Pat does.

We drove back to the house, and Shaun helped us with the tree. Okay, that's hot, watching my boyfriend unload a tree from the roof of a car.

"Less drooling and more working. You can drool later," Parker remarked.

My brother is a tool.

Pat

Britt and I finished wrapping gifts, and my brothers and Shaun brought in the tree. We got it set up and helped Ma decorate it. Pops helped Ma with the tree topper as he lifted her so she could put it on. Pops lowered Ma and kissed her as we looked at our parents and smiled.

"Okay, we'll spend Christmas at Ma and Dad's house along with some cousins, the aunts, and uncles. It includes my crazy ass sisters," Pops announced.

"Is Aunt Lakin coming in with Aunt Mia and Larissa?" I asked.

Pops looked at me. I knew that look. Aunt Lakin and Aunt Mia weren't coming for Christmas.

"Lakin can't get time off this year. Her caseload increased," Pops explained.

I nodded as my family looked at me. Out of the aunts, I was closest to Lakin.

"Uncle Nathan will be there," I reasoned.

"Pat," Ma said.

"Uncle Nathan, isn't coming?" I questioned.

"The boys can't come this year, and Aunt Macey wants to spend time with them," Ma answered.

I furrowed my brows. The two people who understood me best won't be here for Christmas. Matthew isn't coming because of Nora, and Nora is celebrating with Skylar. Britt and I looked at each other.

"I made cookies," Shaun mentioned, picking up a plate of sugar cookies.

"We have Christmas movies," Payton mentioned.

"And Christmas music," Parker added.

"We have gifts," Presley said.

"I'm celebrating the holidays," Pax told me.

I looked at everyone.

"Honey, we can video chat with Nathan and Lakin," Ma suggested.

"Yeah, sure," I mumbled as I went up to my bedroom. To me, the holidays weren't about cookies, movies, music, gifts, or trees. It was about spending time with my family. Plus, I wanted to introduce my girl to Lakin and Nathan.

Lakin

I helped Mia and Larissa pack.

"Do you think it's a good idea to lie to everyone?" Larissa asked me.

"Sometimes, you lie to surprise everyone," I answered.

"Lakin, did you get my favorite PJs?" Mia asked, yelling from the closet.

"Yes, baby girl. I packed everything," I replied.

Mia came out of the closet, looking confused.

"What?" I asked.

"Did you see my hoodie?" Mia questioned.

"I packed it," I answered.

Mia started questioning different clothes. I assured her I packed everything for her. Mia came a long way since her attack, but she has her moments. Patience and love were crucial for helping her.

My phone rang, and I answered it.

"Yep, we are leaving now, and I will call when we're ready," I said, then hung up. I looked at Mia and Larissa. "Okay, family, let's go give someone their Christmas gift."

Mia and Larissa smiled as we grabbed our bags and left. It took some time, but we arrived at our destination. We got out of the car, and I looked at Mia and Larissa.

"Okay, you both go to the front door, and I will go to the back door," I instructed. Mia and Larissa nodded as I walked around the back. I made a call, and when the person answered, Mia knocked on the front door.

"Hey, Aunt Mia," Payton said, surprised.

Mia and Larissa went inside the house as I waited.

Pat

I heard Payton say Aunt Mia and came out of the kitchen to see Mia and Larissa standing there. Everyone hugged them, including me. I looked past them.

"Where's Aunt Lakin?" I asked.

"Ma couldn't come," Larissa answered as Mia looked at me.

"Oh," I mumbled. Everyone looked at me.

"Pat," Pops said.

"You said Aunt Lakin had a busy schedule. I was hoping to see Aunt Lakin and introduce her to my girl," I said, feeling disappointed.

"Honey, there will be other times," Ma assured me.

"Yeah," I mumbled.

"Why don't we open gifts?" Grandpa suggested. Everyone nodded.

"That is okay. You all go ahead," I replied, masking my disappointment. "Look, I got everyone something." I feigned happiness. I handed everyone a gift I bought. My family looked at me, holding their presents. "Open them," I said.

My family, along with Britt and Sam, opened their gifts. They smiled as I stood there, watching. I wanted nothing except to see Uncle Nathan and Aunt Lakin.

"Thanks, Pat," my family said, admiring their gifts.

"No problem," I said, shrugging.

Material things meant nothing to me. They never did. I prefer spending time with people. That's why I picked a teaching career.

"Patton, this is thoughtful of you. You deserve a special gift," Grandpa said.

"I need nothing. It's the thought that counts, isn't it?" I asked.

"Yeah, but sometimes the most thoughtful person deserves a present," Nana said with a smile.

Grandpa opened the kitchen door. "Okay, it's time," he announced as I stood there.

I watched as Lakin came out of the kitchen holding her phone.

"Ready?" Lakin asked.

"Ready," Nathan said.

Lakin walked over to me and turned the phone to reveal Uncle Nathan on video chat.

"Merry Christmas, Patton," both said.

"Merry Christmas," I said, shocked.

"Sorry that I couldn't be there, but we heard you felt upset, so Nash made a call," Nathan explained.

"We know how close you are to us. We thought you deserve something special for Christmas," Lakin said, smiling.

"Having time to talk to both of you is the best Christmas present ever," I said, my voice cracking.

"Good, now we heard you have a girl you wanted us to meet," Nathan mentioned.

I wiped my face and got Britt. I introduced Britt to Lakin and Nathan. Britt's last name surprised them, but they accepted it. That made me happy because Nathan and Lakin meant a lot to me.

We talked for a while, then hung up with Nathan. This Christmas turned out great, and I couldn't ask for a better day.

CHAPTER 65

BACK TO SCHOOL, WE GO

Pat

We returned to school, and Mason asked Skylar out on a date with my cousins' encouragement.

"Okay, here's your chance. Walk up to Skylar and ask her out," Kaxon advised, rubbing Mason's shoulders.

"Is that necessary?" Pax asked.

"Is what necessary?" Kaxon questioned.

"That you're rubbing Mason's shoulders," I answered.

Kaxon and Mason looked at Pax and me as we gave them a strange look. Mason smacked Kaxon's hands away, then cracked his neck, which made us groan. I hate that sound.

"Here I go," Mason said, walking towards Skylar, who was talking to someone.

We watched and took bets. Mason walked towards Skylar. He reached Skylar, and she looked at him. Mason smiled as Skylar smiled. That's a good sign. Then Mason turned and walked back to us.

"That was quick," Pax mentioned.

"Mason said nothing," Kaxon huffed.

I held out my hand. "Pay up," I demanded. Pax and Kaxon each put a five-dollar bill in my hand. I shoved the money into my back jean pocket, then walked towards Mason. I stopped Mason and turned him around as Kaxon and Pax watched us.

I pushed Mason towards Skylar. We reached Skylar.

"Mason wants to take you on a date. Say yes," I told Skylar.

Mason gave me a weird look.

"I already won the bet," I mentioned, shrugging.

Mason rolled his eyes.

"Yes, I would like to go on a date with you," Skylar said.

"Who? Pat?" Mason questioned.

I smacked Mason on the back of the head. He glared at me and rubbed his head.

"Not me, tool. I have a girl," I said.

"Oh," Mason said, confused. Then the lightbulb turned on in his brain. "Oh," Mason exclaimed.

My cousin is slow on the uptake. I shook my head and walked away, then walked over to Pax and Kaxon.

"Mason spent too much time in cornfields," Kaxon mentioned.

"You think?" I asked.

"How did you make valedictorian?" Pax questioned Kaxon.

"Are you still pissy that you shared the title with me?" Kaxon asked Pax.

"The title belongs to us fair and square," Pax told Kaxon, referring to Pax and me.

"Not if I earned it," Kaxon smirked.

Pax looked at Kaxon, annoyed. Pax hated sharing valedictorian with Kaxon. It didn't matter to me since we left high school.

"What does it matter? We left high school and all the bullshit that went with it," I reasoned.

"When did you become philosophical?" Pax asked me.

"The minute he got his cherry popped," Kaxon answered.

Pax and Kaxon looked at me. I looked at them with annoyance.

"No, dipshit. I learned some things aren't as important as others," I replied.

"Uh, huh, sure," Pax and Kaxon said, shaking their hands.

"Let's get back to the Mason issue. Do you think he will screw this up?" Kaxon asked.

"Yep," Pax and I agreed.

"I thought so," Kaxon mentioned.

It's not that we don't have faith in our cousin. Oh, who am I kidding? We have no faith in our cousin. Mason dated Nora with the notion he's in love with her and destined to stay together. You can't base love on dating someone for a short time. Even my brothers knew this, and my brothers are twits.

While the three of us stood in the hallway and talked, Presley ran into us, hurrying.

"What the hell?" Pax yelled.

"Sorry, I'm running late!" Presley yelled back.

We shook our heads.

"I can't believe Presley will save lives. Those poor souls will croak before he makes it to them," Kaxon remarked. We chuckled as we walked.

Presley

I hurried home and changed into my uniform, then made my way to the ambulance company.

"You're late, probie," the chief said, irritated.

"Sorry, my class ran over at school," I apologized.

The chief walked over to me. "Do you want to become a paramedic?" He questioned.

"Yes, chief," I answered.

"Then show up on-time. Lives depend on us to keep them alive until we reach the hospital. Carelessness will cost you in the field. Now, restock the truck with supplies," the chief ordered. He left, and I sighed.

I walked over to the truck and found Eliza writing numbers down on a sheet. I climbed into the back of the ambulance. She handed me the clipboard.

"Presley, you can't keep running late," Eliza told me.

"I know. The professor wouldn't shut up," I said, counting supplies.

"Well, this summer, we do our ride-along, then become certified," Eliza reasoned.

I smiled. We were taking a course to earn our certifications as paramedics. We completed our EMT course in the summer after graduation. Uncle Cayson explained the difficulties of a paramedic to us. He said you work to save people, but sometimes you lose someone.

We finished counting and restocked the truck. The next thing is cleaning the bathrooms and doing what probies do at the company. A call came in, and two guys left to take it.

"Probie!" The chief yelled.

I walked over to the chief.

"I need you to run these items to the hospital," the chief said, handing me a box.

I took the box and walked over to a rescue truck. I set it in the backseat. Eliza went with me to take it to the hospital. We pulled up to an entrance and went inside as Parker met us. I handed him the box.

"Thanks," Parker said, taking the box. "Supplies are running low," Parker called for someone to come and get the box of supplies. The emergency room's shipment ran late, and someone called over to us to get some items.

Parker looked at me. "How's it going?" He asked.

"The chief is riding my ass," I answered with a look.

"Presley, the chief wants to make sure your head is in this job. People's lives are depending on it," Parker explained.

"I know," I said.

"Look, at the end of summer, you will become certified. Hang in there," Parker advised as I nodded.

"Gray! We need you!" A woman yelled.

"I got to go. We have an accident victim incoming," Parker said, rushing to another room.

Eliza and I went back to the truck. We got in and went back to the station. I know that I have to work my ass off to get certified, but I hated it when the chief rode my ass. Next year, I can split a shift with my classes.

After Eliza and I finished our training, I'm proposing to her. Who better to understand your job than your wife, who will work alongside you. We returned and finished our shift. We left and went back to the house.

Once we got back, Eliza went upstairs to take a bath. Pat, Pax, Britt, and Shaun were watching a movie. Pat looked at me.

"How was work?" Pat asked me.

"Rough, but it will be worth it. Plus, at the end of this summer, when we complete our certification, I'm proposing to Eliza," I mentioned.

The four of them looked at me with surprise.

"Are you sure you're ready to take that step?" Pat asked me.

"Yeah, I love Eliza," I answered, smiling.

My brothers smiled at me, then got up and congratulated me. Both hugged me. I know people think that I'm crazy for wanting to settle down so young. I didn't care, because Eliza is everything to me.

Pat

It didn't surprise me that Presley would propose to Eliza. After what happened, we realized Presley loves Eliza. You never know what happens between a couple unless you're one.

Take Pax, for example. He thought the wrong thing with Shaun. His anxiety helped create scenarios ten times worse than they are. Parker assumes Selena would be another Sable. Parker was wrong on that one. Selena is nothing like Sable, and we like Selena. Then you have Payton, who couldn't get his head out of his ass to see that Josie was perfect for him. Both are neurotic, so they work as a couple.

I differed from my brothers. Britt and I started as friends, and our friendship grew more with each other. I wished Britt didn't pretend as a guy and make me think I was into guys. Do you know how unnerving that is to feel attracted to someone who you think is a guy? I have no interest in guys. That is Pax's area.

As this year came to a close and the summer arrived, we were in for a rude awakening. Call it a gut feeling, but I couldn't shake the feeling that something significant will happen. It's a situation that would forever alter us.

CHAPTER 66

VALENTINE'S DAY MIXED WITH CRAZY

Kaxon

Valentine's Day arrived, and I planned a romantic night for Jesse, except for sex. I heard about Pat's butt cramp incident. That was a hell no, and if I can make it a romantic night, excluding sex, even better.

Markus went out with Hayden, and Mason had a date with Skylar. I set everything up at the house and ordered food. Okay, that's a lie. I know nothing about romance, so I called Dad.

We video chatted, and he guided me on what to do for my evening, then told me to buy a box of raincoats.

"Why do I need raincoats? I'm not having sex," I reasoned.

"Do you ever plan on having sex?" Dad asked me.

I thought about it. "Define planning and sex," I answered.

"Erin? Are you sure Kaxon is my kid?" Dad asked Ma.

"You were there when we conceived Kaxon," Ma exclaimed.

"Was I asleep?" Dad questioned.

"I don't think so," Ma answered.

"Can you two discuss my conception later and not around me?" I asked.

"Listen, Frack, Jr., I don't have time for your shenanigans. Do you want my help or not?" Dad questioned.

"I should call Uncle Kaiden," I suggested.

"That's blasphemy," Dad exclaimed.

"Do you understand what blasphemy means?" I asked.

That question earned a look from Dad.

"Look, order some food because we know you suck at cooking. Get flowers, chocolates, and a teddy bear," Dad told me.

"Why flowers, chocolates, and a teddy bear?" I asked.

"Flowers will make the house smell nice. Women love chocolates, especially when Aunt Flo visits," Dad said.

I cringed. Ew, gross, no guy wants to discuss a woman's monthly.

"The teddy bear is for when you screw up, and Jesse can beat you with it. It's soft, so it won't hurt much," Dad reasoned.

Dad has a point on that. I would prefer to get hit with a teddy bear than a fist.

"Now, go onward, Frack, Jr., and make me proud, but not a grandpa," Dad ordered.

I hung up the phone and shook my head. I went and bought everything, then returned home and set the stage. After I finished, I waited. I sat at the table, waiting on Jesse to show us for our date. I checked my watch, and time passed as the food got cold.

I looked at my phone and sighed. I stood up and blew out the candles on the table, then started cleaning up. As I took food into the kitchen, I heard a knock at the door. I set the plates on the counter and answered the door to see Jesse standing there.

"Oh, hey, what's up?" I asked.

Jesse walked into the house as I closed the door behind her.

"Sorry that I'm late. I got a lecture from Dad. You know the whole don't have the sex talk," Jesse said, rolling her eyes.

"Oh, no biggie," I said, acting casual.

Jesse looked at the table and furrowed her brows.

"Kax," Jesse said.

I walked away and picked up the plates and forks on the table.

"Your gifts are on a chair," I said as I went into the kitchen. I put stuff away as Jesse picked up the items I bought. I walked out of the kitchen and moved things off the table.

"Thank you for the gifts," Jesse said.

"Yeah, sure," I mumbled as I finished cleaning up.

"Kaxon, will you talk to me?" Jesse asked.

I stopped and looked at Jesse. "What do you want me to say? That I called my dad, asking for tips for tonight. I worked my ass to make tonight special and sat at the table alone, waiting for you," I said, frowning.

Jesse looked at me.

"All I wanted was not to screw this up tonight. I even made sure that the night was simple," I explained. I looked at Jesse. "Enjoy your gifts," I said as I turned and walked away.

Jesse put the stuff down and ran after me. She grabbed my arm. "Kaxon," Jesse said, stopping me.

I spun around and yelled, "What?"

Jesse crashed her lips into my lips, surprising me. The kiss heated, and the next thing I knew, we were upstairs in my room. It got crazy between us as we made quick work of our clothes. Then we fell onto the bed. As it got intense between us, I stopped.

I got up, and Jesse looked at me as I left the bedroom. I went to Markus's bedroom. I rummaged through his nightstand, naked, finding raincoats. I hurried back to my bedroom and put protection on before continuing with Jesse.

Everything went well until I got a butt cramp. I got up, trying to walk it off. The minute the pain stopped, I went back to previous activities.

I laid there as Jesse looked at me. I played with her hair.

"That was a lot different from I expected," Jesse mentioned.

"If it makes you feel any better, I expected nothing," I replied, making Jesse chuckled.

I pulled her into a kiss as we gave into a passion again. Porn gets sex wrong because it doesn't account for butt cramps.

Nora

I spent Valentine's Day working. Everyone has plans for the Day, and I'm learning that not everyone has someone. After I finished my shift, I left the hotel. I bundled my coat as I walked back to my dorm room.

I passed a flower shop. I looked at the different arrangements of flowers. I went inside and bought a bouquet. I carried the bag home, then stopped and got a box of chocolates. When I returned, I put the flowers in a vase and sat down on my bed, turning on my laptop. I hit play as I indulged in my chocolates.

Every girl deserves flowers and candies on Valentine's Day, even if you buy the items yourself. One Day, I will meet someone and share days like these with the person. Now, I will enjoy myself, learning to love myself.

Matthew

I had dinner and held a picture in my hand. I stared at it as I ate. What did I do? I let my past rule my present. I didn't know if I will ever see Nora again, but I hoped.

I looked at Nora's picture and smiled.

"Let me go," I heard someone say.

I turned and saw Sadie stand there. I put the picture down on the table and looked at Sadie with furrowed brows.

"I'm your past, but someone else is your future," Sadie said.

I stood there, confused.

"One Day, your future will come, don't let it go. Be happy, Matthew," Sadie finished as I turned and looked at Nora's picture. I turned back, and Sadie disappeared.

I cleaned up my dishes, then picked up the picture. I put it in my shirt pocket as I went upstairs. I went into the bedroom and opened a closet door. I brought down the box, carried it over to the bed, and then opened it to reveal Sadie's items.

I rummaged through the box and found an envelope addressed to me. I opened it.

Matthew,

If you're reading this, then you know why? I couldn't tell you I was sick. I didn't want to hurt you. The doctor diagnosed me with schizophrenia and put me on medication. It's not working. The voices tell me things, and they're loud.

I can't tell my parents, or they will lock me up, keeping me from you. I want the voices to stop, and I don't want you worrying about me. If that makes me selfish, I understand. Sometimes there's no other way but out.

You loved me when I couldn't love myself. You have the biggest heart, and I'm grateful to have time to enjoy it. I'm sorry, Matthew. I tried, but nothing's working. Please forgive me.

Sadie

I lowered the note as tears fell down my face. I threw the letter into the box and picked it up. I carried it out of my bedroom and out to the backyard. I put it in the fire pit and grabbed some lighter fluid. I sprayed the box with it, then lit a match, tossing it into the pit. The box ignited and burned. I stood there and watched it burned.

People can say whatever they want, but when someone commits suicide, that's the final decision. Sadie made a choice; now, I'm making mine.

"Goodbye, Sadie," I whispered, watching the fire.

I'm not sure what will happen now, but find love again with someone one day. I have a feeling one day; I will. I turned and went back inside the house, letting the fire burn out.

We need to let go of our past to find our future. When I lost the necklace, that made me realize that there was a reason for it. Someday I will understand the reason.

CHAPTER 67

MOVING FORWARD

Mason

I have my first date with Skylar. I kept it simple and acted like a gentleman. I didn't want to make the same mistake with Skylar as I did with Nora. The date was okay, but I don't think Skylar likes me in a romantic sense. Skylar didn't say it, but I could tell she hesitated with me because of Nora.

"What do you mean the date didn't go well?" Kaxon asked me.

"Well, we went to dinner, then a movie and Skylar kissed my cheek. I tried to hold her hand, and she moved it away," I answered.

"Did you act like a tool?" Pax questioned.

I looked at Pax. "Are you kidding me?" I asked, annoyance filling my tone.

"Well, you have that effect on people," Pax said, shrugging.

I became irritated.

"Did you talk to Skylar?" Pat asked me.

"I called Skylar the next day, and she said she couldn't talk. Later on, I sent a text. She replied she was busy. I saw Skylar at school, and she avoids me," I answered with a look.

My cousins looked at me, speechless. I give up. What's the point? It didn't matter anymore. I focused on school since love isn't working for me. While my cousins were busy with their significant others, I studied.

I sat in the library, working on a paper, then got up to find a book I needed. I scoured the bookcase and found it, then flipped through the pages. I walked back to the table, not paying attention, bumping into someone.

"Sorry," I mumbled.

"No worries," someone said.

I looked up from my book to see Skylar standing there, smiling.

"I came over to your house, and Kaxon said you were at the library," Skylar mentioned.

"I figure I could work on my paper," I said.

We stood there with awkwardness.

"Can we talk?" Skylar asked.

I dreaded that question. Any time someone asks can we talk, it means one thing. I nodded as we went to another section of the library.

"What did you want to talk about, Skylar?" I asked, playing dumb.

"It's about the date we went on the other night," Skylar answered.

"Okay," I said, not sure where Skylar was going with this.

"I had fun, but it doesn't seem you're into me," Skylar told me.

I looked at Skylar, confused.

"Did I do something wrong?" Skylar asked.

"What?" I asked.

"I mean, is it because you're still hung up on Nora?" Skylar questioned.

"No," I answered.

"Then, do you dislike me?" Skylar inquired.

"What?" I asked with confusion.

Skylar turned and paced. "You're keeping your distance because of what happened with Nora. That's okay because I know it seems weird that Nora is my best friend and your ex. I don't want you to think that you have an obligation to me or anything," Skylar rambled.

While Skylar rambled, I took a chance. I made my way to her and pulled Skylar into a kiss. The kiss started small. Then, I deepened it. I dropped my book and placed my other hand on her cheek as I kissed Skylar. She put her hands on my waist, kissing me back.

I pulled back and looked at Skylar.

"You were rambling," I said.

"Yeah, I do that when I'm nervous," Skylar mentioned, giggling.

I smiled as I leaned in and kissed Skylar again. I'm happy that I was wrong about this situation. I like Skylar and wanted to be with her.

After that incident in the library, Skylar and I connected on a whole different level. We spent more time together, and for once, I'm happy.

Sam

I went to the diner often to see Leslie. I know Leslie was older, but I liked her. I talked to Hayden to see how he would feel if I asked Leslie out on a date? He gave me his blessing. That was a relief. Then I thought she might have a boyfriend. Well, shit.

Hayden assured me that his sister is single. Yeah, I want to listen to the guy who pants me. I don't trust Hayden's word. I would find out for myself if Leslie was single.

I went to the diner and sat down at the counter. I looked to see if Leslie was working. I didn't see her. I stopped a server.

"Excuse me," I said, getting a server's attention.

"Yes," the server said.

I looked at the name tag. "Rhonda?" I asked.

"That is my name, Sugar. What can I get for you?" Rhonda asked me.

"Is Leslie working tonight?" I asked.

Rhonda looked at me. She leaned on the countertop with her elbows.

"Do you have a thing for Leslie?" Rhonda questioned.

"I don't know," I answered.

Rhonda looked at me and smiled. I furrowed my brows.

"Sugar, I know you don't come here for the food. I know that you come for the company," Rhonda informed me.

"Is it that obvious?" I asked.

Rhonda smiled. "You seem like a nice guy, and Leslie is single, if you're wondering?" Rhonda mentioned, winking at me.

I looked at Rhonda and smiled.

"Speak of the devil," Rhonda whispered.

I turned to see Leslie come into the diner. I got off the stool and walked towards her. She looked at me with curiosity.

"Hey," I said.

"Hey, Sam. Are you having dinner?" Leslie asked me.

"Well, I planned to but thought it would be nice to have company," I mentioned.

Leslie looked at me and smiled.

"If you have plans, I understand," I reasoned.

"No plans," Leslie said.

"Would you care to join me for dinner?" I asked.

"Sure," Leslie said, smiling.

We walked to a booth and sat down. Rhonda took our orders, and we sat there, talking. We laughed as we talked about different things. Rhonda brought our food to the table.

When I came home, I didn't know what to expect. I'm glad that I returned. I reconnected with my sisters, made friends, and met someone. I learned from the Gray family that family isn't always blood and come to the least likely people.

Parker

My brothers and I were hanging out with Shaun and the girls when my phone rang. I saw Pops calling me.

"Hey, Pops," I answered.

I sat there, listening to Pops as everyone watched me.

"What?" I asked, sounding surprised. Pops had me put him on speakerphone. "Okay, Pops, you're on speaker."

Jaime called and informed us that Sable and Tristan took the deal he offered. Not only will they serve jail time, but both will register as sex offenders. Boys, it's over.

My brothers looked at me as I sat there, stunned. I looked at Pax as he looked at me.

Boys? Is anyone there? Piper, the boys are plotting something because it got quiet!

We heard Ma's voice. *Lex, our boys, aren't plotting! You stunned them into silence!*

We let it rip as we cheered, making Pops chuckle. What? Did you think we would cry? Yeah, we didn't this time. That crazy bitch got hers, and she deserved it. I hope Sable says hi to Bertha when Bertha makes Sable her bitch. People should never mess with the Gray family; it never ends well. It couldn't have happened to a better person.

CHAPTER 68

SPRING BREAK

Pat

We went to Myrtle Beach for spring break and dragged Nora with us. Sam invited Leslie this time. Payton, Parker, Markus, Josie, Selena, and Hayden would be seniors next year. Everyone warned Mason to behave towards Nora. We didn't need drama on spring break.

We arrived at the beach house and got settled into our rooms, then hit the beach.

"How long has your family owned the beach house?" Britt asked as we walked along the beach.

"Granddad's family owned it before he married Grammy Gray. After they got married, Grammy brought the family here for vacation," I explained.

"I love reading your Grammy Gray and Grammy Pat's journals. It's refreshing to know they looked at life with a realistic view," Britt told me.

"Even if Grammy Gray was bat shit crazy?" I asked with a look.

Britt smiled. "Even if she was bat shit crazy. It's sweet that your Grammy Gray endure people to her. It shows people loved her," Britt reasoned.

"Hey!" Payton yelled to us. We walked over to him. "We found something," Payton mentioned.

We followed Payton to the house as everyone was in the living room. We walked over and sat down on the couch. Parker pressed play on the remote control.

"Nathaniel! Watch your brother! No, I didn't say drown him! Damn kids," Grammy grumbled.

Grandpa Grayson chuckled as Grammy walked towards Grampa Nate and Uncle Jonas.

"Cayson! What are you doing?" Granddad yelled at Uncle Cayson.

"I'm shoving Patty's head in the sand!" Cayson yelled.

"Danny!" Grammy Pat yelled as Uncle Danny helped her.

"Luci!" Granddad yelled.

"Ooh, you will get it, Nathaniel!" Grammy threatened Grampa as he stuck his tongue out at her. She walked over to Uncle Cayson. "Leave Patty alone, Cayson!" Grammy yelled.

"Why?" Cayson asked.

"Because she isn't a doll!" Grammy yelled as Cayson shrugged.

We laughed, watching the home movie when Grammy and Granddad lived in their old house. The video changed.

"Happy birthday, Nate," Grammy said, handing a bag to Grampa.

"Thanks, Patty," Grampa said, hugging Grammy.

"I know it's not much," Grammy mentioned.

Grampa pulled a toy car out of the bag.

"I know how much you love cars," Grammy said.

"It's perfect," Grampa whispered as Grammy smiled. Grampa hugged Grammy.

Britt and I smiled, knowing Grammy was fifteen. You could see that Grampa liked her.

"Happy birthday, Patty," Grampa said as Grammy Pat turned around to see Grampa standing in front of her.

Grampa walked over to Grammy. "Remember when I said I wanted to wait until your eighteen to kiss you?" Grampa asked.

"Yeah," Grammy breathed.

Grampa leaned into Grammy, then said, "I'm kidding."

Grammy's face contorted to horror, then a frown formed. She grabbed some cake and smashed into Grampa's face.

"Why did you do that?" Grampa barked.

"You shouldn't tease someone!" Grammy spat.

Then Grampa pulled Grammy to him and crashed his lips into her lips.

"Damn, Grampa has game," Pax remarked as we laughed.

We watched home movies of everyone, including Grandpa Nash and Nana.

"And where do you think you're going?" Grandpa asked, chasing after a little boy. The little boy laughed. "Lex, you stay close. We need not lose you," Grandpa said, holding Pops, who grinned.

"Nash! Catch Larkin!" Nana yelled.

Grandpa spun and caught Aunt Larkin as she ran to towards him. He picked Aunt Larkin up, then carried Pops and Larkin to the cage with the other aunts. Lakin was half-way over the plastic fence as Grampa set Pops and Larkin down on the floor and put Lakin back.

"Listen, you five, there will be no great escape today," Grampa told Pops and our aunts.

The quints smiled at Grandpa as he chuckled.

We laughed, seeing our parents as toddlers. The movies ended, and we sat there.

"I can't believe they got all that on film," Payton mentioned.

"It's cool to see your family when they're younger," Josie said.

"If you think about it, one day, that's all you have left of people in film and pictures," I reasoned.

Everyone looked at me.

"Life is about living, and our family loved life," I added.

"Look at you becoming philosophical," Parker commented.

"It's not about philosophy or any of that junk. It's reminding us that one day, future generations will only have videos and pictures of us," I explained.

"Pat's right," Pax said.

We looked at Pax.

"Last year, I spent most of it dealing with anxiety, which is a bitch. I missed out on a lot of things because I let my mind rule me. This year, I learned that there are bigger things to worry about in life," Pax.

"What's that?" Presley asked.

"Buy a damn cup, or my boys will suffer," Pax answered, making us laugh.

"Yeah, sorry about that," Britt apologized, earning a look from Pax.

"I don't know about any of you, but I learned sex is a lot of fun," Kaxon said, getting up and walking away.

We did a double-take as Jesse rolled her eyes.

"I learned you let go of the past and move on with the future," Mason mentioned, looking at Skylar, who smiled.

We sat around and talked. Yep, we learned many things these last two years and feel next year will be the hardest yet. Someone special will help a family member understand our legacy.

Presley

After the trip down memory lane, we ate and then had a game of volleyball. The guys played as the girls watched and talked. I'm glad Eliza and I worked out our differences, even if my family caused them.

My brothers and I played against my cousins, Sam and Hayden. Shaun refereed us as the girls kept score. Sometimes it's nice to spend time with the family and argue over who cheats in volleyball.

Yeah, Pax and Kaxon argued. Pax accused Kaxon of cheating as he did in high school. Kaxon threw the ball at Pax. Fists went flying, and Pax fell onto the ground after Kaxon nailed in the balls. Good thing my brother is gay because reproducing is out with him.

After our game, I walked over to Eliza. "Did anyone tell you how lucky I am?" Eliza asked me.

"No, because I'm the lucky one," I replied, pulling Eliza into a kiss. I couldn't wait until next year. After we completed our training, I planned to propose to Eliza. I couldn't wait.

Parker

"You seem quieter than usual," Payton mentioned, bringing his plate into the kitchen.

I looked at Payton. "Do you ever get the feeling something bad will happen?" I asked with a look.

Payton looked at me. "You're starting to sound like Pax," Payton mentioned.

"No, I sound like myself. Pay, I have this feeling about something, and I can't shake it," I explained.

Payton furrowed his brows. The last time I got this feeling, Sable humiliated me at homecoming with her video. It's the same feeling, but worse.

"I wouldn't worry about it. Next year, we will be seniors. You're stressed with working at the hospital," Payton reasoned.

I looked at Payton. People say if you have a bad feeling about something, you shouldn't ignore it. You should listen to your gut because it's usually right. I will regret my decision not to listen to my instincts.

There is always the calm before the storm, and our storm will hit when we least expected it. It will be our greatest challenge and defining moment in the family, showing our legacy.

CHAPTER 69

KAYLEE

Kaylee

I put things into boxes as I packed. Someone knocked on my bedroom door as I looked at Dad. He walked into the bedroom.

"Are you all set?" Dad asked me.

"Yep," I answered.

Dad looked at me. "You will make David proud," Dad said.

"I know. David is the reason I became a paramedic," I reasoned.

"Are you sure you want to leave, honey? You can train close to home," Dad suggested.

I looked at my dad dressed in his paramedic uniform. "I don't want special treatment. If people knew the chief is my dad, they would treat me differently," I reasoned.

Dad nodded.

"So, how are the recruits doing?" I asked.

"I have this probie that shows up late and can't get it together. I'm reassigning the recruit to another firehouse," Dad answered.

"You expect too much," I reasoned.

"You sound like David," Dad reminded me.

"Give the guy a chance. He might surprise you. Plus, after I finish my training, I will return to work at the station with you. Then, I can work with your probie," I reasoned, smirking.

Dad chuckled as I grabbed my stuff, and he helped me take it to the car. I'm training at another station, then joining Dad's team. Dad told us about his recruits. Dad mentioned the girl seemed promising, but he doubted the guy.

David and I would tease Dad about it. It was a running joke with us. Then came that fateful night when I was on a ride-along. A call came over the radio about an accident. We took the call and found out it was David. He was working a shift and on his way to a call. A semi-truck slammed into his rig because the truck driver exceeded his hours on the road.

It was the worst night of my life. I promised David that I would continue my training and become the best paramedic. I intend to keep my promise.

I pulled up to the station and grabbed my stuff. I met with the lieutenant, and he showed me around it. I would spend the summer finishing my training, then become a certified paramedic. I can't wait.

Pat

The school year ended, and we packed. Britt was returning with us. Sam was staying at school and taking summer courses, while Nora stayed to work at the hotel. We took the summer off except for Presley and Eliza. They worked on completing their certification course.

We packed up the cars and made our way home. All I wanted to do when we got there was sleep. This year was crazy, and it was good to have the downtime. It took us three hours to return home.

When we got home, we hugged our parents. We missed them as much as they missed us. We took our bags to our bedrooms. I crawled onto my bed and crashed.

My brothers saw me and laughed. Yeah, I'm not ashamed to admit that I missed my bed or sleep. Britt joined me and cuddled up to me as we slept.

Presley

As my brothers took the summer off, I didn't. Eliza and I continued our training when we got home. Next year, I want to prove to Chief Hayes that I could do the job. I didn't understand why he rides my ass?

Uncle Cayson explained that it's our superior's job to make sure we do our job or people die. I trusted Uncle Cayson since he spent years working as a paramedic.

I reported to the station and did everything the job entailed. Our training comprised testing and field action. The timing was crucial for us on the job. We had to make it to the call and stay professional.

Eliza trained with female paramedics while I trained with males. We would work together unless we got a station at different firehouses. That also meant staying at the firehouse. When a call came in, we dressed and left for it.

I have a feeling this summer will end with unexpected results.

Kaylee

Every day, I trained and worked side by side with experienced paramedics. The tests were brutal, with all the terminology you have to know. I studied my ass off for every test, including field tests.

At the end of summer, I will become an official paramedic. I'm attending courses at Saintwood College, then joining Dad's team.

"Hayes, let's go," someone ordered me as I ran downstairs and climbed into the back of the rig.

A call came in on an accident. We were on our way to the scene. I took deep breaths and remembered what David told me.

"Never let the crew see you rattle. Keep your head, because one mistake will cost someone their life," David told me.

I nodded.

"Kaylee, you got this," David assured me.

"What if I mess up?" I asked.

"Don't think like that. Everyone is nervous during training, but we save people's lives. Plus, you come from a lineage of paramedics," David said, grinning.

I chuckled.

"Kaylee, our legacy is saving lives. One day, you will understand what that means," David told me.

I nodded.

I smiled at that memory. David had confidence in me when I didn't, which he got that from Dad. I won't let you down, big brother.

Presley

Eliza and I took our last test, passing and becoming certified. The station had a ceremony, presenting our certifications. My family acted like a bunch of nuts when I accepted my paper.

After the presentation, I walked over to my family.

"Well, little brother, it looks like we will work side by side," Parker mentioned.

"Yep," I said.

"So, what now?" Payton asked me.

"Eliza and I are returning in the fall to continue with classes and training," I answered as Eliza walked over to me.

I pulled Eliza into a kiss, and my family congratulated her.

"This moment calls for a celebration before you all return to school," Pops announced. We yelled as he rolled his eyes.

Pops and Ma planned a party to celebrate our achievement. We have some time before returning to school. I didn't know that something significant was coming our way. It will be a defining moment in our family.

CHAPTER 70

A BEGINNING AND AN ENDING

Presley

My parents set up a party and invited family and Eliza to it. They did a joint party for Eliza and me. Grandpa helped with the food while Nana supplied the desserts. I helped my brothers set everything up, then my phone rang.

I answered it, talked to the person, then hung up. My brothers looked at me.

"I got to go. The station is short because two guys are out in injuries," I said.

"Presley," Payton said.

"It's a life of a paramedic," I said, shrugging. I walked away and went inside the house.

Pops looked at me. "Where are you going?" Pops asked.

"The station called. They're short-handed," I answered.

"Presley," Pops said.

"My shift shouldn't last long. Save me some food," I said, going upstairs to change. I put my uniform on and left the house, then drove to the station and reported for my shift. Eliza arrived and is out on a call.

I climbed into the back of a rig and closed the door.

"Good of you to join us, Gray," Anderson mentioned.

I rolled my eyes. "Stop busting my balls, Anderson," I ordered. He laughed as we went on a call.

My brothers finished setting up for the party. My shift would end when other paramedics showed up to relieve Eliza and me. People started arriving for the party while we were on runs. The runs weren't bad as we answered calls.

We returned to the station as a few guys showed up to relieve Eliza and me. Tonight, I planned to propose to Eliza at the party. Eliza and I were leaving when the bell sounded.

"All hands on deck, there's a fire at an apartment building at West Road and Fourth Street," the captain announced.

Eliza and I suited up in fire gear as we climbed into a rig. We sat in the back as the dispatcher came over the radio.

Attention all rescue, fire is escalating, and we have reports of children missing.

"Paramedic Anderson en route to a fire. Ladder 52 is following," Anderson called in to the dispatcher.

Copy that.

Sirens blared as we made our way to the apartment fire. We arrived as firefighters took the lead.

"Gray, you're with me. Shields will stay with Roberts," Anderson ordered.

I nodded as I pulled on a mask along with a tank. Our job was to go in, find life, and keep the person alive. I followed Anderson along with the firefighters. As the firefighters busted doors in with axes, they checked for people. Any person we found, we administered medical help. Firefighters took them out of the building.

We hurried through the building, searching for people. I came across a child and pulled out a mask. I put it on the child, then lifted the little girl into my arms as I carried her through the burning building.

"I want my mommy," the little girl said through her mask.

"Stay with me, and I will find your mommy," I assured the little girl as I hurried.

Get everyone out of the building! It's ready to collapse! I heard someone yell over the radio. The smoke became thick and engulfed us as I moved. I shielded the little girl.

"Everyone, get out now!" The fire chief yelled as we rushed through the building. I heard a crackling and turned to see the ceiling collapsed.

Lex

Everyone arrived at the party, and we waited on Presley and Eliza. Nolan's phone rang. He answered it.

"What do you mean you're working, Brody?" Nolan asked.

We looked at Nolan.

"Okay, be safe," Nolan said, hanging up.

We looked at Nolan.

"An apartment building caught fire. Brody has to report to the scene to make sure there aren't any casualties," Nolan explained.

The party continued for a few more hours. Nolan went into the house and heard a knock at the door. He answered it to see Brody standing there.

"I thought you were working?" Nolan asked Brody.

"I am. I need to speak with Lex and Piper," Brody said.

Nolan and Brody came out to the backyard.

"Lex!" Nolan yelled, waving me over to him.

Piper and I walked over to Nolan and Brody.

"I thought you were working," I mentioned.

"I am. I'm here on official police business. It's Presley," Brody said as everyone stopped and looked at him.

My heart sank. Piper and I left with Brody, leaving everyone worried.

The boys walked over to Nolan as Nolan looked at the boys along with the family. What happens next will alter everything with our family. It will show what the Gray legacy means.

To continue in The Gray Family: Legacies.

Printed in Great Britain
by Amazon